PRAISE FOR
THE GOLDEN CITY

"Cheney's debut is a masterpiece of historical fantasy. . . . The fascinating mannerisms of the age and the extreme formality of two people growing fonder of each other add a charmingly fresh appeal that will cross over to romance fans as well as to period fantasy readers."

—*Library Journal*

"Pulls readers in right off the bat. . . . Oriana's 'extra' abilities are thoroughly intriguing and readers will love the crackling banter and working relationship between Oriana and Duilio."

—*Romantic Times*

"An ambitious debut from Cheney: part fantasy, part romance, part police procedural, and part love letter. . . . [The author] does a lovely job connecting magical, historical, and romantic elements."

—*Kirkus Reviews*

Books by J. Kathleen Cheney

The Golden City

The Seat of Magic

THE
SEAT
OF
MAGIC

A Novel of the Golden City

J. KATHLEEN CHENEY

A ROC BOOK

ROC
Published by the Penguin Group
Penguin Group (USA) LLC, 375 Hudson Street,
New York, New York 10014

USA | Canada | UK | Ireland | Australia | New Zealand | India | South Africa | China
penguin.com
A Penguin Random House Company

First published by Roc, an imprint of New American Library,
a division of Penguin Group (USA) LLC

First Printing, July 2014

 REGISTERED TRADEMARK—MARCA REGISTRADA

LIBRARY OF CONGRESS CATALOGING-IN-PUBLICATION DATA:

Cheney, J. Kathleen.
The seat of magic: a novel of the Golden City/J. Kathleen Cheney.
p. cm.
ISBN 978-0-451-41776-3 (pbk.)
1. Imaginary places—Fiction.   2. Murder—Investigation—Fiction.   3. Selkies—Fiction.
4. Magic—Fiction.   5. Portugal—Fiction.   I. Title.   II. Title: Novel of the Golden City.
PS3603.H4574S43 2014
813'.6—dc23   2014001394

Printed in the United States of America
10 9 8 7 6 5 4 3 2 1

Set in LTD Kennerley
Designed by Spring Hoteling

In memory of Jennifer Schwabach

ACKNOWLEDGMENTS

With thanks to my editor, Danielle Stockley, for working so hard to make my words presentable, to Christopher Kastensmidt for his endless patience with my Portuguese translation questions, to Sue Burke for her help with Spanish, and to the writers of Codex and Novelocity who soothed my nerves and reassured me that it will all work out in the end.

THE
SEAT
OF
MAGIC

CHAPTER I

The library of the Ferreira home housed a collection of items Duilio's father had brought back to the Golden City from his travels on the sea. A large round table stood in the center of the room, the polished marquetry surface half hidden by a collection of sun-bleached giant clamshells. The chandelier of white coral above it had never been refitted for gas lighting and so held candles that Duilio rarely lit. He kept the thing for its beauty instead. The shelves were lined with books of varying antiquity and origin, purportedly filched from this or that hidden stockpile during his father's many adventures with the prince's father years and years ago.

Duilio didn't concern himself over the books' provenances; he was more interested in reading them. Neither his father nor his elder brother had been fond of books, and his mother preferred to read her newspapers in her sunny front sitting room, so he usually had the chillier library to himself.

He'd selected a volume in French, cheaply bound in dark blue fabric—*Les sirènes du Portugal*—that called itself a truthful account of life among the sea folk, the sereia. The gold lettering on the spine was nearly illegible, worn from the many times he'd read the book as a young man. Duilio doubted its accuracy, but it served better than nothing. Even so, the cities of the sereia's islands were depicted therein as pale reflections of human cities like the Golden City and Lisboa. There had to be more to their civilization, Duilio reckoned, but the author—one Monsieur Mathieu Matelot, a pseudonym if he'd ever seen one—apparently hadn't had the access needed to make a decent study of their culture. Given how little most humans knew of sereia, the author wasn't bound by the truth. Duilio set the volume on the small table next to his chair, wondering what Oriana would think of it.

Almost two weeks now, and he'd not heard a word. He leaned back in the leather chair and sighed, well aware that fretting did no good. Perhaps he should have gone to Mass with Joaquim this morning and prayed.

"Duilinho?" His mother had come into the library, a coffee cup and saucer in one hand, her newspaper in the other. Near fifty, she bore her age well—better than a human woman would. She wore a brown wool day dress that showed that despite having borne three sons, she'd retained her figure. Her dark hair, worn in a high bun this afternoon, likely didn't require any padding, an innate advantage of being a selkie. She regarded him with troubled brown eyes. "Hiding again?"

Yes, he was. He'd returned from a late lunch with his cousin Rafael Pinheiro only to learn his mother had a visitor, Genoveva Carvalho. He'd ducked into the library rather than face the girl. The eldest Carvalho daughter had recently shown an interest in him, an interest that wasn't reciprocated. True, she was a lovely girl from a good family. Her father *had* spoken to Duilio early that summer about arranging a marriage between them, but Duilio had declined the proposition. Unfortunately, the young lady appeared to believe persistence would wear him down. She'd visited five times over the last two weeks, an uncalled-for number of visits when it was obvious his mother didn't care for society.

Duilio rose, laying down his book. "I'm afraid so, Mother. Thank you for dealing with her."

"What else am I to do? I know you haven't encouraged her." She held out the paper. "I realize it's Sunday, but I'm surprised no one has come to tell you. Maraval is dead."

Duilio took the newspaper. She'd folded it so one column showed, headed by an article proclaiming that the Marquis of Maraval, the Minister of Culture, had been killed. Duilio scanned the printed words, grimacing when the newsprint smeared onto his fingers.

In a misguided attempt to recapture the past glory of the Portuguese Empire, Maraval had conspired to create a Great Magic, one that would change history. But his grand spell had been fueled by the deaths of dozens of servants. They'd been placed in pairs inside a large work of art under the waters of the Douro River, left to drown when the river's water seeped into their prisons of cork and wood. The plot had only begun to unravel when the conspirators chose the wrong pair of girls to sacrifice—Lady Isabel Amaral and her hired companion, Oriana Paredes. Miss Paredes was one of the few servants on the Street of Flowers who, when placed under water, would survive. A sereia, or *sirène* as the French book called them, she had gills and could breathe water, which gave her time to escape. Unfortunately she hadn't been able to save her mistress. She'd done her best to bring Lady Isabel's killers to justice instead. The newspaper stated that the young lady's father had gone one step further. The usually indolent Lord Amaral had gained entrance to the prison the previous evening and delivered the marquis up to a higher court of justice. Given that Duilio had been instrumental in the capture of the marquis, the police should have sent him a note at the very least.

"This doesn't say what's been done to Lady Isabel's father," he noted. "I'm relieved there's no mention of the man's motive."

The Golden City's newspapers, elated over a scandal to report, had been surprisingly circumspect in one regard—they hadn't mentioned the names of Lady Isabel or her companion in connection with Mara-val's plot. Instead they'd published that Isabel had been murdered by bandits who grabbed her off the street for her jewelry. It was the only concession Duilio had asked of the Special Police handling the case, a request made to protect Oriana Paredes rather than Lady Isabel. Oriana would not have withstood the attention of the media. Nonhumans had been banned from the Golden City for almost two decades now, and the fact that she was a sereia would have been exposed as the reason she'd survived when Lady Isabel hadn't.

His mother took the paper when he handed it back. "I noted that as well. It will make things easier when Miss Paredes returns."

Duilio frowned, wishing he knew when that return would oc-cur. Oriana hadn't been certain what reception she would receive when she reached her people's islands. He hoped things hadn't gone badly.

His mother touched the polished table and then frowned when her fingers left inky streaks behind. Since much of the staff was off on Sunday mornings, the newspaper must not have been ironed to set the ink. "Duilinho, sitting here and fretting is not going to bring Miss Paredes back."

He'd been thinking the same thing only a moment before. He drew a linen handkerchief from the inside pocket of his charcoal morning coat and handed it to her. "I know, Mother, but she told me she would try to return to us. It worries me that we've heard nothing."

One arched brow rose. "To us?"

Duilio pressed his lips together, refusing to rise to his moth-er's bait.

She sighed, wiped the table with the handkerchief, and then in-spected her fingers. "I cannot tell you what keeps her. I wish I could."

Despite sharing the ocean, his mother's people rarely interacted with the sereia. He sighed. "I should have convinced her not to go."

His mother looked up at him, her limpid brown eyes thoughtful. She had delicate features and a pointed jaw, neither of which he'd inherited. He had his father's rectangular face, very human in appearance, with a wide brow and square jaw. He often wished he looked more like her, as his elder brother Alessio had.

"Do you believe you could have dissuaded her?" she asked.

"I had a bad feeling, Mother." Like his father and brother before him, he was a witch—a seer. His gift was erratic and refused to answer the questions he most wanted answered, but when he *did* have an answer, it was reliable. "I wish I'd begged her to stay."

"She would not have given in, Duilinho," Lady Ferreira said as she handed back the smudged handkerchief. "Do not think her weaker merely because she is female."

He'd never been one to believe women weak and helpless. His mother, with her soft voice and gentle ways, was far stronger than others guessed. "I will keep that in mind, Mother."

"Good." She took a deep breath, as if preparing to launch into a speech. "Now, I wish to ask a favor."

She rarely asked anything for herself. "What is it?"

"I would like you to take me to see Erdano," she said. "I think I am ready."

Her eldest son, Erdano, lived north of the city at Braga Bay. A small bay, inaccessible to larger boats, it was a safe place for the selkie harem to call their own. But as it lay north of the river's mouth, the trip was safest made by boat. For all of her familiarity with the sea, his mother wasn't a sailor. One of the perquisites of being a gentleman, though, was that he was frequently at leisure to indulge his mother's whims. "When do you want to go?"

"Tomorrow morning, I think," she said. "Before I lose my nerve. I . . ."

A discreet cough in the hallway heralded the approach of Cardenas, the family's elderly butler. A vigorous man in his seventies, he was the longtime guardian of the family's consequence—whether or not that was merited. Duilio stepped forward, since Cardenas looked to him first.

"A visitor," he told Duilio, his voice tight with disapproval. "One of *those*. He didn't give his name."

For the last two weeks Duilio had been facing down a string of Alessio's old lovers. They'd slipped cautiously up to the door of the Ferreira house, the ladies veiled and the gentlemen with their hats lowered to hide their faces. At the Carvalho ball a couple of weeks ago, Duilio had revealed to an acquaintance that Alessio had kept journals of his romantic exploits. He'd not realized then how much time he would have to spend smoothing ruffled feathers as a result. He touched his mother's elbow. "I'd better go take care of this, Mother. We'll go in the morning, after breakfast if you'd like."

She nodded gracefully, and Duilio accompanied the butler down the hallway toward the front sitting room. "Would you inform João that I'll need the paddleboat in the morning?"

"Of course, Mr. Duilio," the butler said. He withdrew a note from his waistcoat's pocket. "And this came from Mr. Joaquim while you were out."

Duilio stashed the note in a pocket. Probably the news about Maraval's death that he should have seen earlier. He thanked the butler and stepped over the threshold into the sunny front sitting room. Like most of the rooms in the house, this showed the touch of his mother's taste, all soft browns and ivories. Before the unlit hearth a pale beige sofa in leather and a group of chairs upholstered in ivory brocade surrounded a low table that served to invite conversation. The windows on the far wall looked out toward the Queirós house, but from the right spot Duilio could catch the glittering of the sun on the Douro River.

His newest visitor rose from the armchair in which he'd been sitting. A tall gentleman near his own age, the visitor looked familiar, but Duilio couldn't quite place him. He was a striking man, with a handsome face and a marked widow's peak from which black hair swept back neatly. His fine frock coat, matching waistcoat, and pin-striped trousers marked him as a gentleman. He had a charismatic air, which made Duilio wonder who he was. People like him usually attracted attention. But as Duilio had been abroad for a few years following his departure from the university at Coimbra, there were always people in society he didn't know—although he'd worked hard in the last year to overcome that. Knowing society was his specialty.

"I'm afraid I don't recall your name, sir," Duilio began.

The visitor's lips twisted in amusement. "I've never told you my name."

That implied they *had* met before. "Do we know each other?"

"I was a friend of your brother's."

Duilio felt a sudden flare of recognition, placing where he'd seen that face before—years ago in Coimbra, where students from the same town would often rent a house together. On his arrival at the university, Duilio hadn't wanted to live in his brother's shadow so he'd found a different house to live in, but this man had been one of Alessio's housemates. His widow's peak and aquiline nose were a distinctive combination. "You and Alessio lived in the same *república* at Coimbra," Duilio said. "I recall seeing you there when I visited him, but I don't believe he ever introduced us."

"Very good." The man nodded approvingly, as if Duilio had passed a test. "I was not, by the way, one of his lovers."

Duilio turned toward the marble mantelpiece to hide his smile. He was always amused by the swiftness with which others felt they had to inform him of that. It usually came within a few sentences of admitting they'd known Alessio. He suspected many of those quick denials were false. "So is this visit concerning his journals? I have no intention of publishing them, nor are they for sale."

"May we sit down?" the gentleman asked.

Duilio stared back at him expectantly. "May I ask your name?"

"You may call me Bastião," his visitor said after a split-second hesitation.

That definitely wasn't the man's name. Duilio gestured toward the pale leather couch anyway. The man settled there, and Duilio sat in the chair across from him. "Now, Bastião, what brings you to my house?"

"A number of things," the man said, "but primarily to discover if you know why Alessio was murdered."

Duilio did his best to keep his reaction from reaching his face. "My brother was killed during a duel. Why would you say he was murdered?"

"From what I understand," the man said, "his opponent fired into the air, making one question how Alessio could have been shot in the chest. We know that the Marquis of Maraval had it done, fearing that Alessio would seduce the prince out from under his influence. That, however, was not the true reason behind Alessio's occasional visits to the palace. He was working as an agent of the infante."

Duilio kept from gripping the arms of the chair only by sheer will. Following Maraval's arrest by the Special Police, their inspection of his private papers had revealed his mistaken assumption and decision to have Alessio killed. That last claim, though, was new. "I was unaware the infante has agents. He's under house arrest in the palace. No one is allowed to visit him."

Strictly speaking, that was a lie. In the last month Duilio had met a team of four investigators who were, as far as he could tell, working for the infante. That could be viewed as treason so long as his elder brother, Prince Fabricio, held the throne. When Duilio asked, the group of investigators hadn't admitted the association. They hadn't denied it either.

Bastião crossed one long leg over the other. "Alessio was acting as a messenger between the infante and Dinis. That was what took him to Lisboa so often."

Cold spread through Duilio's stomach. What had Alessio been up to? Prince Dinis II ruled *Southern* Portugal, which Alessio had visited regularly in the last year of his life. Perhaps this Bastião was trying to determine whether Alessio had revealed any such activities in his journals. But if Alessio had worked for the infante, he'd not recorded a word about it. "Why would my brother do so? He was never fond of the throne."

Bastião smiled. "No, he believed things needed to change."

Alessio hadn't been a revolutionary, but he'd thought the usefulness of the twin monarchies of Northern and Southern Portugal was long past. "And you're suggesting his efforts in the infante's name were . . . ultimately intended to reform the monarchies?"

Bastião interlaced his fingers over his knee, looking perfectly at ease as he talked about treason. "Are you asking if I know the infante's leanings?"

Duilio watched him carefully. His gift spoke into his mind, warning him that this meeting—this man—was *important*. Unfortunately, it didn't tell him *how*. "Do you?"

"I also act in his name at times," Bastião said, "so I know his mind on certain matters."

Duilio pressed his lips together. Why had this man come to tell him this? That the infante of Northern Portugal was bypassing his elder brother didn't concern Duilio overmuch. He'd walked that line for years himself. He was half selkie; living in the city at all was illegal for him. And he'd willingly harbored Oriana Paredes, a sereia spy, in his household.

"I know where the infante stands on the issue of nonhumans as well," Bastião added, as if he'd read the path of Duilio's thoughts.

"How interesting," Duilio said in what he hoped was a neutral tone. He had a feeling this man Bastião was trying to winnow out his personal leanings on the matter. He didn't intend to be drawn. Not when he didn't know who this man was.

Bastião smiled at his vague comment, apparently recognizing it for evasion. "The infante could not, after all, be friends with Alessio Ferreira if he felt nonhumans were to be abhorred." His eyes flicked downward to consider the kid-gloved fingers laced over his knee. "The ban on nonhumans is a ridiculous abuse of power by the prince."

Did that mean this Bastião was aware the Ferreira family wasn't purely human? Or had he thought Alessio a Sympathizer? "Seers have predicted the prince will be killed by a nonhuman," Duilio pointed out. "Is that not sufficient reason for the ban?"

"Something will kill each of us one day," Bastião said with a shrug. "Shall we banish the river to assure no one drowns?"

That was, word for word, what Alessio had said once when speaking of the ban. This man had to have known him.

Duilio rose and crossed to the mantel again. At least he now had a better answer to why his brother had been killed, a reason more dignified than being killed in a duel over a lover or because of Maraval's strange idea that Alessio would seduce the prince. This new information made sense of what had previously seemed a pointless death . . . even if it meant that Alessio had been committing treason. "So if you're not here about Alessio's journals, what do you want from me?"

"Society seems to have painted you as a dullard, you know, Ferreira," Bastião said. As he'd worked hard to cultivate that image, Duilio didn't argue. "Yet Alessio once told me you got all the brains in the family, while he got all the beauty. I wanted to see for myself if that was true."

Alessio *had* been fond of saying that, even if it was insulting to both of them. "Very well, you've seen me."

"And if your infante needs your services, will he be able to call on you?"

Now *that* was a dangerous question. Duilio considered Bastião with narrowed eyes. Someone had sent this man to pry into Duilio Ferreira's political leanings—a fruitless task, since he wasn't entirely sure of them himself. Would he serve the infante in defiance of a prince he found detestable? Was his distaste for the current prince grounds to risk his life as Alessio had? Duilio decided evasion was his safest course. "I'll answer that when the infante asks me himself."

Bastião rose, a wry smile twisting his lips. "I'll leave you then, to decide that another day. I'll show myself out." Nodding once in farewell, he walked out of the sitting room. A moment later, Duilio heard Cardenas speaking to the man, and the front door closed behind him.

Duilio paced the strip of Persian rug behind the couch, trying to parse out what had just happened. He'd endured enough bizarre interviews in the last two weeks that not much surprised him, but this one had been different. The fact that Bastião had known Alessio at Coimbra a decade ago wasn't enough to ensure his loyalties. Duilio had no way to know for whom the man worked now.

After a moment Duilio stopped pacing and withdrew Joaquim's note from his coat pocket. He read the contents and quickly stepped out into the hall, calling for Cardenas.

The butler emerged from the end of the hallway. "Yes, sir?"

"I need my gloves and hat immediately. I'm heading out to the cemetery."

Cardenas frowned. "It's Sunday, Mr. Duilio."

"Unfortunately, the dead don't honor the day of rest."

CHAPTER 2

Inspector Joaquim Tavares perched on a stool at the far end of the barren stone cell. It was chilly in these rooms. This row of cells with their unadorned granite walls, once dedicated to prayer and meditation, was perfectly suited for preparing the poor of the city for burial. The Monastery of the Brothers of Mercy had once stood on the Street of Flowers not far from where Duilio's house was now, but had been moved to this spot high above the river, outside the Golden City's medieval walls. That placed it close to the city's seminary for orphans. When the city had set a new cemetery in this area in the mid-nineteenth century, the brothers had been the natural choice to handle the final disposition of paupers.

The girl on the stone slab was destined for one of those pauper's graves marked with a small stone cross. Slim and pretty, with her dark hair trailing off to one side, she lay on the slab as if asleep. Joaquim knew her name—Lena Sousa—but little more. It likely wasn't her real name anyway. She'd been found Saturday, crumpled in a doorway on Firmeza Street, by the elderly woman who owned the home. There had been no blood, no sign of any injury, and her small coin purse had still been in a pocket sewn into the seam of her skirt. If Joaquim hadn't been notified, she would have gone to her grave nameless. Her disappearance had been reported to the police by another prostitute the afternoon before. Her life had come down to a few lines written on a report and a tattered photograph, quickly forgotten, one of too many dead in a city of this size. The paperwork had been handed off to Joaquim but he had no way to find her family, not without her true name or hometown, so the police turned the body over to the brothers.

But something had told Joaquim not to let this one go.

When he'd asked to have the body autopsied, his captain shrugged it off. The police didn't have the funds for a skilled physician's services every time a prostitute died, particularly when there was no indication of violent death. Joaquim had considered applying to the medical college but that would have taken longer than he liked. So he'd taken a step he wouldn't have been willing to pursue if he hadn't needed answers—he asked Duilio to pay for the doctor's time. The money was nothing to Duilio, so now Joaquim sat in this cold cell on a sunny Sunday afternoon, his jaw clenched and his stomach churning.

The girl hadn't been dead long so there was surprisingly little smell, but watching a doctor take apart a young woman and put her back together always bothered Joaquim. He had never developed the strong stomach he needed for this job.

A discreet tap at the door preceded portly Brother Manoel opening it to allow Duilio inside. Joaquim gestured him over to another empty stool, and Duilio came, looking winded as if he'd run all the way from his house. Likely he had. He shifted his morning coat as he settled atop one of the other stools, then adjusted his well-tied necktie. Joaquim might accuse his cousin of being a dandy if Duilio's up-to-the-mark garb didn't make him self-conscious about the shabbiness of his own brown tweed suit.

Joaquim shot a glance at the doctor's square shoulders. He didn't know Dr. Teixeira well, but he'd run across the older man at Mass several times. Teixeira hadn't looked up from his work at Duilio's intrusion, occupied with replacing things he'd previously removed. Joaquim turned away, glad he hadn't eaten lunch.

"How long have you been here?" Duilio asked.

"Hours," Joaquim said with a heavy sigh. "I'm sorry I didn't get to see Rafael before he headed back to Lisboa. But I caught Dr. Teixeira at Mass and he preferred to do this right away. You'll be paying extra, by the way, for doing this on a Sunday."

Duilio shrugged. "So what has he found?"

"Nothing. Not yet."

"Poison?"

"No sign of it," the doctor intoned without glancing over. "There's surprisingly little bloating, though, despite the time passed since her death. I don't know that it's pertinent."

Duilio got to his feet and crossed the room to where the doctor was replacing the last of the organs he'd removed. Not willing to miss anything exchanged there, Joaquim followed, doing his best not to look at the body lying on the table.

"There are, of course, poisons we can't trace," Teixeira added, "but we usually see some damage in the affected organ. Nothing here looks out of the norm except for the heart."

Duilio leaned closer to peer down at the body, probably looking *inside*, which was a ghastly thought.

"Is there a poison that affects only the heart?" Joaquim asked.

The doctor shook his head. "Not this way. Not that I've ever seen before. It's possible one exists, but . . ." He exhaled and said, "If you look at the damage to the heart and the tissues around it, it resembles damage done by a bolt of lightning. But that's not what happened to her."

"Why not?" Duilio asked.

The doctor laid his hand somewhere on the body and Joaquim forced himself to look. The doctor had pulled the sheet back up to cover most of the girl's body and her skin had been pulled closed, saving Joaquim from casting up the nonexistent contents of his stomach, but the long incision running down the center of her chest and up to each shoulder was grisly enough. The doctor pointed to the skin above the girl's left breast. "No evidence of an entry or exit.

When lightning strikes, the electricity passes through the body and usually leaves a burn on each end. This is localized to the tissues directly around the heart."

Joaquim looked up at him. "And what would do that?"

Teixeira glanced over at Duilio and then back. "How familiar are you with healers?"

"A healer did this?" Duilio asked before Joaquim had the chance.

The doctor shook his head. "That's not what I said. But"—he scowled down at the body—"keep in mind that I haven't seen this kind of thing in a very long time. When I was a young man at the medical college, I had a chance to observe a healer at work. They don't actually heal, you know. Instead they encourage the body to heal itself. They can control the flow of not only the blood, but of energies in the body."

Joaquim estimated Teixeira's age between forty-five and fifty, although on the younger end of that spectrum. Teixeira's dark hair had little gray in it and he seemed in the prime of his life. That would put this memory of the medical college twenty years or so past.

Duilio crossed his arms over his chest. "Do you mean electricity?"

"That isn't the term they use for it," the doctor said patiently, "but there are *similarities* between tissues that have been damaged by an accidental electrical discharge and tissues that have been . . . manipulated . . . by a healer."

"And you think a healer could have killed this girl without leaving any external mark?"

While Duilio continued questioning the doctor, Joaquim gazed down at the girl's peaceful face, trying to ignore the neat incision just past the edge of her scalp. She hadn't been more than eighteen. She'd come to the Golden City from the country—unfortunately, her friend hadn't known from what town—looking for work. It saddened him that prostitution was the only work she'd been able to find. He should stop by a church tonight and light a candle for her.

Since her family couldn't know she was dead, he doubted anyone else would be praying for her soul.

Duilio had gone on with his questions. ". . . unethical to use their abilities to take a life? Like doctors and their oath to do no harm?"

"There is no regulating body for witches," Joaquim reminded him.

Duilio cast an exasperated look his direction, one not entirely unearned. Being a seer, even one of limited ability, Duilio was considered a witch as well. The gift passed to all the males of the Ferreira line, father to son, so it bypassed the Tavares family. There were times that Joaquim had been envious of Duilio's talent, since Duilio used his ability to help solve crimes. But those with such gifts had an equal potential to use them wrongly. Although the Church had tried to control them in the past, now that was usually left to the Public Security Police, a body with little experience dealing with such people.

"Inspector Tavares is correct about that," the doctor said with a shake of his head. "This could, conceivably, have been an accident. But if it happens again, we may have a predator of sorts on our hands."

Joaquim licked his lips. The doctor didn't need to know this wasn't the first girl to die without any apparent cause. In the last two weeks, the brothers had buried two other girls, both of whom Joaquim had identified as prostitutes who'd gone missing. Neither had any mark on their bodies, making it possible they'd died the same way. He took a deep breath and asked, "Was she raped?"

The doctor shifted from one foot to the other, brow rumpling. "She recently had relations with a man, but not directly before death and my best guess is that it was . . . consensual."

"The vast majority of healers *are* female," Duilio pointed out.

Had he known that? Joaquim mentally ran through reasons one woman might kill others, but they were very much the same reasons men might kill. He didn't see how that changed the equation. Even so, according to the brothers neither of the other two girls had shown signs of rape. That linked the deaths more closely. Joaquim puffed out his cheeks. "Duilio? Any more questions?"

Duilio pressed his lips together, considering. "Can the brothers leave her until tomorrow afternoon, perhaps? I was wondering if the Lady might come and take a look at her."

Joaquim had wondered if Duilio would think of her. The Lady—who was literally nameless as far as they knew—was one of four investigators who'd arrived in Northern Portugal only a couple of months ago. They'd been brought in to clean out some of the less desirable elements of the Special Police, apparently at the behest of the infante. Their inquiries had become entangled with his and Duilio's investigation of *The City Under the Sea*, that work of art and death being assembled under the river's waters. Each of the four investigators had a particular skill that made them more suitable for chasing down witches than Joaquim himself. "But the Lady specializes in witchcraft, not healers."

"I'd bet she knows more about healers than we do," Duilio pointed out. "How this might have happened, and if it was intentional."

The Church held that there was a clear distinction between witches and witchcraft. Craft was learned, a way of augmenting one's inborn abilities instead of working only with what was given by God. Witches like Duilio, so long as they didn't seek to increase their natural abilities through witchcraft, were tolerated by the Portuguese Church, even though the Spanish Church still hunted them. And while the Lady had studied witchcraft all her life, she'd claimed she'd never *practiced* the art, which made her blameless in the eyes of the Church.

Joaquim scowled. It wasn't the Lady who bothered him so much as the Lady's usual escort, Miguel Gaspar. An inspector brought from the former colony of Cabo Verde, Gaspar had eyes that saw too much. He was a *meter*, a witch who could merely glance at another and know what gifts that person possessed. When he'd first started to work with the man, Joaquim hadn't found that too disturbing, but it had become clear as the days progressed that Gaspar wanted something from him. The man was convinced he was a witch, and wanted Joaquim to admit it, surely unaware of the questions such an admission would raise. And Joaquim wasn't convinced of it himself. Not quite.

"I don't want to hand this case over to the Special Police," he protested weakly.

"Just a consultation," Duilio said. "I'll talk to Brother Manoel and see if they can put off preparing the body until afterward."

And with that, Duilio left the cell, leaving Joaquim alone with the doctor. Joaquim turned back to Dr. Teixeira. "Do you know any healers in the area who might have done this?"

"Well"—the doctor cleared his throat—"science tends not to get along with magic, Inspector. We doctors rarely meet up with healers, and I have to admit there's a growing tendency in the field to think of them as . . . charlatans."

There were dozens of healers to be found in the Golden City, and Joaquim suspected half of them had no talent at all. Then again, not all doctors were as competent as Dr. Teixeira, either. "If you do think of anything else," he said, "please let me know."

The doctor nodded his head vaguely. "I'll go ahead and close her up," he said, "and the brothers can decide what to do from there."

So Joaquim thanked the man again, reminded him to send his bill to Duilio's man of business, and took one last look down at Lena Sousa's still features. He wished he could have prevented this, but the doctor believed she'd been dead even before her friend reported her missing. If the Lady could help them pinpoint Lena's killer, then he would go along with it.

Joaquim nodded one last time to Dr. Teixeira and let himself out into the cool hallway. He retrieved his hat from the low table near the entry door, where Brother Manoel waited on the hard wooden bench, and made his way outside into the crisp fall air.

Duilio lounged against the monastery wall, gazing out over the cemetery, the Prado do Repouso, in the late-afternoon sunshine, top hat pulled low to shade his eyes. The Ferreira family had a mausoleum there among the collection of stern granite and gleaming whitewashed edifices. Duilio's brother Alessio and their father were interred there in appropriate splendor. Joaquim's own mother lay in this cemetery as well, in one of the less ostentatious sections. He needed to visit her grave; it had been months. But today he had to get back to the station out in Massarelos Parish and see what could be done about finding a killer.

"Do you want to stop and get something to eat?" Duilio asked him, as if they'd just visited the market instead of viewing an autopsy.

Joaquim considered his roiling stomach. It might actually feel better if he put something in it. "Where do you suggest?"

Duilio smoothed his hair and resettled his top hat on his head. "That new place on Santa Catarina Street?"

Joaquim guessed he could find something appropriately bland there. He fell into step beside Duilio as he headed up toward Heroismo Street. From where they walked they could see the cathedral with its subdued gray walls standing high over the river, and beyond that the elegant white Bishop's Palace, which now housed many of the government's ministries. Representing the other major power in the Golden City, the fanciful royal palace rose atop a hill farther inland from the river. An imitation of a palace built by the royal family of Southern Portugal, it had crenellated walls painted in gold and red. The hill on which it stood had been built up to assure that the clock tower of the royal palace rose higher than the Torre dos Clérigos, exerting the claim of the throne over the city.

Joaquim wasn't sure either power, Church or State, was watching over the commoners who bustled along the Golden City's cobbled streets, rode its trams, and sailed the river. There were too many beggars on the streets, and too many children with neither schooling nor trade. Having lived much of his early life in the Ferreira household, he knew what wealth was like, but as a police inspector he saw a great deal of poverty.

On Heroismo Street, they walked toward the older parts of the city, the road lined by houses of three and four floors, their whitewashed facades gleaming in the sun. Pedestrians strolled the street, men and women in their Sunday finery, children dashing around and through their elders. A gold-painted tram rattled past, heading out toward the train station on the far eastern edge of the city. Joaquim glanced up in time to spot a lovely young woman out on her small balcony, leaning on the wrought iron railing not far over their heads, a basket of laundry at her feet. Her dark eyes caught his and she smiled at him. He tipped his hat to her, but walked on.

"Not even going to ask her name?" Duilio asked with a laugh in his tone. "She's pretty."

He wasn't going to court women met while hanging their laundry. Joaquim changed the topic. "Have you heard anything from Miss Paredes?"

Duilio's eyes drifted to the cobbles, his shoulders hunched as he walked along, an uncharacteristically resigned posture. "No, still nothing."

Upon meeting the sereia woman, it hadn't taken long for Joaquim to see that Duilio was smitten with her. And although she wasn't to *his* taste, he thought she suited his cousin well. Unfortunately, she'd been forced to leave by her superiors, and Joaquim wasn't sure she would ever come back. He wasn't going to say that to Duilio, though. "And how is your mother?"

That got a smile out of him. "Very well. She wants to try to swim tomorrow, so we'll sail out to Braga Bay in the morning. We should be back by early afternoon. I can ask if the Lady will meet me at the monastery at, perhaps, three? Would you be able to come then?"

Joaquim chewed on his lower lip. He could avoid the meeting altogether, but that would be awkward since it was his investigation. Duilio was merely helping out. "I'll try to be there."

M rs. Rodriguez lived in the back of her shop near the Ribeira. Duilio had come down the steep streets to the quay in hopes of talking with the old Spanish woman, and she was happy to sit with him for a few moments. Since he'd come to her a dozen times over the last year with this or that minor injury, she knew he would pay her well for her time.

The shop wasn't on the quay itself, but on one of the narrow twisted streets that led away from the quay, Fonte Taurina Street. Her store was wedged between a tavern and a pastry shop, the first hosting a number of men drinking at their counter and the second, several customers picking up pastries to enjoy in the fall sunshine on the stone quay itself. Mrs. Rodriguez limped over to draw the white linen curtains at the front of the building, granting them a modicum of privacy. "Now how can I help you today, Mr. Ferreira?"

"I've come to ask a few questions about healers," he told her. "Is that acceptable?"

She made her way over to the high counter from behind which she sold her herbs and infusions, and eased onto the tall stool so her eyes were nearly level with his own. "Certainly, Mr. Ferreira, although I can only answer for myself."

He'd always liked Mrs. Rodriguez, so he chose his words carefully, hoping not to offend. "Is it possible for a healer to hurt someone? Not you, but healers in general?"

She shook her head. "Without a doubt. Take on a task too big and you're assuring your client's death."

That didn't sound to him like what had happened to the dead girl in the monastery. "What kind of task?"

"Well, if I were to try to heal over a deep cut, it might go septic," she said. "So I send anyone with a deep wound on to the hospital. If they're infected inside, it's always better to send them on. That manner of problem."

He nodded slowly, his lips twisting as he worked through that idea. He knew healers couldn't mend certain types of injuries, witnessed by the fact that Mrs. Rodriguez used a cane. As a girl she'd endured a savage beating from the villagers in the Spanish town from which she came. Her broken leg had never healed properly. But that sort of lapse wasn't what he was after. "What if a healer *intended* to harm someone? Could they do so?"

Her dark eyes slitted and she drew her black shawl closer about her shoulders. "That's not the way God meant us to work, Mr. Ferreira."

Duilio had an uneasy relationship with God on the best of days. He doubted God had anything to do with *this* situation. "If one decided they wished to harm others," he persisted, "could they use their gift to do so?"

She shifted uncomfortably on her stool, eyes on the counter. Then she took a deep breath and answered. "It's possible. A healer can, if they're particularly strong, stop their patient's blood in its tracks. They could stop the heart that way. Or they could steal the patient's energies, which would do much the same."

Energies. That could be what had happened to the dead girl. "Why would someone do that?"

"Kill?" The old woman shook her head. "I don't know myself, but people seem to do so with frightening regularity, and they don't need a healer's power to do it."

She did have a point there. Why had the killer chosen to kill in this manner? Why not a knife or a gun? *It does keep the hands clean, but . . .*

Duilio felt his jaw clenching as another idea formed in his mind. "You said *steal*. Do you mean the healer could take another person's energy . . . and keep it?"

"I have never done that," she said firmly. "It is the worst sin for a healer, a corruption of one's gift."

That had been a *yes*. "What could they do with that energy?"

"I do not know. I heard stories from my mother, of healers who stole from others, but . . ." She made the sign of the cross, muttering a prayer under her breath. "Those are demons if it's true, Mr. Ferreira."

CHAPTER 3

Duilio guided the boat north, along the rocky coastline. He'd received a note that morning informing him the Lady would meet him at the monastery as requested at three that afternoon, which gave them several hours to get up the coast and back. The paddleboat had a shallow draught, making it a good choice for hugging the shore so long as the sea remained calm. Fortunately, since the storm on the day of Oriana's departure, mild weather had ruled.

His mother's pelt lay at her feet in the small boat. Like all selkies, she was tied to her pelt. A little over three years before, a footman had found it in the house and stolen it. Duilio's father had immediately blamed his bastard half brother, Paolo Silva, the prince's favored seer. The footman *had* been hired by Silva, it turned out, but he'd sold the pelt instead to a collector of magical items, none other than the Marquis of Maraval. Duilio had found the pelt on the man's yacht two weeks ago, nailed to the wall of the captain's cabin.

Now that she had it back, his mother would be able to take seal form for the first time in years . . . but at a price. Since there were nail holes in the fur, when his mother donned her pelt again, she would have open wounds there. They would heal in time, Erdano insisted, but in the interim they would bleed and seep—an unpleasant prospect in either seal or human form. Nevertheless, his mother was determined to go back to the water, and Duilio would never deny her that.

Even aware of the pain she would have to endure, she smiled up at the brown-winged gulls peppering the rocky headlands and trailed a hand in the calm water. Duilio hadn't seen her this happy in years.

As they approached the opening of the secluded bay, seals slid by the boat, dark shapes in the water. Erdano's harem had come out to welcome them. One thumped the side of the boat with her tail. Duilio opened the valve and let the engine die, then slipped out a pair of oars to take them the rest of the way into the bay—a safer approach for the sake of the bay's inhabitants. While the adults knew to keep a safe distance from the boat's paddles, Erdano had several children too young to be wary.

Duilio had once attempted to count them. He'd estimated between twenty-five and thirty females in the bay, although his mother had told him a handful of those were true seals, living within the selkie harem for safety. He hadn't inquired further into that. As much as he liked his half brother, he truly did not understand the way Erdano's mind worked when it came to females.

Duilio rowed the boat into the bay and shipped the oars. Rocky cliffs as high as a three-story house surrounded the circle of beach—a narrow strip of pale sands. The bay itself was shallow, so Duilio slipped off his rubber-soled shoes and jumped over the side to drag the boat onto the beach. Several pups sunning themselves there cried in dismay at the sight of a human until a pair of females came up onto the sand to comfort them.

Duilio helped his mother off the boat. Her bare feet still in the water, she stopped to watch as, in the center of the beach, a bull seal heaved his bulk awkwardly onto the sands—Erdano. He rose on his hind flippers and stripped off his pelt, dropping it there where a couple of the females could watch over it. Unabashed as always, he strode naked along the beach toward where their mother waited.

Try as he might, Duilio had never gotten used to their complete lack of concern over nudity. He'd spent too many of his childhood years clothed. He had, however, become adept at *pretending* it didn't bother him. As they also spent much of their lives in the water, Oriana's people shared the seal folk's nonchalance about nudity. Duilio had succeeded in hiding his blushes around her, mainly due to his olive skin.

A roaring voice brought his attention back to the present. "Mother! Little brother!"

Erdano's handsome face lit with a smile. He embraced their mother, dwarfing her—selkie females never had the bulk the males did—and then slapped one beefy hand onto Duilio's shoulder. "What are you doing here?"

In human form, Erdano was a large man, a hand taller than Duilio and half again as wide. His dark hair hung in damp curls over his shoulders to the middle of his back. There was little resemblance between them, save about the eyes—they had both inherited their mother's eyes.

Duilio smiled up at his brother. "Mother asked me to bring her out today to try her pelt."

Erdano's thick brows drew together. "Are you certain, Mother?"

"Yes," she said with a brisk nod. "If I'm going to heal, I must start sometime."

Erdano looked to Duilio, brown eyes wide. Reading his brother's expression as a request for verification, Duilio simply nodded. If his mother had made up her mind, he didn't intend to fight her. Erdano made a barking call then, and several of his harem came swimming over.

Duilio watched as three of the seals rose out of the water, removing their pelts as they did so. It still baffled his eyes, that moment when one of the seal folk slid a flipper across their chest to draw off their pelt. The shape of their bodies altered as they did so, and they withdrew first human arms and then shoulders from within the sealskin. It was a feat he would never be able to imitate; he had been born human, with no pelt to remove.

As the women waited in the gently rolling water, Duilio's mother undressed on the shore, pulled her pelt from the boat, and began to wrap it around herself. Then she shrank down next to the water, a seal again. Duilio hadn't seen her do that for years. He folded his arms across his chest, worried, even though he'd held his tongue in front of her.

Dark blood seeped from her flippers onto the sand. She shivered, ripples running along her dull pelt, but shuffled out to the water anyway. She barked when the salt water came up over her wounds, then dove farther in, swimming on her own.

The other females donned their pelts again, all save one. That one boldly walked over to the sands where Duilio waited—Tigana, Erdano's queen. She had beauty to equal his, her nearly black hair streaming over slender shoulders. Like Duilio's mother, she had borne a son, which gave her superior standing among the harem. She settled gracefully on the beach with her pelt laid across her lap and patted the damp sand next to her as an indication that she wanted Duilio to join her there.

Erdano eyed him sharply, but went back to the center of the beach to retrieve his own pelt. Duilio sat on the sand, carefully picking a spot where he wasn't looking too directly at Tigana's nude body. Erdano did have limits to his permissiveness.

Tigana's fingers stroked the dark pelt in her lap. "Erdano has not noticed," she said in her velvety voice, "but one of the girls is missing—Gita. She followed him into the city two nights ago and didn't return."

Duilio didn't pretend to understand the dynamics of the harem. Why so many females stayed attached to one man—who was not *by his nature* faithful to any of them—eluded him. Erdano wasn't even faithful to his harem as a whole, since he had several human lovers as well. Two of the housemaids were in that group, despite the fact that his mother had previously asked Erdano not to seduce their staff. Yet for some reason Tigana and the others didn't seem to mind his excesses. "Why would she have gone into the city?"

"She was following him. Gita thought if she could approach him outside the harem, he would lie with her. Foolish."

It had never occurred to Duilio that his brother didn't mate with all the females of his harem. Erdano had never mentioned that curious fact. "Why would he not?"

Tigana's eyes flicked up toward his and her hands stilled. Her rigid posture suggested offense, although her expression didn't show it. It was often the case with the seal folk that they didn't display their feelings the same way. "She is too young. She is only thirteen."

"Ah," Duilio said quickly. "I didn't realize there were females that young in his harem."

"She became disoriented in the recent storm and washed up here," Tigana said with a graceful roll of one shoulder. "It was either kill her or take her in."

Duilio wondered if his own mother had ever said such a harsh thing when she lived on these sands, when she'd been the queen of Erdano's father's harem. "So she's new here," he said. "Does she know anything about the city? About the laws there?"

"She has been warned," Tigana said, "but I doubt she listened. Too young."

Duilio's gift presented him with a feeling of ill-fatedness for the missing girl. He shook his head to drive it out. "Did you want me to look for her?"

Tigana's brows drew together slightly. "Why else would I tell you?"

Conversation was not one of her amusements, Duilio remembered. "What can you tell me about her, then? What does she look like?"

"As a human?" When he nodded, she continued, "Small like Darina. Brown hair, lighter than Guisa's. Paler than me."

He tried to recall either of those females, but failed. "How tall would she be if she stood next to you?"

Tigana held her hand just above her dark-tipped breasts, which told Duilio the girl fell short of five feet. Short, with brown hair and fair skin, slight build—that described far too many of the young girls of the city to be helpful to him. "Did she have any scars? Marks?"

Tigana considered for a moment and then shrugged. "I do not recall. I will ask the children if they remember."

Duilio hoped she didn't expect him to provide a miracle. The girl would likely have been nude when she came up on the docks, and that would serve as the only point of distinction for describing her. Without her pelt, she would appear completely human. He would have to start at the quays and track her from there. "Do you know where Erdano went that night?"

"She works in a tavern. Her name is"—Tigana scowled again, but Duilio suspected that was frustration, not dislike of the other woman involved—"Zenaide."

That would help him retrace Erdano's path, as he knew in which tavern Erdano had met that girl . . . unless there were two tavern girls named Zenaide in Erdano's life, which seemed unlikely. "That's helpful. I will try, Tigana, but I do not think I will find her."

"You are better to look for her than Erdano. He is too easily distracted." She rose, bundling her pelt under one arm, her delicate feet white against the black sands. Duilio managed to keep his eyes on those feet. "I will ask the children," she said, and left him alone on the sand.

The day felt chillier then as Duilio contemplated the impossibility of hunting a nonhuman girl in the Golden City. Young Gita must be strong-willed if she'd defied Tigana and set off on her own after Erdano, but that didn't mean she could make her own way in the city, not in the harsher parts of it, and not when revealing her identity would mean her death.

The city had once welcomed all of the peoples, human and sereia, selkie or otter folk. Duilio was old enough to remember that time. He remembered sereia walking through the streets among humans, with no enmity between. When the prince's father died, young Prince Fabricio had closed the city to nonhumans after ascending the throne. The Ferreira family had always kept his mother's bloodlines secret— simple enough to do since she wore human form—but from that day on they had lived with the fear of exposure.

It was more dangerous for one of the sereia. When Duilio had noticed Oriana back in the spring, though, it had never occurred to him to expose her. He'd noted the reddish cast of her curling brown hair, her large and dark eyes, her hands always hidden in silk mitts rather than gloves. He hadn't been certain, though, until he saw her in the bathtub. He'd walked in on her there intentionally, citing a need to know the truth. Her skin bared, she could never pass for human. Her belly and thighs had a silvery coloration that mimicked a fish's scales. Her webbed fingers had been visible as well, the pink-edged gill slits on the side of her neck vibrating as she lay with her eyes closed under the surface of the water, singing to herself. And while the teeth hidden behind her full lips resembled a human's, he knew them to be much sharper.

Only when she'd dived into the water that last morning had he gotten a glimpse of her dorsal stripe. She had never turned her back on him before that. A glittering black band several inches wide, it stretched from a point beneath her shoulder blades and tapered down again to her heels, defined by a narrow edging of royal blue. Golden stippling ran down her sides and thighs. A strikingly attractive combination, even though it was merely an imitation of a tuna's markings. The memory of that morning made him smile . . . and then fret again when he thought of her continued absence.

Sighing, he leaned back and watched the seals in the bay breaking the surface as they swam. He didn't know enough of the females to make any sense of what was going on, but it seemed as if they supported one of their number. That had to be his mother, even though he couldn't see enough of her pelt to be certain. Over at the center of the beach where the pups sunned themselves, he saw one larger female moving among them, her almost-black fur marking her as Tigana. Seagulls flew overhead, enjoying the warm morning.

Water rushed up toward the spot where Duilio sat, warning him a second before Erdano threw himself up on the beach, bearing a wave of seal musk with him that offended Duilio's nose; he'd never liked the scent of other males. The bull seal waddled onto the sands and rose up out of seal form, slipping off his pelt once more. With a grin, Erdano came and settled nearby. He reclined propped up on an elbow, his pose reminding Duilio of an odalisque, as if he was displaying himself for his harem's enjoyment. Duilio resisted the urge to roll his eyes.

"She come back yet?" Erdano asked. "Oriana?"

"No, she hasn't returned," Duilio admitted. Erdano had more than once hinted he wouldn't mind seducing Oriana. Duilio didn't think she'd give in, but women *did* seem to find Erdano irresistible, part of his selkie charm.

"Too bad." Erdano smiled past him. "Mother is in pain, but swimming strong. That's good. She will stay at the house if the other one comes back, won't she?"

How could he answer that? "There isn't any understanding between myself and Oriana."

Erdano rolled his eyes dramatically and snorted. "I'm not that stupid, little brother."

She'd agreed she would try to come back, no more. Somehow Duilio doubted Erdano would believe him. "Of course, Mother would stay," he said. "It never occurred to me that she would leave."

"Good. She doesn't fit in here anymore. Been among humans too long." Erdano nodded his head, watching the seals in the water now. "Did Tigana tell you one of the young ones is missing?"

So much for Erdano not noticing. "She mentioned it to me."

"Can you find her?"

Duilio pressed his lips together. "I can try, Erdano, but I have a bad feeling about her."

Erdano fixed him with a worried gaze. "Is she dead?"

Birds chattered in the rocks above them. The sun went behind the clouds for a moment, taking the glare off the surface of the water, and Duilio could see the seals swimming calmly in the midst of the shallow bay—a peaceful scene. "I believe so."

"Then find out who killed her," Erdano ordered.

CHAPTER 4

Duilio's mother, exhausted and in pain, huddled on the boat's deck all the way back, swathed in a blanket and dozing lightly. On each hand an area of raw and reddened flesh marked the tips of her fingers, with matching injuries on her feet. She managed a pair of his felt slippers for as long as it took to get her into a cab on the quay, but Duilio was grateful when they reached the alley behind the house. He carried his mother to the servant's entrance and along the halls up to her room, trailed by their butler.

"Duilinho, put me down," she protested. She craned her neck around to catch the butler's attention. "Cardenas, could you send for Felis for me?"

The butler leaned toward the hallway and beckoned over a foot-man while Duilio set his mother on the delicate wooden-backed set-tee at the foot of her ivory-draped bed. She'd held her fingers tucked into the sleeves of her blouse, hiding the worst of the injuries, and he cringed when he saw the raw flesh. But she'd prepared salve and bandages, expecting this.

He still worried. "Can you do that yourself, Mother?"

"Felis will take care of me," she insisted, naming her maid of many years. "Aren't you to go back to the monastery today, Duilinho?"

Duilio ran a hand through his salt-spiked hair. It was almost two, and he needed to bathe and dress before meeting with Joaquim and the Lady. So he gave in, leaving his mother and her pelt in the hands of her maid.

Not an hour later he was bathed and striding up the Street of Flowers toward the monastery. His valet Marcellin had rigged him out in a three-piece suit in dark gray. The man had been arguing that since his mother had left off her mourning, Duilio should do the same. The truth was that Duilio simply didn't care to wear color. Gray and black suited him fine. But saying so to Marcellin would have given the elderly Frenchman a fit of apoplexy, so he'd vaguely promised to consider purchasing a few waistcoats and neckties in brighter colors. *Poor Marcellin.*

Duilio walked up the steep street, amazed they'd had two sunny days in a row. He reached the Monastery of São Bento de Avé Maria, its white-painted and granite walls bright in the sunshine. The square before the monastery was full of traffic, mule carts vying for space with fine carriages. Near the heart of the old city, this intersection held a collection of granite buildings, most in the neoclassical or baroque style. Businessmen strode by at a purposeful clip, for this *was* the city of business. Several moved with the same intent as he—to catch the tram at the intersection. Duilio had to jog the last bit but managed to jump on in time. The tram trundled away from the square, carrying them on to Batalha Square with its old palace and theater, and then turning out in the direction of the cemetery.

Duilio jumped off in front of the cemetery and walked down toward the Monastery of the Brothers of Mercy. When he reached it, he spotted Inspector Gaspar waiting for him outside the cells. A *mestiço*—part Portuguese and part African—Gaspar was hard to miss in conservative Northern Portugal. And while his darker skin surely made him stand out, his specialized abilities would have earned him a place in any police force in the world. Gaspar was a *meter*, able to measure others' powers with a single glance. Supposedly the meter was the rarest form of witch known to history, perhaps one born per generation in the whole world. Duilio had initially found the man's direct gaze unsettling, but he'd quickly grown to like him.

Gaspar gestured for Duilio to accompany him inside. "Good to see you, Ferreira. I suppose you've heard about Maraval's death?"

The hallway was cold, making him jealous of Gaspar's tweed overcoat. Gaspar always dressed particularly well, his dark suit revealing an excellent tailor's touch. Duilio tilted his head to one side, wondering why Gaspar had waited outside in the hallway. The man certainly wasn't squeamish, as Joaquim sometimes was. "Yes, although belatedly."

Gaspar stroked his chin thoughtfully, his green eyes narrowing. "A setback there. He took a great deal of information with him to the grave that we would rather have had."

They'd had the man in custody for two weeks, so that was surprising. "I thought Inspector Anjos and Miss Vladimirova could get anything out of him."

"Anjos needed to rest," Gaspar said with a shrug. "His illness has good days and bad days."

Duilio suspected he was staring blankly. He'd noted before that the Brazilian inspector often looked tired, but he'd put that down to overwork. "Illness?"

"Tuberculosis," Gaspar said. "He's been better for the last couple of days, but he was pretty weak for several before that."

Tuberculosis was an indiscriminate illness, often inflicting differing symptoms on its victims. While Duilio had noted that Anjos coughed at times, the man also smoked more cigarettes than could be healthy. He'd ascribed the coughing to that. He tried to recall whether he'd ever been in direct contact with the inspector, but in their previous interactions, Anjos had always kept his distance. Duilio had thought him aloof. Perhaps the man had been trying not to pass his illness to anyone else. "What do his doctors say?"

Gaspar set his hat on the long table next to the outside door. "He doesn't see a doctor."

What could doctors do anyway? They would simply stick the inspector in a sanatorium, and Duilio doubted Anjos wanted that. "Why are you waiting out here?"

"I'm sure Tavares would prefer I keep my distance." Gaspar smiled wryly. "Shall we?"

Duilio waited while Brother Manoel opened the door and then followed Gaspar inside the stone cell. The smell was worse than the previous day, although not nearly as bad as it should be. Duilio made do with pressing a gloved finger under his nose. The body on the stone table was still covered with a sheet. Joaquim stood to one side, speaking urgently with the Lady, a striking woman with black hair, pale blue eyes, and a very fine wardrobe. Today she wore a fashionable suit in dark blue, the hem of her box-pleated skirt brushing along the granite floor.

She cast her pale eyes over Duilio and nodded regally to him. Then she turned toward Gaspar. "Miguel, I think *you* need to look at her."

The inspector crossed to her side and carefully drew back the sheet. The doctor had neatly sewn up the Y-incision on the girl's chest, but Gaspar's eyes immediately fixed on the girl's left breast. The pallid skin over her heart showed no sign of the damage the doctor had mentioned. Gaspar stretched his hand over the girl's heart, an inch above her skin.

"This isn't good. Someone drew her life force out of her." His eyes rose to meet the Lady's. "A healer did this, or a witch with very similar powers. Someone who can drain another's life away."

The Lady's mouth tightened into a thin line. "What are you saying?"

"I spoke to a healer last night," Duilio interposed. "She told me a healer can do that, but it goes against everything they're taught. That the ones who do this are like demons."

Joaquim shot him an annoyed look that accused him of withholding information. Duilio shrugged apologetically. The cathedral bells began to toll the hour, and the Lady discreetly laid her gloved hands over her ears, even though at this distance the sound wasn't overly loud. Once they'd announced the time, she dropped her hands and shook herself.

"The question isn't whether it's possible for a healer to kill," Gaspar said quickly. "It is, I assure you. I can see the print of the killer's hand on her skin. The question is why. Why steal her life?"

Duilio had a feeling Gaspar was leading them slowly to his point. He nudged Joaquim's shoulder. "Tell him."

Joaquim scowled at him and then turned back to Gaspar. "When you released me from the investigation of *The City Under the Sea*, I returned to the Massarelos station and picked up working on my list of missing persons again. The officer who does morgue duty usually calls me to look at unidentified bodies. We've had three girls turn up dead on the streets like this in the last two weeks. There might have been more we've missed."

Gaspar stroked his chin. "So we have a predator in the city, one who was probably a healer at one point in their life. One who can kill by touch."

The Lady's eyes flicked toward Gaspar. She rubbed one gloved hand down her dark skirt. "It can't be," she protested softly. "We would know if Nadezhda . . ."

Gaspar held out one hand, almost a gesture to hush her.

Duilio still wasn't sure of the hierarchy between the four members of their team. He'd thought Anjos—their Truthsayer—was nominally in charge of Gaspar, and they both seemed to answer to the Lady. Now he wondered if Gaspar was actually at the head of the pack, especially with Anjos being ill.

If he recalled correctly, though, Nadezhda Vladimirova was the full name of the fourth member of their team—the *rusalka*. When Rafael Pinheiro had been questioned by Miss Vladimirova during the early days of their attempt to clear undesirables out of the Special Police, he'd been uneasy. He'd called her unnatural. Paolo Silva,

Rafael's father, called the woman *undead*. That matched with what Duilio had learned about *rusalki* in the previous two weeks. Various legends abounded about them, but a common strain held they were the spirits of young women who'd been murdered or drowned . . . which suggested *undead* might be the best description.

The Lady stepped away from the stone table as Gaspar pulled the sheet back over the girl's body.

"Why would they be doing this, then?" Duilio asked him. "Why steal others' lives?"

Gaspar gave him a level look. "If they're stealing others' lives, there are a few possibilities. It could be they crave the illusion of life they feel when they've consumed another's life force. Or they could be passing that life to someone else."

"Passing it?"

The Lady opened her mouth and shut it quickly.

"Earlier this year Anjos was shot while in the countryside near Lisboa," Gaspar said. "Miss Vladimirova actually has no life to share, which is a healer's primary tool. She was able to save his life, though, by killing a bull in a nearby field and using that strength to heal him."

Duilio puzzled over that. Using a death sacrifice to enhance her own abilities had to be considered necromancy and forbidden, but did it count if she'd killed an animal? Joaquim's brows were drawn together with disapproval.

"She saved his life," the Lady said to Gaspar, facing him with a level stare. "Don't forget that."

Duilio had the feeling they'd argued this before, and often.

"I'm not convinced that Nadezhda actually is dead," she said to Duilio, as if he needed to hear her justification. "I believe her life is paused instead."

"My gift tells me she's dead," Gaspar told them. "Totally devoid of life. Empty."

"A healer, first and foremost, controls her own body," the Lady argued. "I believe she chose to stop her life rather than die at her husband's hands."

Gaspar regarded her with raised brows. "And how is that any different?"

"Control," the Lady said. "She's of the Vladimirov bloodline, the most powerful family of healers known."

"I don't understand," Joaquim inserted. "How does that pertain to this case?"

"Some healers are stronger than others," Gaspar said. "Like any other gift, there are gradations. Few healers, however, have the strength to contain the energies stolen from another person inside them. It essentially overheats them, although it temporarily allows them greater abilities, to heal things a normal healer couldn't. They can even knit bones or clear infections or . . . make a heart beat again. Or not. As Miss Vladimirova is empty of life, stealing someone's life wouldn't overwhelm her. No one would know the difference."

"You would have *seen* it," the Lady pointed out.

"Only if I'd seen her before it dissipated," Gaspar allowed. He turned back to Joaquim. "In any case, Inspector Tavares, leave the hunting of this killer to me. I'm immune to a healer's touch, so what would kill you won't hurt me."

Duilio had known that witchcraft didn't work on Gaspar, nor had he seemed susceptible to Oriana's *call*, but he hadn't realized the man was unaffected by natural witches as well. "So a healer can't heal you?"

Gaspar's head tilted. "No. I have to rely on doctors if I'm hurt."

The Lady shook her head as if exasperated.

Joaquim's hands clenched into fists. "You want me to drop this?"

Gaspar sighed, looking guilty. "I am aware there's no one more likely to find this killer than you, Inspector. But she can do to you exactly what was done to that girl," he said, pointing to the covered body on the table, "with only a touch. I'm trying to save your life."

Joaquim didn't look too happy at that pronouncement, no matter the reason.

Half an hour later, Duilio and Joaquim walked back along Santo Ildefonso Street toward their more regular haunts.

"I thought you and Gaspar were getting along," Duilio said after they'd walked in silence for some way. "What happened?"

"Nothing," Joaquim said, shoving his hands in his coat pockets.

Duilio recognized that pose, the one Joaquim adopted when he didn't want to talk about something. He wasn't going to get an answer out of him. When Joaquim didn't want to talk about something, he didn't. Ever. He'd grown up with Joaquim, so he knew.

A second cousin, Joaquim's father had been mate on one of Duilio's father's ships. While the elder Tavares was at sea, his wife had died giving birth to Joaquim's younger brother, Cristiano. Duilio's mother insisted that the two boys should live with the Ferreira family until their father returned, and that fostering had carried on for the next eight years. Joaquim had become Duilio's closest friend, more like a brother than a cousin, closer than either Alessio or Erdano. He and Joaquim simply had more in common.

When Joaquim's father left the sea for good to take up boatbuilding, Joaquim decided to enter seminary to study for the priesthood, not having any interest in boats—or building them, at least. It hadn't surprised Duilio too much, though, when Joaquim left seminary to join the police force—no more than Joaquim had been surprised when Duilio left the university. Neither of them was well suited for a life of reflection or legal bickering. They both preferred to be doing instead. So Duilio understood why Joaquim found the order not to pursue this killer irritating. But he could offer Joaquim an alternative.

"I have a case you can help me with," Duilio said. "I'm hunting a lost girl." He described the girl missing from Erdano's harem.

"And that's it?" Joaquim's eyes held doubt. "Small, fair-skinned, brown hair? That could be anyone."

"Well, the girl might have a scarred left foot," Duilio added. Tigana had come up with the information that the girl's left hind flipper was split—the unfortunate result of a past meeting with a shark. It made Gita lame as a human, which gave Duilio the most useful lead he had so far. "Split was the word used. She limped, noticeably so. And she probably would have been nude when she showed up on the quays."

"The quays?" Joaquim rubbed a hand over his face and groaned. "Is this the sort of pursuit I would be ordered to abandon if my superiors heard about it?"

Trust Joaquim to see through to what I'm not saying. The fact that Gita wasn't human meant that the police weren't supposed to render aid. They were supposed to refer nonhuman cases to the Special Police, whose mandate from the prince was more concerned with capturing and executing nonhumans than helping them. "Yes. I'm afraid so."

Joaquim puffed out his cheeks. "I'm going to lose my job."

But he didn't refuse to help. Joaquim had a very egalitarian view of justice. In truth, many of the police officers Duilio knew fell on that side of the prince's law.

"I thought to search out her trail tonight if I can," Duilio said as they passed the Church of Santo Ildefonso. "I expect she followed Erdano to The Lusty Siren." Duilio mentally cringed. He would be willing to bet a great deal that Oriana found that stereotype offensive.

"I know the place."

"I could use your help. I don't know that part of the city all that well." Joaquim lived on the edge of that parish and knew it far better.

"After hours, right?" Joaquim peered up at the skies where clouds were scudding in. "Very well. I'll tag along."

Duilio knew this part of the riverside well. His own boats—a yacht, a twenty-seven-foot sailboat, and the paddleboat—were moored not far from the quay near the treelined Alameda de Massarelos. The few miles to the mouth of the river had been dredged to reduce the silting of the river's channel, and several marinas were tucked along the old quays past the Ribeira where the river turned and widened. This side of the river housed mostly private boats and those belonging to smaller businesses, while the winemakers used the opposite shore over at Vila Nova de Gaia.

Duilio's family had rented this particular space near the quay for three generations, back to the time when the family had smuggled French goods. Now the Ferreira boats were nestled between the yacht owned by Mr. Cezar Tome Guilherme, and on the other side the Ramires Fishing Company, a family interest with a dozen moderately sized boats, each lashed to the next parallel to the quay. Even after nightfall, that business had men coming and going. Lanterns lit the masts of the boats and the windows of their office next to the stone slip that led down to the moored boats. As they had always been good neighbors, Duilio didn't mind the lingering odor of fish. Guilherme supposedly complained about it every time he visited his yacht.

Dressed now in the same seal-smelling garments he'd worn to visit Erdano that morning, Duilio waited as Joaquim cajoled one of the fishermen dozing on his deck into bestirring his tired memory. As it turned out, the fisherman had seen the girl on Saturday night. It was evidently difficult to miss a girl climbing naked onto the quay. One of the other fishermen had hurriedly given her a blanket, thinking she'd fallen into the river.

It was, as Duilio suspected, not far down from where his own boats were moored. Erdano kept a few changes of clothing in the yacht, which also provided him a relatively safe spot to leave his pelt while in the city. But a search of the yacht didn't reveal the girl's pelt.

João, the young boatman who maintained the family's boats, had an apartment just off the quay and came down to ask if he could help. Since they'd finished searching the boats, Duilio settled for asking the young man to keep an ear out for any word of the missing pelt. As João's lover, Aga, was a selkie, the young man understood the importance of the missing item.

"The fisherman didn't say anything about her carrying a pelt around," Joaquim noted once João had gone back home. "How big would that be?"

Since Gita's must be smaller, Duilio extrapolated down from the size of his mother's pelt bundled tightly, and gestured with his hands. "About this big."

"So she hid it somewhere. On one of the Ramires boats? Or Mr. Guilherme's?"

They didn't have time to search all those boats. "She wouldn't know which ones were mine, so she might have picked any of them. I can look again later, but this is the one Erdano always uses."

Joaquim nodded. "Where did he go from here?"

"To the Lusty Siren, I believe," Duilio said. "There's a girl there named Zenaide that he favors."

Joaquim peered up at the clouds coming in from the sea. "Where is there a girl he doesn't favor?"

Duilio climbed up from the sailboat's deck and then jumped over to the stone slip. Joaquim didn't approve of Erdano's excesses when it came to women. He didn't approve of Duilio's past connections with women either, despite the far smaller number of women involved. It amused Duilio that Joaquim had grown up so straitlaced—particularly when compared to Alessio and Erdano. He'd never figured out how that happened. "It's selkie charm," he said. "Erdano can't help it."

Joaquim rolled his eyes. They headed up from the docks toward the tavern. The Lusty Siren was located off the Largo do Mirante. The prevailing winds carried the smells of a fish seller's wares along the street. Finer businesses had fled that area for cleaner and wealthier environs. Even so, according to Erdano, the women there were still as fine.

"So you meet Erdano here?" Joaquim asked as they made their way through the dining area of the Lusty Siren. It was a crowded place with no more than a dozen small tables. But the sounds of the mournful singing of the black-shawled woman near the soot-stained stone hearth carried over the murmur of voices as patrons went about their business and ate their suppers.

"I've been here a few times," Duilio admitted. "His choice."

Joaquim snorted. "No, I didn't think it was yours."

The lovely Zenaide didn't prove any more helpful than the fisherman. The buxom young woman led them back into the cramped kitchen to keep out of her employer's eye and turned her hand to drying glasses with her apron. "Yes, Erdano came to see me that night, but I didn't see any girl."

Joaquim sniffed dubiously at a large pot of soup bubbling on the stove. It smelled of cabbage, but Duilio wasn't going to investigate. "Is anyone else here who might have seen her?"

Zenaide appeared to consider that as she loaded the glasses onto a tray. "You know, Old Timoteo was outside that night. He would have seen anyone who came in."

"The beggar who sits on the fountain?" Joaquim asked, proving he did know the area.

Zenaide put her hands on her rounded hips. "Not a fine gentleman like you, sir," she said, surveying Joaquim in a way that caused a dull flush to spread across his skin. "But he has sharp eyes. He remembers everyone who comes or goes. Keeps an eye on us girls, too."

Duilio shot Joaquim a dry look over the woman's head. He pressed a couple of milreis into her hand. "Thank you. We'll see if he saw anything. We appreciate your help."

She pocketed the coins and simpered at him. "A pleasure, Mr. Ferreira."

"Selkie charm," Joaquim whispered under his breath.

Duilio laughed as they walked out the back door of the tavern. "More a case of my regularly paying Erdano's tab here."

The street on the far side of the tavern was dark, lit only by the faint glow of a streetlamp on the corner. And this side of the building reeked of urine, so Duilio watched where he set his feet. When they came out into the triangular area formed by the juncture of three streets, he could see the beggar perched on the edge of a half-circle fountain built onto the side of one of the buildings.

Timoteo was a wizened old man, dressed in a ragtag assortment of clothes, but his eyes were indeed sharp. He clutched a glass of beer as they described their missing girl. "Two nights ago she came here, the poor girl."

"What do you mean, poor?" Joaquim asked.

"Only had a blanket about her." Timoteo took a swig of beer. "Thought she must be mad."

The blanket was a telling detail, matching the fisherman's claim. "Did she go into the tavern?"

"No," Timoteo said. "Not the front door. Went into the back-street like you did."

Which proved the old man had been watching them, as well. Sharp eyes, as Zenaide said. "Did she come back out again?"

The man set down his glass and held out his hand. "Fine gentlemen like you two have enough to spare."

True, even if neither of them was dressed like a "fine gentleman" at the moment. "The price will be based on your answer, then."

The old man grinned, showing only a handful of teeth. "A man gagged her, carried her into a coach over there." He pointed at the intersection through which they'd just walked. The square's traffic appeared to be mainly pedestrian, folk out at night moving from tavern to tavern, so a coach would likely have drawn attention. "Thought it might be a family problem. A nice coach, not tatty, so richer folk, like you."

Duilio dug out his wallet and located another pair of milreis. He held them up for the man to see. "Tell us everything you can remember about this man and his coach."

Joaquim drew out a notebook and jotted down the man's words. Unfortunately, he described a man almost as difficult to distinguish as Gita had been. He was very average—brown hair, fair complexion, shorter than Duilio or Joaquim and older, wearing a dark jacket and trousers. The coach was black with no arms on the side. Timoteo hadn't seen the driver clearly, but he'd been stocky. Duilio pressed his lips together, frustrated.

"Wish I could tell you more," the old man said.

Duilio handed over the coins, and the old man secreted them inside his shirt. He winked up at them. "Hope you find her, fine gentlemen. She looked lost."

Lost, indeed. Duilio clapped Joaquim on the shoulder. "Let's head back to the house."

Joaquim folded up his notebook, nodded to the old man, and followed.

"Do you think he's a good witness?" Duilio asked.

"Actually, I know his name," Joaquim said. "He's been helpful to the police in the past, so I suspect he earned that money."

A hired cab took them through the crowded area around the hospital and down to the Street of Flowers. Once there, they settled in the library at the house, each with a glass of brandy. *It's nice to be somewhere quiet,* Duilio thought, away from the crowds and the smells of nighttime revelry. He'd never been much of a reveler himself.

Duilio sat at one of the chairs set around the polished table in the center of the library, cradling his brandy in his hands. "I feel like we asked all the right questions, but came away without answers."

"I hate this part," Joaquim said. "I can ask discreetly if anyone has heard about such an incident that night, but don't expect an answer, Duilio. It's too vague."

"I know." Duilio swirled the brandy in the glass, letting it take on the warmth of his hand. He rarely drank much; that had been one of Alessio's excesses. "She's dead, Joaquim."

Joaquim set his glass down and dragged one hand over his face wearily. "Why were we wasting our time, then? For heaven's sake, Duilio."

"Erdano asked me to find the killer," he admitted.

"And you couldn't tell him no. Why couldn't you say no?"

Duilio fixed him with a level gaze. "Could you?"

Joaquim leaned back in his chair and put his feet up on the polished wood table. "No."

Duilio swirled the brandy again. "Did you know Alessio knew the infante?"

Joaquim cast him a glance that suggested he'd drunk too much. "Where would he have met the infante?"

"No idea." Duilio hadn't told Joaquim about his Sunday visitor the day before, not in a venue like the restaurant where they'd eaten. Some things were too risky to say in public. But his own library was the safest place he knew, so he told Joaquim of his incognito visitor and their rambling conversation, which made Joaquim scowl.

"I accused Alessio of going to Lisboa so often because he'd run out of aristocrats to bed here," Joaquim said in a regretful tone. "Well . . . I didn't use those words."

Joaquim and Alessio hadn't gotten along well for the last few years Joaquim had lived in this house. Duilio never had known why. "You were on speaking terms then?"

"I'd come by to report on my hunt for your mother's pelt."

When his mother's pelt had been stolen over three years before, his father and Alessio had chosen not to inform Duilio what was missing. Nor had they told Joaquim, despite the fact that his police ties would surely have helped in the search. Alessio had informed him a couple of years after the fact, and then had died less than a month later. It frustrated Duilio that they hadn't gotten along better. But commenting further on the estrangement would only make Joaquim stop talking, so he dropped the subject.

"Did you hear anything from Miss Paredes today?" Joaquim asked after a long silence.

"No. I feel like I should be doing something, but . . . I don't have any idea what needs doing." Duilio slid down farther in his chair and rubbed his hands over his face. "I've got things to keep me busy. Finding Erdano's girl. Taking care of Mother. I even went to the boxing salon for the first time in a month or so. But it all feels like I'm treading water, just waiting for her to come back. Like my life is . . . paused midstream."

Joaquim's brows drew together. "You only met her three weeks ago, and two of those she's been gone. Don't you think you're over-reacting?"

Duilio laughed softly. He was moderately certain Joaquim had never been in love; he was waiting for the *perfect* woman. "No, I don't."

Joaquim raised one hand. "Hear me out, Duilio. Is it possible that she's bewitched you? A sereia can do that with her voice."

"No." Duilio smiled, grateful for Joaquim's concern. "I have heard her sing, but I felt this way long before that."

"Also remember, their *call* draws human men," his mother said, "which you are not, Duilinho. Not completely." She stood at the library's door, wearing a quilted dressing gown in pastel yellow. Her hair hung in a loose braid over her shoulder. She kept her hands behind her.

Joaquim hastily slid his feet off the table, looking sheepish.

"No, don't get up," she told them. "I didn't realize you were here, Filho. I only came down to ask Duilio if there was any news."

She always called Joaquim *Filho*, since he shared his father's name. According to Joaquim, it had the same effect as when she called him "Duilinho"—that of making him feel like a small child. "Nothing yet, Mother."

She turned her eyes on Joaquim. "How is your father? And Cristiano?"

Joaquim inclined his head. "They're both well. Now that he's back from Coimbra, Cristiano is working at the shop full-time. He loves it there, for which I am glad."

"As am I." She cast a hesitant glance at Duilio before addressing Joaquim again. "I wonder if you and your family would join us for dinner sometime soon. So that I might catch up on your news."

That was the first Duilio had heard of such an idea.

"We would be very pleased to do so," Joaquim said. "Father especially has worried about how you're getting on."

"I'm much better now," she said. "I will send an invitation, although we should plan our dinner *after* Miss Paredes returns, don't you think, Duilio?"

Joaquim turned curious eyes on Duilio.

"Of course, we should wait. Mother, were *you* aware that Alessio knew the infante?"

"Yes." She shifted and folded her arms, apparently only remembering as she did so that large sheepskin mittens still covered her hands—mittens usually reserved for the cook's frequent bouts of arthritis. She cast a guilty glance at Joaquim and said, "My hands are tender, but you do not need to tell your father, Filho. I don't want him to worry."

Joaquim cast a conspiratorial glance in her direction. "Certainly not."

She turned back to Duilio. "Your brother knew him from school. The infante studied Latin with him, but he actually studied while your brother did not. They remained friends, I believe, until Alessio died."

Had he spotted the infante in some corner tavern or in the library and never known he was looking at royalty? "Why didn't I know that?" Duilio mused.

"Because you and your brother never talked," she said with some asperity.

He should have expected that answer. "I'm sorry, Mother."

She laughed softly. "He didn't make it easy, did he? Now, I shall leave the two of you to your commiseration over whatever requires brandy at this time of night."

With that she inclined her head toward the two of them and slipped into the dark hallway. Joaquim turned guilty eyes on Duilio. "I had my feet up on the table."

Duilio shrugged. His mother had never been one to fight with boys over mistreatment of the furniture. "It's not as if she's never seen you do that before."

After casting a swift glance at the hallway, Joaquim put his feet up on one of the other chairs rather than the table itself. "Father is halfway in love with her, you know. I'm not certain this is a good idea, a social call."

Duilio settled back in his chair. Although his mother would never have betrayed her wedding vows, he'd always known she admired the elder Joaquim Tavares. She had, after all, raised his two sons after his wife died. "I'll see if I can subtly remind her not to dazzle him too much."

CHAPTER 5

In the darkness, a light rain began to fall. Oriana shifted onto her back, crying out when sand pressed against her burned skin. She let her mouth fall open, catching as much rain as she could, buying precious time. Enough for a few more hours, that was all she needed. She had to survive a few more hours.

She heard the waves rushing onto the rocks, too far away to do more than tantalize her. The post loomed over her, a dark shadow with something pale at the top—the albatross. Her eyes were failing. Her gills ached, so very dry, and the rain wasn't enough to ease the pain.

There was no one, she knew. No one would come for her. It would be the will of the gods if she died here alone. Only she had done nothing to deserve this punishment. By all rights, the gods should send her rescue.

The rain, meager though it might be, refreshed her hope. A few more hours. She only had to survive a few more hours.

CHAPTER 6

Duilio stood in the doorway of the front sitting room. His mother hadn't come down for breakfast, so their morning visitor was left to him to handle, even if she'd asked for his mother. Lady Pereira de Santos sat alone on the pale leather couch, a small figure in unrelieved black. She wore a lace mantilla over her neatly coiffed black hair. The lace was turned back to expose her face, but the veil's presence told Duilio that the lady, who lived much farther up the Street of Flowers, had made the visit secretly. He couldn't see any reason for the subterfuge; he was sure she wasn't one of Alessio's conquests.

There had been some scandal in her family, though, several years ago when he was at Coimbra, a break with her stepson. He'd met the Marquis de Sesimbre, a puppy of a nobleman who thought a mere gentleman like Duilio Ferreira far beneath his noble family's notice. The young aristocrat surely wouldn't approve of this visit, so perhaps that was her reason. There was a daughter as well, unmarried and unlikely to be so soon. Despite having seen her at many balls, Duilio didn't think he'd ever heard tall Lady Ana speak—or seen her dance—with anyone.

When she saw him at the door, Lady Pereira de Santos rose. Nowhere near her daughter's height, the lady barely reached his shoulder. "Mr. Ferreira," she said with a small curtsy. "I trust Lady Ferreira is not too ill?"

He gestured for the lady to sit again, and she settled once more on the couch, a dark blot against the leather. "We were sailing yesterday," he offered, leaning against the corner of the marble mantelpiece. "She burned her fingers on a rope. It is uncomfortable, but she'll soon be fully recovered. I'll convey your concern."

The lady turned her long eyes on him, a measuring glance. "You didn't take a crew?"

He had difficulty imagining the lady sailing her own boat, all swathed in black. "My father—bless his soul—would never forgive me should I not man the sails myself."

"Of course," she said, her eyes drifting down toward her black-gloved hands where they lay in her lap. "I'd forgotten he was a sailor."

Duilio controlled his annoyance. "Sailor" was far too simple a word for his father, who'd *captained* ships for the prince's father and transformed his trading business into large investments when he no longer wished to sail. "Adventurer" would have suited him better. Duilio smiled at her anyway. "He was most adamant, my lady, that I learn to sail."

She went still, as if deciding what to say next. The light fell across her face, glinting across a metallic thread in the lace of her mantilla. She was truly lovely, although in a hard way, like one who wore her beauty as a shield. She'd been widowed young, and while she wore mourning for her husband still, black flattered her fair complexion. She lifted her face to his then, and he saw that her eyes were hazel, not brown. "I am looking for Miss Oriana Paredes. I hoped you or your mother might know what's become of her."

That was not, in any way, what he'd expected. He kept his breathing calm only by virtue of reminding himself not to give anything away. Why was this woman asking after Oriana? The lady's home stood next to the Amaral house, where Oriana had worked longer than a year. And the woman had attempted to speak with Oriana at the Carvalho ball, but Oriana had seemed very uncomfortable being the focus of the lady's attention.

He wished he had an answer, although he wasn't sure he would share it if he did. "Has Miss Paredes offended you somehow?"

"No, Mr. Ferreira." The lady's chin lifted in a stubborn tilt. "But I need to find her and I don't have access to the palace. You might."

The palace? The lady had a reputation for being disturbingly direct, but she'd just gone three steps past direct and straight to insanity. "I don't understand. Why are you seeking Miss Paredes?"

She rose and paced the length of the rug before the couch. When she turned to him again, her jaw was set. "I am in an uncomfortable position, Mr. Ferreira," she said, her voice cross. "I'm here on the behalf of another, someone whom I cannot reveal, who is concerned for the young woman's welfare. He hasn't been able to discover her whereabouts and needs someone to intervene on her behalf. Someone with greater access. As Miss Paredes was employed here, I had hoped that *you* might be willing."

He stared at the woman. What was truly going on behind that lovely face? "Access to the palace?"

"I have reason to believe that . . ." She paused and he guessed she'd reached the truly awkward part. She started over. "I believe Ambassador Alvaro might have some idea where the young lady is. Or he could find out."

That name set off warning bells in Duilio's head. Alvaro was the ambassador of Oriana's people to the prince's court. The lady's request meant she knew Oriana wasn't human—or that this unnamed person on whose behalf she'd come did. And while the idea of going to the ambassador for information had occurred to Duilio, he didn't know whether the man would be inclined to help Oriana.

"I am a widow and have no reason to request a meeting with

the man," Lady Pereira de Santos added when he didn't respond. "But you might do so, Mr. Ferreira. You're a man, and can go where you like."

Had she thought through what she was asking of him? Sympathy for the cause of the various sea folk was often difficult to prove, but visiting Ambassador Alvaro would surely be considered a sign of Duilio's leanings, inviting scrutiny his not-completely-human family could ill afford. And while he now had friends in the Special Police, that body was divided between the new powers and the old members who'd abused their authority. He couldn't be sure the *second* group wouldn't get their hands on him, and therefore, his mother.

His hesitation must have shown, because the lady stepped closer, the scent of roses drifting with her. "You have no reason to trust me, I know, Mr. Ferreira. But I swear I only have the young woman's safety in mind. My friend believes she's in great danger. There are rumors starting in certain quarters that . . . something has happened to her."

Duilio swallowed and pressed his eyes closed. His gift agreed with that statement. Something had happened. But when he asked himself if Oriana was still alive, his gift told him she was. He met the lady's eyes. "What makes you think you can trust *me*?"

"I saw you with her at the Carvalho ball."

That was the only social event Oriana had attended as his mother's companion, a single ball where Oriana had sat quietly in the shadows among the old women and hired companions. Lady Pereira de Santos had tried to speak with her there. Duilio didn't remember singling Oriana out himself, though. "She is my mother's companion," he pointed out. "I was not escorting her."

Lady Pereira de Santos regarded him with narrowed eyes. "Those of us who lie to society, we all keep a certain distance from others. The face you showed her was not a lie. You trust her, which tells me she has some value to you, beyond that of a mere servant."

"Everyone in society lies, lady," he said softly.

She took a deep breath, pressing one hand to her belly. "I have a husband," she told him. "No one knows, but he and I have been secretly married for seven years now."

Now *that* surprised him. She still wore mourning for her first husband; it was not unusual in the more traditional families for a widow to dress so for the remainder of her life, and to remain a widow as well. And although Duilio had heard that the lady had a lover, he had no idea she'd married the man, a commoner who ran a clerk's office in the city—her man of business. "Monteiro."

She cast a startled look at him, but didn't deny it. "You can imagine my stepson would be displeased, and society rather disapproving, should it get out."

Both true. Even if the remarriage were not an issue itself, her first husband had been a marquis and her father a duke. She came from a long line of nobles who would find her marriage to a commoner shocking. Yet she'd married Monteiro knowing there would be scandal and opposition. Her gesture of trust in revealing that secret decided him. "What should I ask the ambassador?"

Her shoulders slumped in relief, and she laid one black-gloved hand against the mantel. "If he knows where she is," she said, "and if he can intercede if she's been imprisoned."

Imprisoned? Duilio swallowed. "It may take me a couple of days to get an audience at the palace. Even with the ambassador."

"I understand. All I ask is that you send word if you learn anything. My butler is in my confidence and can be trusted with any message you have for us." She faced him squarely. "I am very grateful, Mr. Ferreira."

"No need," Duilio said, giving her a wry smile. "I was considering going to him anyway. I didn't know where else to turn." He'd known that Oriana reported to a spymaster in the city, a man disguised as a fisherman. But the spymaster's fishing boat was no longer at its previous mooring, and Duilio had no way to know if the man would help Oriana anyway.

Lady Pereira de Santos laughed softly, seeming friendlier now that she had her way. "I was right about you, then, that you hold her in esteem."

"I think very highly of Miss Paredes," he admitted.

She held out one hand. "Again, my thanks. Even if you learn nothing at all, you will have tried. It's all we can ask."

He bowed over her slender hand and a moment later, the lady was gone.

D uilio wrote his request for the fourth time, this time finally aligning the wording correctly so that nothing spilled into a margin. He sanded the paper and set it aside to dry. It was at times like this that he considered hiring a secretary, but finding one he could trust with his family's secrets posed difficulties.

He'd wrapped a fine leather-bound book carefully in brown parchment, neither too rich nor too plain. It was only one of several volumes from his library written in an unfamiliar script supposedly belonging to the ancestors of the sereia. His father had told him that, making him doubt the claim. The unknown book held little value to Duilio—he certainly couldn't read it himself—but he hoped it would provide an *excuse* to talk to the ambassador without causing too much suspicion.

His mother waited at the door of the library, her bandaged feet tucked into felt slippers and her hands hidden in the sheepskin mittens. Once Duilio gathered his things, she laid a hand on his arm and kissed his cheek. "Be cautious," she told him, an unnecessary warning.

"Stay off your feet, Mother," he bid her in turn, equally without need.

The family's carriage had been readied to transport him to the palace gate. He could have taken the tram or walked, but arriving in a carriage would grant him an air of importance. Posturing was everything when it came to dealing with bureaucracy. He would have to deal with guards and secretaries, all of whom considered every petitioner an inconvenience. So he chose the carriage, hoping to start off on the right foot.

The ride to the entrance of the palace grounds wasn't long, only a couple of miles up the Street of Flowers. The road served as the primary thoroughfare between the water and the palace, though, and was heavily used. The driver wended his way through the early-afternoon traffic, likely more slowly than Duilio could have walked. The tram would have certainly been faster. The delay gave Duilio time to fidget with his black frock coat, his linen cuffs, and the creases of his charcoal pinstriped trousers. His valet would have exploded in a flurry of French curses had he known Duilio did anything other than sit perfectly still.

But it was one of those moments when Duilio's gift warned that his imminent choices would mean his life or death. So far he'd always made the correct choice. He wasn't sure this time.

CHAPTER 7

After passing through the densely wooded park that surrounded the palace grounds, the coach stopped before the first gate. Duilio stepped down, tucking the paper-wrapped book under one arm. He gazed up at the walls of the palace, asking himself whether he wanted to walk inside and practically proclaim himself a Sympathizer . . . but it was a moot point. He had no other way to seek out information about Oriana, so to the ambassador he would go.

The palace rose above him, its fanciful turrets and walls painted in red and gold. Merlons topped each wall, suggesting a military usefulness that this palace had never actually exercised. It was decorative rather than defensible. It was also a maze, Duilio had heard, with several different levels, dozens of stairwells, and patios that looked out over the Golden City. The newest addition to the palace, built by the current prince's father, was a square structure rising two stories above the clock tower that had once been the palace's highest point. Its whitewashed walls failed to capture the whimsical spirit that the older parts of the jumble displayed.

Duilio cast a glance up at the ornate entry gate with its tiles and arches. The source of the emblem on the Special Police's badge, an open hand on the arch's keystone, warned the intruder of the palace's magical properties. Whatever those were, their secret remained unknown to the general populace. Not swayed, Duilio walked up to the gates to present himself to the guards.

Unlike the building, the guards *did* have a martial air, making Duilio glad he hadn't attempted any weapons. Their blue uniforms with red sashes and gold braid hailed back to the previous century, the cutaway coats revealing very businesslike sabers and formal daggers. He wouldn't be surprised if each guard had a pistol secreted somewhere on their person as well.

His request went over more easily than he'd expected. One of the guards eyed him narrowly from under the brim of his shako, escorted him through the tunnel and up to the next level, and then through the next two gateways. The main terrace surrounding the palace afforded a view of the city to the south, although he would have had to go to the very edge of it to see the Street of Flowers. Instead, they crossed the terrace and walked under an archway set in the middle of that part of the palace, leading to the patio on the opposite side of the building.

A frightening bust supported the bay window over that archway—a depiction of the sea god on his clamshell. He had wild hair and wide, pained eyes, and his mouth seemed frozen in a grimace. Duilio almost asked the guard to stop so he could get a better look at the thing, but decided the guard must see it every day and would think him easily awed. So he followed the man up a small spiral staircase on one side of that arch and out into a second-floor hallway.

"If you'll wait in there, Mr. Ferreira," the guard said in a cool voice, "the secretary will get to you eventually. That may be a while, though."

In there proved to be a long hall, the sitting area for all petitioners. Chairs lined the walls, with a thick runner between them leading up to a large desk at the far end of the room where the secretary held his court. Duilio inclined his head, aware that he had a long wait ahead of him. He counted two dozen other petitioners there. He sat obediently in one of the chairs while the guard went up to the front to give Duilio's name to the secretary.

The chair was hard—no doubt intentionally so—and the hall over-warm, but since removing his coat would be inappropriate, Duilio sat back and sweltered without complaint.

The hall's ceiling and upper walls were ornately tiled in blue and white, with arches and keystones in gray granite. Workers for the court occasionally strode past, intent on this or that task. Most of the petitioners were of a common stripe, wearing their best church garb, dark and serious save for the occasional red sash. A white-haired man sat to Duilio's right, clutching a sheaf of papers and rolling them in nervous fingers. His thin frame hinted at frailty and a lack of wealth. An issue of unpaid taxes, Duilio suspected, and when he spoke to the old man, he found that confirmed. Ignorance of the law, the man claimed, a likely thing as their tax laws were often convoluted.

His gift supplied confirmation that the man's cause would prove just, so Duilio took a slim notebook from the inside pocket of his coat and made a note of the man's name and direction, thinking he might check on him later.

"Are you a lawyer?" the old man, a Mr. Bastos, asked upon see-ing that, brows drawn together in a worried knot.

"No," Duilio told him, sliding the notebook back into his pocket. "But I know someone who is willing to help with issues like this. I'll give him your name if you wish."

The old man grasped Duilio's hand with papery-skinned fingers, his grip light. "Oh, bless you, sir."

Duilio was about to return the blessing when he was forestalled.

"Ferreira?" The deep voice belonged to a tall man who stood on the burgundy runner in front of Duilio's chair. Glossy black hair was brushed back from a widow's peak, framing a pensive face with an aquiline nose. It was his visitor from Sunday—Bastião—only today the man wore a blue and red sash about his chest, an acknowledg-ment of his station as a member of the royal house of Aviz. Two guards waited behind him, escorts from their stance.

Duilio gazed at him for a second, trying to decide how to react, but good manners outweighed his annoyance. Now he knew why his gift had viewed the man's visit to the house as an important one. He rose and bowed properly. "Your Highness."

Infante Raimundo de Bragança Angeja, Duke of Coimbra, shot a cautionary glance at his guards and then said, "Walk with me."

Duilio shoved the wrapped book into a coat pocket and fell into step with the man, wondering where he intended to go. The infante was under house arrest. *Where exactly is he allowed to go?*

"I walk," the infante said as if in answer to Duilio's thoughts. "It's all I can do. There are days when I walk every floor of the palace, every wing, the terrace, the patio. I am allowed visitors on rare occasions, but as I have no power, I am not worth anyone's time."

Perhaps this man's doppelgänger had visited him instead. But no, this was the man who'd come to his house on the Street of Flowers, so clearly the house arrest wasn't as effective as was widely believed. "I'm certain that must not be the case, Your Highness," Duilio murmured.

The infante snorted. They stepped out of the long receiving hall and walked down the hallway that looked out over the patio. The two guards had fallen back, possibly a courtesy. "Tell me, Ferreira. What brought you here?"

"I came to speak with someone."

They turned another corner and headed into the new portion of the palace, a section that was—judging by the abundance of guards—not open to visitors. The infante stopped. His two guards were now more than a dozen feet away, and none of the ones stationed in the hallway stood close enough to overhear. "Who?"

Duilio had stopped; he could hardly keep walking. As the infante had all but told him he found the ban on nonhumans insupportable, Duilio took a chance. "Ambassador Alvaro."

"An odd choice, but I think I can arrange it," the infante said gravely. "May I ask a favor in return? I used to talk to Alessio often. I found his perspective refreshing."

"I expect you did, Your Highness," Duilio said. *Refreshing* might be the most benign term ever applied to his brother.

"I tried to keep him apprised of Paolo Silva's doings. In return he told me what he knew, what he foresaw, and more recently, he helped with other matters," he said vaguely as a bespectacled court functionary passed them in the hall, eyes politely averted. The infante waited until the man was several feet away to continue. "Now with Silva out of favor, I have no such trade to offer. But I might be able to get you in to see the ambassador."

"Silva's out of favor?" Duilio hadn't heard anything about his bastard uncle since the last time their paths had crossed.

"Because he helped bring down Maraval," the infante said. "My brother punished him by turning him out of his room in the palace. Thus the prince has lost two of his more rational advisors. Despite his infernal plans, Maraval did give my brother sound political advice."

Prince Fabricio rarely made decisions of state any longer, the majority of power in Northern Portugal having been slowly appropriated by the various government ministries instead. It actually made for a more stable government, but there was always the possibility the prince would attempt to retake his lawful powers and make some new nonsensical decree like the ban. "I see. And what favor can I do for you?"

The infante crossed his arms over his chest. "I feel as if the palace is ill. Is it?"

Ill? A bizarre question. But if the palace had magical properties, then perhaps it wasn't so strange after all. Duilio closed his eyes, trying to ask himself the correct questions. His talent supplied him only with a sense of danger. Vaguer than normal, it was still unformed—a *nascent* danger. He let loose his breath and opened his eyes. "I have no specific answer for you, Your Highness. You are right, though. There is something wrong."

"Thank you, Ferreira. Glad to know I'm not losing my mind. The palace is bound to the royal family, and lately it's felt . . . upset."

The infante turned and resumed walking, his expression pensive. "There is a rumor that my mother was a witch and ensnared my father."

"I hadn't heard that," Duilio said, an untruth. But if the mother had done so, it hadn't profited her much. She'd lived less than a year after her marriage, dying at the infante's birth.

They came to a halt before the intersection of two hallways. The infante held out one hand, gesturing for Duilio to step back. Duilio obeyed, backing away from that crossroads, the infante moving after him until they stood several feet from the intersection.

And Duilio quickly realized why. Prince Fabricio walked along that perpendicular hallway, a huddle of men following close behind him. The prince, fifteen years Duilio's senior, appeared closer to fifty than forty-five, or older. His hair had once been as black as the infante's, but was now heavily streaked with gray. Worn overlong, it also hadn't been brushed out or tied back, making the prince look unkempt. Under a dark blue velvet dressing gown, he wore what appeared to be pajamas and scuffed along the hallway in felt slippers.

A madman. The prince rarely appeared in public any longer, but rumors of his madness had circulated about the city for years. If the prince chose to spend his days thus, there must be truth behind those rumors. Judging by the ornamentation that bedecked their purple robes—stars and planets stitched carefully in threads of gold and silver—those sycophants must be the prince's astrologers. Most were older men, white-haired and spectacled, wise men, perhaps. One plain black coat stood out among that bunch, a man of about fifty, still dark-haired and clear-eyed.

Duilio waited for the prince to notice them, waited for one of the followers to ask for his purpose there, but they walked on as if none had seen the infante or Duilio standing to one side. He turned to the silent infante. "Your Highness?"

The infante jerked as if Duilio had startled him. "The astrologers," he said, his voice harsh. "And Dr. Serpa. I'm not overfond of any of them."

It was as well, then, that they hadn't been noticed. Serpa would have been the plainly dressed man, then, as doctors wished to be taken seriously. Black coats were expected of them.

With a sigh, the infante crossed the intersection and they continued on their original tack. "Their stars are in ascendancy at the moment. Whatever one might say of Maraval, he and Silva did keep my brother's superstitious excesses under control. They could reason with him, even if they often tugged him in different directions. These men bow to whatever strange demands my brother makes and tell him whatever he wants to hear."

Duilio walked beside the infante, his footfalls muffled on the thick runner. In front of a spiral staircase that led up to the next level, the infante stopped again and turned a furrowed brow on Duilio. "I can get you in to see Alvaro without being seen. That should keep your name off the list of Sympathizers."

"Thank you, Your Highness."

"That's going to grow tiresome," the infante said. "Please address me as Raimundo."

There were levels in society, with the nobility far above mere gentlemen like him, to say nothing of royalty. The familiarity implied the infante considered Duilio an equal, though.

"I am honored, Raimundo," Duilio managed. It sounded odd to say that aloud, but none of the guards moved away from their posts to arrest him for his effrontery.

The infante gestured at the two guards who followed them—his own personal watchdogs—and they stopped in the hallway, leaving the infante unwatched. A subtle matter, but one of great importance. That told Duilio the infante had control of his guards, whether or not they were legally required to obey him.

He led Duilio up a straight stair and, after holding one finger to his lips, proceeded in silence down a side hallway. Guards stood unmoving, seemingly lost in contemplation. They didn't respond as the two intruders slipped past.

When they'd gotten beyond the guards' hearing, the infante quietly said, "They only follow Alvaro if he comes out of his suite. Otherwise they leave him alone. He still receives and sends diplomatic correspondences, but little more. No one talks to him. No one listens to him, either, I'm afraid."

They rounded one more corner, ending up in a cul-de-sac that had only one door leading off it. The infante crossed to the door and rapped on it.

"No, I will *not* let you examine me," a low voice snarled from within.

The infante shot a glance back in the direction they'd come, and then rapped again. "Open the door, Braz."

A second later the door jerked open. The middle-aged man within seemed frazzled. His coppery hair was a wild mass of curls that looked as if they hadn't seen a comb in some time. A few inches shorter than Duilio, he had dark eyes that looked overlarge in his angular face and paler skin than most residents of the Golden City. Translucent webbing showed between the fingers of the hand that held open the door. "Come in."

The infante obediently stepped inside, Duilio following his example. Like many rooms in the palace, the ceiling of this one was breathtakingly beautiful. Delicately painted plaster leaves and vines wound up and around the beams, joining into an elaborate rosette at the keystone. But the room was sparsely furnished, only a single pair of stiff-backed chairs set by a small lacquered tea table adorned with an inkwell and a pen. A narrow bed waited in the corner halfway hidden behind an oriental screen. While that barrenness highlighted the ornate craftsmanship of the arches overhead, Duilio doubted that was the reason behind it.

"Has Dr. Serpa asked to examine you again?" the infante asked.

The ambassador threw up his hands and made a series of ob-scure gestures. "The arrogant fool thinks I should be honored by his desire to poke and provoke me. Who is this?"

"Duilio Ferreira," the infante answered. "A friend of mine, and trustworthy."

The ambassador turned his dark eyes on Duilio. "Would you be willing to carry a message out of the palace for me?"

That could get him hanged, but Duilio didn't flinch. "Yes, sir, for I've come to ask *your* help."

"What is your price?" the ambassador asked without hesitation. The collar on his open-necked shirt didn't hide his gill slits com-pletely. Their edges seemed red and inflamed, as if he'd not been in water recently.

"I'm trying to find a missing woman," Duilio said. "One of your people, Oriana Paredes."

Alvaro's eyes narrowed. "What is she to you?"

"My mother's companion." That sounded insufficient, so Duilio added, "When she left the city she told me she would try to return, but I've heard nothing. Can you tell me where she is?"

Alvaro looked to the infante. "Are you certain of him?"

The infante nodded. "I'll vouch for him, Braz. He has reason not to bend to my brother's whims. Familial concerns."

The ambassador's brows drew together. He stepped closer to Duilio and sniffed. "Ah," he said, realization lightening his expression.

Duilio felt a flush creeping across his cheekbones. He had a sel-kie's smell, a hint of musk about him. Oriana had once told him she'd mistaken it at first for ambergris cologne.

Alvaro spun about and disappeared behind the screen. He re-turned after only a few seconds, a large book in his hands—an atlas. He set it on the fragile tea table and started flipping through the pages. "I was sent a message late this morning in the post," he said, not looking up from his quest. "I haven't had any chance to get word to anyone, so your coming is a god gift."

Duilio stepped closer. "You know where she is?"

The ambassador glanced up at him, one hand splayed on the open page. "The message was cryptic, but I'm certain it referred to her. She's been left on one of the Ilhas de Morte. Perhaps three days now. I can't even say she's still alive."

Oh, God. Duilio swallowed. "The islands of death? Where are they?"

The ambassador picked up the pen, dipped it in the ink, and using the coastlines as a guide, drew a pair of lines that crossed. Near that intersection he drew in a constellation of seven points, each marked by an x. "This string of islands. The note said she'd been chained there. I don't know when, exactly. It only takes a few days before one of us dehydrates."

"Chained?" Duilio repeated, his breath short.

"Traditional execution," the ambassador said, shaking his head. "It's a warning, I think. Not for anything she's done. A reminder to me not to talk."

Duilio didn't care about the *why*. "How many guards are there on these islands?"

"None, although it's said a leviathan haunts those waters."

Duilio shut his eyes, fighting for calm. He knew now the meaning of that sense of foreboding he'd had. The urge to run down the hallways and all the way down the Street of Flowers to the river itself screamed through his nerves, but the pale voice of reason in his head reminded him he needed to plan. He wasn't going to worry about the chance of a sea serpent showing up; the creatures preferred shipwrecks. They rarely bothered ships above the water. "So I simply go there and bring her back?"

"Yes," the ambassador said in a guarded voice. "Do you have a boat? Are you willing to help me?"

He wasn't doing this for the ambassador. "Yes. Is there anything else I need to know?"

The ambassador set his webbed hand on Duilio's sleeve. "They

waited to inform me until they thought it too late for me to interfere. They didn't say which island she's on, but visiting them all will
take a day or so, so pick carefully."

Duilio closed his eyes and tried to concentrate, but he was too
upset now to get anything coherent out of his gift. Was she still
alive? His gift sent a twinge that confirmed it, but his sense of foreboding didn't fade. "I can't waste any time. I have to go now. Your
message, sir?"

The ambassador let go of Duilio's arm, ripped the page out of
the atlas and handed it to him. "You are my message. Gods speed you."

Hastily folding the torn map, Duilio cast a helpless look at the
infante, who'd remained silent throughout. "What is the quickest
way out of here?"

"Follow me." The infante headed for the door, and then startled
Duilio by running down the hallway, down the flight of stairs,
through a side hall and down that to another set of stairs.

None of the guards moved to stop them along the way, not even
when they reached what must have been the "secret" tunnel that
led up from the entryway arch. Near the end of the tunnel, the infante came to a halt, and grabbed Duilio's arm. "Walk straight out.
They won't question your coming out of the tunnel if you act as if
everything is normal."

Duilio almost walked on but remembered his manners. "Thank
you, Raimundo."

The infante touched his shoulder. "Who is this woman?"

Duilio took a slow breath, concentrating on not appearing
winded. "A good question."

The infante nodded and disappeared into the shadows of the
tunnel. Duilio turned and walked out into the afternoon light. It
was all he could do not to run from the palace.

CHAPTER 8

Duilio stopped at the house, hoping only to be a moment. Most everything he needed could be found in the sailboat, save blankets. It was times like this that he wished the older parts of the city had telephone service. He would like to have had Joaquim along but didn't have time to go looking for him. He'd sent his most reliable footman, Gustavo, to Coimbra a week ago, and the other, Luís, didn't sail. Perhaps he could take his young boatman, João, with him. He went to the library to leave a note for his mother—who was reportedly visiting a dressmaker—while Cardenas found blankets and his valet dug up a warm coat.

I'm going after Oriana, he wrote. He pressed his lips together, trying to decide what else he could say to his mother that wouldn't upset her overmuch.

"What are you doing?" Joaquim stood at the library doorway, overcoat folded over his arm.

"What are you doing here?" Duilio asked in turn. "You're supposed to be at the station."

"I came by to see if you needed me. . . ." Joaquim waved one hand vaguely.

"Actually, I do." Duilio spread the torn map on the polished table and pointed to the series of marks Ambassador Alvaro had made. "Have you been out to these islands before?"

Joaquim looked over his shoulder. "I don't think so. Why?"

"I need to get out there. Oriana's trapped on one of them, but I don't know which, so I'm going to have to start with the closest." Duilio noted the distance and bearing on the edge of the torn map with a pencil.

Joaquim remained silent a moment, then leaned past Duilio. He touched the second island in the string. "This one," he said. "We should go to this one."

Duilio glanced over when Cardenas arrived at the library door, blankets bundled in his arms. "I've sent Luís down to warn João you're coming, Mr. Duilio."

Duilio took the blankets and pointed with his chin toward the table. "Grab the map."

Joaquim didn't move. He surveyed Duilio's court garb. "Haste is the enemy of perfection. Go change into something suitable for sailing," he ordered calmly. "Mr. Cardenas, can you ask Mrs. Cardoza to throw together food and water for us. We'll probably not be back until early morning at best."

"We don't have time," Duilio snapped.

"Yes, we do." Joaquim set a firm hand on his arm. "João will be getting the sailboat ready to cast off. I promise we'd only be waiting on that end if we hurried now. Go."

Joaquim's only being sensible, Duilio reminded himself. Letting go a pent breath, he dumped the blankets atop the map and obeyed.

The winds *were* in their favor. Joaquim tried to engage him in conversation, but Duilio was too tightly wound to answer in more than monosyllables. He kept scanning the water, ignoring the birds crying out above them, the sparse clouds drifting about. Normally he would have enjoyed being out on the water, but now all he wanted was to find Oriana, and that made him poor company.

Once the sun set, Joaquim watched the stars and kept them on course, making notes on a small pad of paper by the light of his lantern. Navigation was one of Joaquim's native skills, almost a gift. He never got lost. "We're close," he said, pointing. "Stay on this course."

Holding the tiller steady, Duilio gazed that way, searching for a landmark he could follow. The moon hadn't risen yet. Since the islands weren't large enough to appear on the map, they were hunting something small in a vast ocean, likely no more than rocky outcroppings. When something pale fluttered high above the level of the water, Duilio pointed. "What's that?"

Joaquim peered at the light-colored object. "Albatross."

Duilio hoped the creature didn't move. He guided the boat closer and when they'd nearly reached the shore, he dropped the mainsail. Together he and Joaquim jumped into the water and tugged the boat high enough to keep it from slipping away into the water. The sailboat leaned to one side as the keel dug into the sand.

Duilio grabbed up his kit and lantern and headed onto the beach. The island looked small—smaller than the palace grounds. In the ring of light from the lantern, Duilio could make out a slope and, at the top of it, a pale form. He ran.

The albatross flew away with a heavy beating of his wings. A wooden post had been erected at the highest point of the small island, chains affixed to it, and curled about its base he saw Oriana's unmoving form. She'd managed to half bury herself under sand and small rocks, scant protection against the sun.

Afraid of what he would find, Duilio went to his knees beside her. Her pained breathing tore at his heart, but she was *alive*. He let go a breath he hadn't realized he'd been holding. Her gills were distended and red, and in the lantern's light her pale skin seemed burned and crusted with salt. No, that was sand. White blotches stood out against the reddened flesh of the side that had been facing upward. He glanced up at Joaquim and dug the blankets from his kit. "Go soak these."

Joaquim grabbed them and jogged back to the boat. Duilio

withdrew a canteen from the kit and, after a moment's consideration, dribbled water onto Oriana's distended gills. She shuddered, but the sound of her breathing eased. He picked free the stones wedged about her body, and then carefully turned her onto her back so he could rinse the gills on the other side of her neck. Her eyes opened but appeared to be filmed over, staring blindly upward in the darkness. A heavy metal cuff on one wrist was fixed by a chain to the post, but her other hand reached out toward him. She made a sound that might be his name.

"It's me, Oriana," he told her touching her cheek. "It's Duilio."

Can she even see me? Surely she'd heard him. She seemed to relax at the sound of his voice. He irrigated the gills on the other side of her neck, and then held the canteen to her lips. She managed only a sip before beginning to cough. Duilio dribbled some water into her eyes, and by then Joaquim had returned with the soaked blankets.

Oriana whimpered as the wet wool touched her burned skin—a sound of relief rather than pain. Duilio tucked them about her carefully, talking softly to her all the while.

Then he dug in the kit again and retrieved the bolt cutters.

While Duilio settled Oriana in the sailboat's tiny cabin, Joaquim shoved the boat away from the shore. The waning moon had risen, giving him light to work. He jumped aboard and paused, listening to the rising wind. It had shifted in their favor again. It pushed to the southeast now, so they'd be running with the wind. The sound of a sail snapping made him cast a glance at the mainsail . . . only to recall that Duilio had dropped it when they approached the little island.

A frisson of alarm ran down his spine. Where had that sound come from? "We need to get out of here," he called to Duilio. "Help with the sails."

Duilio didn't look like he wanted to leave Oriana's side, but he must have heard the urgency in Joaquim's voice. He started to haul on the main halyard while Joaquim settled at the tiller. The small boat bobbed as the mainsail rose, flapping in the wind, and they began pulling away from the island.

"Can you hear it?" Joaquim asked. "There's another boat out there. No lights."

Duilio stopped amid securing the halyard, his head tilting. "On the other side of the island."

Clutching the tiller, Joaquim peered into the distant darkness while Duilio finished securing the halyard and raised the jib. He couldn't make out anything in the moon's feeble glow yet, but that boat had to be running without lights. That made it dangerous.

"We've got the wind," Duilio said. "Run with it. They'll have to come around the island if they want to follow us."

Joaquim let the mainsheet out and the boat leapt forward toward home. "What is a boat doing out here, anyway? We're out of the trade lanes."

"What are *we* doing out here?" Duilio headed for the bow of the boat.

Joaquim shook his head and didn't answer. For several minutes, he concentrated on keeping the boat headed toward the Golden City, hoping they could get there without drawing any curious patrols. They wouldn't be able to explain away a sereia on their boat.

"I still hear it!" Duilio called back to him after a few minutes.

Duilio's ears were better than his. Joaquim held his breath. There, in the distance, he heard sails again. *More* sails this time. That couldn't be a small sailboat. It had to be a yacht or something even larger.

And it was faster than they were. The island was already gone from his sight, but this ship had come around the island and was gaining on them. *In pursuit.*

Had Duilio been wrong? Did the sereia have a navy that guarded these infernal executions after all? Or were there pirates in these waters?

Joaquim weighed the chances of their dropping the sails and closing their lanterns to escape notice, but figured that the vessel already had its eyes on them. With white sails they would be easy to spot in the moonlight. He could try changing course, but in any other direction, they would lose speed.

Then something bumped the side of the boat, sending the stern of the boat heaving upward.

Joaquim grabbed at the rail with his free hand, heart pounding. "What the hell was that?"

Duilio slid back toward the cabin to check on Oriana. "I don't know!"

The thump came again, closer to the bow this time, sending water splashing about when the boat's hull slammed back down to the water's surface. There was no chance that was accidental. *A whale?*

"They're coming!" Duilio yelled at him.

Casting a glance over his shoulder, Joaquim finally saw the other ship clearly. Light glinted on bits of metal and panes of glass. It was a shadow-wrapped vessel with sails of blue or black—a steam corvette, judging by the size and set of the sails. And it was closing fast.

A voice boomed out of the darkness, the words garbled in the wind.

But Joaquim had no doubts about the ship's intention. It was going to ram them, and this sailboat wouldn't survive. Duilio lifted Oriana out of the cabin and carried her to the rail, preparing to push her overboard. Joaquim couldn't blame him. Once in the water, she had a chance of living through this.

A gunshot whizzed through the night, followed by another. Duilio fell back toward the hatch atop Oriana, covering her body again.

The voice boomed out of the darkness, clearer this time, calling for them to surrender. The ship would be on them soon. He could make out the figurehead now, the gilt shape of a woman with a fish's tail—a creature of myth nothing like the woman they were trying to save.

Jaw clenched, Joaquim kept his course. What could they do? They couldn't outrun a ship this size. They couldn't fight. And clearly someone on the deck of the other ship had his sights on Oriana, which meant Duilio couldn't get her overboard.

And then the terrifying sound of splintering wood filled Joaquim's ears. The other ship, almost atop them, began to list alarmingly to port. Joaquim shoved the tiller to the left, sending the sailboat slipping off in the opposite direction. The sails fell slack and the boom swung toward him.

The corvette began to right itself amid panicked cries on the deck, and then keeled to starboard when the wood-splintering sound came again. With so much forward momentum, it sped past them, far too close for Joaquim's comfort. Their horn sounded, and sailors ran along the deck, moving to strike the sails, dark forms that Joaquim could barely make out amid all the spray.

Joaquim dragged the tiller back, and the sailboat's boom swung to full reach. Whatever trouble the corvette was having, they had to take advantage of it. The sailboat sprang forward unhindered. More gunshots rang out.

"Look!" Duilio yelled from the hatch, pointing.

The moon's light struck the sinuous coils of a leviathan as it wrapped its pale length about the bowsprit of the corvette. The muzzles of rifles flashed. The creature didn't seem to notice the guns firing in its direction. Its muscular body twisted like the coils of a python, and there was a boom as the bowsprit snapped, followed by the crack and whistle of breaking ropes amid the cries of frightened sailors. The leviathan fell back into the water with its wooden prize.

Joaquim felt the boat bob on the wake of that motion. Their sailboat continued its run on the wind while the crippled corvette slowed, listing to one side. Joaquim watched it until the darkness enfolded it, waiting for his breathing to calm. He said a silent prayer for the safety of the sailors on that ship and, for good measure, another for the health of the leviathan who'd stopped it.

Unwilling to let Oriana go, Duilio asked Joaquim to sail the boat home to the Golden City. Joaquim unerringly led them back to the mouth of the river. They passed the lighthouses on the breakwaters before dawn and sailed the last few miles to the city. Joaquim pulled the boat directly up the stone ramps that led to the Ribeira quay. "Go on," he said. "I'll moor the boat and stow the sails."

Duilio didn't fight him. There would still be revelers out at the quay, even in the early hours. He climbed up onto the ramp and Joaquim carefully lifted Oriana into his arms so he could get her up to the quay. Then Joaquim cast off again to take the boat back to its normal mooring.

A breathless Duilio carried Oriana's blanket-wrapped form up to the quay and even found an oxcart—one that was waiting to unload cargo—willing to carry them back home. Without question, the driver took them into the mews area behind the houses on the Street of Flowers. When Duilio carried Oriana up the servant's entrance steps, his mother came running from the front of the house. Still dressed, she must have waited hours for their return. She rushed to Duilio's side. "Is she all right?"

"I don't know, Mother," he admitted, so relieved by her presence that he wanted to cry. Oriana hadn't woken again since that initial response to their arrival on the island. She seemed to have slipped into a deeper sleep, mouth slightly open and eyes closed. If it hadn't been for the occasional movement of her gills, he would have thought her gone. And God help him, that would have been too painful to bear. "I don't know what to do for her."

His mother stroked Oriana's chalky-pale cheek with her raw fingers. "We should get her into water. Come, take her back to her room, and I'll fill the tub."

Duilio followed his mother into that bedroom. He sat on the

edge of the bed, Oriana still in his arms, to wait while the water ran. Once his mother had the temperature where she wanted it, she bid him to bring Oriana into the bathroom. He stripped off the damp blankets and carefully laid Oriana in the rising water, on her side just as she'd lain next to that post. The metal shackle on her wrist banged against the porcelain with a dull clank. The worst of her burned skin was exposed to his mother's eyes.

"Now go away," his mother said firmly.

Duilio turned his eyes on her, startled. "Mother, I need—"

"No, you don't." She pointed toward the bedroom. "There is nothing for you to do now. I want you to go bathe and get some sleep. I'll stay with her."

She wore a resolute expression. He took a last look at Oriana, who lay motionless in the slowly rising water. Then he turned and walked out of the bathroom.

He stopped out in the hallway and set his back to the wall, shaking. Then he slid down against the wall until he sat on the floor. He had been so focused on bringing her back to the house that he'd refused to let himself think she might not survive. Now that he'd reached the end of what he could do, that worry welled up again, making his throat tighten.

Duilio had no idea where he could turn for aid. There was no doctor he could send for; none would treat nonhumans for fear of rousing the prince's ire. All he could do was hope and pray that water was what Oriana needed. He had to believe his mother knew what was best.

After some time sitting there on the cold floor—minutes or hours, he wasn't sure—a hand wrapped around his arm and hauled him to his feet. "Come on, Duilio," Joaquim said. "Let's get some brandy. Just what you need right now."

Oriana woke in water. It flowed through her aching gills and caressed her burned skin. Her eyes, painfully stressed, couldn't focus, but she knew where she was. The muted glow of a skylight above and the faint taste of bicarbonate of soda in the water told her she was in the oversized bathtub back at the Ferreira household.

A dark blur shifted above the surface, someone watching her. By the gracefulness of the movement, she decided it was Lady Ferreira. An irony, since Oriana herself had come to this house to be the lady's paid companion—a glorified servant. Now the lady was waiting on her.

Oriana tried to raise one hand under the water in greeting. It felt exceptionally heavy, and she realized dully that it still bore the shackle that had secured her to the post. The metal thunked against the side of the tub, and the sound reverberated painfully through the water. Oriana squeezed her eyes shut.

CHAPTER 9

WEDNESDAY, 22 OCTOBER 1902

Duilio woke to a painful stab of light from the curtains in his bedroom being thrown open. For a second he rubbed his temples, and then rolled off the bed and got to his feet. His mother stood at the window, wearing the same dress she'd worn the night before. "I told you to bathe, Duilinho."

He sniffed and caught a whiff of his stale clothes and self. Then he shook his head to clear it. "Is she . . ."

"She's asleep," his mother said.

Feeling a wave of relief, Duilio sat down again. Joaquim must have dumped him on his bed, and he hadn't managed to get under the coverlet. Salt and sand sprinkled the brown silk. "Thank God," he finally managed, crossing himself. "Do you think she'll be all right?"

The window's light cast his mother into silhouette, so her expression was hidden from him. "She woke for a moment, but fell asleep again. I can't be certain she's seeing normally. I've made her as comfortable as I can. For now she needs sleep, water, and time."

"I'll go watch her for a while, Mother."

She laid one hand on his shoulder. "I left Felis sitting with her.

Get cleaned up, and get something to eat. Miss Paredes isn't going anywhere for now."

Duilio gazed down at his bare feet—he had no idea where his shoes were—and nodded. He needed to send a message to Lady Pereira de Santos, so he pushed himself up from the bed.

Once bathed, he had to admit he felt better. It was nearly eleven by then, so he dressed casually in trousers and an open-necked shirt and made his way to the dining room. His mother wasn't there. Given the time, that made sense, although he'd hoped to question her further. But he could smell food in the warming trays, the staff working hard to accommodate the unraveling of his normal schedule. Duilio spotted Cardenas in the hallway and, when asked, the butler confirmed that Lady Ferreira had retired to her own bed.

Duilio rubbed his temples. "Is Joaquim still here?"

Joaquim had tried to discuss last night's events with him, but Duilio had been so worried over Oriana that he hadn't paid much attention. The brandy hadn't helped. While stowing the sails Joaquim had found a bullet hole in the mainsail; the crew of the mysterious ship had been sincere in their threats. That raised questions to which neither of them had answers.

"Mr. Joaquim has left, sir," Cardenas said.

"Thank you, Cardenas." The butler bowed and went on his way. Duilio sighed, resigned to eating alone, and went to select his breakfast.

Once he'd written and dispatched his note to the Pereira de Santos home, Duilio headed back to Alessio's old bedroom. He found Felis sitting primly in a straight-backed chair, half in and half out of the bathroom. She effectively blocked his entry, so he couldn't even see the tub, much less whether Oriana was still in it. The elderly maid busied herself plying a needle through a hooped section of linen, embroidering a subtle pattern of flowers around the neckline of a garment. She believed the devil had use for idle hands.

Duilio tried to look past her. "Felis, do you need better light for that?"

"I am not an old woman yet, Duilinho," she lied tartly. She had been his mother's maid his entire life, so the familiarity was expected. She pointed her needle at him. "You shouldn't be in here."

He felt his brows draw together. *Ah, because Oriana isn't clothed.* "I brought her back here, Felis," he said, vexation creeping into his voice. "I only want to see her."

"It isn't proper," the woman groused.

This from the same woman who'd read the cards dozens of times for him. She'd predicted his attachment to Oriana that way. Duilio pressed his hands together. "Please, Felis. You know how important she is to me."

And since she'd chided him about letting Oriana leave, she gave in . . . partially. She moved the wooden chair out of the doorway and then surprised Duilio by going back into the bathroom and shutting the door on him. He was about to knock when the door opened again, and she emerged, thin nose held in the air. "You can go in now."

Duilio stepped into the bathroom and almost laughed out loud. Felis had taken several of the towels from the shelves on the other side of the room and draped them across the tub, allowing him only a view of Oriana's head and neck.

Oriana still lay on her side, facing away from where he stood. Water dribbled into the tub, the spigot left running slightly so she wouldn't suffocate in still water. Under the illumination of the skylight, he saw that her hair had been cleaned, the water bringing out the burgundy highlights among the brown strands. Her eyes were closed, but the faint motion of the gill slits on the side of her neck told him she was breathing. The sunburned side of her face seemed less red now, and Duilio let loose a sigh of relief. He sat down on the rug, close enough to gaze over the lip of the tub. He reached into the water and gently stroked her cheek, but she didn't respond. "Has she roused at all?"

"No, Duilinho." The maid set a gnarled hand on his shoulder. "Your mother says to let the girl sleep."

"I'll stay here," he said. "In case she does wake."

He felt her hand slip from his shoulder, and then he was alone. For a time he simply gazed down at Oriana's face. He saw that the back of her neck was bruised, as if someone had grabbed her that way. He had to wonder if there were other marks, if she had been tortured before being left to die. The light had been poor when he'd carried her to this room, and his mother had sent him away before he'd had the chance to see the answer to that himself.

Oriana hadn't committed any crime, had she? She didn't deserve treatment like this.

The ambassador had said this was done as a warning not to talk. Duilio hadn't asked about what; he'd been too agitated at the time to think it through. Alvaro claimed he'd been notified too late, an intentional oversight. Yet it had been clear that the ambassador had someone specific in mind when he asked Duilio to carry a message out of the palace. That meant someone in the city might have gone to Oriana's aid. Unfortunately, Duilio had no way of knowing who that was. He didn't know whom he could trust on her behalf.

He set his shoulder against the side of the tub and stretched out his legs, preparing to wait until Oriana woke. He had no commitment pressing enough to make him leave, so he let his thoughts chase the problem around in his mind, a futile exercise. The sound of falling water and the smell of sea salt comforted him, wrapping him in familiarity.

It was only when Felis shook his shoulder that he realized he must have dozed off, leaning there against the tub.

The maid stood over him, a stern figure in her black dress. She shook him again. "Wake up, Duilinho."

"I'm awake." He pushed himself up off the rug and cast a glance back to see if Oriana still breathed. Once reassured, he turned to his mother's maid. "What did you need, Felis?"

"There's a gentleman asking to see you," she said, casting a disapproving eye over his casual garb. "He's in the front sitting room."

Three visitors in four days—a crowd by their standards. He was going to have to start having Cardenas turn away callers. "Will you stay here until I can come back?"

"Yes." She pushed at him with one hand. "Go on, boy."

After one last glance at the towel-shrouded tub, Duilio walked out into the hallway and down the stairs toward the front of the house. He wasn't dressed properly to receive visitors, but he didn't care. He would just get rid of this guest as quickly as possible and head back upstairs.

Instead of Lady Pereira de Santos, her paramour—or husband, according to her own confession—waited for him. Adriano Monteiro paced behind the couch, rubbing one gloved hand with the other as if he'd been writing too much. A handsome man with dark hair and a lean build, he was elegantly dressed in a black frock coat and striped trousers, gray waistcoat, and black tie. A touch of silver at each temple lent him an air of distinction. Although he wasn't a gentleman, he certainly had the demeanor of one. He and Lady Pereira de Santos would make an attractive couple if ever they were seen in public together.

This man had to be the "friend" who begged Lady Pereira de Santos to seek him out in the first place. Duilio wanted to know why. "Mr. Monteiro, what has brought you to our door?"

The man inclined his head, his expression grim. "I came to speak to you."

"That's obvious. What did you want?" Duilio asked, irritation making him snap.

The man's nostrils flared, betraying a hot temper, but he said nothing.

Duilio sighed and, in a more civil tone, tried again. "I apologize for not being more formally dressed, but I hadn't planned on entertaining today. How can I help you?"

Monteiro didn't seem interested in his cordiality either. "I want to know how she's faring."

Duilio leaned against the mantelpiece. He wasn't going to quibble with the man over whom he meant by *she*. "Who put her there?"

"I don't know," Monteiro said with a quick shake of his head. "The rumor is going about that it was a warning not to talk, but I don't know what we're not to talk about."

Duilio looked back at the man. Was he a sereia spy? Monteiro wore gloves, but Oriana had said most spies had their webbing cut away to allow them to pass more easily as human. "They knew she would die there."

"Of course they did," Monteiro snapped. "Is she still alive?"

Duilio doubted he could keep it secret long; the staff knew she was here . . . and he hadn't asked them not to talk. "Yes."

Monteiro's dark eyes flicked up to the ceiling, and he made the sign of the cross. "Is she blinded?"

Who exactly is this man? "We don't know yet. What concern is she of yours?"

Monteiro gave Duilio a hard look. He tugged off one of his gloves and held up his bared hand for Duilio to see. Scar tissue ran along both sides of his fingers where the webbing between them had been cut away and the edges cauterized. "I'm her father."

Duilio gazed at Monteiro's handsome face. The scars indicated only that he was a sereia, not that he was Oriana's father. The man didn't look much like her. Then again, Alessio hadn't resembled their father either. "Then why weren't *you* the one to go get her?"

Monteiro replaced his glove. "Do you think I wouldn't have if I'd known where she was? I heard nothing of this until your message reached the Pereira de Santos household this morning. I never thought they would go to that extreme. There's no reason to hurt

Oriana—not in order to intimidate *me*. I know nothing worth threatening over."

It was convoluted logic, but Duilio understood blackmail well enough. "Why didn't you come to me yourself? Why send Lady Pereira de Santos?"

"She wished to protect me," Monteiro said. "We had no way of knowing how you might react to such a request, and you had no reason to see me. I'm not your man of business, after all."

Lady Pereira de Santos had refused to name Monteiro, even after Duilio indicated he knew of their relationship. He certainly wouldn't have turned Monteiro away unheard, but the man had no way to know that. If Monteiro judged gentlemen by the actions of the lady's aristocratic stepson, he wouldn't have expected a hearing. "I understand," Duilio finally said.

"Can I see her?" Monteiro asked.

"No," Duilio answered without hesitation. He folded his arms over his chest. "I only have your word that you're related. Until she can confirm it, I will not let anyone see her."

Monteiro's nostrils flared again, but he reined in whatever outburst he was considering. "Understandable. I know of a doctor. One who's willing to see one of our people."

Duilio tamped down his pride. "If you'll give me his name and direction, I'll send for him if he's needed."

Monteiro drew a slim notebook out of a coat pocket and jotted something down with a pencil. He tore out the page and handed it over. "He's a good man, discreet."

Duilio glanced down at Monteiro's gloved hand, thinking that the name on the page likely belonged to the man who'd cut those fingers apart. *Dr. Esteves.* "I pray that he's not needed."

Monteiro crossed himself again, and Duilio copied the motion reflexively. Oriana had told him a small percentage of her people were Christian due to the Church's persistence in sending them missionaries over the centuries. Had she said that about her father, though?

"Please send word to Lady Pereira de Santos when Oriana regains consciousness," Monteiro said. "I do want to see her . . . even if she's not eager to see me."

"I will do nothing against her wishes," Duilio warned. "I'll talk to her first, then decide."

Monteiro inclined his head. "Fair enough. I'll be on my way, then."

Duilio showed him the door and tried hard not to slam it behind the man. He leaned against it and rubbed a hand over his face, teasing out the ramifications of what he'd just learned . . . if it was true.

Oriana's attempted execution had been a warning aimed at her father and the ambassador both, and in which her life was considered insignificant. That indicated a great deal was at stake, made all the more apparent by the fact that someone had attempted to prevent her rescue. Yet neither of them seemed to know what that warning concerned.

And it was curious to Duilio that Oriana had never mentioned that her father lived in the Golden City. She'd said he lived in Portugal, but not that he was a businessman secretly married to Lady Pereira de Santos. The Amaral household, in which Oriana had been employed for a year, stood next to the home of Lady Pereira de Santos, where Monteiro would have come and gone on a regular basis. Yet when Isabel Amaral was murdered, Oriana hadn't gone to *him* for help. Surely they were estranged—but not enough that the man didn't care what happened to her. There was, without doubt, a great deal Duilio didn't understand about her family.

He hadn't been there for the last few years of Alessio's life, but Duilio had known of the increasing rift between his father and brother, both from his mother's letters and Joaquim's. He hated to think of any family fractured like that. Sighing, he started back toward the stairs, but hadn't quite reached them when he spotted Joaquim striding up from the kitchens in his direction.

Joaquim paused when he saw Duilio, and then headed toward him with a resolute step. "I've got something I need you to come see. We think we might have found her, Duilio. Your missing girl."

Gita? He hated to ask, but did anyway. "Is she alive?"

Joaquim's jaw clenched. "A girl's body was dumped last night in an alleyway behind the Dried Cod," he said, naming a brothel in the northern part of the city. "We think her foot had been previously injured, which is what made me believe it might be your girl."

"You *think* her foot had been injured?" Duilio repeated. How could they not know?

"It's complicated." Joaquim took a breath and said, "She was skinned."

The police headquarters sat beyond the cathedral, to the north of the two-level iron bridge that crossed the Douro River. Although Joaquim usually operated out of the station that sat between Massarelos and the half-completed hospital, he often visited the headquarters. There the police kept their own morgue, a small detached building with whitewashed walls and a red-tiled roof, whose windows remained shuttered even on the sunniest of days.

The only body the police currently found curious enough to hold was that of a girl, but they knew little more. What remained of her didn't tell them hair color or skin tone, and although she'd once had warm brown eyes, they were clouded over in death.

"They found her early in the morning," Joaquim said, covering a yawn. "The police chief has ordered us not to discuss it, in the hope that it won't get into the newspapers."

Duilio felt a flare of worry—not his gift, but his native cynicism. There would be no stilling the talk once it did get out; the newspapers loved anything sensational. "How do they think she died?"

"By losing her skin," Joaquim said.

Which meant she was alive when that happened. Duilio stifled a shudder. "When?"

"Likely Monday, midday."

On Monday morning, Tigana had been asking him to find the girl. Gita had come into the city on Saturday night, meaning that an entire day had passed between her arrival in the city and her death. "Will they turn the body over to the Church?"

"Clearly not a suicide," Joaquim said as he pushed open the door to the back room, "so it's likely."

Erdano wouldn't like that. His people had their own ways of dealing with their dead. Duilio couldn't think of any way he could interfere, and Erdano could hardly come into the city and claim the girl as one of his own.

"I'll talk to Brother Manoel," Joaquim volunteered, "but I can't promise anything."

Brother Manoel received all the bodies at the monastery, but might help, given the girl's identity. There was little chance she was a Christian. "Thank you."

They opened the door and stepped into the anteroom where visitors to the morgue were greeted, a deceptively cheerful room with blue-and-white-painted tiles ringing the lower half of the walls. A young police officer sat at a desk with a pair of chairs in front of it, his curling hair tumbled and his lean face set in an expression of concentration as he sketched on a pad of paper. He glanced up when they entered. "Back to look at her again, Inspector Tavares?"

Joaquim nodded. "Just the feet, Gonzalo."

"It might help if I see her eyes," Duilio offered. Selkies generally had the same color eyes, much like his own.

Joaquim set a hand on Duilio's sleeve. "You don't want to."

Duilio didn't argue. "Very well. Just the feet."

The young officer rose and led them back toward an inner room where bodies were held prior to turning them over to family or the Church. As soon as he opened the door, Duilio pressed a finger under his nose, his stomach turned by a smell terribly similar to rotting meat. Only one of the tables set around the perimeter of the square room held a body.

The officer went to the table and started folding back the sheet, exposing what looked like illustrations from an anatomy book Duilio had once studied. For a brief instant, his mind told him it was a hoax, that someone had made a clay model and painted it for their benefit. The girl's skin had been flayed off, laying bare muscle and tendons in gruesome detail that none should ever see.

Duilio forced himself to look at those bared feet. The left had a gap between the second and third toes that extended halfway to the arch of the foot. The muscles and tendons didn't look newly torn, but as if they'd healed that way, thickened and twisted in spots. That could have come from the grasp of a shark's teeth, where the victim had escaped by tearing her foot—or flipper—free. "This has got to be her," he said to Joaquim.

"You know who this is?" the young officer asked as he covered the naked feet again.

Duilio spun out a tale, keeping it vague to save trouble. "An acquaintance requested that I look for a girl, a young relative who'd become lost in the city. But there's no way to be sure."

"No." The young officer crossed himself. "And not much here to tell us about the unholy bastard who killed her, either. The body was only wrapped in a sheet and dumped."

Duilio pressed his lips together. Tigana had charged him with finding the girl, but Erdano had asked him to find the girl's *killer*, a different matter. "Thank you for letting me view the body, Gonzalo."

"Sorry it didn't have a better outcome for you, Mr. Ferreira." The officer returned to his sketching, and Duilio followed Joaquim out of the building into the evening air.

They walked along the street together, Joaquim listing off what he did know about the girl's death—which proved to be very little. Her body had been dumped behind the brothel sometime during the previous night. There hadn't been much blood there, a sure sign she'd been killed elsewhere. Her missing skin wasn't in the alleyway, either. The killer had apparently kept that.

That brought to mind another question Duilio hadn't answered. "We still don't know where her *pelt* is."

Joaquim walked along with his hands behind his back, a pose that usually meant he was troubled. Duilio couldn't blame him.

"As long as no one knows she's one of your brother's people," Joaquim said, "I'll still be permitted to investigate her death, so the pelt can't figure in anything I do. If word gets out I'm looking for such a thing, any investigation will be terminated."

"I'll look for the pelt myself, then. I'll talk to Mother to see if she's ever heard of anything like this."

Joaquim set a hand on his sleeve. "Don't worry her, Duilio."

Duilio stopped in the street near where the paving ended. A clump of road workers in dust-marked trousers and shirtsleeves approached, so he waited until they'd passed to say, "She needs to know. Even if it has nothing to do with her people, she needs to be warned."

"She doesn't need to know exactly what happened, though, does she?"

Sometimes Joaquim was more protective of his mother than he was himself. "I'll try. She's not likely to go out for a while anyway."

"Is she still . . . hurting?"

"Not too much any longer, but now she's helping take care of Oriana."

Joaquim smiled. "She must like her. How is she, by the way?"

So they walked down the Street of Flowers toward the house, discussing Oriana, the surprising visit of Monteiro, and the possible relationship between the two.

T he intricately carved wooden kneeler in the library didn't see a great deal of use. Duilio's mother had only a tentative adherence to the Church, and Duilio himself had never been particularly devout in his practices. But he lit the candle there anyway, hoping that God would forgive his regular lapses in piety and restore Oriana to them. Well, *to him*, actually.

He prayed for the dead girl Gita as well, little though she might appreciate it. No one deserved such a death. He only hoped her soul had found some peace with the god of the sea. He kept his words short, figuring whichever saint carried *that* prayer to heaven wouldn't appreciate the burden of excess words in addition to the blasphemy. Then Duilio rose, blew out the candle, and headed back upstairs to Alessio's old room.

When he stepped into the bedroom he heard water dribbling into the tub, which told him Oriana was still under that water. He found his mother sitting on the floor in the bathroom, gazing over the tub's rim at Oriana's unmoving form, her brown silk skirts billowing about her. He touched her shoulder and settled on the rug nearby. "Has she woken?"

"No." His mother gave him a direct look. "Why do you think they did this?"

"I still don't know, Mother. Alvaro and Monteiro each thought it was done to keep them from talking, although Monteiro didn't know what he wasn't supposed to talk about."

"It will be hard to forgive what her own people have done to her," she said, her voice sad.

Duilio sat back against the wall. "She's safe here," he said. "We'll keep her safe."

His mother touched his cheek with a damp hand, her fingertips still reddened and raw, and rose from the floor. "I'll have Teresa bring up a dinner tray for you, Duilinho."

"Thank you, Mother." He shifted over to where she'd been sitting and gazed over the edge at Oriana's sleeping face under the water.

She lay on her side, facing him. Her full lips were parted, and the steady movement of her gills told him she was breathing. Although his mother had left the towels wrapping the tub for Felis' sake, Duilio pushed them back enough to locate Oriana's hand. He drew it up out of the water, metal shackle and all. Her long fingers curled against his in reaction, hiding away the webbing between them. He wrapped his hand around hers and rested them on the lip of the tub. He just wanted her to know he was there, waiting on her.

CHAPTER 10

Oriana woke sore and achy, with an empty stomach. Her eyes seemed more willing to focus, showing her that the glow had left the skylight above. Now a pair of fainter lights shone. Gaslights—it must be night. She was still in the Ferreira household, a miracle of sorts.

She could tell the water in the tub had been changed, as there was less salt from her own body in it. Pure sea salt instead. The dull burning in her gills had faded. She was determined not to dwell on the rest. Grasping the lip of the tub in her right hand, she pulled herself into a sitting position. It took all her strength to accomplish that. As the water sloshed around her, she took a deep breath of air into her lungs. Her head spun.

Her motion had dislodged several thick ivory towels laid over the top of the tub, sending them slithering either into the tub or off onto the floor. She plucked at one that had fallen over her legs, frustrated by the wet weight of it, and finally succeeded in freeing herself from its grasp.

The sun had left her right side tender, but the blistering and crusting of salt were gone, as were the deposits the damned albatross had left. Where not red, her skin had transformed from the chalky white of dehydration to its normal opalescence. Her thighs and belly had regained their silvery coloration. She let out a shuddering sob, relieved it wasn't worse.

She was alive. She had survived, when someone had meant her to die.

She heard a soft sigh then and gazed over the side of the tub. On the fine silk rug next to the tub, Duilio slept. He wore only a linen shirt and trousers. His dark hair was tousled. He was unshaven as well, his square jaw darkening with stubble. For a moment, she stared down at him with her head propped on her folded arms. Then a drop of water from her hair splashed onto his wide forehead.

His seal-brown eyes blinked open. "Oriana?" He sat up quickly, his face level with hers. "Can you see?"

"Yes," she managed. *Ah, gods, I sound so feeble.*

His shoulders slumped in relief. "Thank God. We feared it might be permanent." His eyes searched her face and then he moved closer, setting his warm cheek against her chilled, damp one. His arms went around her, holding her to him even though the wall of the tub remained between them.

Her throat ached, and she shuddered as if she'd come in from the cold. She'd forgotten what that felt like, to have someone hold her. To have someone wanting to care for her, rather than the other way around. For a long while, she pressed her face into the crook of his neck, smelling the light musky scent of his skin. She wanted to stay there forever. "I knew you would come for me," she whispered.

He backed away and set one hand on each of her cheeks. "I wish I had come sooner. I've never been so afraid in my life."

"Soon enough. I'm still alive." That would be her mantra for the rest of her days—the gods had given her a second chance. They hadn't thought her deserving of death. It was proof of innocence that none of her people could dispute. "How did you know where I was?"

"The ambassador told me," Duilio said.

"Uncle?" she asked, mind spinning. How had her uncle intervened? As the ambassador, he was trapped up at the palace. "You went to see him?"

Duilio stroked a lock of hair back from her face and tucked it behind one ear. "We can have a long talk about that later. Do you think you could eat something?"

Her mouth immediately began to water and her stomach clenched. "Oh, yes. How long have I been asleep?"

"Almost a full day round," he said, pulling away from her and rising. "I'll go to the kitchens and see what I can find at this hour."

She nodded, and dropped her head onto her arms again. He was gone an instant later. She stared at the manacle affixed to her right wrist, a couple of links of chain dangling from it.

Then Duilio was gently shaking her shoulder to get her attention. "You drifted off."

She shook her head, and the room spun.

Duilio settled cross-legged on the floor and set a plate in his lap. He had a selection of cold baked cod and smoked salmon, along with a crusty hunk of bread. "It's been a while since you've eaten, so take it slow."

She managed to untangle her arms and took a piece of cod when he held it out to her. It tasted heavenly to her starved mouth, and she dutifully chewed while he watched her with concerned eyes. "Why are there towels in the tub?" she asked once she'd swallowed.

He handed her another piece of fish and flashed an embarrassed smile. "Felis has been helping watch over you. If she knew I'd seen you unclothed she'd cane me."

"But you have before," she pointed out. Despite having lived among humans for two years, their prudishness regarding nudity still surprised her.

"Felis doesn't know that," he said. "No questions. Eat."

She obeyed. He talked about his mother's trip out to Braga Bay and her taking seal form for the first time in years. Every time Oriana took a breath to ask a question, he handed her another piece of food. The salmon had a delicious smoky flavor, the bread was perfectly baked, and after he switched to his mother's plans for a dinner party—in which she was evidently expected to participate—Oriana realized the plate was empty. She moved her right wrist and was dismayed when the heavy cuff dragged it off the bathtub's edge. Her arm dangled there. "How do I get this off?"

"We'll take care of it later," he promised, lifting her arm back to the rim. "Now, do you want to stay in the tub, or should I move you to the bed?"

After a full day in water, her gills could use a rest. "The bed."

He set the plate to one side, got up, and left the bathroom. He returned a moment later with the old nightgown she'd left behind. "Felis laid this out for you," he said. "If I help you out of the tub, can you dry off and put it on?"

"I can try." He got one arm under hers and lifted her out of the tub, getting water all over the rug and the floor. When her feet hit the ground, though, Oriana discovered exactly how weak she was. Her head spun dizzily again, and she had to hang on to his shirt to stay upright. "No, I don't think I can."

"Well, Felis doesn't have to know." Duilio picked her up and carried her out to the darkened bedroom. He laid her on the sheets, still wet, and drew the blanket and coverlet over her. He tucked them neatly beneath her arms.

The sheets lost their chill after a moment, and she felt warm for the first time since she'd left this house. She was safe.

"Thank you," she managed. It was insufficient for everything he'd done, by any measure.

He smiled down at her. "I'm going to go sop up the mess you made in there. You'll be asleep before I'm done."

She was.

D uilio carried the armchair over and set it next to the bed. He'd left the lights turned up in the bathroom, and in that glow he could see Oriana's face. As he'd predicted, she'd fallen asleep, so he just settled into the chair.

He wanted more than anything to join her on that bed. Only to hold her, he told himself. But she needed rest now. Everything else they could work out later.

He couldn't imagine what would drive someone to take Oriana out to that island and chain her there to die. He had a better chance of understanding why someone would kill a lost young selkie girl by skinning her.

He slid down farther in the chair, thinking dark thoughts.

CHAPTER 11

Felis came to Oriana's bedroom with the dawn and chided Duilio for sitting up all night. Oriana slept on, looking peaceful, so Duilio went back to his own room to dress. After a quick breakfast with his mother, he walked down to the quay where his boats were moored to see whether his boatman João had heard anything about Gita's missing pelt. The young man had no news, so Duilio headed up to the police station to find Joaquim.

Joaquim's office held only a wide desk, a couple of plain wooden chairs, and a modern metal filing cabinet. More important, it was private. Duilio could hear other policemen walking past in the hallway outside and a faint murmur of voices, but experience had taught him they wouldn't actually be overheard by anyone in that hallway. "How is Miss Paredes?" Joaquim asked. "Any better?"

"Much," Duilio admitted. "She was sleeping in her bed when I left the house. I talked to her last night, although she was very tired."

"That's good. I hate to take you away from her, but I have something interesting to show you." Joaquim handed him a sketch torn from a notebook, what looked to be another dead girl.

Duilio peered at the drawing. The young officer from the morgue must have done this. He was quite talented. "What am I looking at?"

Behind his desk, Joaquim sighed. "Another unknown girl. Her body was found on a backstreet Saturday."

Duilio scowled at the drawing. "The same day Gita disappeared? Any relationship?"

"Gonzalo doesn't know, but it occurred to him to remind me of it this morning. She was killed Friday." Joaquim tapped the drawing with a pencil. "What that doesn't show is that she was missing some of her skin, too."

Duilio peered at the sketch, which didn't show that. "What was she missing?"

"Gonzalo said that part of her buttocks had been skinned, running up to a point in the middle of her back."

Since the sketch showed a frontal view of the body, that detail was absent. But the likelihood of two such incidents occurring without connection seemed slim; surely the first girl was tied to the second somehow. After a moment of studying the drawing, Duilio decided the dead girl's features didn't look right for a selkie. He commented on that to Joaquim, who said, "Better to assume they didn't know Gita was a selkie. I'll proceed like the killer picked two girls at random."

"Was this first girl picked up to sell to a brothel?"

"No one near where she was dumped had any idea who she was, and no one ever claimed the body. Also, my inquiries about the men who picked up your girl Gita have gone nowhere. I've had half a dozen officers asking around about it."

Duilio peered at a smaller sketch on the corner of the sheet—a hand, the nails curving down like claws. "Is this supposed to be this girl's hand?"

"Yes," Joaquim said. "Gonzalo told me she had ugly nails—his words, not mine—so he drew that."

Duilio rubbed one finger absently over the sketch. A sereia's nails would curve downward like that if allowed to grow out, but if that girl had been a sereia, Officer Gonzalo would have noted the silver coloring of her belly and thighs. Duilio studied the girl's face again, her rounded cheekbones and pointed chin. "Joaquim, have you ever seen an otter girl in human form?"

Joaquim's brows shot up. "Have you?"

"No," Duilio admitted. The otter folk rarely entered human territories, keeping to the rivers and the sea. They couldn't pass for a true human, if he recalled correctly. "Otter folk still have tails in their human form, don't they?"

Joaquim ran a hand through his short, dark hair. "How am I supposed to know?"

Duilio glanced down at the sketch again. "Can I show this to Mother? She might have met one before."

Joaquim didn't look pleased, but nodded. "Meet me for dinner and let me know."

Duilio took a moment before answering. He wanted to stay at the house to keep an eye on Oriana—but he couldn't do that forever. "Fine. I'll meet you at eight."

His mother couldn't shed any light on the situation. He found her at her bedroom's dressing table, putting salve on her sore fingers. The fragrance of unfamiliar herbs drifted up from the blue glass jar. "I've never met one of the otter folk, Duilinho. They don't share beaches with my kind. They prefer the rivers. And they travel a great deal, I think. They don't remain in one place long."

Duilio didn't bother to take the sketch out of his coat pocket. He drew over a delicate chair to sit down behind her where he could see her face in the mirror. "Do you recall ever hearing of one coming into the city?"

"No," she said, tugging on one of the sheepskin mittens. "Has one?"

He shook his head. "A stray inquiry Joaquim and I are pursuing."

She looked into the mirror to see his expression. "Does this have anything to do with Erdano's girl?"

"Perhaps," he admitted. "I think we've found her, Mother, but . . ."

"But she's dead, as you predicted." She sighed heavily.

Duilio reached over to the dressing table and grabbed the jar of ointment. He sniffed it and then put the lid on it, wondering if it might benefit Oriana's burns. "Mother, I need to ask you an upsetting question."

She gazed at him from under a lowered brow. "Duilinho, honestly."

He sometimes forgot that although his mother had been raised among humans, she'd spent a couple of years living in the sea, a very different life from the one she had now—a harsher life. "The girl was skinned," he said. "Not her pelt, we haven't found that, but her *skin*. Does that have any significance to you?"

She turned halfway about on her seat to face him. "Our skin and our pelts are inseparable." She held up her uncovered hand to display the reddened fingertips. Better, but still far from healed. "Damage to one is damage to the other. But there's no value to taking the skin rather than the pelt. The pelt can be sold. Skin can't."

She had a point. A human skin couldn't be sold. *Well, one can be*, he admitted to himself, if done in absolute secrecy.

"Miss Paredes ate this morning," his mother said, interrupting his thoughts. "But fell asleep again directly afterward. Felis told me you'd made a dreadful mess of the bathroom."

He almost laughed at the exasperation in her voice. "Miss Paredes asked to sleep in her bed to rest her gills. Getting another person out of a bathtub is far more difficult to do neatly than I expected, Mother. I did try to mop it up."

"You're smiling," she said, a glint of laughter in her warm eyes.

"Felis reports that Miss Paredes was put to bed without her nightgown."

He could well imagine Felis reporting to his mother, her spine stiff, wrapped in offended propriety. "You do understand that wasn't embarrassing to Miss Paredes at all, don't you?"

"Yes, of course, Duilinho," she said, "but Felis is lurking in the halls, waiting to box your ears, so be warned."

Fortunately Felis was with Oriana at the moment, so Duilio didn't have to worry about avoiding his mother's maid on his way to the library. Cardenas had left a handful of correspondence on his desk, and Duilio thumbed through the pile. He found a pair of worried inquiries, both related to Alessio's journals, and sighed. He set them aside and sorted through his other correspondence, a handful of invitations to this ball and that soiree, when he had no time or stomach for such frivolity.

His man of business had also sent a baffling note, asking if there was some matter Duilio didn't find him capable of handling. It took a moment to determine that the man had heard of the visit by Lady Pereira de Santos' man of business—Monteiro—and feared replacement. Duilio penned a calming note to the man, explaining that Monteiro had called on a personal matter rather than a professional one.

That train of thought brought something else to mind, though, and Duilio opened the drawer and located the note Monteiro had given him. The man's handwriting was exceptionally neat, a good thing in a businessman. Duilio folded the slip of paper and secured it in a pocket.

He stopped by to check on Oriana before leaving the house again. She slept peacefully while Felis scowled at him over her needlework. Softly, so as not to wake her, he told the maid, "I'll look in on her again tonight after dinner."

The old woman's eyes narrowed, but she didn't argue.

Dr. Esteves had his office on Fábrica Street, not far from the

Torre dos Clérigos, so Duilio headed up to that part of the city afoot. The doctor's thin-faced receptionist wasn't any friendlier than Felis, but after Duilio promised to take no more than a few minutes, she reluctantly agreed to let him in to see the man. He settled in an anteroom that smelled of lye and ammonia. Three women sat there, one an elderly and wizened creature in mourning garb, clutching a driftwood cane. The other two were younger, one pretty, one not as much. None of the trio looked to be particularly wealthy. The pretty one sniffled and clutched her handbag close to her, making Duilio suspect she was afraid. Not so much of the doctor, but perhaps of his diagnosis, or the cure.

After a short while spent in uncomfortable silence, the doctor came to the doorway. He was an older man—likely in his late fifties. His graying hair and black coat gave him a serious air. He glanced at the three women, and said, "This is a professional inquiry, ladies. He'll only be a moment. Miss Victore," he added to the receptionist, "no interruptions, please."

The doctor turned his eyes on Duilio and gestured for him to follow. Duilio pursued the man back to an office, where a cup of tea sat cooling on a desk. "Mr. Ferreira? Can I assume this has something to do with a police inquiry?"

He hadn't said as much to the receptionist, so that startled Duilio. "You're aware I work with the police?"

"Dr. Teixeira told me you paid him to perform an autopsy for the police." He gestured for Duilio to sit. "I for one find it refreshing when a gentleman uses his influence for good, or his funds. My father was the Duke of Heranas, but my family doesn't approve of my clientele and they no longer associate with me."

The current duke lived farther up the Street of Flowers, close to the palace. Duilio could imagine the man's horror at seeing the collection of impecunious women in his brother's waiting room. "I see."

"I imagine you do," Esteves said. "Now, young man, what brings you to this part of town?"

Duilio shifted on his chair, then straightened his necktie. "I have questions of a delicate nature," he said. "Ones a police officer would be forbidden to ask, but as a private citizen I can."

The doctor sat in a straight-backed chair across from him. "Is this regarding my practice here?"

"Not directly, sir. I wanted to ask if you've ever treated one of the otter folk."

"It's been a very long time," the doctor said, "but yes. Before the ban on nonhumans, I did have one come into the hospital where I was working. That was the only time."

Duilio slipped the sketch from his pocket and began to unfold it. "In human form, I assume."

The doctor looked amused by the question. "Well, as human as they get. He did have an impressive tail."

Since that confirmed Duilio's suspicion, it led to other questions. He passed the sketch to the doctor. "If you look at that hand, could it, in your opinion, be the hand of one of the otter folk?"

"Who is she?" the doctor asked, pushing the drawing back toward Duilio. "If you're trying to hunt her down, I won't help you."

He had to admire that resolve. "She was found dead in an alley five days ago, Doctor," he said, "partially skinned. In the area where a tail might have been, if she had one."

The doctor appeared to be weighing his honesty. "Why come to *me* with this matter?"

"You were recommended to me as a discreet doctor, should a certain member of my household need care. By a Mr. Adriano Monteiro." The statement was essentially an admission that there was a sereia living in his household. He hoped the display of trust would buy the doctor's willingness.

The doctor nodded, apparently appeased. He picked up the sketch, drew a pair of spectacles out of a pocket and set them on his nose, then peered at the paper. "The nails in this drawing," he said, pointing. "The sereia have similar nails, but they're far more fastidious about such things. I can't see a sereia allowing her hygiene to lapse to this point. The girl's facial structure could belong to a selkie, I suppose, but selkies don't have nails like this in human form—or a tail. Given this drawing, I would say it's a *possibility* she was one of the otter folk, but that's as far as I'll go. Without a tail, you have no proof."

Duilio tucked that statement away in his mind. "She was missing skin about her buttocks and part of the way up her back. Would it be difficult to remove that much skin?"

"Hunters do it all the time," Esteves said matter-of-factly, handing the sketch back to Duilio. "Is that what you came to ask after?"

"Yes." Duilio rose. "Thank you for your time, Doctor."

Esteves escorted him to the door, but Duilio's mind suggested another question. "If this *was* an otter girl, do you know of any reason for removing her tail?"

The doctor shook his graying head, his brows drawn together as he considered the last-minute question. "There are those who believe the magic of the otter folk is in their tail, but so little is known of them that it can't be substantiated."

A strange thought occurred to Duilio. "What about the selkies? Where is their magic?"

"Ah. It's said to be in their skin."

"You mean their pelts?" Without their pelt, a selkie couldn't resume seal form, a fact his family knew all too well.

"No, their skin," Esteves said firmly. "Have you ever seen the pelt of a selkie? By itself it isn't magic. It's the bond between the pelt and their skin that allows them to take on seal form. So even without her pelt, a selkie is still a magical creature, which is thought to be why they're so seductive in human form."

Duilio stared at the doctor, disturbed. His mother had said the skin and pelt were *inseparable*. "How do you know that?"

The doctor gave a sheepish shrug. "Medical college, Mr. Ferreira. While students don't officially study nonhumans, they always gather and whisper about them when they should be studying more pertinent topics."

Since he hadn't always studied what he should at university either, Duilio didn't doubt the man's word on that.

CHAPTER 12

Oriana's old clothes still hung in the dressing room where she'd left them before heading back to the islands. It wasn't a vast selection.

When she'd been companion to Lady Isabel Amaral, she'd had several dark and severe gowns, as well as enough day wear in somber colors to accompany Isabel on whatever mischievous course that young lady decided to pursue. But when Isabel was murdered, Oriana had been forced to flee the Amaral household with almost nothing—only what she had previously packed in one bag. So the overlarge dressing room in the Ferreira household held only two shirtwaists, two skirts, and the out-of-date blue gown of Lady Ferreira's that Oriana had altered to wear at the Carvalho ball.

"We'll definitely need to have the seamstress in," Lady Ferreira said with a shake of her head. "Why you didn't mention this to me before escapes me, dear."

Standing at the door of the dressing room, Oriana clutched her borrowed dressing gown. Her head ached, and if she moved too swiftly, the dizziness returned. The links of the chain attached to the manacle on her wrist clinked together, a sound she was beginning to hate. "Lady, I didn't have need of more."

"Nonsense." Lady Ferreira opened a large armoire full of a man's garments. "We need to get Alessio's clothes out of here. There's no reason to keep all of this. Felis?"

The elderly maid bustled into the dressing room, the scent of rose water drifting with her in a heavy wave as she passed Oriana. "Yes, lady?"

"Felis, I'd like a couple of the footmen to remove this clothing. Tell Cardenas to distribute it as he sees fit among the servants. Anything not wanted should go to the poor."

Felis made a quick bob, then sailed out of the dressing room and away.

Oriana watched Lady Ferreira with wide eyes. When she'd been hired as the woman's companion, the lady had been perpetually distracted, responding to very little beyond her son's urgings. With her pelt restored to her, she had regained a vitality that Oriana found most startling. This new Lady Ferreira was a gentle whirlwind.

The lady in question fixed her eyes on Oriana again. "Now, if you are to be my companion, I expect you to be better garbed than this. I'll have my seamstress come in the morning." Her eyes drifted down to Oriana's bare silvery feet. "And you need more shoes."

Oriana gazed sheepishly at her toes. Shoes were always a problem, as her feet were wider than a human woman's. In her two weeks imprisoned aboard ship, her nails had grown longer than she liked. They were beginning to curl down at the tips. "I already have . . ."

Lady Ferreira cocked her head. "I wager they don't fit properly. I'll have my shoemaker in tomorrow morning as well."

Why am I arguing? In the last two years, she'd never owned custom-made shoes. While the idea of a shoemaker handling her wide feet made her feel self-conscious, the prospect of having shoes that fit properly was too tempting to pass up.

The lady had already moved on anyway. "Now, I want you to prepare a list of any toiletries you need. I'll be sending Felis out later to the druggist, so I'll simply put your list with mine."

Oriana ran her fingertips across her aching forehead. "My lady, I don't have any way to pay."

Lady Ferreira waved that protest away with a sweep of one

delicate hand. "You're in my employ, Oriana. Your expenses will be folded into mine. Aspirin, I think."

And Duilio would end up paying. Oriana had no idea what relationship Lady Ferreira believed existed between her and Duilio. She didn't know the answer to that herself. The man who'd laid his cheek next to hers, who had fed her with his own hands, who'd tucked her under her coverlet so carefully—that man had been gone when she woke. She didn't know where. He'd said they needed to talk, and he'd promised to get the damned iron cuff off her wrist. Other than that, she was certain of nothing about him.

But he *had* come to save her. When she hadn't had any faith left, she'd still hoped he would come after her. She had forced herself to believe it, even when there was no way for him to know what had happened to her, or even much reason for him to intercede. He was wealthy, and a gentleman. He was human—mostly. She was none of those things.

"I cannot believe Alessio bought this," Lady Ferreira said, holding up a frock coat so Oriana could see it. The red crepe coat was heavily trimmed with swirls of black soutache. "Must be a gift from one of his admirers. Duilio would die before wearing something like this."

Oriana nearly laughed at the image of Duilio Ferreira in that jacket. Had she ever seen him in any color other than black, white, or gray? No, he must be naturally somber, which could not have been true of his brother. "What was he like?"

Lady Ferreira stroked a white-gloved finger along the trim on the colorful jacket. "Alessio? He was his father's son in many ways," she said. "Volatile, charismatic, charming when he wished to be. He had far too many lovers, all of whom laid their hearts at his feet to be trampled—which was what he usually did." She set the coat back in the armoire. "He had a selkie's charm, you know, in a very human world that didn't approve."

Duilio had told Oriana his brother was killed during a scandalous duel over a lover, but the way the lady spoke, every word sounded like a caress, as if each trait was a favorable one.

Lady Ferreira smiled sadly. "He had few honest friends, and managed to alienate his brother and father and the Tavares boys as well. He fled the university and scandalized society until he was no longer accepted anywhere. He drank far too much, especially after he broke with his father."

"What provoked that?" Oriana asked softly.

"My husband wanted him to marry. They argued over that regularly, but Alessio's tastes never ran to domesticity. He enjoyed falling in love, but had no intention of working at *staying* in love for more than a week or two. One night his father told him that if he was going to carry on in that manner, it would not be under his roof. Alessio took him at his word and left."

"Oh. I am sorry." It was unusual for an unmarried child to leave the family home, so that must have been a great trial for Lady Ferreira.

"He came to visit me regularly when he knew his father was out. I did not agree with his choices, but I still loved him." She smiled at Oriana then, a warm look holding only a tinge of regret. "Why don't you get dressed, and we'll sit down to a civilized meal. Duilio is still out, so it will just be the two of us, but I would enjoy that."

"Yes, my lady." Oriana was actually beginning to feel lightheaded, so eating was a good idea. "If you'll give me a few minutes."

It actually took far longer. While she managed to dress quickly enough, the footmen arrived soon after to begin removing Alessio's clothing and, before they were quite done, Felis returned, determined to arrange Oriana's hair and cut her nails for her. It was strange to have such a fuss made over her—as if she were the lady rather than the servant. Fortunately, the elderly maid had brought along a tray with cookies and a glass of water with lemon, which helped Oriana endure her ministrations.

"Such an unusual color," Felis said as she combed out Oriana's hair. "I would suggest you wear blue. Or pinks, Miss Paredes. Not light ones, but the deep rosy shades, or ones with a golden undertone."

Most people who noted her hair color hinted that there had been a terrible accident involving henna, so Oriana had no ready answer for a compliment. "Thank you, Felis," she mumbled.

The maid continued to comb Oriana's hair, being very careful near the bruising on the back of her neck. In the dressing table's mirror, Oriana could see that her split lower lip had scabbed over. Her cheeks looked thinner than normal, and her eyes bigger in her pale face. Felis smiled at her in the mirror, and Oriana managed to return the gesture.

Her afternoon of dealing with Lady Ferreira's plans hadn't completely done her in, but she wouldn't have any trouble getting to sleep that night. Even so, she should attempt dinner first. Felis put up her hair and produced a pair of teardrop-shaped opal earrings that must belong to Lady Ferreira. Oriana slid on the silk mitts she wore to disguise her webbed fingers and, with the cambric blouse's high neck covering her gill slits and her wide feet neatly hidden by a pinching pair of shoes, saw what could be a human woman in the mirror, albeit an exhausted one.

Was this what the rest of her life would be? Passing herself off as human? She didn't much like the idea.

D inner with Joaquim brought bad news and good. The officers working on finding the men who'd taken up Gita still hadn't turned up any information. Evidently the behavior hadn't been repeated anywhere—making it unlikely the men involved sold women for their living.

When Duilio shared what the doctor had told him about the possibility of the first girl being one of the otter folk, Joaquim groaned. They would have to be careful that the information about the two dead girls being nonhumans didn't slip out. Fortunately, the press hadn't caught wind of either death, so the police had been lucky so far.

The better news was that Brother Manoel had given in to Joaquim's urging and agreed to release Gita's body to Duilio. He could retrieve her shrouded body in the morning and take her back to Braga Bay. He would be happier if he'd been able to find her pelt . . . and her skin. That would give him closure of one concern. Sailing to Braga Bay and back would take a few hours, and then he could visit the palace, since he hadn't yet informed the ambassador that Oriana was safe. Joaquim rolled his eyes when Duilio mentioned that, but Duilio's gift continued to tell him the infante was important, so he intended to foster the new acquaintance. After all, the man had asked him to call him by his given name. Coming from royalty, that was a great privilege.

When Duilio got home, he found his mother in the library, her feet tucked up under her on the couch and a clothbound book in her gloved hands. The lights in the room weren't turned up high, but that didn't present a problem for her eyes. "What are you reading, Mother?"

"I think you must have left this out, Duilinho," she said, showing it to him. "Surely there must be something more accurate. And in our language. How irritating."

Ah, now he recognized it. She held Monsieur Matelot's certainly erroneous volume about Oriana's people. His mother thought French an annoying language, primarily because it wasn't her native one. "Yes, I have to wonder if he ever came near her people's islands."

"Well, someone must trade with them. And perhaps the sereia in French-held territories are different," she said with a shrug. "Miss Paredes should write a book. Or you. Either of you would do a far better job."

That wasn't necessarily high praise. He pulled one of the chairs from against the wall and sat facing her. "Speaking of Miss Paredes—did she get out of bed today?"

"Yes. We just finished with our dinner an hour ago, and she went back to her room. She's tired, but much improved." His mother set the offending book on the table next to the couch. "I fear she's a bit lost, Duilinho."

"Lost?" His mother read people well, so that must be the case. "What do you mean?"

She sighed. "When you first brought Miss Paredes here, she came as my companion, but that wasn't her true function. She was seeking a killer and was a spy for her people." When he nodded, she continued. "Now neither is true. Now she must try to figure out who she is, and what she must do to survive. That will take time, I think."

"I've told her she's welcome to stay here as long as she wants."

"As what, Duilinho? As a servant? As your pet, perhaps?" His mother shook her head. "She is a proud, intelligent young woman. As much as I like her, I don't believe she's cut out to be a hired companion for the remainder of her life."

He had meant for Oriana to be a *guest*, but his mother was right. Oriana would want to be doing something. "So she needs time to decide what she wants."

"I agree." His mother glanced up at him from under a lowered brow. "I don't want her forced into . . . making any precipitous decisions."

She meant *into his bed*. He felt a flush heating his face. A gentleman didn't take advantage of women in his employ, but apparently his mother felt he needed reminding of that. Perhaps he did. "Of course not, Mother."

"Good," she said. "Now, didn't you promise to get that thing off her wrist? It's annoying her terribly."

Duilio groaned. Why hadn't he taken care of that? If nothing else, he could have instructed Luís to do it. "Is she still awake, do you think?"

"Probably." His mother made a gesture clearly intended to shoo him on his way, and then picked up the offensive book from the table with a scowl, as if determined to read the whole thing.

Aware that he'd been dismissed, Duilio made his way upstairs to Alessio's room. He knocked on the door, and when there was no answer, peeked inside. Oriana reclined on the leather chaise before the tea table, asleep. She had replaced her shoes with a pair of Alessio's old felt slippers and her silk mitts lay on the table, but otherwise she was still dressed. She must have been waiting for him.

He went to wake her but he stopped before his hand touched her shoulder. He had seen her sleeping endlessly in the last two days, when she'd been ill and exhausted. Her burned skin had faded from red to its normal ivory, and save for the bruising on her face and a split lip, she looked normal. Her hair trailed in a neat braid over one shoulder. It was as if she were a different woman from the one who'd lain ill for the last two days.

He touched her shoulder, waking her. "You should have gone back to bed."

She lifted her wrist to display the shackle. "I want this off, Duilio. Please."

"I'll take you to the kitchen." He helped her to her feet. "I've got tools down there, and Mrs. Cardoza can make you some chocolate while I work on it."

The kitchen was warm, courtesy of the oversized stoves, and the scents of dinner still lingered: fish soup, bread, and garlic. Oriana settled at the servants' table on the far side of the room while Duilio had a quick word with the cook. Mrs. Cardoza was more than willing to warm some milk for chocolate.

He didn't want to use bolt cutters that close to her hand, so he fetched the heavy pliers and iron spike he'd located in the tool kit on the sailboat that first night. He returned to the table to find Oriana staring dully at the oaken surface.

He sat down on the bench next to her and considered how best to pry open the first link on the chain. Once he did that, he could slip the link out and open the cuff. He took off his tie and slid it between the iron of the cuff and her wrist to protect her skin. "Now be still."

Oriana seemed disinclined to move at all. "Your valet will be displeased, I suspect. Such an abuse of your tie."

"Marcellin will survive," he said. "If you don't mind, I'd like to ask you some questions."

"Very well," she whispered.

"Monteiro. Who is he?"

Her head lifted. "You know him?"

Duilio slid the spike through the loop for leverage and set to work with the pliers. "I met him two days ago. He came to inquire after you."

"Oh." Her eyes met his, a line forming between her brows. "He's my father."

So that much was true. "He wanted to see you. I couldn't be sure he was telling me the truth, so I sent him away." The loop gave enough that he could loosen the cuff. He slipped the loop through one side of the cuff, enough to let him open the thing and remove it. Fortunately, her wrist was merely chafed, not raw.

"Thank you," she said, rubbing that wrist with the other hand.

He felt a swell of warmth in his heart. Perhaps this was why he hadn't asked Luís or the coachman to remove the manacle for her. He'd wanted to do it himself to earn her gratitude, a selfish notion. Duilio set the tools aside, shaking his head.

"I'm surprised he told you," Oriana said. "That we're related, I mean."

Ah, back to Monteiro. "He seemed concerned for you."

Her eyes looked pained. "He chose his political beliefs over his children."

Her tone held a frostiness he'd never heard from her before. "What do you mean?"

"He was exiled for sedition when I was sixteen. Marina was only twelve, and I had to take care of her. We became wards of the state and were forced to live on Quitos with our aunts. Why would he do that? He should have been taking care of us. And then he comes here and . . ." She sighed.

Duilio waited for her to finish, but after a moment decided she wasn't going to. "He said he would like to see you. And if he hadn't sent Lady Pereira de Santos to prompt me, I wouldn't have reached you in time."

She didn't respond. Mrs. Cardoza brought the cup of chocolate for Oriana, and she wrapped her bare hands about the mug as if craving its warmth. "Lady Pereira de Santos?" she asked. "There was gossip among the servants—that he is her lover."

That last part came out as a whisper. Oriana didn't know her father and Lady Pereira de Santos were married. Should he be the one to tell her? Or would it be better coming from Monteiro? "She came here first," he began, and told her of the lady's visit.

Oriana listened, her expression pensive. "I see."

That told him nothing. "I can arrange a meeting with your father," he prompted, "whenever you feel you can handle it."

Much as he expected, she lifted her chin and said, "I can handle him anytime." Then her shoulders slumped. "I suppose I should talk to him. He's all the family I have left here."

He couldn't argue that. "You called the ambassador uncle. Are they brothers?"

She took a sip of the chocolate, her eyes downcast. "No. The ambassador is my mother's brother. A different line."

"Line?"

Her brows drew together. "Like a clan? A group of related families. My mother's line is Paredes, by Arenias. My father is Monteiro."

Duilio didn't bother asking why she didn't use her father's name. "Your father seemed to think what was done to you was meant as a warning to *him* not to talk, but the ambassador thought it was a warning for himself."

She cradled the mug of chocolate in her hands. "I have no idea."

"Perhaps if we talk to your father, we can figure it out. Would you like me to arrange a meeting, then?" She regarded the remaining chocolate in her mug with bleak eyes, and finally nodded. "I'll do so, then," he said, "for tomorrow afternoon if possible."

She nodded again and, as he watched, her eyes drifted closed and her head drooped. She shook herself. "There's rum in this chocolate," she managed. "A lot."

Duilio cast a glance at Mrs. Cardoza, winked at the cook, and then turned back to Oriana. "Perhaps I should take you back upstairs."

Oriana's head slowly descended to his shoulder. Duilio pushed the mug away and carefully picked her up in his arms. She tucked her head under his chin as he walked from the kitchen toward the stairs, the scent of her hair filling his nose, a hint of lily of the valley.

When he reached her bedroom, he debated for a moment, and set her on the bench at the end of the bed. He caught his breath—Oriana wasn't a featherweight—then drew back the coverlet and sheet. He removed her slippers and laid her, fully clothed, on the bed and then tucked the bedding back around her.

She reached one hand toward him. "Don't leave me," she whispered.

Gentlemanly behavior demanded that he go, but she sounded lost, just as his mother had said. Duilio suspected he was going to spend the rest of his life unable to resist her whims. He stripped off his frock coat and shoes and pushed the coverlet back so he could lie down next to her on the wide bed. "It's all right," he said. "I'll stay."

She shifted closer, her head coming to rest on his arm. Duilio wrapped his other arm about her and held her close. They hadn't discussed her staying at the house, what she would do now, or anything else important, but he wasn't going to disturb her with that. When she began to cry, he said nothing. He simply held her until the tears faded and she slipped into an exhausted sleep.

CHAPTER 13

Oriana woke slowly, warm and comfortable. Duilio lay next to her, his thick lashes lowered over his seal-brown eyes. Her head rested on his extended arm, and his other hand lay on her hip. Despite her full skirt, one of his legs had tangled with hers. That explained why she was warm even though she'd pushed the coverlet away. She gazed at Duilio's sleeping face. His dark hair swept across his wide brow and his chin was shadowed with stubble.

Something in her chest tightened. She closed her eyes for a moment, feeling an ache that was almost pain. She knew what it was. More foolish than she could ever have predicted, her traitor heart had fallen in love with him.

It wasn't infatuation. She knew better than that. She trusted Duilio. He didn't see her as inferior or an enemy, even though he'd known her for a spy. But before they'd had a common goal—finding Isabel's killer. Now she no longer knew what her goals were.

When she'd been imprisoned on that ship, not knowing what was going to happen to her, she'd told herself that whatever happened, she wanted to come back to the Golden City. She'd wanted to court Duilio Ferreira, even if it didn't make sense at all. She'd promised herself she would try, but that was before she'd been left to die.

Who am I now? Surviving execution expunged any crimes from a criminal's record; it was believed the gods sent rescue only to the innocent. But she had no idea if she could ever go home.

Following orders, she'd climbed aboard a ship that was supposed to take her back home to the inlands. Instead they'd chained her and thrown her in the hold, only leading her out in time to face her execution, with no trial or charges ever read out. She'd been placed on an island to die by someone in the intelligence ministry, her own employers. She'd been used up and thrown away, like so much refuse. And what was she without her home, her avocation? Everything she'd struggled to make of herself had been shattered.

And yet Duilio was still here, like a fixed point in her world, an anchor. Oriana set her hand lightly against his waistcoat, feeling his heart beating slow and strong through her webbing.

His eyes fluttered open at her touch. For a second he seemed disoriented, and then his eyes locked with hers, as if he sought to read her soul through them. The hand on her hip flexed, settling more firmly there. He leaned closer, and his lips brushed hers. His lashes drifted closed, as if he didn't want to think about it, only *feel* as she did—the featherlight touch of his lips on hers, the warmth of his breath against her chilled skin.

He drew away, only far enough that his eyes could focus on her face, trying to gauge her reaction.

Oriana licked her lips. She had never been kissed before. *Can he tell that?* Had she made a terrible fool of herself? Surely he must feel the tie between them. In this light she doubted he could read her expression, so she raised her hand from his heart, slid it behind his neck, and pulled him back to her.

He kissed her again, more firmly this time. Oriana pressed closer. His hand slid to the small of her back, drawing her against him as his lips moved from hers to the line of her jaw. When his lips brushed against her gill slits, she gasped and arched against him.

He drew back immediately. "Did I hurt you?"

Oriana shivered. "No. They're just very sensitive."

Duilio reached up and ran gentle fingers along one side of her neck, his clear eyes shaded by those thick lashes. Oriana pressed her face into his shoulder, trying to control her response to that touch. His thigh lay between her legs, though, and she'd pressed her legs tightly around it, giving away exactly what sort of reaction he'd drawn from her.

He leaned over her and lifted her braid away from her neck. "You're badly bruised here. Who did this?"

"One of the guards," she whispered.

He settled back on the sheets, farther away. His hand touched her face gently, though, easing the sense of rejection she'd felt at that retreat. "You had nightmares," he said. "What happened?"

"It's not important." She wanted to hide now. The physical weakness was bad enough. She didn't want to cry yet again and convince him of her emotional fragility as well.

Duilio ran fingers across her brow, sweeping her hair back. "Did they beat you?"

"No," she whispered. "Not really. I was held prisoner on that ship—the one that was supposed to take me home—for ten days. The guards were afraid to hurt me much because they knew there hadn't been a trial."

"I don't understand. Why would they be afraid?"

She sighed. "If a person is innocent, the gods will find a way to release them. They feared that if they hurt me, I would come back and destroy them. That saved me from worse treatment, I know. It could have been worse."

"Then what is this bruise on your neck? And your cheek?"

"I didn't fight them until they put the chains on me. One of the guards grabbed me by the neck and pushed me into the wall. And then apologized." A bitter laugh welled up from her throat. "When I heard that, I knew I was going to die."

His hand touched her hair. "Did you not think someone would save you?"

That had been the worst part, the knowledge that her fate was out of her own hands. She had never felt so helpless in her life. "It's hard to believe when you're offered the knife."

"The knife?"

"It's tradition. Once the condemned person is chained to the post, they are offered a knife. If they take their own lives with it, it's seen as an admission of guilt. I wouldn't take it." She had opted for a slow death, refusing to validate the implied sentence.

"I'm grateful you didn't," Duilio said.

"I had to tell myself someone would come," she admitted. "I had to believe that or I would have died." Her eyes began to water, and she wiped them quickly.

"I wish I had come sooner," he said regretfully.

"You came soon enough," she whispered.

He stroked her cheek, his eyes searching hers. "Can you get some sleep now?" he asked her then. "If I leave, I mean."

Oriana took a deep breath. She wanted to beg him to stay. "Yes," she said anyway.

He slipped away from her, the warmth of his body going with him. He tugged the coverlet higher to cover her shoulders, and his fingers brushed her cheek. He turned down the gaslights over the mantel and, while Oriana pretended to sleep, gathered his coat and shoes and slipped out the bedroom door.

In the library, Duilio poured himself a glass of brandy, which helped cool the initial flush of his anger. He drank the glass down and poured another. He wasn't a drinker. He'd seen where that reckless path had taken Alessio, but at the moment he wanted to stop thinking.

He had known *before* he let her return to her people. He'd known he was in love with her. But he'd decided to say nothing and let her go. Her treatment at their hands was his fault. He slumped down in one of the chairs, cradling the second glass of brandy and deciding if he wanted to drink it. It shook him to think how frightened Oriana must have been, imprisoned without explanation and then learning they intended to put her to death.

"Duilinho?" His mother stepped into the library, a lamp in her gloved hand. "What are you doing, sitting in here in the dark?"

He set the glass of brandy on the table. "I should never have let her go. When I think how she was treated . . ."

His mother pulled out another chair and sat next to him. "What did she tell you?"

He met his mother's eyes. "It could have been worse. That ship that was supposed to take her back to the islands? They threw her down in the hold instead. The guards were afraid to touch her, she says . . . which is better than the alternative." He heaved out a sigh. "I just hate that . . . that anyone would treat her like that, like she was of no import."

"Especially when she's so important to you." His mother rose and set a hand atop his head. "Try to help her heal. It's a far better use of your time than self-recrimination. Now go upstairs and go to sleep."

His mother, as always, gave very good advice. Duilio left the second glass of brandy untouched on the table and headed upstairs for his own bed.

CHAPTER 14

The sun had barely risen when Brother Manoel greeted Duilio and his family's driver at a side entrance of the monastery. A cold wind carried fog in from the sea, wrapping the riverfront and its surrounds in chilly obscurity.

"Are you certain of this, Mr. Ferreira?" the monk asked. "We can care for her here."

"I can get her back to her family, Brother," Duilio said. "They will be grateful."

The monk gestured for them to take the linen-wrapped form that waited on the stone table inside. The driver crossed himself before lifting the lower end of the body, so Duilio quickly did the same, and they carried the wrapped corpse out into the fog and cold.

The fishing boats hadn't returned to their moorings yet, and the fog made it unlikely anyone would be able to identify the stiff form they carried down the stone slip to the paddleboat. The driver helped Duilio get the body onto the boat's flat deck and cover it, and then headed back up to the city to take Duilio's note to Monteiro's office and a package down to the Tavares boat works—an English revolver that Duilio wanted altered.

Duilio checked the kerosene in the motor, primed it, and then started it. The motor's roar sounded horrendously loud in the silence, but the boat splashed away from the quay unnoticed. It was an easy trip so long as he didn't lose sight of the shore, so he settled on the housing over the motor and kept one hand on the tiller. Once he'd passed the breakwater to the open sea, he kept the boat near the fog-wrapped shore as he headed north toward Braga Bay. A steamer—likely a naval patrol—sounded its horn somewhere nearby. Duilio didn't let it worry him; even if the patrol did spot his boat in the fog, they couldn't come into shallow waters to question him over his peculiar cargo. And as he continued north up the coast, the sounds of other boats faded until he was left with the splash of the waves against the hull and the cries of the seabirds.

He spent the time fretting over Oriana. He had no way to relate to what she'd suffered. He'd been shot more than once, stabbed and beaten, but he had never been made *helpless*, and not by anyone he'd been taught to trust.

Joaquim was right; he hadn't known Oriana all that long. But she was a fighter. She was resolute and resourceful. She would recover. Duilio refused to believe otherwise.

It would help greatly, he suspected, if they could find out the *why* behind what had been done to her. They had held her for ten days, long enough for someone to send a message to the islands asking for either guidance or permission, and get word back. *Someone* had a secret worth killing her over. She didn't know the answer, but he hoped her father might—or the ambassador.

He had been puzzling over that problem for some time when he saw the break in the dark cliffs that lead into Braga Bay. He cut the engine and rowed in as before. The seals on the beach stayed put this time, but Erdano reached him in time to help draw the boat up onto the sand.

Erdano shook his head, spraying Duilio with water from his

wet hair, and then scowled down at the blanket-covered body, his nostrils twitching. "Is that her?"

"I can't be sure," Duilio admitted.

Erdano's expression didn't change. "Well, let me look at her."

When Erdano reached down to remove the blanket, Duilio grabbed his arm. "They skinned her."

Erdano growled, his eyes narrowing. "Who?"

"Joaquim and I are trying to find out. Whoever killed this girl may be hunting for nonhumans." Duilio set a hand on his brother's shoulder to make sure he had his attention. "If you don't want any of your harem in danger, you'll keep them all out of the city until we find out who did this."

Erdano leaned over the side of the boat, dragged the blanket loose and gave the linen-wrapped body a perplexed look. Knowing Erdano's persistence, Duilio climbed back aboard the boat to help him untangle the shroud from the body. He drew the covering back from the dead girl's feet, but Erdano didn't seem put off by the gruesome display. "Why is she wrapped like this?"

Duilio didn't think the answers that immediately came to mind—those concerning tidiness and smell—would appease Erdano. "The priests were going to bury her. Can you tell if this is a selkie?"

Erdano sniffed his hand and nodded. He hadn't actually touched the body, but the smell of it would have permeated the linen and the blanket. He pointed to the split foot. "And her foot was crippled," Erdano said, "like that. I remember it."

That settles that. It would have been awkward had he come all this way only to have Erdano proclaim this wasn't his missing girl.

Erdano lifted the partially unwrapped body off the boat's deck with Duilio's help and set it on the sand. By then Tigana had come to join them, her pelt nearby on the sand and her inky hair still streaming water. She folded her arms over her chest and stared down at the body, her expression unreadable. "Where is her skin?"

"I haven't found that yet," Duilio said, taken aback by her matter-of-fact tone. He repeated the warning he'd made to Erdano about staying away from the city.

Tigana stared at the body a moment longer, then crouched next to it. She continued the work of unraveling the shroud, but spared one glance up at Erdano. "You will stay here as well."

Erdano's lips twisted, vexation on his handsome face, but he didn't argue.

It was, Duilio decided, an interesting lesson in harem dynamics. Evidently Tigana was master here, not Erdano. He elected not to comment. Erdano was larger and could still thrash him soundly. "I'll leave her with you, then."

"Yes, go away," Tigana said, dismissing him.

Duilio pushed the boat back from the sand, and Erdano came to help him. "Thank you, little brother," he said. "For finding her."

"We will find the killer," Duilio promised. "Give us time."

Oriana sat down, relieved that the seamstress had given her a few moments' peace between periods of standing on a stool for measurements and fitting. She had endured the shoemaker's handling of her wide feet and waited through what seemed to be hours of Lady Ferreira conspiring with the seamstress about what colors and fabrics she should wear.

When working for Isabel, all of Oriana's clothing had been ready-made. Having worked for a dressmaker, she could alter them to fit well, but she'd never been able to afford the luxury of having something made specifically for her. She'd merely watched while Isabel was subjected to endless fittings. And when she'd worked for the dressmaker, she'd been hidden away in the back room while some other poor woman was subjected to this. She'd never known how uncomfortable it was to be the victim of the poking, pinning, and measuring. It was, she decided, a form of torture.

Lady Ferreira cast her a sympathetic glance. The lady didn't care for excessive attention, either. Oriana managed to smile back.

Lady Ferreira had applied a dusting of powder to her cheeks to disguise her bruises. It had been the lady's idea to wrap a length of gauze about Oriana's neck, citing a nasty-but-fictitious burn from a pair of curling tongs. That hid her gill slits and the bruises. Oriana sat in one of the sitting room's armchairs, dressed only in her chemise, drawers and underskirt, corset cover, stockings . . . and silk mitts that hid her webbing. To the seamstress and her young assistant, she must look human.

And there had been the argument over the corset. Sereia had air bladders on the outside of their lungs, making those organs smaller than a human's, so wearing a corset left her perpetually short of breath. Lady Ferreira explained that away by telling the seamstress that Oriana suffered from the lingering ravages of a childhood lung ailment. The nimble-fingered seamstress, a slender woman whose own tasteful garb hinted at her skill, had eyed Oriana with vexation, no doubt wanting her creations to be displayed to the greatest advantage. However, after measuring Oriana's small waist again, she'd given her permission, suggesting a lightly boned corset cover rather than the constricting garment itself.

A knock came at the door of the sitting room, and the door opened enough for Duilio to peer inside. The assistant squealed in surprise. The seamstress immediately placed herself between the male invader and Oriana, as stiff as Felis at her worst. "Sir, you cannot come in here."

His head disappeared from the doorway.

"What is it, Duilinho?" his mother called, ignoring the seamstress.

"May I speak with Oriana for a few minutes?" he called back from outside, laughter in his voice.

Oriana got up, walked past the seamstress, and slipped into the hallway, relieved to have any excuse to escape. She shut the sitting room door behind her and set her back against it.

"Not enjoying yourself?" Duilio asked.

His hair appeared slightly damp, as if he'd just bathed. She caught the scent of soap rather than the musky scent of his skin, reinforcing that conclusion. His black satin waistcoat and elegant pinstriped trousers seemed overly fine for day wear. "Are you going out?"

"I am," he said, "but I hope to be back before luncheon. Or by two at the latest. I'm going to visit the palace, to see if I can get word to the ambassador that you're safe. If I can, is there anything you would want me to tell him, or ask him?"

She shook her head. Due to the house arrest, the ambassadorial position was largely a decorative one. "I doubt he'll have anything to tell."

Duilio's lips pressed together, keeping something in. If he was uncomfortable after what had happened between them last night, he didn't show that. In fact, he seemed more likely to burst into laughter. "I received an answer from the Monteiro office," he told her, "saying around three this afternoon was acceptable. Do you think you'll be done with these fittings by then?"

"I had better be," she said, asperity creeping into her voice.

He did laugh then. "My mother's seamstress is probably having spasms right now."

Oriana glanced down at her attire—definitely not appropriate for meeting with a gentleman. And while Duilio had seen her nude several times, making her current state of undress more than adequate, the seamstress couldn't know that. "Oh," she sighed. "I forgot."

"It's a very interesting ensemble," he said, gesturing toward the gauze about her neck. "I think a black velvet ribbon would add more dramatic flair, though."

She must look completely ridiculous. Her hair was braided back out of the way, which would only accentuate the hollowness of her cheeks. White had never flattered her pale skin, either. She wrapped her mostly bare arms about her chest, unable to think of any clever response.

"I was only joking," he said. "You did look like you were suffering in there."

She lifted her eyes to meet his. "Why did you go last night?"

The change of subject didn't seem to surprise him, as if he'd been asking himself the same question. "I needed to leave before I said or did something I would regret later."

Regret? That wasn't what she'd expected him to say. "I see."

"And I didn't want you to . . ." He shifted on his feet. "Remember that before you left, I said you could come back?" When she nodded, he went on. "You are a guest here, for as long as you need. There is nothing required in return, no price. You don't even need to act as my mother's companion, although it does make your presence here easier to explain."

She wasn't certain what he was trying to accomplish with that speech, but felt vaguely appalled. Had he thought she'd let him kiss her as *payment* for saving her?

His shoulders slumped and he turned his eyes toward the ceiling. "Let me try this again. My mother reminded me that since your situation is uncertain, you have probably not yet decided what you want to do with the rest of your life." The words came out very precisely, as if he were assembling a legal defense. "Therefore it would be unkind to pressure you into any sort of relationship you might not find acceptable or desirable after a proper period of consideration. So until you have had time to weigh your options, I should probably . . ."

She mutely stared at him while he appeared to consider how to finish that.

". . . back off," he finally said.

It hadn't been a rejection. He'd been trying to be considerate, which she should have recognized immediately. Oriana wiped at the corner of one eye with her hand. "I enjoy being your mother's companion. The new clothes are unnecessary, though. It's a terrible expense."

He smiled. The moment of awkwardness had clearly passed, like a cloud lifting. "You honestly don't realize how wealthy we are, do you? Although we don't flaunt it, we could buy the Carvalho family three times over, perhaps four. Believe me, Oriana, this is nothing. Mother is enjoying herself. I suggest you simply allow her to do so."

How could she say no to that request? "If I must."

"You'll survive it." A gentle touch on her bruised cheek made her lift her eyes again. He drew his hand away and surveyed his fingertips—now smudged with powder. "Ah, I thought you were healing exceptionally quickly."

"Your mother . . ."

"I have your coat ready, sir." Duilio's stuffy French valet had come walking up from the back of the house, looking down at a black frock coat spread carefully over his outstretched arms. He stopped, mouth open, when he spotted Oriana in the hallway, half-undressed. Duilio gestured for the man to avert his eyes.

He turned back to Oriana. "I do need to go," he said. "But I'll be back in plenty of time. You will be ready by three, won't you?"

The way he phrased that suggested he intended to join her. "Are you coming with me?"

"For moral support."

She had no idea how a meeting between her and her father would go. They hadn't spoken for a decade, and there were too many problems between them to make any discussion simple. She would have to work hard to control her temper. "Thank you. I'll be ready."

"Until later then," Duilio said and turned toward his valet.

Oriana grabbed his hand. He regarded her with raised brows as she caught up a handful of her underskirt and used it to wipe his powder-covered fingers. "Black coat," she whispered when she let go of his hand.

He smiled at her again before going down the hallway to retrieve his coat from his valet.

Oriana watched as Marcellin, his eyes averted from the scandalous sight of her bared shoulders, helped his employer into his coat and handed him a pair of gloves. The valet said something to Duilio in French. He answered in that language, a firm comment, whatever it was.

She had never considered Duilio Ferreira a strikingly handsome man. Viewed objectively, he was attractive perhaps, but nothing out of the ordinary. Joaquim was more handsome, despite having similar features. Duilio's warm eyes were, without doubt, his finest feature. He was above-average height, only an inch or so taller than she was, and he had an athletic leanness nothing like Erdano's muscular bulk. But as Oriana watched him tug on his gloves, she decided he had to be the most handsome man in the world. He glanced up and caught her watching him. He made a shooing gesture with one hand to send her back to the sitting room.

She didn't want to lose sight of him, but since his mother must be waiting for her, she went.

Duilio settled again among the petitioners and tried to be patient. It had been a few days since his last visit to the palace, and the crop of people waiting appeared to have changed—a sign that some progress had been made. He didn't see the elderly gentleman, Mr. Bastos, there. He hoped his man of business had been able to sort out the old man's problems.

He sat pondering what to tell the ambassador, should he actually succeed in seeing the man and was pleasantly surprised when the infante came walking down the wide runner in the hall before even a quarter hour had passed. The infante gestured for Duilio to join him this time and kept moving. Duilio jogged a couple of steps to catch up. The guards fell back, giving them room to speak privately.

"Did you find the girl?" the infante asked.

"Yes. I would like to tell the ambassador so, if possible."

"Not a good idea." The infante moved at a faster walk than normal. "There are guards outside his door now."

Ambassador to Northern Portugal must be an uncomfortable posting. "What's changed?"

The infante pointed toward a spiral stairwell. "The astrologers fed my brother some nonsense about *Alvaro* killing him."

They crossed over the sea-god archway and walked toward the new part of the palace. The infante stopped in the tower to one side of the archway and gazed out the window, gesturing for Duilio to join him there. Out on the terrace below, Prince Fabricio stood staring up at the bust of the sea god that supported the archway. The sun had burned through the fog, and in that light, Duilio could clearly see the prince's rapt expression as he gazed up at the fantastical sculpture. A lean-faced priest in a plain black cassock stood at a distance behind him, the prince's entourage today instead of the astrologers, Duilio supposed.

"Fabricio wants to be the sea god," the infante said softly. "He dreams of controlling the seas, bringing the two princedoms back into one kingdom, conquering Spain, perhaps."

While Duilio didn't see any likelihood of conquering Spain or the seas, there would be value to bringing the two princedoms back under one flag. Portugal had split during the eighteenth century, when two young princes had compromised rather than fight each other for control, leaving the Golden City controlling the north and Lisboa, the south. The reunification of the two princedoms had been part of Maraval's plan, although he'd tried to achieve it through necromancy instead of diplomacy. "How does the prince intend to do that?"

The infante chuckled. "That's the point of dreaming. One need not have a plan."

"Ah." It was the only thing Duilio could say that wouldn't get him in trouble.

"Were I in his shoes," the infante said, "I would spend less time dreaming and more doing."

The priest's eyes lifted toward the window where they stood and for an instant Duilio thought the man was looking at them.

The infante backed farther from the window. "You should get back. I don't want Father Salazar to see you."

Duilio obeyed, losing sight of prince and priest both. "Why not?"

The infante licked his lips, the first sign of reticence he'd displayed thus far. "He watches me. I don't . . . like that."

That didn't make much sense, but Duilio didn't argue. Sometimes people rubbed one the wrong way. It was usually wise to heed those reactions. "Is he the chaplain here?"

"Yes. The former chaplain died a few weeks ago. I miss Father Abreu." With a sigh, the infante stepped away from the window and led Duilio toward another stairwell, into the newest part of the palace, and downward to a level that must be dug into the hillside. "So," the infante said in an inquisitive voice, "do you box?"

Where had that come from? "Excuse me, Your Highness?"

"Raimundo," the infante corrected. "Alessio said you were good at sport. You do *box*, don't you?"

Duilio was far from expert, and admitted as much.

The infante laughed. "I could get Bastião to go up against me," he said, pointing discreetly at the burly guard still following them at a distance, "but he'd flatten me with his first swing. Would you be willing to give it a try? The guards have a gymnasium on this level."

So that bearlike guard was the real Bastião. Duilio wouldn't want to fight the man either. He stood as tall as Erdano and his blue uniform coat strained across his barrel-shaped chest. Duilio drew out his watch and checked the time. If he didn't stay too long, he should be able to get back to the house in time to clean up and take Oriana to her father's office. "If you'd like, Raimundo."

He only hoped he wouldn't regret it.

Oriana sat on the leather chaise near her bedroom door, trying to draw calm from the silence. She was going to talk to her father and the closer the time came the more nervous she became. She was grateful Duilio intended to accompany her. He'd been late getting back to the house and disappeared immediately into his rooms, evidently needing a change of clothes.

She wanted to hate her father. There was ten years of anger built up in her that had never had an outlet. But he *had* come to ask after her. He'd revealed his identity to Duilio, risking his life. She couldn't figure out her father's motives, not without talking to him. And if she did that, how could she stay objective? She and her father had always bickered, but she'd always loved him. Was that enough to make up for his leaving her and Marina behind?

She got up and went into the bathroom to look at her reflection one more time. She wanted to present a strong face. Teresa had styled her hair in a high bun. Powder hid most of the bruising on her skin. The clothes she wore had come from Lady Ferreira's dressing room, quickly made over by the seamstress to fit Oriana's taller frame. The brown silk skirt had an added flounce now that blended with the original fabric well enough that most women wouldn't notice if they hadn't once worked in a dressmaker's shop. She wore a close-fitting pinstriped vest over her high-collared cambric shirt. A borrowed black brooch at her throat and teardrop earrings in carved jet lent her a sophisticated look, and Felis had even found her a flat-brimmed black hat. She looked quite sharp.

"Oriana?"

Duilio's voice came from the hallway, so she took a last look to reassure herself and went to join him. He stood outside her bedroom door. He'd bathed again and changed clothes, yet another black frock coat, but with a simple brown waistcoat now. He held a handkerchief to his lips. When he took it away, she saw that his lip had been split. She went to his side to get a better look and saw swelling along one of his cheekbones as well. "Did the guards at the palace do that?"

He sighed. "No, the infante thrashed me."

The prince's brother? She touched his swelling cheek gently. "Why?"

"Why don't I tell you in the coach?" he asked, looking more exasperated than pained. "You look very well, I should add, even if you have decided to ignore my recommendation of black velvet."

Oriana laid her hand on his offered arm, feeling for a moment that she fit somewhere in this world. "A black velvet ribbon would only be appropriate with evening attire," she said airily.

"I'll keep that in mind," he replied, a laugh in his tone.

They walked down the stairs and he waited while she pinned her hat into place and donned the silk mitts she wore to hide her webbing. Cardenas opened the door for them, and Duilio held out his arm for her to take. The fog had burned off, leaving a crisp chill in the air—something to be appreciated in rainy October.

It was only when they headed down toward the street that they saw a slender woman garbed in a pale green walking gown pushing open the wrought iron gate to enter the small garden in front of the house. A maid in stark black followed at a distance, parasol clutched in her hands. The woman's head lifted when she caught sight of them coming down the steps, revealing a lovely face under her hat's brim.

Oriana felt cold spread through her stomach. *Genoveva Carvalho. What is she doing here?* The last time she'd laid eyes on Miss Carvalho, the young woman had been pressing a kiss to Duilio's cheek, ostensibly in gratitude for his saving her youngest sister.

Miss Carvalho's face lit with delight at the sight of Duilio, but that expression faded when she saw Oriana's hand on his sleeve.

Oriana clutched his arm more tightly, unable to help the reaction. She had no claim on him. *That doesn't mean I'm going to back down.*

Miss Carvalho approached anyway, apparently undaunted by Oriana's presence. Meeting them at the bottom of the steps, she twitched her lace-edged skirt about to keep it from the grasp of the boxwoods. "Mr. Ferreira, I'm pleased to see you," she said in her soft voice. "And Miss Paredes as well. Lady Ferreira told me you'd gone to visit family. I hope you found them well."

Oriana found herself clenching her jaw. Miss Carvalho was only asking a polite question. But that question implied familiarity with Lady Ferreira, perhaps a sly hint that Duilio's mother approved of her as his future wife. "Yes, thank you," she said after hesitating a split second too long. "Is your sister fully recovered from her ordeal?"

Miss Carvalho opened her mouth, her eyes wandering about as if she could find the answer written on the leaves in the garden. "She's well," she finally said.

"That's good," Oriana mumbled. She glanced at Duilio, hoping he could use his silver tongue to extract her from this awkward situation.

"I'm afraid we must miss your visit again, Miss Carvalho," Duilio said quickly. "Miss Paredes and I have an appointment, and we are cutting it close as it is." With truly fortuitous timing, the carriage pulled around from Ferraz Street at that moment. Duilio tipped his hat to Miss Carvalho and her silent maid and led Oriana past them and out the gate to the cobbled street, where the carriage met them. He opened the door and made a show of helping Oriana up into her seat. Then he climbed up and settled next to her without a backward glance at the elegantly gowned young woman on the steps of his house. Once he got the door closed, he rapped on the wall for the driver to move out.

Oriana cast a quick glance at the forlorn figure. "Does she come to visit often?"

"Unfortunately, yes," Duilio said with exasperation in his voice.

"I've been avoiding Miss Carvalho, so I suspect she's been trying to get my mother to like her instead."

She felt an unwelcome surge of sympathy for the girl. Genoveva Carvalho was, without doubt, a good match for him—lovely, well mannered, and from a wealthy family of the older aristocracy that lived farther up the Street of Flowers. But Duilio had been put off because she'd been infatuated with his brother Alessio first. Her interest in him had arisen too late to make a favorable impression. If that hadn't been the case, perhaps they might have married.

Oriana reached up and grasped one of the hand straps. Like everything in the Ferreira household, the coach was of the highest quality, well sprung and clean inside, but somber. Searching about for a new topic, she returned to her earlier question. "What did happen? With the infante, I mean?"

"He is ostensibly in need of a sparring partner," he said, "and asked if I would humor him."

"Do you box?" she asked hesitantly.

His eyebrows rose. "I'm a gentleman, Oriana. Of course I box."

She cast him a doubtful glance from under a lowered brow.

"I box. I fence. I shoot," he added, "with differing degrees of proficiency. I sail and I rowed at university, but I'm no good with horses. I smell wrong to them."

Oriana suppressed a smile. "I see. Forgive me for doubting. How did you fare?"

"With the infante?" Duilio's brow furrowed. "He's very fast. A couple of times I could have sworn he wasn't there a second before."

"I see." That explained the bruising and split lip. "I thought you went to see my uncle."

"That's the bad news, I'm afraid. He's been put under even stricter guard than before."

"Why?"

Duilio exhaled heavily. "Apparently the royal astrologers predicted that the ambassador is going to kill the prince."

Oriana sat back as the coach turned a corner, appalled. "He would never do such a thing."

"I agree," Duilio said. "The infante thought it was nonsense."

The coach hit a rut and bounced, so Oriana hung on to the strap. "Poor Uncle. It can't be true. They're lying."

"The infante seems to think they lie to the prince regularly. They tell him what he wants to hear." He went on to describe his entire visit to the palace, which still didn't make sense of why he'd been sparring with the infante. "He did say he would try to sneak in to tell your uncle, by the way, although he couldn't promise anything. He's asked me to go back on Monday. I'll ask again then."

Well, he'd tried. Oriana felt the carriage slow and come to a full stop. "Are we there already?"

Duilio glanced out the window. "Nearly, we're just stopping in traffic." He rose halfway and pounded on the front of the coach with his fist, signaling the driver to stop. "We can walk from here."

He opened the door carefully and jumped down without using the steps. When she went to follow, he caught her by the waist and lifted her down to the cobbles. Then he shut the door and sent the driver on his way. Oriana slipped past a stalled cart to the side of the road. They were in Bonfim, a newer parish, not as cramped as the older parts of the city. Duilio joined her, offering her his arm.

They didn't have to go far to reach her father's place of business. It was a clerk's office, with a sturdy wooden door, Monteiro and Company stenciled on the glass in gold lettering.

Oriana took a deep breath. "I have always known how to find him, but never did so."

"And today?" Duilio asked.

She turned to him. "Now I have to ask myself if I was wrong not to."

"I can talk to him alone if you wish."

To find out if her father knew why she'd been left to die—Duilio would be a better choice to ask *that*, but she had too many questions for her father. There was so much more she needed to know. "Your mother told me you were always the cautious one, the responsible one, the sensible one."

He rolled his eyes. "Compared to Alessio, how could I not be?"

"Then help me be cautious now," she said. "Or sensible, at the least. I'm not when it comes to my father, you see. You're likely to witness a display of inappropriate behavior in there."

"You?" His raised brows indicated disbelief. He opened the door for her. "Never."

Oriana sighed, brushed her mitt-covered hands down her skirt nervously, and stepped inside. She only hoped she didn't embarrass Duilio too much.

CHAPTER 15

A studious-looking young man met them at the door, neatly dressed and holding a sheaf of papers in one bare hand. He gazed at them over the rims of his spectacles. "May I help you?"

"I have an appointment with Mr. Monteiro," Duilio said.

The young man—human, Duilio decided, by virtue of his unscarred hands—let them inside and led them toward the back of the building. In rooms to either side, a dozen clerks of varying ages tapped away on clattering typewriters, apparently transcribing old records. A side hallway led farther back to a door marked with Monteiro's name. The young clerk knocked on it briskly.

When the door opened, Monteiro stood there, his handsome face expressionless. He leaned close to the young man and spoke softly enough that Duilio could barely make out his words. "When she arrives, will you ask Miss Arenias to wait here until I call her, Narciso? Otherwise I don't want to be interrupted."

The young man nodded, gestured for Duilio and Oriana to enter, and swept himself away. Duilio watched Monteiro, wondering how the man could remain so cool, here with his daughter finally in his presence. The office matched with Duilio's estimation of the man's taste, well appointed, with a fine mahogany desk and framed maps on the walls that suggested a fondness for cartography. Duilio gestured for Oriana to precede him inside.

Oriana's eyes swept the office, but when the door shut, she

turned on her father. "Why now?" she asked, voice choked. "Why do you care about me now?"

Monteiro shot Duilio an annoyed glance. "You don't need to be here, Ferreira."

"He stays or I go," Oriana said, clutching her handbag tighter.

Monteiro folded his arms over his chest but gave in. "I wanted to see that you were well. You are my daughter."

"That hasn't *ever* mattered before," Oriana snapped.

Duilio schooled his expression to neutrality. He'd guessed they were estranged, but he must have underestimated the extent of it . . . vastly so.

"It has *always* mattered," her father said. "But they have been using you against me from the beginning, and I must protect—"

"What? Your fortune? How exactly have you suffered, Father? What have they done *to you*? Were you the one left to die on that island?"

Her voice had grown louder with each question. She opened up her handbag, drew something out, and chucked it at him. The object struck Monteiro's chest before he could bat it away and rebounded to the floor with a metallic clunk. It was the shackle that had bound Oriana to the post. Duilio had wondered why she'd asked to have it. It hadn't occurred to him she'd carry it about with her.

Monteiro cast a glance at the metal cuff and then looked Oriana in the eye, his mouth in a firm line. "When you made your choice to spy for them," he said, "you cut yourself off from me. I regret what happened to you because it was likely aimed at me, but I'm not the one who imprisoned you there. I did not set you on that island."

Oriana didn't seem appeased. "When I made my choice? You left us, and I had to make my way alone. What else was I to do?"

"Once you were an adult," he said, "you could have gone to your grandmother on Amado. You could have come here to me. You chose to follow your aunts' path instead."

Oriana's jaw worked in fury. Duilio nearly stepped in then and there, but before he could, she asked, "Do you even know what happened to Marina?"

The question seemed to baffle Monteiro. "Of course I know."

"Then how can you question my decision?" she asked. "I couldn't save her, but at least I had some hope of avenging her."

Monteiro let out a gusty sigh and closed his eyes. "Ferreira, this would be easier for us all if you waited outside."

"No." Duilio stood his ground. He wasn't going to leave Oriana alone to face what clearly wasn't turning into a happy reunion.

"Well," Monteiro said, "it looks like you're going to have to endure this." He walked to the door and gestured for someone to join them.

A young woman stepped inside. She was dressed like a working woman, her dark skirts and vest finer than a factory worker's, her brown hair caught up in a sensible bun. Her delicate features and petite stature were dissimilar, but her dark eyes were so like Oriana's that Duilio knew they had to be related.

The young woman turned to Oriana, who looked as if she'd seen a ghost, and reached out kid-gloved hands and to grasp Oriana's. "Ori? Father said you'd been rescued, but I wanted to see for myself."

Oriana's eyes began to water, and she seemed to be at a loss for words.

Oh, damnation. Duilio pressed his lips together. The young woman must be Oriana's sister, Marina, the one who'd been taken aboard a human ship and murdered. Or that was what Oriana had been *told*. That was the reason Oriana had become a spy—her sister's murder. He couldn't imagine what she must be feeling, but betrayal must figure in with the relief.

"I was told you were dead," Oriana whispered.

Her sister seemed taken aback by that claim, but Duilio noted that Monteiro wasn't.

"I told you I was coming here to find Father," the other girl said.

Oriana gazed down at Marina's gloved hands, still clasped in her own. "You cut yourself," she said, her voice breaking.

The webbing, Duilio surmised. The girl couldn't wear gloves otherwise.

"It was necessary." Marina drew her hands away and rubbed them together, as Duilio had seen Monteiro do, like her hands ached. "It's not so bad."

Oriana's eyes closed, and Duilio guessed she was fighting tears. He turned to the younger girl. "Miss Arenias, I presume? Duilio Ferreira."

Her gloved hand slid into his, and she clasped her other hand over his in an ardent grip. "I know who you are. Father told me you rescued my sister. I will always be grateful."

"It was my pleasure," Duilio managed, which sounded idiotic.

Seen together, the two women bore some resemblance to each other, but Marina's brown hair lacked the burgundy highlights that made Oriana's so unusual. Somehow she looked more completely . . . *human*.

Seeming to have collected herself, Oriana stepped forward to touch her sister's elbow. "Where are you living?"

"In a boardinghouse," Marina said, "at 309 Virtudes Street."

Duilio drew a slim notebook and pencil from the inside pocket of his frock coat and wrote that down for Oriana. Marina seemed terribly innocent, unaffected by the trials Oriana had borne. How old was she? Had Oriana told him?

"May I come visit you?" Oriana asked.

The younger sister glanced at her father, as if asking for approval. Only when he nodded did she give Oriana permission to visit.

Oriana hadn't missed that exchange. "Why didn't you tell me? Why not write me a note?" Oriana asked her father. "Why let me think she was dead all this time?"

Monteiro picked the cuff off the wooden floor and laid it on his desk. "Heriberto. You chose to work for him, but she didn't."

Oriana's eyes blazed. "Did you believe I would turn her over to him?"

"You were certainly obedient enough until a few weeks ago."

"You thought I would expose my own sister?" Oriana pressed her hands to her face. The younger girl wrapped an arm around her waist to reassure her.

"We chose to make our lives here, Oriana," her father said stiffly, "outside any of the government's political games, outside the plots and petty arguments. We want to be left alone. That's all. If Heriberto got wind of her true identity, he could force her into serving him as well. If she'd ever met with you, he would have put two and two together. As it is, he thought she was only another clerk in this office."

Oriana's eyes lifted. "And you? Because I know he was blackmailing you."

"You were the one thing he had to hold against me. So yes, I gave him information when he pressed me."

"I heard him tell you he knew about your girl," she said. "He meant Marina, didn't he?"

Her father's jaw clenched. "Yes. He found out somehow."

Oriana took her sister's hand in her own. "Has he threatened her?"

"No. He's gone," Monteiro said. "He disappeared about the same time you did. His boat's gone, and the woman he'd been seeing is too. The rumor is that he's fled to Brazil."

That made Duilio's brows draw together. His footman Gustavo had told him the man's boat was gone from its mooring, but it was news that he'd left the city altogether. Duilio found that odd. "You said to me, sir, that you were told not to talk. If not by him, then whom?"

"This is not your concern, Ferreira," Monteiro snapped.

"It *is* his concern," Oriana said quickly. "When I was out on that island, he was the one who came to rescue me, not you."

Monteiro pointed at Duilio and his hands moved fluidly as he snapped, "The only reason Ferreira went rather than me was that he got to your uncle. If I'd known, I would have gone."

Duilio puzzled over that gesture. He had a feeling he might know what it meant.

"Oh, no, Father," Oriana said, making the same gesture back at him, emphatically. "You don't want to be bothered. You have your fine business here and your lover, and you'd rather ignore what happens to us back on the islands."

"Leave Alma out of this," he said, his voice going quiet.

Oriana pulled away from her sister's grasp. "It was so much easier when you didn't have any children to worry about, wasn't it? When you left us alone there?"

"Do you think I would have left you two behind if I'd had a choice?"

Duilio pressed his lips together. Now they were talking about his exile. If they were going to rehash events of a decade ago, this wouldn't help anyone.

"I wasn't given a choice," Monteiro went on. "You were handed over to your aunts' custody without a word to me."

"Coffee would be nice right now," Duilio interrupted.

And for a moment silence ruled. Marina gazed at him as if she'd forgotten he had the ability to speak. Oriana laid one silk-covered hand over her eyes. Her father settled for glaring at Duilio.

"There's a small café around the corner," Duilio added. "We could sit down and have a pleasant drink."

"Stay out of this," Monteiro said. "I didn't want you here in the first place and . . ."

Oriana didn't wait for him to finish his statement. She turned and strode out of the office.

"Too much at once," Duilio said softly. He nodded to Marina and fished out a card. "It was a pleasure meeting you. You're welcome to visit our home anytime. My mother is very fond of your sister, and I'm certain she would love to meet you as well. Your father can provide you with the address."

Monteiro settled on the edge of his desk, his arms folded over his chest. "You have no right to interfere."

Duilio hesitated at the office door, but turned back. "My brother and father fought incessantly, so much so that when the opportunity came for me to go abroad, I jumped at the chance."

Monteiro shot a glance at his younger daughter, who stood in the corner, eyes glistening.

"No matter how bad it got," Duilio said to her, "it never meant they didn't love each other." He nodded once to Monteiro, and let himself out.

Oriana waited on the cobbles outside the office, barely able to keep the tears from her eyes. She had let all the anger of the last ten years boil over. Until the last few weeks she'd always been able to keep her temper under control. Until then, when her world had come crashing down about her. And now she could see how much of what she'd known, or thought she'd known, was all wrong. She wanted to scream at someone, to make someone pay for all the lies and secrets, only she didn't know where to start.

Duilio emerged from the office door and came to where she waited. "Do you want to catch a cab back to the house or would you rather try the coffee?"

He wore an innocent look, as if he didn't know he'd ruined what had been shaping up to be a screaming match. She didn't know why it went that way with her father, but it always had. It was childish, and she knew better. "I need something stronger than coffee."

Duilio held out his arm and, once she'd taken it, led her along the street toward a hotel entry where several cabs waited. The afternoon hadn't warmed up, so the chill air helped cool her temper.

He selected a cab, paid the driver, and settled next to her on the tired leather bench.

"They need to change this out," he said, peering down at the soiled straw under his fine shoes. "I think one of last night's patrons left part of his dinner behind."

She felt slightly nauseated, although it was due more to the fight than the scent. She managed a nod as the cab lurched into motion. Fortunately it wouldn't be a long ride.

Keeping his hands low enough that it wouldn't be visible to someone outside, Duilio imitated the gesture she'd turned back on her father. "What does this mean?"

"Oh," she said softly, "that."

"It seemed to annoy him."

Making such a gesture should have been unthinkable for a Portuguese gentlewoman. After a moment of silence, she admitted, "I told him to do to himself what he'd suggested you were doing to me."

He laughed softly. "You truly do have trouble controlling yourself around your father."

"I warned you," she reminded him contritely.

He smiled as if her display of bad temper was insignificant. "I thought you were exaggerating."

She gazed out the window as the cab came around onto the Street of Flowers, heading past the larger mansions down in the direction of the river. She couldn't think of anything to say that wouldn't sound petulant, and she'd already subjected Duilio to enough of *that* for one day. Fortunately the cab soon jerked to a stop, and Duilio helped her down in front of the Ferreira home. Cardenas appeared at the door, as if he'd been watching for their return.

Oriana made her way wearily up the stone steps and inside the house. She tossed her hat onto the entryway table and went straight to the library, not waiting for Duilio. When she tried to open the liquor cabinet, she discovered her hands were shaking. The mitts didn't help. Duilio had caught her up, though, and steered her to the sofa while he poured a couple of glasses.

The day's discoveries were all jumbled in her head, triggering a mass of conflicting feelings. She didn't know whether to feel happy or sad, angry or relieved. At the moment, she felt worn thin. Oriana swallowed the brandy, a fire in her tight throat and gills. She set the glass down on the table next to the sofa and as a distraction, while Duilio refilled her glass, picked up one of books that lay there. She frowned down at it. Embossed in fine rose gold, the script on the leather spine looked familiar, but it certainly wasn't Portuguese. "Where did you get this?"

Duilio settled on the other end of the couch. "My father bought a batch of books from a merchant in North Africa. Marrakech, I think. He claimed they came from your people's islands, although the alphabet is vaguely reminiscent of Greek, not ours."

She flipped through the first few pages. "These do come from our islands, but they're written in the language of our scholars, not Portuguese, so I can't read them."

He made a speculative humming sound. "I'm surprised they're actually what Father claimed. I took this one up to the palace to use as a pretext to talk to the ambassador, but didn't need it after all. I must have left it in my coat pocket. I'll wager Marcellin put it in here."

Oriana imagined the snooty valet's offense at Duilio's mistreatment of his coat.

"I've wondered," Duilio said, "why your people would speak Portuguese if you already had your own language."

"Accessibility," she answered. "Most of my people weren't allowed to read or write this tongue. Reading was reserved for scholars. When the Portuguese priests came, they were willing to teach us to read their language, and after only a century, it became the tongue of the masses."

He nodded, his mouth in an "o" as if that made sense of an old mystery. For too long, her people's government had chosen to control their lives. It often turned out to be shortsighted. "You must be thinking I'm a fool," she said aloud. "We went there to find out one thing, but I ended up acting like a harpy, and we never got the answer."

Duilio shifted closer on the sofa. "Don't worry about that now. You have a right to be upset. Someone has clearly lied to you."

Her three aunts were surely to blame for this. They had wanted her to join the intelligence ministry, but she'd refused. When Marina had run away, they must have seen that as an opportunity to draw her in by concocting the story of Marina's supposed death. Once in the ministry, she'd been kept in inferior postings, mostly because she'd dragged her feet about having her webbing cut. From her father's point of view, it must seem she'd been dangled in front of him all this time, in their grasp and willingly serving the government that had exiled him. It was humiliating to think he'd been right, and *she'd* been the fool—especially after so long thinking the opposite. She sighed. "I can't figure out who used me against him, or why. Well, Heriberto obviously. But the note not to talk? That doesn't sound like him."

"But you don't think your father's lying to you."

She shook her head. Her father wasn't a liar.

Duilio regarded her with those earnest eyes. "What was he like when you were a child?"

Oriana took another burning sip of brandy. She had never talked with anyone about her family. Not in the last few years. She hadn't had any friends save Isabel, and Isabel hadn't been interested in the truth. Isabel had held some childish notion of the sereia playing in the waves all day. "He and my mother were very happy, I thought. I suppose I was wrong about that, too."

"I doubt it," Duilio said, head tilting. "Children can always tell."

"Yet when he came here he took up with . . . with Lady Pereira de Santos. My mother must not have meant that much to him after all."

He gazed at her with a troubled brow. "Do you think his current relationship negates what he felt for your mother?"

She tugged off the silk mitts and spread her fingers to stretch the webbing, briefly sensing the beat of Duilio's heart. "I don't know anymore."

"My mother has spoken of remarrying," he told her.

Lady Ferreira hadn't mentioned that to her, but his mother had clearly abandoned her mourning. Duilio's father had been a *philanderer*—to use Felis' word—so she certainly didn't blame the lady. But did it mean she'd never loved Duilio's father, either?

Duilio stared down into his untouched glass of brandy. He swirled it around a couple of times and then said, "She told me they were married. I thought it should be their secret to reveal when they chose, but given today's conversation, I've changed my mind. I'd rather you hear it before you talk to him again."

"You mean Lady Pereira de Santos?" Her voice sounded faint when she said that.

He nodded. "She said it's been seven years. They've kept it secret that long."

She didn't know why that seemed even worse than thinking her father had taken a lover, but it did. Her dismay must have shown on her face, because Duilio shifted over on the couch. He wrapped an arm about her shoulders, and she clung to his coat, eyes screwed tightly shut to keep tears at bay. After only a moment, she pushed herself away and drank down the rest of her brandy in one gulp, setting her gills to burning. "I'm just so tired."

And as if he accepted that weak explanation for her distress, Duilio rose and helped her to her feet. "I think you've had enough news for one day," he said. "You should take a long nap before dinner. Everything will seem clearer after you wake up."

She *was* exhausted. But she didn't want to be by herself, and she hated the idea of begging. "Would you . . . ?" she heard her traitor voice ask anyway.

"I'll stay with you, if you like," he said, sparing her from asking it. "Until you sleep."

So he walked with her up to the bedroom. He left the door open and sat down in the chair next to her bed. She removed her shoes and her borrowed jewelry and curled up on the brown coverlet, facing him. "Do you not have appointments?"

He gingerly touched his split lip where it had scabbed over, a match for her own torn lip. "No. I'm at your disposal for the rest of the day."

It was as if he'd known meeting with her father would overset her. There was so much buzzing around in her mind, too many problems all at once. One had been bothering her since their morning discussion in the hallway. "Duilio, from what are you . . . backing off?"

He rose, picked up a heavy woolen throw from the foot of the bed and laid it over her, and settled in the chair again. He touched her outstretched hand, wrapping his warm fingers around hers. "Right now, I am your friend, and that's all."

And for the moment, she suspected a friend was what she needed most.

O riana was asleep in only a few minutes, her hand slipping out of his grasp. Duilio rose and made his way out of the room, closing the door softly behind him. He had notes to dispatch and plans to make, so he made his way down to his desk in the library. But his mind kept drifting, far away from the tasks at hand.

Now that Oriana seemed to be feeling better—temper not withstanding—she wouldn't be satisfied waiting in the house and trying on new clothes all day. Duilio couldn't see her remaining a hired companion. His mother was right about that. Oriana had to figure out what her new calling in life would be. She was resourceful and intelligent, both qualities he admired in her. She was, he suspected, the equal of a man in every way.

From the first time he'd laid eyes on her, he'd sensed her importance. He'd felt Oriana would play some part in the rest of his life.

He'd had women before. He had always chosen carefully, seeking lovers who would be interested in an affair but nothing more—women who didn't need his money, who had no interest in marriage, and who were discreet. Unlike Alessio, he had never enjoyed *the pursuit*. He preferred a comfortable relationship, one that provided companionship and offered an outlet for his physical needs. Most of those relationships had lasted for some time—months, or even a year—before he had moved to another city. But when he returned home, he hadn't wanted to risk his family's safety by taking up with a woman who might not be a Sympathizer. So there hadn't been a woman in his life—or his bed—for well over a year now.

Oriana had asked what he was backing away from. He pinched his nose as he considered that. He'd been considering it for weeks, actually. There was only one acceptable answer. He wanted her to *marry* him.

That wasn't going to be easy. There were legal bars to marrying one of her people, although Monteiro had worked around that, hadn't he?

"I would like Oriana to marry me," he said softly, trying out the words in the library's silence. *Yes, I like the sound of that.*

But he needed to give her time and space to make up her mind about her own life before he asked her for more. So for now, he decided, he would be good. He would strive for propriety in his interactions with her. *I will wait.*

He didn't like the sound of *that*, but he would survive.

CHAPTER 16

Joaquim Tavares made his way along Fábrica Street, pondering his most recent meeting with Inspector Gaspar. Much as the man unnerved him, he had to admit that Gaspar was a thorough investigator. He'd carefully studied the list of missing women, most of whom were prostitutes or beggars—the sort of women policemen didn't usually worry over. They were often transient, moving from one place to another, so most officers felt their disappearances could be explained away. Others felt women like that weren't worth their time, that their "sins" relegated them to a less-than-human status.

Joaquim had never looked at them that way. His own mother had sold herself on the streets of Barcelona, forced into it by none other than her father, a man who should have taken care of her but used her instead to finance his careless life. She'd married anyway, to a man who was kind to her and brought her to Portugal, far away from her past—the elder Joaquim Tavares. No one knew that part of her history save her husband and the Ferreira family, and they never spoke of it. But Joaquim never forgot, so he was grateful that Gaspar seemed to be taking the women's deaths as seriously as he did.

And as much as Gaspar bothered him, he was beginning to suspect that the man was right. Gaspar had confronted him two weeks before when Duilio had been lost in the river after his rowboat had been hit broadside by a yacht. Gaspar had yelled at him to *find* Duilio, and he'd supplied the answer without thinking. Duilio and Miss Paredes had been located the next morning exactly where he'd predicted, on the beach near the southern breakwater at the mouth of the river. It probably wasn't a coincidence.

Gaspar, whose own gift was to recognize those of others, believed that Joaquim was a *finder*, a witch who could locate people, particularly if they knew the other well. He had been able to take Duilio directly to the island where Oriana was held. He never got lost. And his own mother had never lost track of him when he was a child. She had to be the one from whom he inherited the gift.

It made sense, in a way, but he hated being forced to deal with the notion of being a witch. He'd spent most of his life denying it.

He shoved his hands into his pockets, mind ticking away as he walked along.

He had other problems to solve, ones larger than his personal issues. He hadn't mentioned the dead selkie to Gaspar, or the otter girl. Those deaths were disturbing in a different way. What recourse did a selkie have if a crime was committed against her? If a selkie— or a sereia or whatever else—came to *him* to report a crime, he would never turn them over to the Special Police to be prosecuted for the mere act of living in the Golden City.

Was he the only officer who felt that way? Were there others, each keeping their investigations secret from their superiors and other officers? There probably were. He couldn't be the only one. Surely they could all find a way to work together.

He stopped on the cobbles.

Something is wrong.

He couldn't pinpoint what made him so sure of that, but it seemed he'd played out this day before, as if he knew he was going to . . .

A cry caught his ear, a woman calling for help.

Joaquim ran, bolting toward the voice. He ran past half a dozen houses and turned into a vacant lot created by the removal of a narrow building. A smartly dressed young woman struggled with a stocky man there, her hands in his grasp.

"Let her go!" Joaquim yelled.

The man spotted him and dropped her hands. He ran away from the street and was out of Joaquim's sight almost instantly.

Joaquim went to the frightened girl. She was tugging her gloves on with shaking hands, revealing that one had torn in her attacker's grasp. The man had knocked off her hat in the struggle and her braid had come loose, trailing down over her shoulder now. Her head was bowed as she gazed at her hands. He couldn't see her face from that angle.

"Are you hurt, miss?" Joaquim asked as he retrieved her felt hat from near a pile of old cobbles. He dusted it off with one hand.

She looked about as if she'd lost something else. "He threw my handbag away," she mumbled. "Where is my handbag?"

Joaquim peered down the narrow slot between the two buildings, no more than ten feet across. Vegetation ruled the center of the block, hedged about by old houses, and he couldn't see any sign of her attacker now. Surely the man had taken her bag with him. But no, he spotted a small beaded handbag not far from where her hat had landed. He made his way around the pile of cobbles and retrieved it. She wiped her cheeks with the side of one gloved finger, valiantly trying to put the fright behind her. When he held out her bag, she reached out one small hand, her eyes lifting to meet his for the first time.

Joaquim forgot to breathe.

"Thank you, sir," she said as he mechanically deposited the bag in her hand.

He *knew* that face.

Not from a photograph of her, not a drawing from a friend's description. She wasn't one of the missing women in his files. But he knew her face like the back of his own hands: the deep brown eyes, the curl that had come loose from her braid and curved against her cheek, that ivory-pale skin, the soft lips. *How can she be here, this woman from my dreams?*

"I must thank you, Mr. . . . ?" she said in a voice that he recognized now. A narrow line formed between her smoothly arched brows.

How long had he been gaping at her like an idiot? Joaquim mentally shook himself and rubbed a hand over his face. "Tavares," he answered. "There's no need, miss. I was walking this way anyway. Did he hurt you?"

She shook her head quickly. "No, no. He ripped my glove, but . . ." She lifted her chin and favored him with a shy smile. "But he didn't take anything, Mr. Tavares. Thanks to you."

Joaquim felt a flush warm his cheeks. "Can I escort you, then, to make certain you get home safely?"

"Yes," she said after a brief hesitation, those beautiful brown eyes lifting to his again. "I would like that."

When Oriana appeared in the front sitting room before dinner, her hair had been neatly done up into a very proper bun. She once more wore the jet earrings and brooch set. Her brown skirt didn't look rumpled, which made Duilio suspect Teresa—who was acting as Oriana's maid—had insisted on pressing it again. Oriana seemed composed now and answered his mother's queries about the visit to the Monteiro office with as little detail as possible. His mother quickly caught her unease and moved to another topic. She picked up the French book about the sereia. "I have been meaning to discuss this book with you, Miss Paredes. I suspect its validity."

Oriana took the offending text from her, squinted at the nearly unreadable lettering on the cloth-covered spine, and then glanced at the frontispiece. "I don't have French, Lady Ferreira."

His mother waved away that objection. "I suspect the author drew the wrong conclusions about many things. As Duilinho has informed me he intends to let Filho chase murderers on his own tonight, he can read some of it for us."

Oriana shot a quizzical glance at Duilio and mouthed, "*Murderers?*"

"*Later,*" he mouthed back at her. He had written to Joaquim, begging off for the evening. He wanted to be available should Oriana wish to talk about her visit to her father's office. He was grateful, though, that his mother had hit on such an excellent distraction. Aloud, he explained, "I've mentioned this book to you before, but I couldn't find it. It turns out that Erdano somehow managed to break one leg of his bed and filched a pile of books from the library to prop it up, this one among them. Probably the best use for the thing, as it *is* truly awful. Mother thinks someone should write a more accurate book about your people."

"And that would be you?" Oriana asked.

"I lack the experience needed, Miss Paredes. I've never even seen the islands. You, however . . ."

"Ah," she said, "I'm to be the expert."

Cardenas appeared in the doorway to announce that dinner was ready. Duilio held out an arm for his mother, but inclined his head in Oriana's direction. "Perhaps after dinner, I can read the first chapter to you, Miss Paredes."

"Of course, Mr. Ferreira," she said, a hint of laughter in her voice.

"The writer says there are very few males," Lady Ferreira commented once they'd retired to the front sitting room after dinner. "Does that disparity exist?"

"Yes," Oriana said. They had discussed Monsieur Matelot's questionable book over dinner, a topic that seemed likely to last all night. "Among our people there are approximately two females born for every male. In the past it was closer to three to one but over the last several generations, that's been changing."

Duilio made a note in the margin of the book itself. Apparently he didn't share her father's horror of writing *in* books. "I don't think human numbers are exactly even, either," he commented aloud, "although I'm not certain what the percentages are."

"Among selkies," his mother offered, "it's closer to ten to one."

The lady sat on the other end of the pale beige couch, so Oriana shifted about to face her more directly, tugging at her brown skirt to get it to cooperate. "Is that why the females live in harems? Because there aren't enough males?"

Lady Ferreira's eyes slid to her gloved hands. "The harems are principally for protection. It's safer to live in a group. The male is there for . . . breeding purposes. They're honestly not that useful otherwise."

Oriana couldn't hold in the peal of laughter that bubbled out. She could only image Erdano's offense should anyone tell him that. Duilio had a studiously uninterested look on his face, but Oriana wasn't fooled for a moment. His lips were pressed into a thin line, barely keeping his amusement inside. She turned back to Lady Ferreira. "So they don't provide protection?"

"Not much," the lady said, the corners of her eyes crinkling. "They're so often gone hunting new females that it's usually up to the queen to prevent that sort of predation."

That sounded harsh, but Oriana had learned that many things about selkie life were. "It seems unfair to his queen."

Lady Ferreira smiled at her. "It *is* difficult. I was not well suited to that life."

Of course, she'd been queen of a harem at one point. "Because you were raised among humans?"

"Yes," Lady Ferreira said. "I have to admit, when a human man offered himself, I found the idea terribly attractive."

"And your mate didn't fight to keep you in the harem?"

"I don't think mate is the correct word, Miss Paredes. Mate implies a one-to-one relationship, does it not? But no, Guidano feared that should another female want to be his queen, she would kill me to have my place. So when Duilio's father took an interest in me, Guidano encouraged it."

And that explained why, despite having borne him a son, the selkie male had given her up to a human lover. Oriana *had* wondered. "Did you love him?"

"Guidano?" She waved one hand vaguely. "I was fond of him. He was kind, but not terribly clever."

That told Oriana a great deal about that relationship. She caught Duilio's eye. He didn't seem upset, so she suspected he'd heard all of this before.

"Forgive me for asking," Lady Ferreira said, "but selkies deal with the numerical imbalance by having many females sharing one male. Do your people do the same? I had the impression monogamy was practiced among them."

What an awkward topic. Oriana sighed inwardly. She would have to take her ire out on the inconvenient Monsieur Matelot, should she ever run across him. "More or less. Our people are taught there's a mate intended for them from the very moment they are born. Even before. If there is to be one."

Duilio regarded her with brows drawn together. He opened his mouth to ask a question, and then apparently thought better of it.

"Then what becomes of the other females?" Lady Ferreira asked. "Are half the females meant not to have mates?"

"Yes," Oriana admitted. "Those are meant to serve their people."

"As spies, perhaps?" Duilio closed the book and set it aside.

Oriana nodded again.

"I find that terribly shortsighted," Lady Ferreira said. "Why not choose a human male, as there are plenty of them running about."

Oriana tried not to look at Duilio. It was a terribly complicated subject. Choosing a human mate meant diluting the bloodlines, although none were all that pure anyway. At the same time, beauty in a male was often defined by how *human* he looked. "I suppose it's convention," she answered weakly. "Most selkie females don't leave the harem, do they?"

"No. They usually stick together. Most of the young males leave, though, and many end up living among humans if they aren't successful at attracting a harem." She rose regally. "Now, I've had a long day. Please don't get up, Duilinho. I will see you both in the morning."

Duilio had risen with her anyway. "Good night, Mother."

She shut the sitting room door on the way out, leaving them alone in the room—an improper thing to do. Oriana doubted anyone was going to raise eyebrows at that, not when Duilio had already spent an inordinate amount of time alone with her. He returned to the chair across from the sofa.

"Murderers?" she asked, brows rising.

Duilio didn't argue with her effort to escape the previous discussion. His features went solemn like he was debating how much to tell her. "Joaquim and I have been searching for someone who murdered a selkie girl, one of Erdano's harem."

Oriana caught her lower lip between her teeth. It had to happen in cities of this size. People died, and some small percentage of them probably weren't human. "I didn't think the police were interested in nonhumans."

Duilio shrugged. "His superiors believe she was human. Erdano had asked me to look for her, so when Joaquim came across her body, he had a good idea she was the one. Another girl was killed several days before that in a related manner. Possibly an otter girl, although we can't be certain."

"The otter folk have tails," she said. He was holding something back. "It would be hard to miss that."

He cast an apologetic look at her. "If she had a tail, it was removed."

"Removed?" Oriana sat back, horrified. *What kind of person would do that?* "And the selkie?"

"They removed her skin. All of it." He paused a moment, jaw working, and then asked, "Does that mean anything to you?"

Her stomach churned. "No, nothing. Are they only after non-humans?"

"It seems likely that the two murders are related, given the manner of death. The killer would have known about the otter girl, if she was that. We can't know if he was aware Gita was a selkie. We're not sure what's unfolding here."

Oriana looked down at hands, which clearly marked her as a nonhuman. Had Duilio been staying so close out of concern for her safety? "Please, tell me everything."

After a brief pause, he began to speak, starting with the day before he'd come to find her. The web of incidents and evidence didn't make sense to her, but with Isabel's death she'd learned that things often looked far different in hindsight. What had seemed a random abduction that night turned out to be only one in a long series of murders.

"So there's a healer out there killing prostitutes," she summed up, "and someone is mutilating nonhuman girls. Both are classes of women the authorities generally ignore."

"Not us," Duilio said. "Gaspar is looking into the healer, although he seemed to suspect . . ."

She waited for him to finish that.

"Well, he's got a few ideas," Duilio equivocated. "Apparently the number of people who can do that is limited."

Oriana found herself nodding, although she had no idea if that was true. Her people didn't have healers. "I'd like to tell my father, so he can get the word out among the exiles. Would you mind?"

"No," he said quickly, sitting up. "I think it's an excellent idea."

Surely she could do that without falling into a disagreement. Oriana's eyes fixed on the bruise darkening Duilio's cheek. "What does your infante have to do with all of this?"

Duilio groaned. "He wants something from me. He came to the house this past Sunday, but I didn't know who he was then. He asked me if I would serve the infante as Alessio had. Apparently Alessio was a courier of sorts for him. I don't think he wants me to take over Alessio's work, but I don't know what else he'd need me for."

"Other than a sparring partner?" She gestured toward the bruise. "What did that prove?"

"Well, it showed me that the guards allow him to practice with them. That suggests they prefer him over the prince. There were several present in their practice room when he sparred with me. They cheered when he scored that hit. It was genuine friendliness, not false praise."

She sat for a moment in silence, puzzling at the mystery the infante posed and trying to pull together pieces. It was actually a relief to have something else to think about beyond her own problems. "He's the one who told you about the astrologers, is that right? What they claimed about my uncle killing the prince."

"Yes. And if the prince were to die, the infante would inherit the throne."

"But that's always been more a case of *when* the prince dies, hasn't it?" she pointed out. "He doesn't have any other heir."

Duilio shook his head. "A moot point. However, if the astrologers were right, it will be sooner rather than later."

"My uncle would never . . ."

He held up his hand as if something had just occurred to him. "What if someone did intend to kill the prince, perhaps one of your people *other* than the ambassador?"

"An assassin?" She thought immediately of Maria Melo, the sereia woman who had chosen her and Isabel to be among Maraval's victims. Heriberto had been afraid of Melo, and had warned Oriana against her, claiming that Melo's mission outweighed his authority. He'd believed the woman would kill her own people to protect her mission . . . and now he'd apparently fled. "Did the Special Police ever find Maria Melo?"

"No," Duilio said softly. "Do you think she could be an assassin?"

Oriana weighed what little she knew about the woman. "She could be. But I can't imagine who in the government would sanction such a thing. We don't have a history of aggression against your people, and we stand no chance of winning an outright war, should an assassination trigger one." Oriana rose and went to the hearth, her hands going cold. The death of the prince might benefit her and all the exiles, but it could be disastrous for her people as a whole. "Do you want the prince to live?"

Duilio stayed in his chair. "Not particularly, I admit."

He *was* willing to ignore the rules if he believed the greater good was served, she knew. They had circumvented the prince's edicts when they'd gone after Isabel's killer. And she had ignored her own orders as well. "Mrs. Melo might have wanted to be rid of me. If she's high enough in the ministry, she would have the influence to order my execution."

"Could she send a ship there to keep us from rescuing you?"

Oriana turned back to stare at him. "What do you mean?"

He shook his head dismissively as if it was nothing. "When Joaquim and I found you, a ship chased us away from the island—a steam corvette or something about that size. They seemed to want to board us."

"No, our navy's ships are small, built for stealth. I don't think we have anything that size."

Duilio licked his lips. "The men aboard didn't speak Portuguese well, so we doubted it."

Oriana shook her head. They'd been discussing the gender disparity among her people earlier that same evening, but apparently he hadn't worked out all the ramifications yet. "Men, Duilio. You said they were *men*. Our navy is almost all female."

His mouth fell open into a rather comical "o." "So the guards on the ship you were held on?"

"Were all female," she said patiently.

"But your spymaster, Heriberto, was male," he pointed out.

"Yes. Our government knows that humans expect to interact with males, so they bring in a few older males, mostly ones who've lost their mates . . . as figureheads."

He gazed at her a moment longer as if all his understanding of her people had been overset. "So your father . . ."

"Holds the radical belief that males should have the same rights as females. That was why he was exiled."

Duilio seemed to process that for a moment, then nodded. "Your father is an exception, then."

"As is your mother, I think."

He tilted his head and nodded as if allowing that truth. "She is. As to the ship, Joaquim has made inquiries, but hasn't heard of any vessel that size limping into a nearby port. Since we didn't see a flag, we wondered if they might be pirates instead, coming to collect a sereia who was too exhausted to defend herself."

"Gods, I hope not." Oriana laid a hand over her mouth, appalled. *What a horrid thought.* "How did you get away?"

"A leviathan attacked them," he said. "The ambassador had warned me there was a leviathan near those islands. . . ."

Oriana gaped at him. "Are you sure?"

"We didn't get a good look at it, but I can't imagine what else it could have been."

"Leviathans serve the gods," she told him. "If it came to interfere, they would never have succeeded in taking me."

Duilio nodded, although she guessed he didn't credit that. Leviathans were generally too shy to bother moving ships. This one had acted out of character, but Duilio wouldn't attribute that to the gods, or even to *his* God. He preferred scientific answers to his problems.

But if a leviathan had interfered to save her, it meant the gods had a plan for her. She needed to figure out what that was. Oriana returned to the couch and sat squarely facing him. "Let me help you try to find the truth, find out if my father knows anything."

He didn't argue about letting her get involved. "No more rude gestures?"

"I promise I can be civil," she said.

He didn't smile, but the corners of his eyes gave away his merriment. "Keep your hands behind your back," he suggested.

She lifted her chin. "I will if he does."

CHAPTER 17

SATURDAY, 25 OCTOBER 1902

"It seems to me," Lady Ferreira said the next morning at the break-fast table, "it might be better if Miss Paredes didn't speak with her father at all."

She wore a cream-colored silk day dress with lace undersleeves, one of her new ones, the height of fashion. Oriana's garb was new as well, Duilio noted, a heathered teal skirt paired with a tailored teal jacket that emphasized her lovely figure.

"Mother, we do need to speak to him again."

His mother sighed. "I meant that *you* should speak to him, Duilinho. Miss Paredes can talk to her sister. Does the girl not work in the same office?"

Duilio had been hesitant to suggest that, for fear Oriana might think he doubted her ability to control her temper. He was grateful his mother had done so. "Would he talk to me alone?"

"He might," Oriana said hesitantly. "There might not be so many sparks." Her sheepish expression hinted that she regretted her exhibition of temper on the previous visit. "I sat down last night and wrote out a list of questions I have for him. I could give *you* that, and I'll try to get Marina to talk instead."

When they were preparing to leave, his mother drew him to one side. She brushed the lapels of his morning coat with her gloved fingers and sighed. "You have reason to be upset with this man, Duilinho, but I would counsel you to try to get along with him."

He looked heavenward—or toward the plastered ceiling. "I know, Mother. He is her family."

She leaned up and kissed his cheek. "And don't walk away from him."

So chastened, half an hour later he stood in the chilly morning fog at the gold-lettered door of Monteiro and Company, Oriana at his side. She seemed calm enough, and even managed to don a smile when he opened the door for her.

The same clerk met them inside the doorway, his expression quizzical.

Duilio supposed no one ever visited on two consecutive days— or else Monteiro never met with people on Saturdays. "I'd like to speak with Mr. Monteiro. And is Miss Arenias here?"

"Mr. Monteiro is with a client," the clerk said, "but Miss Arenias is in the back room."

"If you'll inform him I'd like to speak to him, I would appreciate it," Duilio said.

"I'll talk to Miss Arenias," Oriana added.

Oriana disappeared down the long hallway toward the back room, leaving Duilio perched on a wooden bench in the hallway. He was surprised when the clerk emerged from Monteiro's office with word that his employer would see him immediately. Duilio rose and walked into the office and was even more surprised to find that the previous client hadn't left; Lady Pereira de Santos sat in a chair to one side of the desk. He'd been correct; the two of them did make a handsome couple.

"Mr. Ferreira," Monteiro began, his tone not as frosty as Duilio had expected. "I was surprised when Narciso told me you'd returned so quickly."

As he didn't ask after Oriana, Duilio guessed Narciso had informed his employer where Oriana had gone. Duilio inclined his head toward Lady Pereira de Santos—who'd remained in her seat—and turned back to Monteiro. "Yesterday's meeting was not as productive as I'd hoped it would be. However, I have two objectives today, simple ones, and I'll be out of your way, sir."

Monteiro gestured toward one of the chairs before the desk. Duilio sat as Monteiro settled in his own chair, his shoulders squared. "And what are those objectives, Mr. Ferreira?"

Ah, this is going to be civil. "First, to give you a warning. We believe someone has murdered a selkie and one of the otter folk in the last week or so."

"We?" Monteiro's tone was cool.

"I work with the police," Duilio said.

Monteiro's eyes narrowed. "Do they care whether we live or die?"

Lady Pereira de Santos reached over and laid one black-gloved hand on his arm.

It must have been an admonishment to be polite, because Monteiro sighed. In a conciliatory tone, he added, "I understand the police are forbidden to investigate crimes that concern nonhumans."

Duilio understood the man's vexation. "As long as the identity of the victim cannot be proven conclusively, we—well, *they*—can investigate. Unfortunately, the police don't have any means to get the word out to nonhumans if they are being targeted. I hoped mentioning it to you might help."

Monteiro sat back in his chair, his dark brows drawn together. "I can take care of that."

"I would appreciate it, sir. Unfortunately, the police aren't making much progress with this case, so I have no specific advice other than to be cautious."

Monteiro nodded. "And your second objective?"

The man looked as if he were bracing himself, and Duilio had the impression Monteiro expected a discussion of his intentions to-ward Oriana. He cast a quick glance at Lady Pereira de Santos. Her hopeful expression reinforced that idea. Even so, Duilio didn't plan to ask this man for permission to court his daughter. "Your daughter supplied me with a list of questions. They're personal, so it might be better if I left the list with you and you wrote the answers for her."

Lady Pereira de Santos looked away, her brows drawn together and her lips pursed.

Monteiro seemed taken aback. "Is that all?"

"Well, you might be able to answer *my* questions," Duilio said. "We need to find out who put Oriana on that island to die. Someone used her as a pawn. I want to know who."

Monteiro gave him a measuring glance. "Why would you think I know?"

"Someone told you not to talk. Who was that? They had to have known what happened to her before anyone else did."

Monteiro opened a desk drawer and withdrew an envelope with a broken seal. He held it out. "This was delivered to this office by a beg-gar boy. Narciso didn't get his name, so there's no way to track him."

Duilio leaned forward and took the envelope. "May I give this to Oriana?"

Monteiro nodded. "If I knew who did that to her, I would have already turned them in to the Special Police."

That was, Duilio realized, the only recourse a nonhuman would have. "Do you know a woman named Maria Melo?" he asked. "She's a sereia."

"No," Monteiro said. "Should I?"

It might be easier to come at the topic from the rear. "Are you aware that Oriana and Lady Isabel were among the victims trapped in *The City Under the Sea*?"

Lady Pereira de Santos closed her eyes and shook her head. She must have guessed what had happened to Isabel Amaral, even if the newspapers glossed over that fact.

Monteiro scowled. "We suspected."

"Mrs. Melo was the one who selected her to be there—a saboteur within the organization that built the artwork. She was posing as an upper servant, meeting with servants from along the Street of Flowers at one of the local taverns. She picked Oriana specifically because she wouldn't drown. Heriberto later told Oriana that Mrs. Melo was higher than him in the ministry."

"You're very much in my daughter's confidence," Monteiro said in a guarded tone.

"I am. I was investigating the artwork when Oriana went missing, so I tracked her down. She agreed to help us stop Isabel's killer."

"I see," Monteiro said. "And you think the same woman might have been responsible for what happened to her on that island?"

"It occurred to me that should Oriana reach home, her testimony about being offered up as a sacrifice by a fellow sereia might be damaging. So they made certain she never reached home. She said there was no trial, no charges. Just a sentence of death."

Her father's jaw clenched. "I would help you find the woman if I knew her, Ferreira."

Well, that has to be considered progress. "That gives me a plausible explanation for what happened to Oriana, but I still don't know why you and the ambassador were threatened. The only thing I can think of that would be important enough to warrant silencing you—and others—is an assassination attempt."

"If one of my people were to attempt such a thing, Mr. Ferreira, it could go very badly for us." Monteiro shook his head. "We would not allow it to happen—to protect ourselves and to protect the peace, *not* your prince. The alternative is too terrible to contemplate."

The back room was full of filing cabinets—work relating to various clients, Oriana supposed. It smelled of musty paper and dust. Marina had turned away from her typewriter and sat sideways in her chair, rubbing one hand with the other. "I haven't heard anything about anyone being killed."

"They didn't want the newspapers to know," Oriana told her. "Just remember to be careful. One of the girls was grabbed from a side street, so watch where you walk. Stick to the larger streets and stay with your friends."

"A side street?" Marina's delicate brows drew together.

"That's what Mr. Ferreira told me," Oriana said. Marina's face took on a worried look, her lips pursed and her eyes focused inward, so Oriana pressed further. "What is it?"

Marina shook her head. "You can't tell Father."

Oriana gave her a hard look. "What *is* it?"

Marina swallowed, and then gave in. "Well, yesterday afternoon after you left, I went to see the doctor. My hands were hurting, so I wanted to ask if he could recommend anything. That's why I didn't tell Father. I didn't want him to know."

Oriana waited, trying to decide whether her father needed to be throttled, or Marina.

"Well, after I came out, I was walking down the street when a man grabbed my arm and dragged me into an empty lot." Marina took a deep breath. "He tried to steal my gloves, but another man came running into the alleyway and scared him off. The thief ran away."

Oriana could only think of one reason for a man to steal Marina's gloves; he'd wanted a look at her hands. "He didn't take your handbag?"

"No, I dropped it. Well, I tried to hit him with it, and he grabbed it and threw it away."

At least Marina had tried to defend herself. "Did you cry out for help?"

"Yes," Marina said, flushing—she had thinner skin and actually *could* flush. "The other man, he'd heard me screaming. He found my handbag and walked me back to my flat to be certain I was safe. It was very kind of him. He said he hoped he might see me again."

See her again? "And you didn't mention *him* to Father, either?"

"You know how protective Father is," Marina said with a half shrug.

No, I don't. Oriana pressed her lips together, trying to be like Duilio and limit the things that came out of her mouth. The glow in Marina's eyes hinted she'd found a new hero to worship. As a girl, Marina had always been prone toward mooning over males. Oriana rubbed her temple. "What was his name?"

"Mr. Tavares."

Oriana felt her mouth fall open. *It can't be, can it?* "Did he tell you his given name?"

Marina shook her head.

Tavares wasn't a terribly common name, she supposed, but it wasn't uncommon either. "Did you *call* him?"

Marina rubbed her nose with one gloved finger—a gesture she always made when she was thinking hard. "I don't remember," she finally admitted. "I was so scared. I may have used my voice, but . . . I don't remember."

Oriana sighed. If Marina had used her voice to *call*, any human male nearby would have been compelled to come to her aid. Her attacker could have resisted her only if his ears had been plugged or he was deaf . . . or nonhuman. "Did he say anything to you, the man who grabbed you?"

"No."

There was also the possibility that the two men could have been working together, but Marina wasn't cynical enough to believe that, so Oriana let it drop. "I need you to do something for me," she said. "I'll not tell Father, but I need you to tell Mr. Ferreira about this. He may want you to talk to . . . a friend in the police. Would you be willing to do that?"

"Will it help?" Marina asked.

"I'd rather let them decide." She got up and drew Marina toward the door, wrapping an arm through her younger sister's. "So what does Mr. Tavares look like?"

Marina went along willingly enough. "He's tall and handsome."

That wasn't helpful. "Did he tell you anything about his family, or where he worked?"

"Not so much," Marina admitted. "He did say he had brothers."

"Come on. I'll pry Mr. Ferreira out of Father's office and we can get a cab."

"But I have to work," Marina protested.

"Marina, this could be *very* important. If you'd let me explain to them, I'm sure Father will let you come with us." Oriana marched down the hall and knocked on the office door that bore her father's name before the attentive young clerk could intercept her.

"Come," her father's voice called from inside.

Keeping one hand on Marina's arm, Oriana swung the door open. Duilio came to his feet, apparently unbloodied. He cast her a confused glance. This hadn't been their plan. "Mr. Ferreira, Miss Arenias and I need to talk to you."

He turned back to her father. "Perhaps we can finish this another day, Mr. Monteiro. Thank you for your time."

"Mr. Ferreira, surely we can all hear what Miss Arenias has to say." For the first time Oriana saw that Lady Pereira de Santos was in the room, too, sitting in a chair next to her father's desk. "Why don't you close the door, Miss Paredes?" the lady suggested.

Oriana wasn't certain why it bothered her—the woman was, after all, both his wife and his client—but it did. She found herself obediently pulling the door shut.

Marina sighed dramatically and tugged her arm loose. "You see?" she whispered. "Now you've gotten me in trouble."

Oriana resisted the urge to pinch her. "Tell Father what you told me."

With a resigned glance at her father, Marina described her

encounter with the man who dragged her off the street. The scowl on their father's face grew. Duilio's eyes met Oriana's; he'd clearly understood what Marina had missed, that the robber had been trying to determine if she was a sereia. When Marina mentioned Mr. Tavares coming to her rescue, though, Duilio gazed at her, eyes wide. "Mr. *Joaquim* Tavares?"

"I didn't ask his given name," Marina said. "I didn't think it would be proper."

Their father crossed his arms over his chest. "And did you think it was proper not to tell your own father you'd been assaulted? Marina, for God's sake, you could have been killed!"

Marina's eyes began to glisten, and she sniffled.

Lady Pereira de Santos rose and set her hand on his arm. "Adriano," she said very softly, "she was trying to spare you concern. She didn't know of any potential threat. I probably would have done the same."

Oriana was surprised the woman had stepped in to defend Marina. "She's right, Father. Marina didn't know."

Her father's eyes slid toward Duilio, as if seeking support from the only other male in the room. "Do you know this man?"

"If you're referring to Mr. Tavares," Duilio said, "I can't be certain. But I know a Joaquim Tavares, and it does sound like something he would do."

"He needs to hear this story," Oriana said. "The parts he hasn't heard."

Marina turned on her. "What do you mean?"

"The police need to know that you're a sereia," Duilio answered. "That puts a different complexion on the assault."

Marina's brows drew together. "What does that have to do with Mr. Tavares?"

"I am not going to let her walk into a police station and tell them that," her father snapped.

Duilio raised a hand. "The officer I would take her to see is a

Sympathizer, sir. He's handling the two other murders. I promise he'll keep her name out of any records."

"Can you guarantee his actions?"

Duilio nodded. "I trust him with my life. With my mother's life."

Oriana held her breath.

"He is my . . . cousin, sir," Duilio added. "One of the few who know my mother isn't human. He knows about Oriana as well."

No, that middle statement hadn't slid past her father, nor Lady Pereira de Santos, whose delicate eyebrows rose. Marina's brow remained furrowed.

"Your mother isn't human?" her father asked Duilio.

"No," Duilio said, and turned to Lady Pereira de Santos. "And now you know *my* family secret, as is fair."

The lady inclined her head in his direction.

"You're a selkie?" her father asked, disbelief plain on his features.

"Half," Duilio said calmly.

"I've seen Lady Ferreira. She certainly has nothing of their manner about her."

"She was raised on land," Duilio said, "and only went to the sea later. She was educated as a human would have been."

Her father's brows lifted as if he'd figured out something clever, and he glanced in her direction. "It's not what you think," Oriana snapped before he could say anything. "Mr. Ferreira hasn't ever tried to charm me."

Her father touched one finger to his cheek under his eye—the sign of disbelief.

Oriana raised her own hands to gesture, but caught Duilio looking at her pointedly.

Hands behind your back, he mouthed at her.

Oriana took a deep breath and put her hands behind her back. She could use them to strangle Duilio later.

Duilio shifted to face her father directly. "I told you that, sir, so you would know that my cousin can be trusted. He would never allow any harm to come to Miss Arenias. And it would be helpful for him to talk to her directly, as she might be the only person who can give him adequate descriptions."

Marina, who'd remained silent throughout that exchange, tugged at Oriana's sleeve. "He means the police, right? Or did he mean Mr. Tavares?"

Oriana took her hand. "I believe they are the same."

CHAPTER 18

Duilio kept his mouth shut while Oriana whispered comforting things to her younger sister. He sat on the cab's bench across from them, facing backward, which gave him a clear view of the area they were leaving. It wouldn't be a long journey, and fortunately, this cab didn't smell of vomit.

It was entirely possible that Joaquim had heard a young lady in distress and run to her aid. It would be like him. It was not, however, like him to make a casual statement about seeing that young lady again. Joaquim didn't believe in leading women on.

On the other hand, Duilio suspected Joaquim would find delicate Miss Arenias appealing. He didn't know exactly what made him think that, but his certainty grew as he watched her talking with Oriana.

The girl glanced up and caught him watching her. "Are you truly part selkie? I've never met one before, but you look quite human."

"As do you, Miss Arenias," he replied.

She blushed. Even in the partial light of the cab he could see that—a reaction he hadn't thought possible for a sereia. Their skin was generally too thick to allow it, something to do with the cold temperatures of seawater and circulation of blood. Oriana certainly never blushed. "In human form," he told her, "a selkie is completely human in appearance. If you saw my half brother Erdano, you wouldn't know he was a selkie either."

"Until you smelled him," Oriana added. "He *reeks* of musk."

Duilio stifled a laugh at Oriana's disgusted tone.

"I suspect some women find it attractive," she added, "but I find it overbearing."

"Ah," Duilio said. "Is that why you never succumbed to his subtle attempts to court you, Miss Paredes?"

Oriana opened her mouth, but her sister spoke first. "If you're meant to be her mate," Marina said, "no one would be able to turn her away from you, not even a selkie."

Duilio suspected that if Oriana *could* blush, she would be doing so at that moment. She looked tense now, and uncomfortable. He plastered a smile on his face. "Miss Arenias, I believe you're correct."

Marina was about to add something else when the cab started slowing. Duilio glanced out the window and saw they were near the police station. He opened the door when the cab stopped and, once down, helped the two sisters to the cobbles. Oriana had one arm tucked through Marina's when he turned back from paying the driver, so he held the door open for them to enter the station. Oriana continued to keep her eyes averted from his.

He led them down the hallway toward Joaquim's office and asked them to wait in the hallway outside. That got Oriana to look at him, but she only nodded in a jerky fashion and then her eyes slid away.

Duilio knocked on the door and was relieved when he heard Joaquim call for him to enter; he hadn't dragged the two women to the station in vain. After a quick nod in their direction, he opened the door and slipped into the office.

Joaquim glanced up at him when the door closed, and relief covered his strained features. "I'm glad you're here."

"I'm not alone," Duilio warned. "I've brought Miss Paredes and her sister to talk to you."

Joaquim dragged a hand over his face. "This isn't a good time for social calls."

"This isn't a social call, Joaquim. Oriana's sister might have been a target, only someone came to her rescue before she was dragged off. She was lucky."

"You don't know how lucky. There was another body found this morning—a sereia girl this time."

Duilio felt ill. He'd warned Monteiro too late. "Damn."

Joaquim kicked at the leg of the desk. "There's no hiding this one, Duilio. Gonzalo hasn't said anything, but . . ."

No hiding it? "Was she not skinned?"

"No," Joaquim said. "She was dumped in the same fashion, though. It has to be related."

"What did they do?" Duilio asked.

"Tore out most of her throat." Joaquim grimaced. "That's where a sereia's magic is, isn't it? In their throat?"

If that were true, it clearly established a pattern, despite all the other differences. He should go see Dr. Esteves again. "I don't know, but I'll ask."

Joaquim stood and gestured toward the door. "If the younger Miss Paredes was attacked, she might be our only lead."

Duilio held up a hand to stop him. "She doesn't use Paredes. She uses Arenias."

"Arenias? Is she . . ." Joaquim's eyes focused inward.

And that answered Duilio's question as to whether he'd been the same Mr. Tavares who came to her rescue. Duilio could almost see the wheels of Joaquim's mind turning, recalculating something in light of his new knowledge of the girl's identity.

"The girl who was being robbed?" Joaquim asked. "*That* Miss Arenias?"

"Yes, but she wasn't being robbed. He didn't take her handbag. He was trying to take off her gloves instead, to see if she'd ever had webbing, I suspect."

And then that sunk in, as well. "The dead girl has scars between each finger," Joaquim said. "She had her webbing cut away."

"Oriana's father as well—Monteiro. He looks so human one would never guess."

Joaquim squared his shoulders and straightened his necktie, his lips set in a thin line. "Why don't you ask them to come in?"

Duilio complied, drawing Oriana and her sister into the small office. On seeing Joaquim there, Marina looked eager for an instant . . . but that expression fled into resignation as she seemingly realized her rescuer and the policeman were one and the same, and now he knew her secret. She sank gracefully onto a wooden chair next to the door, with Oriana stepping around to sit next to her.

Duilio started introductions—a formality, but it eased the tension in the room. "Joaquim, I'd like you to meet Miss Marina Arenias, who works for Monteiro and Company." He turned to the younger sister. "And this is my cousin, Joaquim Tavares, who is an inspector."

Joaquim inclined his head. "Of course we've met, Miss Arenias."

Marina nodded, her eyes fixed on the desk. Then she lifted her chin. "I should apologize for not telling you, Mr. Tavares, but I am not human."

Duilio was impressed she'd gathered her courage to do so.

"I understand your choosing not to reveal that, Miss Arenias," Joaquim said in his most polite voice. "There's danger in confiding that information without due consideration."

"That information, however, casts a different light on the attack." Duilio suspected they would be there for a while, so he leaned against the wall.

"It would probably be best, Miss Arenias," Joaquim said, "if we started over from the beginning. I'd like you to tell me everything about that afternoon you can remember. Do you know why he might have suspected you were a sereia in the first place?"

"No," Marina said, shaking her head.

"Very well," Joaquim said. "Why were you walking down that street?"

"I'd been to see the doctor," she began.

Duilio glanced at Oriana. *What is she thinking?* She had eyes only for her sister at the moment, or was studiously avoiding his gaze. He would have to pick her brain when he got her alone.

After Joaquim had exhausted most logical lines of questioning, Duilio frowned down at his shoes. They hadn't accomplished much. Marina described the man who grabbed her as dark haired, brown eyed, and with a stocky build, shorter than Duilio, perhaps thirty, nothing distinctive about his garments. While that could describe many men in the city, it did match the description the beggar had given of the coachman who'd grabbed Gita. The assailant hadn't spoken to Marina at all. And Joaquim, normally the most observant of men, hadn't been paying attention to the robber. He'd apparently been too concerned about Miss Arenias to pursue her assailant.

"Which doctor did you go to see, Miss Arenias?" Duilio asked when Joaquim stalled in his questioning.

Marina seemed surprised at a query from *him*. "Dr. Esteves."

He'd suspected that. After all, her father had recommended the man for Oriana. He had gone to see the man earlier the very same day. "Does he see many of your people?"

"Well, he is very discreet," Marina said, "and knows how to treat . . . certain things."

Joaquim pinched his nose. "What exactly did you go to see him about, Miss Arenias?"

She rubbed her gloved hands together. "My hands were hurting. I asked him if he could recommend anything for that."

Joaquim's brows drew together in concern. "Your hands hurt?"

"Where the webbing was," she said dismissively. "I'm told it's like someone who's lost a leg, and sometimes their foot hurts."

"The webbing is very sensitive," Oriana inserted, "so if it's removed, there's always ghost pain. For the rest of one's life."

Joaquim glanced at Oriana's mitt-covered hands, folded primly together in her lap. "Why do it, then?"

Marina's jaw hardened. "Because I live here and I don't want to die."

Joaquim flushed, hard to do with his darker skin. "I apologize, Miss Arenias. I didn't mean to question your decision."

Marina's fingers grasped her handbag. "I should go back to the office. Is that all, sir?"

Joaquim seemed to consider for a moment. When he didn't answer immediately, she glanced up, and Duilio could see that her dark eyes were glistening again.

"There is something you could do for me, Miss Arenias," Joaquim said, "although it would be unpleasant. A girl was murdered, a sereia girl. Her hands don't have webbing, but her coloration gave that away. We don't have any way to identify her, though, to get her back to her family. If you could look at her . . ."

"We could send for Dr. Esteves," Duilio inserted. "There's a good chance she was one of his patients."

Oriana glanced up. "I'll look, although I'm not certain I would know her."

"I'll do it," Marina said firmly. "There's a better chance I would recognize her."

"Thank you. We can take a cab there." Joaquim rose from his desk and extended a hand. After one doubtful look, Marina set her gloved fingers in his and let him help her to her feet. He laid her hand on his arm and led her toward the doorway.

Duilio extended a hand toward Oriana, who accepted it distractedly. They followed Joaquim and Marina at a slower pace. "Whoever the dead girl is," she whispered, "she's dead because Mr. Tavares saved Marina."

"We can't be certain of that," Duilio reminded her as they stepped outside the police station.

She cast him a bleak look and turned her eyes back on her sister as Marina walked at Joaquim's side down toward the intersection where hired cabs usually picked up their fares. "What do you think they're discussing?"

"Us, of course," Duilio said. "It's only logical since we're talking about them." When she gave him a caustic glance, he said, "He's apologizing for what he said about her hands, and trying to distract her so she doesn't get too upset over the idea of viewing a corpse."

"Oh." They had reached the corner where a cab waited, the driver already talking to Joaquim. He opened the cab's side door and helped Miss Arenias into the seat, and then waited for them to catch up.

Oriana shivered in the chilly air. The fog had burned off, but it was still overcast. "I should have brought a shawl."

"Would you like my coat?"

She shook her head. "We'll be warm enough in the cab."

He handed Oriana up to sit with her sister and settled next to Joaquim, facing backward. "It's not far."

Oriana wrapped her sister's hand in her own as the cab lurched into motion. "It'll be fine, Marina."

Marina held on to the hand strap with her other hand, looking lost and afraid. But she lifted her chin after a moment and resolutely stared out the cab's windows. Fortunately, it wasn't too long before the cab set them down on Arnaldo Gama Street. Joaquim directed them toward the door of the morgue. Marina seemed pale, but her expression was determined.

"We'll need to go to the back of the building," Joaquim explained—mostly for Marina's benefit, Duilio guessed. "It might be better if you hold this over your nose."

He held out his handkerchief, which Marina took, dutifully holding it to her face. The building was, once again, mostly empty. They reached the back room and Officer Gonzalo rose from his desk with a startled expression on his face. His eyes moved from Oriana to Marina, and then settled on Joaquim as if demanding an explanation.

"These two ladies might be able to identify the dead girl," Joaquim said.

Gonzalo's mouth fell open, but he quickly shook himself back to attention. He drew a set of keys out of his desk, then led them through the empty inner morgue to what appeared to be a closet. "I've put this body in the back room. The fewer people who see her, the better."

Duilio agreed. As soon as word got out that the police were holding the body of a sereia, Joaquim's superiors would demand he close down his investigation to avoid violating the terms of the ban. Fortunately, Gonzalo had acted quickly.

The officer held the door open, and Joaquim escorted Marina inside. Duilio followed, one hand on the back of Oriana's waist. The lone table in the room bore a sheet-covered form that smelled of stale blood and death—a scent magnified by the smaller size of the room. Marina pressed the handkerchief tighter her nose, tears starting in her eyes. Joaquim gestured for her to stay by the door.

Duilio followed him to the table and watched as Joaquim lifted the sheet back from the girl's face. She'd been young, near Marina's age, with straight brown hair and a pretty face. Her eyes were closed. The line of her chin had kept the blood from reaching the sheet, but Duilio caught a brief glimpse of the girl's ruined throat. His stomach soured.

Joaquim looked like he felt even worse. He folded the sheet carefully against her chin, not allowing her butchered throat to show. He gestured to Oriana. "Please, Miss Paredes."

Oriana came to Duilio's side and gazed down at that pallid face. "I don't recognize her."

She turned and held out a hand for Marina. Her sister approached more slowly, as if afraid of what lay there. Oriana set an arm about her waist. Marina slowly lifted her eyes to look at the dead girl's pale face. Her response was immediate. She laid both hands over her face and began to sob. Oriana wrapped her arms about Marina and turned her away.

Joaquim caught Duilio's eye. "I'll need to talk to the family."

That would present its own set of challenges, Duilio reckoned. "I'll take the two of them to Marina's flat, and meet you back here."

"No, I'll escort them there," Joaquim said. "I already know where it is. Then we can figure out where the family lives."

Oriana had evidently been listening, because she mouthed something at Duilio over her sister's bowed head. He didn't catch her words though, and returned a confused look.

"Ask my father," Oriana said softly. "Ask him to go with you."

He could swallow his pride and do that. Monteiro would know far better how to handle the situation. Joaquim crossed to where Oriana and her sister stood. Marina had stopped crying. She wiped her cheeks with her borrowed handkerchief.

"She's a friend of mine, Felipa Reyna," Marina said brokenly. "Her family lives on Bragas Street."

Joaquim leaned down to look her in the face. "I'd like to take you and your sister back to your flat, Miss Arenias. Your father will understand."

She nodded, her eyes fixed on the handkerchief that she twisted in her gloved fingers. "We close this afternoon anyway. But Father will be waiting for me."

"Joaquim and I are going there, so we'll explain where you are," Duilio reassured her. "And we'll see that your friend's body is properly taken care of, I promise."

Oriana sat on one of the soft upholstered chairs in Marina's tiny rented flat while her sister heated water for tea in a kettle set atop her radiator. The place suited Marina. There were two rooms— a sitting room and a bedroom with furnishings that looked moderately worn. It was a soft and humanly feminine place, a touch shabby, and quite unlike the masculine brown-and-ivory elegance of the Ferreira household.

Marina settled in the other chair across from her, a tufted-back armchair in a butter-colored floral. "I knew he was human."

Those were the first words Marina had volunteered since they'd come upstairs. She must mean Joaquim Tavares. Oriana had been waiting for Marina to say something, *ask* something. She'd been expecting to talk about the years they'd been separated, when Oriana had thought her sister was dead. No . . . instead Marina wanted to talk about Joaquim Tavares. "But he didn't know you were a sereia. Is that what you're saying?"

"I thought perhaps he might take me for a walk in the park one day, or down to the seashore at Matosinhos to hunt for shells. I thought perhaps dinner in a fine restaurant. It was foolish. Everything's ruined now," Marina said, "because I'm not human."

Oriana managed to hold in her groan. "Marina, you only met him yesterday."

"I felt the tie between us, Ori," Marina protested. "I was so sure."

Oriana could understand her sister placing Joaquim Tavares on a pedestal when he'd come to her aid. No doubt he'd become her hero in that moment, but there was no guarantee he would reciprocate her admiration. Oriana settled for truism, since nothing she said would make Marina feel better. "If your souls are tied together, then everything will work out in the end, Mari, human or not."

The teakettle began making a feeble whistle, probably the best it would manage under the circumstances. Marina opened the top, funneled in a handful of leaves, and set it back on the radiator. "And you and Mr. Ferreira? He must be tied to you or he wouldn't have been the one to go after you."

The soft chair in which Oriana sat abruptly became uncomfortable. She had never felt at ease talking about her feelings. "He's a gentleman, Marina," she said, trying to sound dismissive. "I'm merely a servant."

"You're too smart to be a servant." Marina shrugged then. "Besides, Lady P married our father, and she's a noblewoman."

"Lady P?" Oriana was glad she didn't have her tea yet. She would have choked on it.

"I got tired of saying *Lady Pereira de Santos*." Marina gestured airily with each syllable of the lady's name. "She doesn't mind."

Oriana's stomach felt hollow. Had the lady replaced their mother in Marina's mind? Marina had been only eight when their mother died. Twelve herself, Oriana had become Marina's mother, in a way. Perhaps she'd been replaced as well. "Do you like her?"

"Well, she's actually very nice. She seems unfriendly, but that's because she has to act that way." Marina paused, her lips pursed. "That doesn't sound right. Um . . . it's like a mask that she wears, because she has to be very careful about who learns the truth about her, so she can't make many friends."

Oriana thought of the hard face Lady Pereira de Santos presented to the world, and realized that despite her awkward words, Marina might have hit on the truth. The lady couldn't afford for anyone to find out she'd remarried. Would she become plain Mrs. Monteiro then? Or would she retain her status? Oriana wasn't certain how that worked. And how would it affect the woman's control over her stepson and daughter? "How many people know about her and Father?"

"Not many," Marina admitted. "She has a daughter my age, though. Ana and I became friends after I came here, although Ana's very quiet."

Wallflower was the term generally applied to Lady Ana. Although attractive, Ana had the reputation of being wordless. She was also quite tall, which wasn't fashionable. While Isabel had never mocked Ana, she hadn't made any effort to befriend her either, meaning that Oriana had never had the chance to speak to her. "Does Lady Ana know?"

Marina nodded. "Ana likes Father."

Everyone likes Father. Gods help her, Duilio probably liked her father, too. Oriana sighed.

"Lady P said Mr. Ferreira is interested in you," Marina said brightly. "She went to see him at his house and he was very concerned."

Over the years they'd been separated, Oriana had forgotten her sister's gentle tenacity. Marina would pick one topic and hang on to it like a crab—in the sweetest way possible. Oriana tried changing the subject. "So tell me about the exiles here. How many are there?"

"Not that many," Marina said as she poured tea through a strainer into her cup. "Some decided to go to other cities—too dangerous here. I think Father said there were less than fifty."

The arm of the government that sent spies into the city had estimated that at closer to thirty. Oriana suspected her father's estimate was more accurate. Despite being male, his position in the city had made him a natural leader among the exiles.

"Your Mr. Ferreira is rather handsome," Marina added. "Has he ever kissed you?"

Oriana sank farther down in her chair. She hadn't seen her sister in three years, and Marina wanted to talk about *males*, of all things.

"You should just tell me, because I'm not going to give up." Marina handed her the first cup of tea. "So when did you first meet him? Did you know, then?"

Oriana took a sip of the weak tea, wishing she had coffee to sustain her instead. She had no idea how to answer Marina's last question. She wasn't certain exactly when she'd suspected her tie to him. The feeling had grown slowly. And even if she did feel a tie to Duilio, she wasn't certain how he felt about her. He'd told her he would be her friend. That implied he eventually intended to pursue a closer relationship, after she'd had enough time to decide what she wanted.

But to placate Marina and distract her from the sorrows of the day, Oriana decided to tell her everything that had passed between her and Duilio Ferreira. Well, almost everything. "The first time I met him," she began, "was several days after Isabel Amaral died. It turned out he'd actually been looking for *me*."

She told of Duilio offering her a position as his mother's companion. She'd taken the job because it had been the only way she could afford to stay in the city and hunt for Isabel's murderer. That search had led to Maraval, and in the end Oriana had *called* the marquis and his accomplices into the ocean—most of them to their deaths— to prevent them from shooting Duilio.

Marina clapped. "That's wonderful. Did he kiss you *then*?"

Oriana laid her hands over her face. *It's going to be a long afternoon.*

CHAPTER 19

Monteiro agreed to accompany them to the house of the dead girl's parents. He did, however, demand to look at the body first, to assure that no mistake had been made. It seemed a reasonable request, so once again Duilio visited that quiet back room of the morgue. Gonzalo guarded the door while Joaquim drew back the sheets to expose only the girl's face.

"Damnation," Monteiro said, and then made the sign of the cross. "It is Felipa Reyna. What happened to her?"

"Her throat was torn out, sir," Joaquim said.

Monteiro turned his dark eyes on Joaquim. "When?"

"Gonzalo guessed yesterday, sometime during the evening. He didn't have a doctor come look at her because he knew it would be reported. He's fairly knowledgeable himself, though."

Monteiro turned his eyes on Duilio. "After the attack on Marina. If you'd warned me yesterday about the murders, I still couldn't have gotten the word out in time to save her."

Duilio felt a wave of relief. Although he hadn't intended to point out that fact, he hadn't wanted Oriana's father blaming him either. "No, sir."

Monteiro gazed down at the body. "Will you show me what they did?"

Duilio pulled back the sheet. The girl's throat had been sliced away, not much more than the spine and the bloody flesh around the back of the neck remaining to hold her head to her body. The cuts were clean, so the killer had used a sharp blade. Surely her death had come quickly, some small consolation.

"They took her gills," Monteiro said.

"Is there any significance to that?" Duilio asked.

"I don't know." Monteiro grabbed the edge of the sheet and yanked it back over the girl's waxy face. "She'll be safe here?"

Joaquim nodded. "Gonzalo said he'd stay on duty until someone comes to take the body. He'll keep everyone out of here."

"Then let's get moving," Monteiro said.

The Reyna family lived in a modest three-story house on Bragas Street, but they had the entire first floor, a large home in this part of town. Duilio and Joaquim waited near the parlor door while Monteiro broke the news to the girl's parents. The father covered his face and began to moan. The strong-jawed mother, with her straight brown hair drawn sternly back from a face that looked much like her daughter's, fixed a wrathful eye on Monteiro. "Who killed her?"

Monteiro shot a quick glance at Joaquim, but answered anyway. "They don't know. There have been two other murders of nonhuman girls in the city in the last two weeks—an otter girl and a selkie. Mr. Ferreira and Inspector Tavares suspect this may be related to those." His hands moved fluidly while he spoke, and Duilio could only wonder what he was telling them.

The woman turned angry eyes on Duilio and Joaquim, measuring them. Then she turned back to Monteiro. "And what about my daughter?"

Monteiro touched a finger to his chin and said, "Arrangements need to be made for her body, Rute, as soon as possible. The police are hiding it from themselves. They are bound to notice what they are doing eventually."

The husband continued to moan, his head in his hands. The

woman cast a quick glance at him, took a tight breath and said, "I'll go talk to the mortician. We'll fetch her home."

"It is gruesome," Monteiro added. "Julio shouldn't see her until the mortician has prepared her. The girls either, honestly."

The woman nodded grimly, and then fixed her red-rimmed eyes on Joaquim and Duilio where they stood by the door. "I am aware you aren't required to do this for foreigners like us. You have my gratitude."

While her sentiment sounded grudging, Duilio could hardly blame her.

Joaquim just inclined his head. "I am very sorry for your loss, madam."

Maneuvering the girl's body to the mortician's without anyone noticing the commotion proved more difficult than they'd anticipated. Even so, by four the girl's body was out of the morgue and safely out of police hands. The mortician turned out to be another Sympathizer, a man who'd done this service for nonhumans before.

If nothing else, Duilio's new acquaintance with Monteiro was affording him the opportunity to meet a variety of the Golden City's Sympathizers. While the Ferreira family had always shared that sentiment, they had never sought out others. It was unsafe. Any one of the people they dealt with—the humans, at least—could as easily take the prince's coin to betray them. And while Duilio had always known his family was at risk, making contacts with members of that community made it clearer how much *more* vulnerable those who took an active part in resisting the prince's edict were.

After leaving Joaquim at the police station, Duilio decided he would walk to Miss Arenias' flat to escort Oriana back to the house. He was surprised when Monteiro offered to accompany him. While the man had been grateful to Joaquim for coming to Marina's aid and for their actions concerning the dead girl, it was also clear he remained irritated over something, and Duilio strongly suspected that irritation was with *him*.

"Your help this afternoon was invaluable," Duilio told Monteiro as they proceeded toward Virtudes Street. The afternoon traffic was heavy enough that they didn't have much privacy, so their conversation had been sporadic. People hurried on either side, heading toward their homes, brushing up against them in their rush. Duilio kept an eye on that flow of pedestrians as they walked. "We were unsure how to approach the family."

Monteiro settled his hat on his head more firmly. "It would have been equally difficult if they were human. But the family would not have known your sympathies or those of Mr. Tavares, and so it would have taken much longer. You do smell, by the way."

Monteiro didn't mean the normal perspiration that chasing all over the city would have engendered—he surely meant the musk. "Yes," Duilio admitted, "most people mistake it for cologne. Your daughter did, as well, at first."

"I don't know exactly what that legendary charm consists of," Monteiro said, stepping to one side to let a pair of women garbed like factory workers pass them. "However, I suspect smell plays a part in it."

"I don't know the answer myself," Duilio admitted. "My half brother simply looks at women and they fall all over themselves."

"Have you tried to charm my daughter?"

"I have never tried to charm *anyone*," Duilio said. "Not by anything other than good manners and attentiveness."

Monteiro walked on for a moment. "Have you heard her *call*?"

Duilio looked ahead, trying to count how many more blocks there were until they reached the right building. Two? Three? *Please let it be two.* "I have, sir, although I should tell you that due to my bloodlines, I am not as susceptible to her voice as other men."

"But that's why you're interested in her, is it not?"

Of all the things he didn't need to discuss with Monteiro, the chief one was his relationship with Oriana. "My interest in her predates that incident, sir."

"Ah," Monteiro said.

And because Duilio wanted to make certain the man didn't make any further false assumptions about his daughter or her relationship with him, he said, "And she is not my lover, no matter what you may think."

Monteiro stopped on the cobbles and faced him. "Why tell me that?"

Duilio refused to flinch under Monteiro's anger. "Because in our first meeting in your office, you suggested to her that you believed that."

"And you don't want anyone to associate the two of you?" Monteiro's tone sounded bitter.

Duilio forced a smile, hoping that would emphasize his good intentions. "That's not my reasoning. I don't want *you* to think poorly of her. I admire her more than I can say. I suspect she finds it painful that her own father does not share that admiration."

Monteiro's jaw clenched. "You're very good at rudeness cloaked in fine words."

"Simple truth. In normal circumstances," Duilio said, "I would walk away from this discussion, but my mother asked me not to."

"A dutiful son as well," Monteiro said with a shake of his head. "Oriana and I are both too hot tempered for our own good. We always say things we don't mean."

And at that Duilio felt a real smile tugging at his lips. He had, on first acquaintance, thought Oriana Paredes cool and emotionless. It was only after he'd known her for a time that her true emotions had begun to show. They crossed Taipas Street, now within sight of the door to Marina's building.

"So what exactly are your intentions toward my daughter?"

Monteiro snapped as if he'd been holding back that question all afternoon.

Duilio opened the door of the building, which revealed a narrow stairwell. "Sir, whatever my intentions toward her, I suspect that if I discuss them with *you*, she will kill me."

Monteiro went on inside. "You know her well, then."

They were admitted to the younger sister's rented rooms—a feminine and frilly place that would not suit Oriana at all. And after a round of pleasantries, Duilio extended an invitation for Monteiro and daughter to come visit the Ferreira household, perhaps for dinner some evening. It might set the man's mind at ease and satisfy Marina's all-too-blatant curiosity about Oriana's situation there. But having seen Oriana's face, he quickly excused himself to the younger woman, claiming they had to leave.

"You look tired," he said once they were on the street, Oriana's hand tucked in the crook of his arm.

"She wears me out." Oriana wore a sheepish look when admitting that. "I'd forgotten how quickly. If you please, tell me what happened with the family."

So he spent the remainder of the walk back to the house going over his afternoon with Joaquim and her father, which she wryly noted might have been easier on her nerves.

They arrived back at the Ferreira house in time to change for dinner, so Oriana let Teresa dress her like a doll in a new rose-colored silk gown with a high-collared infill in white that would hide her throat. Teresa arranged her hair into a simple knot, produced a pair of silver earrings with opal drops, and then began to apply powder to Oriana's bruised cheek.

Marina would love this—being treated like a lady, dressed in fine human garments with pretty jewelry that sparkled. Marina would probably be content to live the rest of her life among humans here in the Golden City. She'd always been a retiring girl, never taking the lead in anything. The way women were sheltered in this country must suit her far better. How would her own life have been different if she'd listened to Marina's childish urgings and run away *with* her to find their father after his exile? Would she have a little flat in the city, work at their father's business, and think nothing was more important than finding a mate?

That was unfair, Oriana thought ruefully.

Marina had found the nerve to go alone and find passage on an unfamiliar ship to Northern Portugal. She'd managed to find Father, all on her own. No matter how immature Marina might seem, three years ago she'd had the courage to step off the safe path and make her own destiny. At the same time, Oriana had let herself be entangled further and further in her aunts' web of responsibility and propriety and service. Of the two of them, Marina had more control over her own life. *That makes me the fool, doesn't it?*

"Will that do, Miss Paredes?" Teresa asked brightly as she placed the powder puff back in its tin.

Oriana gazed at her reflection. Teresa had done a good job making her look like a human lady, whether or not that was what she wanted to be. "Yes. Thank you, Teresa."

The girl bobbed her head, collected the clothes Oriana had worn that afternoon, and let herself out of the bedroom.

What exactly do I want? Oriana peered at her reflection, the bruise on her cheek hidden by powder. The split lip had almost healed. She took a deep breath.

I want to find out whoever killed Felipa Reyna and stop them. I want to keep Marina safe from them forever. She had helped find Isabel's killers; she could do this. Fortunately, Duilio didn't believe in coddling females and protecting them from the truth. He wouldn't cut her out of the investigation.

I want to find out who sentenced me to death, she added. *I want to be able to go home.* She suspected that Maria Melo had been behind that, although she wasn't sure why. She'd done everything the spy had asked of her, intentionally or not. So in truth, she wanted to know *why* she'd been sacrificed a second time.

She took a deep breath and let it out slowly. *I want Duilio Ferreira.*

When she'd been held on that boat, she'd decided she would return to the Golden City eventually to court him. But that had been a dream. Faced with the reality of being back in the city, in his house, all the impracticalities of that idea had come back to her. She was an imposter here in his world . . . and he would never fit in hers.

A knock sounded at her bedroom door, Duilio come to escort her down to dinner. Gathering her nerve, she went to meet him at the door. When she opened it, his eyes surveyed her new outfit and he smiled. "I think that color suits you, Oriana."

She thanked him, feeling warmth spreading through her body under his regard. He walked next to her down the stairs, exchanging pleasantries as if they did this every day. Or as if they would do it every day. So she smiled at him and played along. His mother was already waiting in the sitting room, and they all went in to dinner together.

Over the meal he apprised his mother of their activities that day, leaving out the more gruesome parts regarding Felipa Reyna's death, probably out of deference to the venue rather than fear of oversetting his mother. Eventually the lady got around to questioning Oriana about her sister, Marina's unexpected acquaintance with Joaquim Tavares, and asked Duilio some rather pointed questions about the inspector's behavior toward Marina. As she was Joaquim's foster mother, Oriana didn't find that curiosity surprising.

After dinner, they retired to the sitting room, but Lady Ferreira quickly excused herself, leaving Oriana alone with Duilio again.

"You look ready to run away," Duilio said softly.

She didn't know where to start. She should warn him that she'd probably said too much. Marina would doubtless repeat things to

Father, who might come to Duilio with expectations that Duilio had never meant to raise. "It's been a difficult day."

Duilio came and sat in the spot his mother had abandoned. "It would be nice if everything were simple. Unfortunately, not much in my life seems to be."

She gazed down at her hands. "Marina asked me a lot of questions about you, which I may not have answered as clearly as I should have. She may give Father the wrong impression."

"What impression might that be?" Duilio said.

Do I have to say it aloud? "You know what I mean."

"That I'm courting you?" Duilio asked. "He already has that impression. He asked me this afternoon what my intentions were."

Oriana looked up at him, horrified. "He what?"

"And I told him that if I discussed my intentions with him, you would kill me," Duilio said blithely. "Although it's equally possible you might kill *him* instead."

Oriana felt cold seeping through her, rooting her to that spot on the sofa. What intentions *did* he have?

He moved closer until he sat next to her on the sofa. His sympathetic eyes stayed on hers. "I admire him a great deal, Oriana. But it truly isn't your father's concern what our relationship is. We're both adults."

Ah, she understood then. Duilio hadn't made a secret of the fact that he wanted her, even if he'd backed away to give her more time. That was a relationship she could accept. She could be his lover, which was as close as she could get to taking him as her mate.

For a moment he stared into her eyes. Then he was leaning toward her. His lips met hers, warm and firm. Oriana didn't want him to pull away, so she slid one hand around his neck. She felt him smile against her lips.

Ah gods, I like this. No, I love being in his arms. Surely this would be worth all the pain farther down the line.

He pulled away too soon, far enough to lean his forehead against hers. "You have become very precious to me."

Oriana took a shaky breath, catching his scent in her gills. His warmth was all about her. He expected her to say something, but nothing would come out of her mouth. Frustrated, she let him go and sat back. She didn't know what face to let him see now. Surely everything she felt showed on her features anyway, a helpless and terrifying thought.

Duilio wiped a tear from her cheek. "This is frightening for you, isn't it?"

Oh, such deadly accuracy. She hadn't realized she'd been crying. Oriana nodded mutely after a second, unable to put words to her fears—her fear that he wouldn't understand what she offered him, or even worse, that he would spurn it. No, he wouldn't do that. She was certain he wanted her.

"It's like diving off a cliff," he said. "Not so bad once you're in the air, but that moment when you jump is truly terrifying."

Now he's resorting to nonsensical analogies. "What?"

He took her hands again. "When you dive, you're going on faith that there won't be rocks under the water, that there will be enough depth for you to swim away. And that moment before you jump, you're weighing the possibilities and you're afraid because there's a chance you're about to do something supremely stupid. But once you've jumped, you enjoy the fall because the decision is already made."

Oriana laughed wetly. "So the hard part is the decision, not the leap itself?"

"Of course. Once you know where you're going, you just go."

She licked her lips. Talking was so easy for him, whereas she had never possessed a silver tongue. He waited for her to speak, but she could only stare at him helplessly.

Duilio stroked back a loosened lock of her hair, his expression serious. "I would like for you to marry me."

What? Oriana sat back, suddenly unable to catch her breath. He wasn't supposed to ask her that. He wasn't supposed to . . .

She managed to inhale. "What?" she squeaked.

He grasped her hands firmly as if afraid she would run away. "I would like for you to marry me," he repeated. "I don't know if marriage is the same among your people as ours, but I do want to marry you."

"You can't," she blurted out.

His expression stayed calm. "Why not?"

She dragged her hands free of his. This wasn't what she'd planned. Not at all. She was supposed to court him, not the other way around. "It's illegal, for one."

"That didn't stop my mother and my father."

Oriana sat as far away from him as she could. "It wasn't illegal when they married. And your mother can pass for human." She held up her hands, fingers wide to display their webbing. "I can't."

"You lived in the city for two years before you came here," he pointed out.

"Do you want me to spend the rest of my life hiding what I am? Do you want me to be like Marina?"

"No," he said. "There are other cities. Cities where it's not illegal for us to marry. London, Edinburgh, Paris. We could go to one of them. And the prince won't live forever."

He's definitely been giving this some thought. Even so, they were all *human* cities. She shook her head. "You would be shunned if you were involved with me. A gentleman doesn't marry his mother's companion."

"I don't care about society's opinion," he said.

It was a foolish argument anyway, given the example of her father and *his* wife. Lady Pereira de Santos, the daughter of a duke, had married a commoner. Duilio, the son of a mere *cavaleiro*, had far shorter a distance to fall. Her hands started to tremble. She pressed the heels of them against her eyes, trying to quell the urge to sob.

She had cried more in this past week than she had in years. It seemed the only response she had left in her any longer, and she hated that.

Duilio's arms came around her. He folded her close to him, her head tucked against his shoulder. "I have no words for what this is between us," he said softly. "I am amazed you so perfectly match my heart's desires, but you do."

Amazed was the word that came to her mind as well. Whatever lay between her and Duilio, it made no sense. If this was love, it was a terribly confusing and uncomfortable place to be.

"I am willing," she mumbled against his coat, "if you want me." She couldn't look at him when she said that. She had never thought she would say that. *Never.*

He stayed silent for a long time, though, and she finally forced herself to look up at him. His expression hinted something akin to frustration. "Oriana," he said, "I want more than being your lover. I want you as my wife. I don't want . . ."

Why can't he see he's making this more difficult? She jumped up and stamped her foot on the floor. "Why does it have to be *your* way?"

He rose, a rare mulish expression coming over his face. For a second she thought he was going to yell at her in return. His lips were pressed together, holding something in. And when she decided he wasn't going to say it, she swept past him and out of the sitting room, trying to keep her head high and the tears from her eyes.

Duilio stayed in the sitting room long after Oriana had fled back to her own room, trying to place exactly what had gone wrong. He'd never before asked a woman to marry him. Of course, after careful consideration, he realized he'd failed to do so this time. He'd informed her that he wanted to marry her, rather than actually *asking.*

In turn, after throwing up a handful of ridiculous objections, she had asked why it had to be his way, which made him wonder what her way was. She had, he was moderately certain, offered to become his lover. That had taken him by surprise. As much as he'd like to share her bed, he wanted to be clear that he didn't see this as a passing relationship. And he didn't believe she wanted that either, did she?

But she yelled at me.

That was a good sign, he decided. This was important enough for her to yell at him. Taking that thought as comfort, Duilio headed upstairs to his own annoyingly empty bed.

CHAPTER 20

Oriana endured a nearly sleepless night. When the clock in the hallway chimed three, she filled the tub and lay down in the water. The coolness of it lulled her, allaying her frustration enough to let her drop off to sleep to the sound of the constant dribble from the tap. But when she woke, her reflection looked worn and worried anyway.

She didn't know how to answer him.

In actuality, she didn't recall his actually *asking*. He'd spoken of marriage as if it were the only possible course ahead of them.

But it meant giving up who she was. If she were to become Mrs. Ferreira, she would have to pretend to be human all the time. And even though she'd done that for the last two years, *forever* was a different matter. She had lived this long without Duilio Ferreira in her life, surely she could manage without him. She could.

That thought was incredibly bleak.

And foolish.

Oriana looked in the mirror again and smiled at her pallid reflection. *I am going to court him, and we will work out all the details along the way. We will.*

Having made up her mind, she suddenly felt less weary. She felt like anything was possible.

A tap came on the bathroom door. "Miss Paredes, I've left your coffee tray. Is there anything else you'll be needing?"

"No, Teresa. Thank you." She recalled one of Isabel's tricks and yanked open the door. The maid hadn't escaped the bedroom, so Oriana called after her. "Teresa, do we have any cucumbers?"

The girl beamed at her and curtsied. "I'll go see, miss. I'll be right back."

An hour later she was fortified with strong coffee and a headache powder, dressed appropriately, and had slightly less puffy eyes. She would have to apologize to Duilio for losing her temper with him; she wouldn't even mind doing so now. When she reached the breakfast room, the Ferreiras were already sitting down, the mother with her coffee and her newspaper, and Duilio attacking his usual large breakfast.

He looked up when he saw her enter and smiled. It wasn't forced, which made Oriana smile back at him.

"You're looking tired, Oriana," Lady Ferreira said. "Did you not sleep well?"

Oriana settled for equivocation. "Well enough, Lady."

"Perhaps you might take a nap after you eat? I'm not going to Mass and I have no plans this morning, save for some correspondence."

"Actually, Mother," Duilio said, "if you don't mind, I'd like to borrow Miss Paredes for a few minutes after breakfast." He smiled at Oriana again, as if to reassure her.

"Duilinho," his mother said tartly, "that depends entirely on her. Ask *her*."

Oriana found him gazing at her expectantly. "Certainly, sir."

His mother sighed. "Oh, please stop that, both of you. You know each other's names. There's no need for formality in front of me."

Duilio's eyes danced. His lips were pressed together as if he fought to keep from bursting out laughing. "Oriana, will you talk with me after breakfast?"

"Yes, of course, Duilio."

"Much better," his mother said. "Duilinho, let her eat before you spirit her off."

"Yes, Mother."

Oriana busied herself filling her plate, picking more than she normally would have—more like one of Duilio's excessive breakfasts. She *would* need a nap after this. When she came to sit at the table, Duilio kept a straight face, but she suspected he felt as chastised as she did.

Lady Ferreira took mercy on her and changed the topic to the newest taxes on boatbuilding, one of the family's investments, which occupied them throughout breakfast. And after giving her ample time to eat, Duilio escorted Oriana to the sitting room. He held open the door for her, and then closed it behind them.

Oriana waited until he turned back to her. "I need to apologize."

He gestured toward the sofa, indicating that she should sit. "For what?"

Oriana settled on the end. "For losing my temper."

"You wouldn't have done so if it wasn't important to you." He sat down next to her.

She wasn't going to deny that. "You had the best of intentions."

"I did. But I have no idea what your way is. Will you tell me what is done among your people when a man wishes to court a woman?"

She gazed down at her hands, shaking her head. Of course he would assume that. "They don't."

His brow furrowed. "Are all unions arranged, then?"

Oriana laughed. "No. Well, some are, but not a large percentage. It's the opposite, though. Usually the man is courted by the woman."

He took one of her hands in his own, a smile playing at the corner of his lips. "Truly? The men don't do the courting?"

She shook her head.

"Have you ever courted a man before?" he asked.

He's enjoying this. Not her discomfiture, but wheedling out things she'd never told anyone. "I've never seriously entertained the idea," she said. "I was told my bloodlines weren't good enough to attract a mate. My aunts always said I was born to serve instead."

His thumb caressed the back of her hand. "If you were to court me, you might prove your aunts wrong."

Oriana shook her head, more in bemusement than denial.

"What exactly passes for courtship among your people?" he asked then. "If you were to court me, what would you do?"

"Well," she said, "I could give you gifts."

"Gifts? What sort of gifts?" His sly smile showed he knew he was winning.

"All I have is what you and your mother have given me, Duilio."

"Is the man being courted allowed to make suggestions?"

"He can always *suggest*," she said cautiously.

"I would like to learn your people's hand language."

She recalled some of the things he'd seen her father—and her—sign. "It's not a language, Duilio. Just a few words and phrases for talking underwater. Not at all polite."

"I should be able to learn, shouldn't I? I've studied Spanish and French, and English, too."

She wondered if he'd studied those tongues—none of which she had beyond a few words—in his law studies, in his foreign travels, or if he'd just been keen to learn. "Then may I offer to teach you?"

His eyes narrowed. "Is this to be considered a courtship gift?"

She showed him the sign for yes, the closing of a fist. "This is *yes*."

He imitated the gesture thoughtfully. "Does it matter which hand?"

"No." She showed him that one as well, and he imitated it.

"A good start," he said. "What happens after the giving of gifts? In your people's courtship, I mean."

"Well, the man decides which among the females courting him he wants."

"And if there aren't any other females courting him? Do they still go through the same process?"

"Of course they do." A laugh bubbled up out of Oriana's throat at his crestfallen expression. "Besides, isn't Miss Carvalho courting you?"

"That doesn't count," he protested.

"Why not?"

"Because she has absolutely no chance of winning me."

Oriana wet her lips with her tongue. "Well, we are not fond of terribly long courtships as your people are."

He grinned, and then his smile dimmed. "I am not joking, Oriana. I am willing to do this your way, whatever you ask of me, however long it takes."

"I just need time," she whispered. "To figure out . . . how this will work."

He slid the backs of his fingers along her cheek. "I can wait. I only wanted to know that . . . we're heading in the same direction, more or less."

Taking a mate was, in her eyes, the same as marriage, even if the steps to getting to that end might seem different. But Duilio was giving her control over that path, something she suspected most human men wouldn't. It was a relief to have control over *something*. *Surely we can make this work somehow.* "Thank you."

He smiled, and her heart swelled. "Very well," he said. "Joaquim is coming over after Mass. We intend to sit in here until we figure out what we know so far. We could use your thoughts."

"A good idea," she said, and then had to cover her mouth to hide a yawn.

"Why don't you go back to your room?" Duilio said. "You do look like a nap would do you good. And I mean no insult by that."

"I didn't sleep well," she admitted. She managed to tear herself away from that sofa, but stopped at the door of the library and looked back at him. "Send Teresa for me if I oversleep."

Duilio watched her head up the stairs, observing the familiar sway of her hips. He probably had a foolish grin on his face. Whatever form this courtship of hers took, he would do everything possible to make sure she decided to keep him. It would be awkward if this didn't eventually lead to a wedding. Society had its rules, and he couldn't introduce her as his mate here. But even if she didn't agree to *marry* him, he would work around the difficulties that presented.

Rather pleased with himself, he headed toward the library, only to intercept Cardenas laying an envelope on his desk.

"It's good I found you, Mr. Duilio," the butler began. "Our boatman is down in the kitchen, wishing for a word with you. And your man found this in yesterday's jacket." He held out the envelope.

About half of the staff would be at Mass this morning, so that left Cardenas doing a footman's work again. Duilio took the envelope, the one Monteiro had handed to him the day before, the note that warned the man not to talk. "Thank you, Cardenas. I'll go see to João directly."

The butler headed up toward the front door while Duilio turned down the side hall to the stairs that led to the kitchen. As promised, he found João sitting at the servants' table, his cap in his hands. The boatman rose when he saw Duilio entering the empty kitchen.

"What brings you up to the house, João? Is Miss Aga well?"

João flushed at the mention of his inamorata's name. "She's well, sir. I came about the pelt, sir. You asked me to keep an ear to the wind."

"Did someone find it?"

João sat when Duilio indicated he should do so. "Well, sir, I was talking to old Augostinho, who runs one of the Ramires boats."

The Ramires family owned several fishing boats moored close

to Duilio's own. "What did he have to say?" Duilio asked as he sat across from the young man.

"He did find a pelt on his boat, but he'd left it alone."

Fishermen tended to be superstitious. If a selkie's pelt showed up on their boat, they probably wouldn't touch it. "But then . . ."

"He thought it was a bad omen, sir. It started to smell, like it was rotting."

"The girl whose it was is dead, João, so it would."

The young man's lips pursed. "Oh. Was it someone Aga knew?"

Duilio shook his head, feeling guilty. They'd gone to warn Oriana's family about this killer, but he hadn't thought of Aga, who was a selkie as well and Erdano's half sister. "It was a young girl named Gita, but the queen said she washed up on their beach after that last big storm, so Aga wouldn't know her, I think."

"Good." João puffed out his cheeks. "It's strange though, Mr. Ferreira. Old Augostinho told me when he pulled the pelt out of its hiding spot to drop it in the ocean, there was a square of it that wasn't rotting. As big as his hand. He said that spot looked fresh and whole, like a pelt usually does."

Duilio shook his head. How could only a part of the pelt still be . . . *alive*, for lack of a better term? "I don't understand, but thank you for telling me. Since one selkie has already been killed, it may not be safe for Aga to go into the city alone. I would keep her close for the time being."

"I will." Frowning, João turned his cap in his hands. "There's something else, sir. About Aga."

Duilio had half risen, but sat again. "Yes."

"I'm wanting her to marry me, sir," João said in a rush, "but she doesn't want to. I mean . . . she doesn't understand *why* we need to be married. Like she didn't understand about not taking her clothes off at first, sir."

Most selkies had no qualms about nudity and were mystified by the social conventions of the Portuguese that forbade it. João had managed to explain that to her. Prejudice against bastardy was a more complex issue, and it was likely that Aga would fall pregnant eventually. "Let me talk to my mother. If anyone can explain the situation to Aga, my mother can. I'll send a note to you with her answer. Would that help?"

"I'd truly appreciate it, sir." João nodded quickly and rose. "Good day, Mr. Ferreira."

Duilio let the young man out. *Perhaps Mother can talk Oriana into it while she's at it.*

CHAPTER 21

Inspector Tavares arrived promptly at two, making Oriana suspect he shared Duilio's love of punctuality. She felt far more alert than she had that morning; the nap had been a good decision. As she waited in the library, she heard them approaching.

"I have some new information," the inspector was saying.

"So do I," Duilio told him. "Although I have no idea what mine means."

What did he learn while I was napping?

Joaquim Tavares came into the library, an old leather case in each hand. He stopped to nod to her. "Miss Paredes."

"Mr. Tavares." Wearing a suit in a deep mauve shade that accentuated the unusual color of her hair, now neatly tucked up in a bun, she might look human save for the fact that she'd left off the silk mitts he'd always seen her wear before.

He shot a glance in the direction of her bare hands, then looked away. He handed one of the leather cases he held to Duilio. "Father sent this over this morning."

Duilio laid the case on his desk unopened, making Oriana want to sneak a peek. But he retrieved several sheets of foolscap from the map chest in the corner and carried them over to the table in the center of the library while Mr. Tavares carefully lifted one of the giant clamshells off the table and carried it to the corner of the room. Duilio helped him move the last two, and then wiped off the table before they began to lay out the paper. Mr. Tavares drew a sheaf of papers out of the second case and then held out a chair. "Miss Paredes?"

Oriana settled into the chair. "Do you mind my being here?"

Inspector Tavares hesitated only an instant. "I suspect you will bring a fresh perspective to the discussion, Miss Paredes."

"It would be easier then, if you called me Oriana."

"Then perhaps you might call me Joaquim," he said, "as we are almost family."

Family? She decided not to pursue that last statement.

Duilio had retrieved a pencil, a pen and ink, and a ruler from his desk. He began using the straightedge to draw lines across the page first, and then vertical ones. "We're going to lay out everything we know by date. Hopefully some pattern will start to emerge."

"For the murders," she guessed. They'd created a timeline for the murders that Maraval had committed, but she'd only seen it once completed.

"And everything else we think may be pertinent." Duilio finished making his lines, and began numbering across the top of the page, one number in each column. "So we start on the sixth. What happened then?"

The first number he'd written *was* six, Oriana saw. "Maraval was taken into custody."

"And you left." Duilio picked up the pen and ink and began writing in that column. "Let me put some notes in here."

His notes included his first meetings with her father, the infante, the ambassador, and when he'd brought her back. It seemed odd that he was including so much information about her in his list but when she commented, he said they were merely being thorough.

"The otter girl," Joaquim said when Duilio stopped writing, "was named Erdeg, and she was taken on Thursday the sixteenth from the brothel where she lived."

Duilio looked up at him, amazement on his face. "How did you find that out?"

"Some brothels cater to more exotic tastes," Joaquim said delicately, "so I discreetly asked around if there were any otter girls available for a wealthy patron. One of the brothels confessed theirs was missing."

Oriana hadn't thought of that possibility—but now that she considered it, there might be one or two sereia girls working in such places as well. Even so, otters stayed in tight-knit family groups, so it surprised her that an otter had agreed to leave her family. Then again, perhaps she hadn't. "I'm surprised they were willing to speak to the police."

"He's one of the few who will investigate crimes against their workers," Duilio told her. "It's easier to ignore crimes against women who don't hold influence."

Joaquim's jaw worked, his head shaking.

"So this girl Erdeg was probably killed the next day," Duilio said, making a note in the appropriate column.

"And her body dumped in an alley that night," Joaquim agreed. "She was brought into the morgue the next morning, Saturday the eighteenth."

"And that is the same day Gita was grabbed from the alleyway behind the . . . ah, Erdano's favored tavern." Duilio continued to write, his face flushing.

"Which tavern is that?" Oriana asked.

Duilio looked at Joaquim, his mouth open, and then turned back to her. "The Lusty Siren," he confessed.

Oriana groaned. Her people had a questionable reputation among humans. Some of it came from the fact that most sereia couldn't blush and were therefore perceived as shameless. At the moment, a blush would be useful.

"You asked," Duilio reminded her.

Well, I did. "I was going to suggest that we make a map and mark the places where the bodies were found."

"And where they were last seen," Joaquim added with a nod. "We'll do that after this. Gita died Monday," Joaquim said. "Her body was dumped either Monday or Tuesday night, found Wednesday morning."

"Why do you suppose they waited till Monday?" Duilio asked absently.

"Because they didn't want to kill her on a Sunday?" Oriana suggested.

Duilio appeared to consider that. "A murderer observing the Lord's Day?"

"Wait till we're done," Joaquim insisted.

"Fine. Here's the strange bit," Duilio said, looking up from the paper. "Her pelt started to rot, *but not all of it.*"

"Go back," Joaquim said. "You found her pelt? You never told me that."

Duilio waved his hand vaguely, dripping ink onto the paper. "She left her pelt on one of the Ramires boats. It was found by the fisherman, but he didn't touch it until it started to smell. He told João, who told me earlier today. A patch the size of his hand wasn't rotting, while the rest was."

They worked for some time, Duilio writing down details that Oriana saw no reason to include, but she had to bow to their greater experience with this bizarre method of theirs. When they collectively ran out of scraps of information, Duilio sat down next to her and peered at the two sheets of foolscap, now held together by pins to make a continuous sheet. Next to that lay a map of the city Duilio had produced from his map chest, defaced with red spots marking where each girl had been taken and where each body had been left.

"There's not a clear pattern," Joaquim noted, "other than their bodies being dumped in poorer sections of town."

"Well, they did take them one at a time," Duilio said. "Each girl taken after the last body was dumped."

"If there were only the three of them," Oriana pointed out. "Could there be more?"

Joaquim shrugged. "We'll never know. There could have been bodies dumped in the river or the sea. We can only consider what we've got."

"Besides," Duilio said. "They took one of each of the sea peoples. That's a pattern in itself."

"Have they taken a human?" she asked.

"None have been found who've been . . . mutilated like them," Joaquim answered. "I asked Gonzalo to alert me if any showed up." He was staring at her hand, Oriana realized, spread wide on the edge of the paper so that her webbing showed. His eyes turned away, almost guiltily.

She kept her hand where it was. "So they held the otter girl a day before she was killed, the selkie girl two days, but the sereia girl only hours."

"Why did the selkie take so much longer than the others?" Oriana asked.

"You may be right," Duilio said with a nod in her direction. "Perhaps they didn't want to kill her on a Sunday."

"There were three days between the first two killings," Oriana noted, "but four between the second and third."

"No clear pattern," Joaquim agreed. "We *are* dealing with more than one person, by the way. It would take two to get a struggling girl into a coach and drive it away. And someone who knows where to find nonhumans. Someone had to be watching your boats, Duilio, to have seen the girl come up onto the docks. The same with the doctor. They had to know he works with nonhumans."

Duilio's lips narrowed. "A Sympathizer?"

"Or not," Joaquim said. "Someone who hates them."

"And why are they choosing the trophies they are?" Duilio asked. "That hints they know more than most about nonhumans."

Trophies? Oriana cringed at a sudden mental image of jars filled with preserved parts.

Duilio scowled. "Or not. Dr. Esteves wasn't certain an otter's magic is in their tail; it was what he'd heard. Mother agreed a selkie's magic is in their skin, though, or rather in the relationship between the skin and pelt, if that makes sense."

But a sereia couldn't change form like the selkies or the otter folk. A sereia's only magic was in her voice. Oriana laid a hand over her throat, and then snatched it back into her lap when she realized she'd done so. Neither of the two men said anything.

Cardenas rapped softly on the frame of the library's door. When Duilio looked up, he said, "Captain Pinheiro is here, Mr. Duilio. I told him you're occupied, but . . ."

"No, bring him on through," Duilio said with a flash of a smile. "Rafael's been working in Lisboa for the last two weeks."

Pinheiro was a captain in the Special Police, but not a threat in any way to Duilio or her. During their search for Isabel's killer, they'd learned that Pinheiro was Duilio's first cousin, the illegitimate son of Duilio's detestable uncle, Paolo Silva. Oriana found Pinheiro quite likable, despite his questionable father, and from the first he'd seemed unconcerned that she was a sereia.

A moment later, the captain entered the library, stopping to embrace both Duilio and Joaquim. Pinheiro didn't wear his Special Police uniform, making this a social call. "Rafael, you remember Miss Oriana Paredes?"

"Miss Paredes," he said, pressing her hand between his. "It's good to see you again. I'd been worried about you, but I'm glad to see I was right."

Although he was shorter and a bit stocky, there was a strong resemblance to Duilio—and Joaquim as well—in Pinheiro's face. It made her like him by default. "Right?"

"That you would come through your trials safely," he said.

"You knew?" Duilio asked sharply.

Pinheiro laughed shortly. "I have been doing nothing but meditating these last two weeks and trying to control my gift, so yes, I *knew*, after a fashion. Nothing specific."

Oriana hoped she wasn't the only one confused. "Control your gift?"

Pinheiro sat down at Duilio's gesture, picking a seat across from hers. "Anjos sent me to Lisboa to study with the Jesuits there, trying to pull my abilities as a seer into order." He shrugged. "I inherited the gift from my father, but I've always ignored it, and therefore have probably missed more opportunities than I should. When I think of all the people who might have been helped had I worked to use my gift instead of brushing it aside, I cringe."

Duilio shook his head. "You can't fix everything in the world, Rafael."

Joaquim leaned against a bookshelf near the door, his lips pursed in a pensive manner.

"So you're working for Inspector Anjos now?" Oriana asked.

Pinheiro grinned lopsidedly. "Yes, I'm to be their group's seer, although how successful I'll be remains unclear. The Jesuits can train me, but not increase my natural talent."

Oriana nodded. That was similar to how a sereia's *call* worked. There had to be natural talent before it could be trained as hers was. "I see."

"He's actually a much stronger seer than I am," Duilio told her. "Gaspar says my selkie blood limits my seer's talent somehow."

Pinheiro rolled his eyes, but then turned his gaze to the papers on the table. "Is this what you're working on? I think this is why I came by." He glanced over at Joaquim. "Whatever you're working on is related to the case Gaspar is working on. You need to bring him and Anjos in on this one, and combine the two."

Duilio closed his eyes for a second. Asking himself questions,

Oriana decided. A moment later, he opened his eyes. "Damn. I never thought to ask that."

Joaquim stepped away from the bookshelf. "There's nothing in common."

Pinheiro held his hands wide. "Sorry, cousin. I don't know *how* they're related. I spent hours trying to figure that out, but never could chase it down. Perhaps there's someone linking the two cases."

That sounded similar to how Duilio described his gift as working. He had to know the right questions to ask himself, a harder feat than expected unless one understood the criminal's design.

Pinheiro turned back to Duilio, hazel eyes worried. "This is going to turn into a bloody mess. A deadly one."

Duilio pinched the bridge of his nose. "It already is, Rafael."

"No," Pinheiro said. "It's going to get worse, and you're not going to be able to prevent the deaths."

"Then what's the point of knowing?" Joaquim asked.

"You'll be there to clean up the mess afterward," Pinheiro said to him. He swept a hand over the papers on the table. "This is all someone's design. This goes beyond a handful of deaths. The repercussions from whatever they've set in motion, that's what *must* be stopped."

Joaquim folded his arms across his chest. "Those deaths are not negligible."

Pinheiro inclined his head in Joaquim's direction. "Sorry, cousin. I didn't mean to say they were. But they're already gone. Don't lose the city trying to save one house from burning."

Oriana cocked her head to one side, considering. Perhaps they weren't seeing the whole picture, but she had no idea what that whole was likely to be. She turned back to Pinheiro. "Have you talked to Inspector Gaspar or Inspector Anjos yourself?"

Pinheiro shook his head. "I'm only passing through town. I managed to have lunch with my father, and then came here afterward. I did send Gaspar a note, though, so he'll probably get in touch with you."

Duilio came alert at the mention of food. "Do you have plans for dinner?"

Pinheiro checked his pocket watch. "Actually, I need to catch the train for Guimarães. My maternal grandfather has summoned me to his home. I'm expected for dinner *there* tonight." He didn't sound excited at that prospect.

"I thought your mother was estranged from her family," Duilio said as Pinheiro rose. "I mean, after . . ."

"After she bore a bastard?" Pinheiro asked without heat. "Yes, but he asked, and he is my grandfather, so I'm going." He nodded to Oriana and Joaquim. "Good day."

Duilio headed after him to escort him out, but Pinheiro stopped him at the threshold. "I'll see myself out, Duilio." He paused, and then added, "Do me a favor. Talk to Miss Carvalho. I believe her father has been pushing her to pursue you, and she needs be told there's no point."

Duilio crossed his arms. "When did Miss Carvalho become your concern?"

Pinheiro opened his mouth but didn't answer immediately. Oriana could have sworn he was blushing. "I have had ample time," he finally said, "during meditation to think about every last person I've ever met, even Miss Carvalho. Besides, Duilio, it does affect *you*, doesn't it? Do you think the gossips have missed that she keeps visiting your mother?"

Duilio laughed. "Whereas I've been avoiding her for the last two weeks. That should have been telling enough."

"Make it clear, cousin. Please." Pinheiro glanced over at Oriana. "Or you do so, Miss Paredes, since he doesn't want to be alone with her."

And with that, he walked off down the hallway. A second later, the front door of the house closed. Duilio turned back to Joaquim. "Well, that was interesting. Do you think our cousin has an interest in Miss Carvalho?"

"They don't travel in the same social circles," Joaquim said doubtfully. "He is right, though. It would be kinder to tell the girl sooner rather than later."

Duilio sighed theatrically, and Oriana did her best not to laugh. Duilio hated confrontations. He preferred to endlessly avoid them. "Would you prefer I talk to her?"

"And tell her what?" Duilio asked, throwing his hands up. "That she's wasting her time?"

"Yes. Exactly that. I doubt she would see me if I went to her house, but I suppose I can catch her the next time she shows up for tea with your mother."

Duilio's lips pressed together. "Actually, we can find her earlier if my mother agrees. I'll ask in the morning. Short notice, but Mother enjoys a challenge." He turned to Joaquim before Oriana could ask for clarification. "Speaking of which, Mr. Monteiro and his younger daughter have accepted our invitation to join us for dinner tonight. You're staying, aren't you, Joaquim?"

Oriana shot Duilio an irritated look, but he carefully didn't meet her eyes. He must have been sitting on that information for hours, waiting to spring it on her at the last minute.

"It's not a formal dinner," Duilio added to Joaquim. "It's practice for a formal dinner Mother's planning, a chance for Mrs. Cardoza and Cardenas to work out the kinks. It's been a long time since we've entertained."

Lady Ferreira intended to throw a *formal* dinner party and have the Tavares family over, but hadn't arranged it yet. Oriana held in a groan. Dinner parties weren't her favorite event. While other ladies took off their gloves to eat, she couldn't, and neatly handling a fork or spoon while wearing mitts could be challenging. Joaquim seemed to be contemplating the request still, though, so she said, "I'm certain Lady Ferreira would want you to stay. It would make the numbers even."

He shot her a doubtful glance. "I'm not dressed for dinner."

"Marcellin can fix you up," Duilio inserted smoothly. "He can shoehorn you into one of my jackets."

Although Joaquim was heavier, he and Duilio were similar in build. It didn't surprise Oriana that they could wear each other's clothes. In the midst of collecting his notes, Joaquim nodded shortly, defeated. "Do you mind if I head back to my old room and take a nap?"

"No, go on," Duilio said.

Joaquim replaced the last of his notes and closed up his leather case.

"Would you like to look at my hands?" Oriana asked before he left the table.

A silence fell over the room. Duilio frowned but didn't protest.

Joaquim cast a rueful look at her. "I apologize if I was staring, Oriana."

Joaquim had to have seen her naked when they found her on that island, but had likely kept his eyes averted the whole time. She went to stand next to him, noting when she did so that he didn't smell like Duilio, no matter how similar his appearance. "It's natural to be curious about something different."

She lifted her hand for his perusal, spreading her fingers wide so that the translucent webbing showed between them. The webbing anchored at the last knuckle on each finger, and stretched between the index finger and thumb. With her webbing fully spread, she could feel the vibration of his pulse and, more distantly, Duilio's.

"May I?" he asked before touching her hand, indicating that she should turn her hand halfway over. "This is sensitive?"

"Yes. It's how we sense movement in the water . . . the tide, the presence of fish and other animals, even boats. It looks delicate, but it's difficult to tear and heals exceptionally well."

Joaquim's brows drew together. "Do you intend . . . ?"

"No," Duilio said before she could answer.

"No," she echoed. "I am a sereia. I won't live the rest of my life hiding that. Some of my people don't mind living as humans, but I'm too stubborn to do so for long. So I'll not have my webbing cut away."

Joaquin nodded slowly. "Do your gills . . . hurt?"

"No. They're fine as long as I immerse myself regularly. A bath will do, even. Would you like to see them?" When he nodded, she struggled to unbutton the high neck of her blouse. Duilio came to her side, carrying his scent with him, and his fingers eased the two top buttons free. Oriana drew down the high collar of her shirt far enough that her gill slits were exposed on one side. The edges would be visible, but not terribly *noticeable*. "They're closed if I'm not breathing water," she told Joaquim. "Or *calling*."

He moved closer to look and then drew back. "Thank you."

Duilio buttoned the neck of her blouse for her, his breath warm against her skin.

"With those two exceptions," she told Joaquim, "we are more or less human. And the color of our skin, of course."

"Weren't you going to go take a nap?" Duilio asked Joaquim, irritation in his tone.

Joaquim laughed, his eyes meeting hers briefly. "I'll get out of your way."

He picked up his bag and headed out of the library, pointedly leaving the door standing open. Duilio shut it and turned back to her, a vexed expression on his face. "Which one of us are you court-ing anyway?"

CHAPTER 22

Duilio had never considered himself a jealous man, but his visceral reaction to Oriana's offers had been to shove Joaquim out of the library. He knew it was childish, and apparently so did Joaquim and Oriana. "You weren't planning on showing him your dorsal stripe, were you?"

Oriana shot him an exasperated glance. "You know why I let him look at my gills."

The annoying part was that he *did* understand. She wanted Joaquim to get over any nervousness before her sister showed up for dinner. It was that simple. Among her people, nudity was tolerated or even expected in some situations, so Duilio knew plenty of men must have seen her dorsal stripe and her gill slits before. "That doesn't mean I don't mind."

She came to where he stood by the door. "I am not courting him. If you're unclear about that, I must not be trying hard enough."

Duilio touched her cheek, ran his fingers down and along the side of her neck. Her gills slits were covered by her high collar now, but even through that, his touch made her shudder. Stepping closer, he ran a finger over her full lower lip. "How sharp are your teeth, exactly?"

She smiled. "Not sharp as a razor, but sharp enough that you don't want to surprise me."

He pressed one step closer, and her back came up against the door. "Are you going to let me kiss you? You could consider it a gift."

She didn't try to get away. She didn't say no. So he leaned closer and kissed her. Her hands slid under his coat, permission of a sort, and he touched her lips with the tip of his tongue. She opened her mouth, allowing him to slip his tongue inside and run it along the edge of those very sharp teeth. She drew a startled breath and pressed herself against him.

This wasn't like the first time she'd let him kiss her, sleepy and innocent, or the second interlude between them, where she'd been willing if not eager. This was different. He felt that right away. She was sure of herself this time.

So he let her lead, let her guide the kiss. He settled his hands on her hips and firmly reminded them to stay there. She brought one of her hands up to cup his cheek. Her tongue touched his, touched his lips. He shuddered.

When her hand wrapped about the back of his neck and tugged him closer, he didn't fight. His body pressed hers against the door.

It was glorious to feel her against him, her breasts brushing his chest, her legs against his. He reminded himself to stay composed, because this wouldn't lead where he wanted, not today. Her touch calmed then, her lips against his but the passion slowing into a careful exploration as if she'd recalled that constraint as well. She kissed him once more, and then drew back enough to meet his eyes.

He didn't step away. She still held one hand about his neck. The other lay on his back inside his coat. He couldn't decipher her expression, but then she smiled.

"I love you, Oriana," he told her.

Her eyes began to glisten. She licked her lower lip and almost spoke, but then it seemed as if her words were caught in her throat.

Why does that not surprise me? She was far more reticent than he was. Duilio touched his forehead to hers. "That kiss was a per-fect gift."

Her head tilted in the way that always made him think that if only she could, she would be blushing. He stayed there a moment, only holding her. But then he eased away, managing to catch one of her hands. "I have a gift for you, by the way. Is that allowed in this courtship procedure?"

She apparently didn't trust herself to speak, but nodded quickly. He drew her over to his desk where Joaquim's other case waited. He drew a wooden box out of the case and opened it to display the contents for her. She cast him a baffled look.

He picked up the revolver from within. It was smaller than he preferred and unattractive like its name, but it had decent accuracy and had been simple to alter. "It's called a bulldog because it's short and stubby. I picked it up in England."

"Along with your penchant for big breakfasts?" she asked slyly.

"Yes," he admitted. "I also brought back an alarm clock, a bun-dle of books, and a kilt."

Oriana rolled her eyes.

"Very well, I didn't buy a kilt," he admitted. "You didn't look at this, did you? Joaquim had one of the men at the shop take off the trigger guard, so it won't hurt your webbing." That had been the issue before—most guns required stretching the index finger away from the middle finger and thumb, far enough to be uncomfortable for a sereia. The smaller size of this weapon meant less of a stretch for her webbing and now there was no trigger guard to pinch it, either. He pointed out the screw they'd set in front of the trigger. "This can be tightened to keep the gun from firing accidentally."

She took the small revolver pistol gingerly. "Not loaded, is it?"

"No," he told her.

She wrapped her hand around the ivory grip, pulled back the hammer, and set her finger on the trigger. Her manner suggested that she did, as she'd once claimed, have familiarity with firearms. She pulled the trigger, flinching when the hammer sprang forward with a click. But then she smiled widely. "This is a perfect gift."

The dinner went smoothly, with no one resorting to harsh words at the table. Oriana managed to keep her calm. Her father seemed equally determined not to upset either Lady Ferreira or Marina with their normal squabbling.

Joaquim wore a coat that Oriana recognized as one of Duilio's. His white tie and light gray waistcoat flattered his darker complexion. As Duilio had gone to talk to Joaquim after leaving her in the library, he'd evidently gotten over his short-lived fit of jealousy. Oriana smiled to herself. She'd never had a man jealous over her before and, while Duilio had stepped between her and Erdano once or twice, that had been more along the lines of protection than jealousy. Duilio understood that Erdano merely *annoyed* her with his unsubtle attempts at seduction.

It was plain from his behavior during dinner where Joaquim's interests lay. He was seated next to Marina, across from Oriana and her father. He listened attentively to Marina's every word, something that wasn't lost on Lady Ferreira where she sat at the head of the table. While Oriana was eating her soup the lady cast a glance her way that seemed to ask her opinion. Oriana shrugged. She wasn't going to interfere in that situation any further.

Since Lady Ferreira insisted, Oriana didn't wear mitts. Everyone here already knew her secret anyway. It was a relief to sit at the table and eat without having to hide her hands. She didn't drop a single spoon or fumble with a knife.

Lady Ferreira managed to carry most of the conversation with her father, sparing Oriana from talking to him too much. She asked him discreet questions about his business in the city, about Marina's job there, and the current investment atmosphere, which demonstrated that she did read the trade daily from end to end. Oriana didn't even mind when Lady Ferreira invited her father—and Lady Pereira de Santos—to the still-unplanned dinner party.

After dinner Oriana retired to the sitting room with Lady Ferreira and Marina, who seemed awed by everything she saw in the house. Oriana tried to recall if she'd felt the same way when she'd first arrived in the Ferreira household, but she'd been tired and care-worn then. And she'd never had Marina's natural effusiveness.

"Father says I'm not to go anywhere alone," Marina was telling Lady Ferreira as Oriana settled on the couch next to her. "So he'll escort me back to my flat and come back up to check on Lady P."

Oriana saw Lady Ferreira's lips press together exactly as Duilio's would have done on hearing that abbreviation of the lady's name—holding a laugh inside. "I could get Filho to escort you back to your apartment," the lady offered.

Marina flushed. "Oh. I wouldn't want him to go out of his way."

The lady asked after the address and then pronounced, "That won't be a problem, since it's in the same direction as his."

Oriana sighed inwardly, wishing she'd gone off to the library with the men.

Monteiro was going out of his way to be civil, so Duilio steered the conversation away from either of his daughters. He poured a brandy for each of the three of them, and gestured for Monteiro to take his choice of the sofa or a chair at the table. The man chose the table, and took a sip of his brandy as Joaquim moved over to the sofa and sat there—probably still thinking.

"Your mother is a very gracious hostess," Monteiro said.

"She has only been out of mourning for a few weeks," Duilio said, "but she enjoys having company."

"Apparently she does not mind *varied* company," Monteiro said then. "Most fine households would not be so welcoming to my daughters. I am grateful."

"Mother does not care for uninteresting people," Duilio said, "so by that measurement, you and your daughters are the best of guests."

Monteiro seemed to take that as a compliment, which was how he'd meant it. "Thank you, Mr. Ferreira."

Duilio went to the desk and retrieved the leather-bound book he'd intended to show Ambassador Alvaro. "I wanted to ask you about this, sir. My father claimed these books came from your islands. Oriana told me she can't read them—that it would take a scholar."

Monteiro took the book and gazed down at the strange script on the spine. "I'm hardly a scholar," he said, "but I *can* read this. Before I came to live here, I worked converting ancient texts to modern print. This is a history, telling of the reign of Queen Jacona."

"I actually have several books like this," Duilio said. "I considered offering them to the ambassador. I can't make use of them, so it seemed appropriate."

"How many do you have?" Monteiro asked.

Duilio went to the case in which the others were locked. "Six volumes in all, but the bindings are different. They don't appear to be a set."

Monteiro flipped through the pages of the one he still held. "I remember reading this as a child, although in Portuguese. Rather boring."

Duilio drew out the remaining books and set them atop the table for Monteiro's perusal. None were in as pristine shape as the first—which made sense if it was a boring book—but only one could be considered tattered. "Do the islands import their paper?"

"Timber is an abundant resource there, but cutting is limited and most of that is used for construction," Monteiro said as he picked up another book and read the spine. "So yes, most paper is imported. Trading is mostly with Spain and England these days, since we're cut off from Northern Portugal."

That was to be expected. The sereia had long ties to the

Portuguese people, dating back to the claiming of the islands for the Portuguese by Vasco da Gama in 1499. When the Spanish attempted to take the islands by force during the sixteenth century, King Sebastian I had sent ships to protect the sereia. Despite those ties, the ban prevented them from trading with Northern Portugal while superstition kept them out of Southern Portugal. The sereia believed that the 1755 earthquake that destroyed Lisboa—or more precisely the tidal wave that followed it—had been an unfavorable judgment by the gods of the sea. Even so, Duilio disliked hearing that his people had been replaced in favor by the Spanish.

"This is another history and this, a novel." Monteiro laid aside those two books. He picked up the tattered book and peered at the spine. Then he opened it, his dark brows drawing together.

"I've often wondered if tourists were allowed to visit," Duilio said then. "Was that done before the ban?"

Monteiro didn't respond. Instead, he began to flip through the book, stopping briefly on various pages. His lips made a stern line.

"Sir? What is it?"

Monteiro glanced up. "Burn this one."

Joaquim came over to look at the offending book.

Duilio gazed down at the page, the dashes and lines indecipherable to him. "Why?"

Monteiro shook his head. "All copies of this book were destroyed about fifty years ago."

Clearly not *all*. "Then this is one of few copies left?"

"This is the journal of a monster," Monteiro said, casting a glance up at the both of them as they stood over him. "His name was Dr. Castigliani. A Sicilian, I think. He did terrible things in his quest for knowledge. The copies—there were only about fifty printed—were destroyed to prevent anyone from taking ideas from his work. There's some debate as to why they were printed in the first place. He was a human doctor, after all, and male."

Duilio sat again. History was filled with men who thought their goals made the means, however questionable, acceptable. Maraval had thought so. "What did he do?"

Monteiro turned the spine toward him, showing its sereia script in faded gold leaf. "This book is called *The Seat of Magic*. The doctor was searching for the organs in the body that housed magic. This is the journal of his dissections." He shut the book. "Or his vivisections. He kept his victims alive as long as possible to see the results of removing various organs."

Duilio's gift warned him, a jangling of his nerves. Not that he was in danger, but that he was in the presence of something immensely important. "Of sereia?"

Joaquim's hand touched Duilio's shoulder. Clearly he saw the relationship, too.

"Yes," Monteiro said, his jaw clenched. "That's why he came to our islands. He'd already studied otter folk, selkies, fairies. Anything with any magic, he managed to find them and take them apart. Human witches, too, if I recall correctly. Ultimately, he was executed for his experiments on the island, but his notes survived." He pushed the book farther away from him. "This is the transcription of those notes—in the language of our scholars, as a precaution, so the common sereia couldn't read it. Even so, the book was deemed too dangerous and ordered destroyed."

Duilio stared down at the closed book for a moment, noting the tattered edges of the fabric cover. This volume had been read many times. "But not all copies were accounted for?"

"Most, but not all." Monteiro said. "I heard of a scholar caught studying one once. She was exiled because she'd read it."

Duilio pinched the bridge of his nose. Monteiro didn't see the relationship, but that was because he didn't have the information they did.

"Was it ever translated into a human tongue?" Joaquim asked. "Or did his original notes survive?"

Monteiro turned mistrustful eyes on Joaquim. "Why do you ask?"

Joaquim's eyes slid over to meet his, so Duilio explained. "The girls who've been murdered, sir. We didn't tell you how the other two died, but in each case what was done could be seen as removal of what was magic about them, as if someone *removed* that seat of magic from their bodies."

The servants had pulled off the dinner with ease, despite having the morning off. Joaquim dutifully agreed to escort Marina back to her flat, her father had left, and no blood had been spilled.

Oriana wished she'd spoken with her father privately, but he'd brought her a sealed letter that must hold answers to the questions she'd written out. The idea of reading it made her nervous. She wasn't sure she was ready to hear his side.

She found Duilio in the library, pensively staring at a glass of brandy she suspected he would never drink. "What did the three of you talk about?"

He pointed to a book lying next to the giant clamshells on the table. "That thing."

The faded lettering on the spine was in her people's ancient language. "What is it?"

As he told her of her father's description, a sick feeling grew in her stomach. She'd never heard of the book, but that wasn't surprising. She'd never made much effort to become a scholar. "Someone is . . . experimenting?"

"We don't know that," he said. "It's an alternative we'd never considered before."

Thinking of someone *experimenting* on her sister, Oriana shuddered.

"Are you cold?"

"No," she said. "These people sicken me. Like Maraval, they play with people's lives because they think their grand plans are more important than anything else."

He remained quiet for a moment, then apparently recalled

something he'd forgotten. He picked through the pockets of his jacket and produced an envelope. "Your father gave me this yesterday, but I forgot it in the flurry over Felipa Reyna's death. It's the note that warned him not to talk. He received it the day before Lady Pereira de Santos came to see me."

She took the envelope from his hand and turned it over to peer at the broken seal. It seemed familiar. "This looks like the last note I had from Maria Melo. I wonder . . . I left it in my room. Do you think Teresa would have thrown it out?"

Duilio rose and held out one hand to help her up. "Let's find out."

He sent one of the footmen to locate the maid while they headed up to her bedroom. Duilio waited outside, and a moment later the fresh-faced maid came dashing along the hallway.

Teresa looked surprised by Duilio's presence, but when he stood aside, she went on in to speak with Oriana. "Yes, I remember, miss," she said once Oriana explained what she was looking for. "There were two letters. I put them in the little vanity table. I know right where they are." The maid disappeared into the dressing room and emerged a second later with two small envelopes in her hand. "Here they are, miss."

Oriana took the envelopes. The first was still unopened. She'd received it when they were hunting Isabel's killer and hadn't wanted to give up the hunt if her orders told her to leave the city, so she'd never opened it. The second had arrived *after* they'd caught Maraval. That envelope's seal was broken. Oriana shuffled them about in her hands and went out into the hall to show Duilio. She held out the two opened ones. "Same handwriting, and it's the same seal. See the M?"

He slid the unopened one from her grasp. "This one's different."

It bore an M like the other two, but in a different script. The wax was also different. "I guess she used Heriberto's supplies."

"Not the same handwriting, either," Duilio pointed out.

Oriana glanced down at the handwriting on the sealed

envelope. It bore both of her maternal surnames, but Mrs. Melo had intimated that she'd known Oriana's mother. Even so, the longer she looked at it, the more familiar the hand was. Oriana crossed to the table where she'd laid her father's missive earlier that night and turned the envelope over to look at the seal. It matched.

The first missive—the one she'd ignored—had come from her father. M for Monteiro, not Melo. Oriana licked her lips. "It's from my father. He tried to contact me."

"What does that mean?" Duilio asked softly.

"I don't know," she admitted. "I . . . I need to read these."

Duilio handed her the other envelope. "I'll say good night, then."

Teresa, who'd stood quietly to one side, bobbed politely when he wished her a good night as well. Then he was gone, leaving Oriana alone with the maid.

"Thank you for saving these, Teresa," Oriana said. "Um . . . why don't I change for the night and you can go on to bed."

Half an hour later Oriana sat on the leather settee near the bedroom door, the unopened envelopes lying on her lap. The note from Mrs. Melo wasn't surprising. The warning addressed to her father was only one sentence long, saying that if he talked, he would share his daughter's fate. Maria Melo didn't waste words, Oriana recalled.

She then opened the first note from her father, the one she'd ignored.

I'm not supposed to contact you, it said, *but H intimated that you're in danger. If you need, I can hide you, M.*

Her father had offered her a safe haven. He'd done it despite knowing that Heriberto might turn him over to the Special Police if he found out.

Oriana pressed a hand to her stomach, regretting now the angry words she'd said to her father on Friday. She'd accused him of not caring what happened to her. Now she held proof in her hands that she'd been wrong. Sighing, she laid the note on the table at her elbow and broke the seal on his new missive, wherein he'd answered the questions she'd written out for him.

Her father's hand was excellent, something she'd forgotten in the last decade. She smoothed her fingers across the page, flattening it. And then she started to read.

CHAPTER 23

MONDAY, 27 OCTOBER 1902

O riana had tossed and turned much of the night. Lady Ferreira didn't comment on her bleary look when she arrived at the breakfast table, but when Duilio sat across from her a few minutes later, he did. "Did you find out what you wanted to know? It doesn't look like it brought you peace."

His mother's eyes rose from her newspaper. "Find out what?"

"Just questions I had for my father," Oriana said. "Most were . . . things I should have realized, but one answer raised more questions. If you don't mind, Lady Ferreira, I'd like to go talk to him again this morning."

"Questions about?" Duilio prompted.

Oriana gazed down at the small plate before her. "I need to talk to him first."

Cardenas brought the morning's mail and Duilio began thumbing through it, one eye still on her. "I need to go up to the palace this morning," he said, "but I could go with you afterward."

"I'll go alone. I promise I won't lose my temper."

He gazed at her a moment, but let the topic drop. "Mother,

Rafael asked that I talk to Miss Carvalho. Make it clear that I'm not going to take the bait."

Lady Ferreira set her napkin aside. "And you want me to do it for you?"

"Ah, no," Duilio said, flushing. "It might be better if it came from Oriana. I was wondering if you had any idea what might prove a good venue to find Miss Carvalho."

He did have reason not to talk to Genoveva Carvalho himself. Unmarried women of good birth didn't spend time alone with men they weren't about to marry. If he spoke with her privately, it would be taken the wrong way.

Lady Ferreira sat back, eyes fixed on some internal point. "Let me see. There's a dinner party tonight at the Vieira house. I expect she and her mother will be there, but that's not ideal for a private conversation."

"Will she even speak with me?" Oriana asked. "I'm just a servant, after all. . . ."

"Nonsense," Lady Ferreira said with a wave of one hand. "You're my companion. Besides, Genoveva is too well behaved to make a scene. Now, tomorrow night there's a ball at the Simões house, and a card party at the Freitas house. I expect Lady Carvalho will choose the ball, since Genoveva dances so well."

A ball? Oriana almost protested at the idea of preparing for a ball in only two days, but they'd done exactly the same thing once before, and Lady Ferreira had been unwell then. "Are your hands healed enough?"

Lady Ferreira smiled. "Certainly, Oriana. I'll be wearing gloves, so no one will know. And I have a new evening gown on order for you. I'll send Felis around to hurry the dressmaker. Take care of your meeting with your father, and she and I will handle it all."

Oriana puffed out her cheeks. Duilio's expression was apologetic; he clearly recognized that she may have to endure a hideous scene with the younger woman. Perhaps Lady Ferreira would prove correct and Miss Carvalho would be sensible. If her father was the one pushing her to court Duilio, as Pinheiro claimed, surely she would be willing to curtail her pursuit of him.

After breakfast, Duilio caught her in the hallway before she went into her bedroom. "Joaquim is setting up an appointment with Anjos for this afternoon. Will you be done by then?"

"I'll be back before lunch," she promised.

He touched her powdered cheek with gentle fingers. "Please be careful out there."

"Don't let the infante beat you *too* badly," she told him in turn.

The infante's fist connected with his jaw, and Duilio found himself sitting on the wooden floor. It hadn't been a hard hit, but it had taken him by surprise. The handful of guards in the gymnasium at that early hour cheered.

"You aren't paying attention today," the infante said, offering a hand to help Duilio up. He wore a loose pair of linen trousers and an open-necked shirt, casual garb that better suited the practice floor than Duilio's fine pinstriped trousers.

Duilio accepted the man's help up and rubbed at his jaw, hoping it wouldn't bruise later. He was starting to look like a street brawler. He dusted off his trousers. "My apologies, Your Highness."

"Raimundo," the infante reminded him, gesturing for Duilio to accompany him out of the ring. They walked over to one side of the room as two of the guards began to circle each other, fists up. Two other guards stayed close to where they stood, but far enough that they wouldn't overhear. "What has you so distracted, Duilio?"

Duilio chuckled. He didn't intend to tell the infante he'd been thinking of Oriana rather than keeping his mind on the bout. But then again, he couldn't think of anything that would justify his laughter. "A woman," he finally admitted.

"The woman you spoke to the ambassador about?" The infante raked a hand through his straight hair, pulling it back neatly from his forehead. "I spoke to him yesterday, briefly. He was grateful for your help."

"You spoke to him?" Duilio asked.

The infante glanced over at the guards, and answered quietly. "No one knows I got close enough, so do not mention it."

"Is he still under strict guard?"

"Yes, but the guards were temporarily distracted, so I managed to get to his door. Unfortunately, that means I've lost Bastião for a couple of days."

Ah, the faithful guard had created a diversion and paid for it. Duilio had to wonder if the replacement guards—whom he didn't recognize—would bend to the infante's will as easily. "Do they still suspect Alvaro an assassin?"

The infante nodded. "Foolishness."

While the infante dressed in more appropriate garb, Duilio tugged his waistcoat and coat on over his sweaty shirt. "Has Alvaro told you how he heard about her being in danger? He said something about being told not to talk. How would he even get a message like that?"

The infante glanced up. "Official mail from his homeland. It's read before it comes into his hands, but my understanding is that it *does* reach him."

"But only official mail?"

"Yes," he said. "Nothing from family or friends, and nothing from any partisans here in the city."

Duilio chewed his lips for a moment. That meant that both the news about the danger to Oriana and the threat to silence him had come through *official* channels. "There's no chance of my talking to him? I have some questions about the woman involved."

"I'm afraid not. My influence is curtailed without my guards to cover for me." The infante turned his head to watch an approaching guard, one of the new ones. "Why don't you join me for a walk around the halls before you leave, Duilio?"

Duilio rose and tugged at his coat one final time, trying to get it to lie properly across his shoulders over the damp shirt. They left the gymnasium and had reached the second floor of the new section when the infante grabbed his arm and directed him to a narrower hallway on one side of the central thoroughfare. "Stay out of sight."

Staying out of sight wasn't possible in the hallway. There were no doorways in which to stand, no niches, or statues behind which to hide. So Duilio stood unmoving against the side of the white-plastered wall, hoping for inconspicuousness. The infante remained at the head of the hallway, watching the approach of a noisy group.

It was the prince and his entourage again. The prince's long graying hair was still uncombed, but he was properly clothed this time. The astrologers followed at a distance, only the doctor pressing close and speaking urgently. The group swept by the open hallway, ignoring the infante completely. Duilio could have sworn that one of the astrologers looked right at the infante, but the man's eyes passed over him as if he weren't even there.

They didn't see us.

This was the second time that had happened. Duilio didn't have any idea what the talent of not being seen would be called—but he'd seen this particular talent before. The Lady shared it. She could hide herself and others with her from view. And it explained how the infante could have spent years at Coimbra without anyone seeming to know he'd been there. He'd surely used a false identity, but that would have been easier to maintain if no one *noticed* him.

The entourage past, the infante continued down the hallway in the opposite direction from the prince. "One day my brother will die, Duilio. Things will change in ways that will require the service of men more open-minded than those who serve my brother."

Duilio understood what the infante wanted—the same thing he'd asked when he'd first come to the house a couple of weeks ago. But offering his allegiance to another—even the infante—while the prince lived was treason. He could hang for doing so. Then again, he could hang for merely being who he was, for harboring his mother and Erdano, for allowing Oriana in his home. Treason or not, he liked the infante and would have no problem following him. Duilio bowed his head. "I *would* willingly serve you, but I cannot promise anything, Your Highness."

One of the infante's brows rose.

"Not without discussing it with Miss Paredes first," Duilio answered.

"I see," the infante said, a laugh in his tone. "Do you intend to bow to a woman's will in all things?"

"It's very likely," Duilio admitted.

The infante nodded. "Can you come back . . . perhaps Thursday, at the same time, Duilio?"

"It would be my pleasure, Raimundo." Hopefully by then he would have an answer to the man's request.

Lady Ferreira had talked Oriana into taking Teresa along with her, so now they waited in the front room of her father's office. Teresa watched the activity in the office with curious eyes, particularly when one of the girls who worked in the back room passed by. She leaned closer to Oriana. "What do the girls do here?"

"They're typists," Oriana told her. "My sister works here, typing up old files."

Teresa's lips pursed as she considered that, making Oriana wonder if the young woman had aspirations beyond household service.

Her father's assistant Narciso approached them, a folder under one arm. Oriana was beginning to think he carried one around out of habit. "Miss Paredes, Mr. Monteiro will see you now."

Oriana touched Teresa's elbow. "Could you wait here?"

"Of course, miss," Teresa said, simpering up at Narciso instead.

The assistant coughed discreetly, so Oriana rose and followed him down the hallway to her father's office. He held the door open for her. Oriana peered inside, spotting her father sitting alone.

Fortunately, Lady Pereira de Santos wasn't there to confuse the is-sue. Oriana went inside and sat carefully. The door snicked shut, leaving her alone with her father.

She lifted her eyes to face him. He looked brittle and stiff, as if expecting her to rail against him. "I'm not angry any longer. Not at you."

"Your aunts kept the truth from you, didn't they?"

If she believed the words he'd written, then they had lied to her. Egregiously. And she had never suspected, not once. "When they told me Marina was dead, they showed me a body, Father. It had been in the ocean for a couple of days, so there wasn't much, but it was enough to convince me Marina was dead. Why go to that much trouble?"

"I don't know," he said, "but you've seen with your own eyes that she's alive."

Oriana pressed her fist to her lips, thinking. "What about your exile. You claim you *weren't* exiled for sedition, but that's what all the official reports say."

He shook his head. "I became inconvenient to someone."

"To whom?" she asked cautiously.

He rose and went to lean against the wall. "Oriana, I know you. No matter how you might have changed since you went to work for them . . ."

"I have not changed," she insisted.

He regarded her silently, his lips in a thin line.

That was a foolish thing to say. Of course she'd changed. Oriana reminded herself to stay calm. "What then?"

He came closer, perching on the edge of his desk before her. "When your mother died on Quitos," he said, "we had no say in anything."

They'd lived on Amado then, mostly because it was the island that best tolerated educated males like her father. Her mother's fam-ily had lived on Quitos, in the capital. Her mother had traveled between the two islands frequently, and when she'd died it had taken days for the news to reach them. "I remember."

"I had some doubts then," he said, "but nothing to back up my instinct. I couldn't believe she'd just died."

"It was food poisoning."

"Your mother could have lived on hot-spiced squid beaks, Oriana," he said with a fond laugh in his voice. "She could eat anything. It didn't add up for me."

Her mother *had* been fond of overly spicy foods. "But . . ."

"I had no proof. Nothing. Not until we visited your aunts on Quitos four years later. Do you remember that?"

How could I forget? She was sixteen. Her father had managed to get exiled and she and Marina hadn't returned to their grandmother's house on Amado, not for years. "What happened?"

He took a deep breath. "Your mother kept a journal, did you know that? When she was at your aunts' house, she hid it under the floorboard in the bedroom."

"No," Oriana whispered. "I didn't know."

"Neither did your aunts, or they wouldn't have left it there. Your mother worked for the intelligence ministry, checking that new candidates were who they claimed they were."

That much she knew. "So?"

"There were problems with a new member of the ministry. Flaws in her story. Your mother mentioned that in the journal, although she never used the woman's name. That would be unprofessional. She meant to speak with that woman's superior the day she died. I'm certain that's why she's dead. So I went to the ministry and started asking questions. I told them about the journal and the person she'd been investigating. They told me I was disturbed, too grief-stricken to be reasonable, that I was making up lies." He exhaled heavily. "I persisted until I bothered someone too much. One day I was escorted from the ministry's offices directly to the prison.

There was no trial, no chance to make my case to anyone. I was on a ship the next day. Three days later I was dumped in the bay south of here at Nazaré, told that if I returned to the islands, I would die. I thought I would be able to contact you and Marina through my mother, but she could never get through the walls your aunts put about you two. After a few years we decided it was safer for you not to know. We exiles have contacts on Amado, but Quitos is a different world, and you lived *there*."

If he'd told her that story a month before, she wouldn't have believed him. But that had been before she'd lived out a scenario frightfully like his claims. No trial, only judgment.

"They searched the house after you were taken," she told him. "My aunts said they were looking for seditious materials. Pamphlets or something."

"The journal," he said. "I made the mistake of telling them that your mother had written it down."

Oriana sat back in her chair, trying to organize her thoughts. "The woman who wrote to you and warned you not to talk, Maria Melo. Do you know anything about her?"

His brows drew together angrily. "Ferreira told me about her."

"Heriberto hinted she did so because Maraval's plot threatened *her* mission. Her mission, whatever was important enough that I became expendable. That's what Heriberto wanted to warn me about."

Her father crossed his arms over his chest, scowling now. "That's probably why he's fled. If one spy is expendable, all are. Ferreira seemed to think she might be an assassin."

"Yes. What else could this be?"

He shook his head. "It would provoke a war with Northern Portugal, and probably Southern Portugal as well. Unless the navy has grown vastly more robust since I was exiled—which I doubt—it would be suicide. Your government can't be that foolish."

"I don't think it's my government any longer," she said softly. "What happened to Mother's journal?"

"I sent it to your grandmother on Amado. I didn't think it would be safe to keep it on Quitos, where the government might find it and destroy it. I assume she still has it."

There were those who argued that sereia males were incapable of reasonable thought. Her father was surely evidence to the contrary.

Oriana wistfully recalled the beach on Amado near her grandmother's home. She missed those summers there. She'd last visited three years ago, when Marina had disappeared. She would have done better to remain there. "Why did Grandmother not tell me? Why not tell me why you were exiled?"

"After what happened to me? Do you think that either of us wanted that for *you*, Oriana? There was nothing to be gained by telling you the truth. I know you. You wouldn't have been able to leave it alone once you found out."

Oriana wanted to rail at him for hiding the truth from her. She wanted to, but she would have been just as willing to hide the truth from Marina, wouldn't she? Her father and grandmother had been trying to protect them. "Are you still in contact with Grandmother?"

"Of course," he said. "She's talked about coming here, although I've counseled against it. She can do more good there."

"Tell her to hide it, then," Oriana said, rising. "And give her my love."

He grasped her hand. "Oriana, there's no name in the journal, and no one in the ministry will help you track that woman down."

"Mrs. Melo came to the Ferreira house before I left the city. She threatened you to get me to go back to the islands. She said if I didn't go, she would expose you."

"I'm sorry," her father said. "But that threat has always hung over you and me both."

"That's not my point, Father," Oriana said. "As she was leaving, she said that I had Mother's look about me. She said that Mother didn't understand the rules of the game."

He leaned back away from her. "She knew your mother."

Oriana nodded slowly, feeling the strands of the rope twisting together in her mind. "That's why you were threatened," she said aloud. "And Uncle Braz. Someone high up in the ministry is protecting this woman. They don't know what's in Mother's journal. They don't know what happened to it, or whom you've told. But they're afraid it's proof of how far they were willing to go to protect Maria Melo, to protect her mission."

Her father rubbed fingers across his brow. "Oriana, don't pursue this further."

"I have to," she told him. "Did Duilio tell you that a ship tried to keep them from rescuing me?"

"Whose ship?"

"They don't know, Father, but that ship was stopped by a leviathan." Her father may be mostly Christian, but he would understand the significance of that creature's interference. "The gods wanted to ensure my rescue, and that means they have a mission for me. Now I know what it is."

Joaquim strode out of the police station in the late-morning sun, clutching his hat under his arm since there was no likelihood of its staying put in the rising wind. Fortunately, Duilio was coming in the opposite direction, arriving only a few minutes late. He wore one of his finer jackets, showing that he'd gone to the palace to meet with the infante as planned. Together they headed back in the direction from which Duilio had just come.

"You didn't bring Miss Paredes with you?" Joaquim asked.

"She had something she wished to discuss with her father," Duilio told him. "I don't know what."

Joaquim raised a brow. "We've got an appointment to meet Anjos at the morgue at three. Two more bodies turned up last night."

Duilio walked toward the intersection where one could always find a cab. A few minutes later their cab trundled up Torrinha Street toward the doctor's office. "Human?" Duilio asked.

"Yes. Like the earlier ones. No apparent cause of death."

Duilio groaned. "I wish Rafael would have told us how the cases are connected. It would make things so much easier."

Joaquim chuckled. "Being a seer doesn't make *anything* easier, does it?"

"No," Duilio said. "It just gives you more responsibility."

Duilio might have thought Pinheiro's comments on Sunday about his gift were merely flippant remarks, but Joaquim had a strong feeling that Pinheiro had meant those words for *him*. He glanced over at Duilio's face in the light coming through the cab's windows. "I never thought I was prejudiced until Saturday."

Duilio gave him a quizzical look. "Comparatively, you're not," he pointed out unhelpfully. "Certainly far less than most."

Duilio couldn't have missed his reaction to learning that Marina Arenias wasn't human. Joaquim was still ashamed at his hesitation to speak with Miss Arenias after that. He'd always believed in equality for everyone, no matter their class, gender, or race. "Does it never give you pause that you're courting a sereia woman?"

"She's courting me. A custom among her people—the woman courts the man."

Joaquim cast him a dry look. "So you're courting her by allowing her to court you. Semantics, Duilio."

Duilio shrugged. "I love her. It's that simple."

Joaquim grabbed on to the cab's door as it swung around the corner onto Carmo Street a bit too quickly. "Your mind's made up, then?"

"Yes. I let her get away once. I'm not going to make that mistake again."

"When will we be having the wedding?"

"Good question," Duilio said. "Among her people, it's a private agreement as far as I can tell. No wedding, and I've agreed to comply with her people's customs." He sighed as he watched the buildings slip by. "If I insist on marriage, it would sound like an implication that her people's customs aren't as valid as ours."

Joaquim remained silent as the cab rattled on up the street toward the Torre dos Clérigos, then said, "I can see her point. It would be easier to argue, though, that each of you should bind yourselves under your respective traditions, rather than choosing one or the other."

"I'll let *you* tell her that, then," Duilio said with half a laugh.

The cab stopped near the doctor's address before Joaquim could press him further on the issue. The waiting room was empty, and the doctor's spinsterish secretary turned a sour eye on them, but eventually Dr. Esteves came to their rescue. Duilio introduced Joaquim as they followed the older man back to his office.

The doctor gestured for them to sit. "So what strange inquiries do you have for me today, gentlemen?"

Joaquim kept an eye on the doctor, trying to read his reactions. He'd asked around at the station about this doctor, and no one had heard anything ill about him. That wasn't always a reliable gauge of a man's actions.

"Have you ever heard of a book called *The Seat of Magic*?" Duilio asked.

The doctor frowned. "I've heard of it, although I've never seen a copy."

"Do you know what it contains?"

Esteves paused halfway around his desk, his lip curling upward in distaste. "It's supposed to be the record of a doctor who tried to find the biological source of magic in various peoples and remove it." He sat down behind his desk, heavily. "The greatest breach of ethical conduct imaginable. Do you suspect the murder of that otter girl had something to do with it?"

"There have been two other deaths," Duilio told him. "A selkie, who was skinned completely, and a sereia whose throat was cut out. She might have been a patient of yours, a girl named Felipa Reyna."

The doctor's shoulders slumped and he crossed himself. "Ah, how terrible. I know the Reyna family. She came to me for her hands, about five or six years ago?"

Joaquim looked away, his mouth a narrow line. This was the man who'd cut the girl's webbing away. It had been done to protect her life, but the girl hadn't had much choice, had she?

"Has she been here since?" Duilio asked.

The doctor's expression went pensive. "I suppose it won't do any harm to divulge that at this point. She was here last week, one afternoon. A feminine concern."

"Thursday? The day I visited?"

The doctor rose and called for his secretary to bring his agenda to him. When she'd done so, he flipped through a couple of pages of entries and laid it open for them to see. Felipa Reyna had visited the doctor that afternoon, his last patient.

Joaquim spotted the name of Marina Arenias above hers. "Miss Arenias was here shortly before her and was assaulted down the street from this office. Were you aware of that?"

The doctor appeared genuinely surprised. "Was she hurt?"

"No," Duilio said. "Inspector Tavares happened to be nearby and stopped her assailant. She was more frightened than anything else."

"And was Miss Reyna taken from near here as well? Is that what you're thinking?"

"We don't know," Joaquim said. "How many doctors in the city treat nonhumans?"

"I honestly can't say. It's not something we talk about, for obvious reasons."

Joaquim didn't doubt that answer. "Do you know of any doctors who might show an interest in procedures like those outlined in that book?"

Esteves appeared taken aback. "You suspect a *doctor* is responsible for this?"

Joaquim didn't back down. "The officer who received the girl's body noted that the cuts on her throat were neatly done with a sharp implement."

The doctor's mouth pursed. "Would it be possible for me to see the bodies?"

"The otter girl has been buried, and the selkie given to the sea," Duilio said.

"And Felipa Reyna was buried this morning at the Prado do Repouso," Joaquim said.

Esteves shook his head. "Well, then, I suppose not. As to the book you mentioned, I can't recall anyone offhand who showed an inordinate interest in the topic. I can make some discreet inquiries, gentlemen, but I don't want to arouse the attention of the Special Police."

Duilio rose. "That's all we can ask. Thank you for your help, Doctor."

When they headed out of the office, the doctor walked along with them. "I'm on my way to the cemetery myself," he said, "so I'll lay some flowers on Miss Reyna's grave as well."

A chill went down Joaquim's spine. "The cemetery?"

"A friend of mine passed a couple of days ago," he said. "His funeral is today."

Duilio glanced over at Joaquim, lips pursed.

Joaquim knew that expression. There was something *important* about this. "Who, sir?"

"Dr. Teixeira," Esteves said. "You've met him, Inspector. You hired him to perform an autopsy last week."

That can't be a coincidence, can it? "How did he die?" Joaquim asked. "He seemed in good health."

"In his sleep," Esteves told them. "It happens sometimes. The heart gives out. If you'll excuse me, gentlemen, I don't want to be late."

With a few words to his nurse, Esteves escorted them out his front door and locked it behind him. Joaquim walked toward the spot where Marina Arenias had been assaulted, waiting there for Duilio to catch up. The empty lot smelled faintly of urine and the gravel was rutted with wheel tracks now. "Dr. Teixeira's death is the first clear tie between these two cases," he said when Duilio reached him. "Could it be a coincidence?"

Duilio scuffed the sole of his patent shoe on the pile of cobbles lying to one side. "I don't have much faith in coincidence, Joaquim."

There were a lot of things Duilio didn't have faith in. Joaquim didn't bother to say that.

"Speaking of coincidence, what were you doing on this street that afternoon?" Duilio asked suddenly. "When Miss Arenias was attacked."

"Walking home. I'd been making inquiries about Gita's abductors."

"So you wouldn't have been walking down this street in time to help Miss Arenias if you hadn't been investigating Gita's murder," Duilio pointed out. "Fate, perhaps?"

Joaquim licked his lips. "I've asked myself if she might have *called* me."

Duilio peered down the crowded street as pedestrians wove their way about them. "Did anyone other than you run to her aid?"

"No," Joaquim said.

"Marina Arenias didn't use her *call*, then, not if you were the only man who responded."

Joaquim surveyed the overgrown vegetation in the court created between the backs of houses on different streets. "We need to talk about that."

Duilio looked at him expectantly. "What?"

"I left seminary because of this," he said. "Because of her— Marina Arenias."

"That was a decade ago," Duilio protested. "You didn't know her."

"Exactly," Joaquim said. "Father Santiago doubted my vocation.

He asked me to meditate on why I wanted to enter the priesthood. So I did, for three days. I'm not sure I achieved enlightenment, but I did dream. Of a woman, so I decided I must want a wife and children more than I wanted to be a priest. I joined the police instead."

"Ah." Duilio folded his arms loosely over his chest, prepared to wait.

"I never thought they were real, Duilio—*the dreams.* Just wishful thinking. But I wondered if I would ever meet a woman who lived up to those memories." Joaquim laughed, and then was tempted to cry. He'd known forever, hadn't he? But he didn't know how to say it to Duilio, not when Duilio was his closest friend and he'd lied to him all these years, even without intent. "I thought for a minute that my heart had stopped, Duilio. I couldn't breathe. It was so hard to believe she was real."

Duilio stared at him, waiting.

Joaquim rubbed a hand down his face, gathering his nerve. "It was *her*, Duilio. The woman from my dreams. Marina Arenias— every strand of hair, every eyelash, perfectly in place. The color of her skin, the sun and shadow. It wasn't only her that I'd dreamed. It was this alleyway with that pile of cobbles, the smell in the air that afternoon, the wheel marks. The way she was tugging on her gloves. Everything was exactly how I remembered it from my dream so long ago."

Joaquim wished he knew what Duilio was thinking. He forced his eyes to meet Duilio's. "Do you understand what I'm saying?"

Duilio laid one hand on his shoulder, his expression somber. "That you're a seer, which means you're actually my brother, not my cousin?" he asked, then grinned. "I can't imagine any brother I'd rather have. I certainly get along better with you than Alessio or Erdano."

Joaquim laughed despite himself, the weight of worry lifting from his shoulders. He'd feared that Duilio would deny his claim or perhaps protest that he was wrong in his conclusions. How foolish that had been; Duilio always took everything in stride.

"Are you hungry?" Duilio asked then. "Because it's not that far to the café. We could have a nice lunch before meeting with Anjos at the morgue."

How like Duilio to think of eating before visiting a morgue. "Sounds like a good idea."

CHAPTER 24

Oriana had ink stains on her fingertips, the result of writing out invitations for Lady Ferreira that morning. There had been invitations for the three gentlemen of the Tavares family, Rafael Pinheiro, her own father and sister, Lady Pereira de Santos, and one for Lady Ana as well. If everyone showed up, the numbers would be uneven, but Lady Ferreira said they would manage.

She'd been happy to do the writing for Lady Ferreira, whose hands still ached. It gave her something to do other than pacing the floor in her bedroom. Her mind was still whirling with the implications of her father's words. What was she supposed to do? Her tenure in the Ministry of Intelligence was over—she no longer even had citizenship. And even if Maria Melo was still in Northern Portugal, the woman had contacts within the ministry who hadn't flinched at destroying lives to keep her secrets.

It was a relief when Duilio returned to the house, Joaquim Tavares with him. "How did your discussion with your father go?" Duilio crossed the sitting room to her side. "Any bloodshed?"

She sighed when she noted the new bruise forming on Duilio's chin. Evidently the infante favored his left hand. "Nothing I want to discuss at the moment. I understand a few things better now."

"That's good, isn't it?" He tilted his head trying to meet her eyes. "Or not?"

Oriana lowered her eyes. "Let it alone for now."

He would hate that. He liked to talk about things, but she simply wasn't ready. She hadn't decided what she was going to do about all of this. Or about him. She couldn't draw him into this mess.

He acquiesced. "We are supposed to meet Anjos and his team at the morgue at three. I need to change shirts, but after that we could walk on up there."

Strange that a visit to a morgue sounds like an acceptable diversion. Oriana cast a glance at the table where her invitations were neatly stacked now, finished. "Let me get my mitts, and I'll be right back down."

A few minutes later the three of them were walking along the Street of Flowers in the sunshine. As they made their way up the steep street, Duilio regaled her with the tale of his continued inability to keep the infante from bruising his face, and then discussed their brief meeting with Dr. Esteves.

"If Castigliani's journal was left on my people's islands," Oriana said softly, glancing about to make certain she wasn't overheard, "I don't see how human doctors would have heard of it in the first place. It would take a scholar to translate it."

"Once an idea's written down," Duilio said, "it's damnably hard to eradicate. Something always escapes destruction. One copy hitting human shores would be all it needed."

Like her mother's journal. One single idea in it had provoked a backlash against her family, even though no one in the Ministry of Intelligence had ever seen the thing. They'd only had her father's assertion that it even existed. And yet . . .

"The library at Alexandria was destroyed," Joaquim pointed out. "Countless texts were wiped out, never to be seen again."

"But that was before printing presses made multiple copies available to the common man," Duilio argued. "Now everyone can read them."

"Only two out of ten men in this country are literate, Duilio, if that. For the common man it's all still rumor and hearsay. They have to lean on the word of their so-called betters."

They'd gone beyond the specific text in question, Oriana decided, and were going to start arguing about rights and education now. She only half listened as the two men discussed the country's educational system. Fortunately the morgue wasn't much farther and soon they walked through the doors into the unpleasant air of the small building. Oriana pressed the side of her hand under her nose, not caring how improper that looked.

Inspector Gaspar was already there. Duilio went to greet him, leaving Joaquim standing with her.

Officer Gonzalo came to lock the door behind them, but paused when a carriage stopped before the door. Oriana watched as Inspector Anjos opened the carriage door and stepped down and turned to help the other passenger out. Miss Vladimirova took his hand and descended from the carriage, draped and veiled in black as always. And as it had the first time she'd encountered the woman, a shiver made its way down Oriana's spine. Her throat tightened and her heart began to race.

Miss Vladimirova was *unnatural* and clearly her mind recognized that fact. Oriana took a few deep breaths in an effort to quell her panicked reaction as Anjos greeted them politely. The man looked even more tired than the last time she'd seen him, a couple of weeks ago at the Carvalho house.

"Now, shall we get this in the open?" he asked, his eyes on Gaspar.

Gaspar gestured for them all to follow Officer Gonzalo. Inside the same back room where Felipa Reyna had lain only two days ago, two tables were set up side by side, and on each lay a fabric-draped body. Oriana pressed her finger under her nose again. Officer Gonzalo went to the first table, cast a quick glance at Anjos as if to ask permission, and then carefully folded back the sheet. A young woman lay there, her dark hair still pinned up and her eyes closed.

Gaspar crossed to that first body, gesturing for Anjos and his black-draped companion to approach.

Duilio laid a hand over Oriana's on his sleeve and whispered, "Stay here."

No need to worry. She had no intention of going over there.

Anjos led Miss Vladimirova to the table. Oriana couldn't make out the petite woman's features since she went so heavily veiled, but she didn't recoil from the sight of the body. Miss Vladimirova reached out one black-gloved hand and touched the dead girl's bare shoulder.

"You think I did this, Gaspar?" Miss Vladimirova asked. No emotion tinged her voice, reinforcing her strangeness.

"Did I say that?" Gaspar asked.

Anjos lifted his gaze to Gaspar's, accusation in his tired eyes. Apparently Gaspar believed Miss Vladimirova was involved in the deaths, but Anjos didn't agree.

"You wouldn't have brought me to see a corpse otherwise," she went on. "There are no marks, but I can feel it on her. She was killed by a healer. Her life didn't drain slowly away as it usually does, but was taken all at once."

"So our killer *is* a healer?" Duilio asked.

"There are things other than a healer that can do this," she said, "but this has the feel of a healer about it. A signature, more or less."

"I've talked to every healer I could find in the city," Gaspar said. "None of them had enough strength to do this."

"Then you haven't found her yet," Anjos said, a hint of irritation in his normally civil tone.

Gonzalo covered the body and moved to the other table to reveal a second woman, older than the first. Miss Vladimirova confirmed the second had died the same way. Then she walked back in the direction of the receiving area. Oriana tried not to draw back as the woman neared, but a chill went through her anyway. She caught the scent of river water when Miss Vladimirova passed, strangely out of place in this room.

"You should know," Duilio said as the others moved away from the two tables, "that the doctor who did the autopsy for us last week apparently died in his sleep Thursday night."

Anjos paused at the threshold of the anteroom. "When did you learn this?"

"We went to speak with another doctor this morning about our case," Joaquim said. "He was leaving to attend the funeral."

Gaspar indicated that Anjos should go on into the anteroom, and they all followed. There were only two chairs—one on each side of Gonzalo's desk—so Oriana remained standing while Miss Vladimirova sat. She didn't want to approach the black-veiled woman anyway.

Anjos lit a cigarette and turned his gaze on Joaquim. "Can I assume you suspect the same killer was involved?"

"It could be a coincidence," Joaquim began.

"But my gift tells me we'll learn it's not," Duilio finished for him.

"If our healer has been killing nameless women"—Gaspar held up one hand to forestall Joaquim's protest of that terminology—"women with relatively no status in society, I should have said, why suddenly switch to the doctor? How could she have known that he performed the autopsy?"

"I spoke to a healer I know afterward," Duilio said reluctantly, "although I don't recall mentioning either the doctor or autopsy to her."

Gaspar leaned forward. "Which one?"

Duilio sighed, but said, "Mrs. Rodriguez, on Fonte Taurina Street."

"It's not her," Gaspar said quickly. "I checked her off my list."

Oriana saw the tension leave Duilio's shoulders. He would have hated to have gotten his source in trouble. "Could the doctor have told someone himself?" she asked.

"That's our best likelihood," Anjos said. "We'll start with the doctor's records, speak to his nurse, and find out if he did anything out of his normal patterns. Do you want the doctor's body exhumed?" he asked Joaquim.

Joaquim shook his head. "We won't gain any evidence to present to the courts."

Anjos nodded slowly. "Pinheiro told us these cases are connected, so we should proceed as if they are. So if you'll tell me about *your* dead girls, that will give us a place to start."

Oriana leaned back against the tiled wall, content to wait while they discussed the two cases as a group. She'd heard all of this the day before, so she found her mind drifting. Her eyes landed on Miss Vladimirova's unmoving form. The conversation went on, the gentlemen rehashing the two sets of murders. It took a few minutes before Oriana realized what was wrong—Miss Vladimirova wasn't breathing.

No, it's not an overly tight corset. The woman was *not* breathing. Her chest didn't move at all until she was about to speak . . . then she drew in a breath, spoke, and stopped breathing again.

Oriana swallowed. The woman was supposedly a water spirit of some sort, a claim strengthened by the scent of river water that Oriana had smelled on her. She'd been interrogating officers of the Special Police, using her abilities to influence them to talk—a talent for suggestion similar to a sereia's *call*—but Oriana found the idea that they might be related repugnant. She looked away, catching Duilio's eye as she did so. One of his dark brows rose as if to ask what was wrong, but she shook her head.

"The healer who's killing our first set of victims is letting them lie where they fall," Joaquim pointed out. "The second killer is moving the bodies from wherever he killed them, stripped and wrapped in sheets. Why not drop them in the river instead of leaving the bodies where they'll be found? There are plenty of places where that can be done without being seen."

Anjos ground out his cigarette in an ashtray on Gonzalo's desk. "Our first killer isn't hiding anything, but the second almost appears to be making an effort to be seen. One seems to be targeting prostitutes, one nonhumans. I expect the first killer is opportunistic. The other is deliberate in his choice of victims. So far I'm not seeing a link."

"Only Dr. Teixeira." Duilio glanced over at Joaquim. "He said he once observed a healer while he was at the medical college. Could we track down who that healer was?"

"We can visit the medical school in the morning," Joaquim offered.

That seemed to serve as a plan for the next day's search. Joaquim and Gaspar worked out a few further details to assure they wouldn't be duplicating efforts. Anjos approved their idea and suggested they all leave.

Oriana stopped him. "Sir, have your people had any luck finding Maria Melo?"

"No," he said. "It appears that entire identity was fabricated for the purpose of infiltrating the Open Hand. We don't know where she came from or where she's gone."

Oriana took a deep breath. She had no qualms about exposing the woman—not now—but it still violated years of training. "Would it help to know she's a sereia spy?"

Anjos went still. Apparently he grasped the import of what she'd just done, revealing one of her people's spies to the police. "That's how she knew about your being a sereia in the first place, I suppose."

No point in denying it now. "Yes."

"Then we'll redouble our efforts to find her," Anjos said, "but don't count on success. We've never actually set eyes on her. If she's a spy, she's likely to have disappeared into another identity. Unless we know where to start, we have nothing to go on."

"I can talk to some people," she offered. Surely someone among the sereia community here in the city had an idea who Maria Melo truly was.

Anjos accepted that offer gracefully, not complaining that she'd withheld information that might have helped their search for the woman in the first place.

It was possible Maria Melo hadn't figured out that she'd returned to the Golden City. Oriana suspected instead that the arrest of *any* sereia would draw attention Mrs. Melo didn't want right now. The Special Police wouldn't be kind to Mrs. Melo if they found her. They wouldn't be kind to Oriana Paredes, either, but she had friends in the Special Police now, didn't she?

"Oriana?"

Oriana realized that Duilio was holding out his arm for her to take. How long had he been standing there while she chased down the woman in her mind? Belatedly, she laid her fingertips on his arm and let him lead her out into the sunshine.

D uilio sat impatiently through dinner that night. He hadn't had much time to talk to Oriana alone. He wanted to know what her father had said that had brought about her change of heart, but Joaquim had wanted to talk to his mother first, so Oriana had gone meekly off to her bedroom to change for dinner. That worried him.

She'd come down to dinner an hour later, dressed in a new creation in pale blue. She looked serene and distant, an attitude he recalled from her earliest days in this house when she hadn't trusted him. Something *had* happened, and he desperately wanted to know what it was.

His mother didn't miss Oriana's distracted manner, and managed to keep the conversation moving over dinner, mostly discussing plans for the next evening's outing. Duilio was relieved when his mother pled tiredness after the meal and took herself up to her bed early. That left him and Oriana alone in the sitting room, the first time he'd managed to speak to her alone all day.

Oriana crossed to the far window and pulled the curtain back to gaze out at the darkened street. She glanced over her shoulder at him. "What did Joaquim want to talk to your mother about?"

Well, I should get that out of the way. Oriana needed to know, and he trusted her not to discuss it with anyone inappropriate. "I don't know if my mother's ever mentioned Joaquim's mother to you," he said, "but Rosa Tavares came from Spain. She married Joaquim's father about six months before he was born."

"Oh," Oriana said softly, apparently grasping the import of that number. She turned her back to the window and leaned against the wall, eyes troubled. "I didn't realize."

"Given his resemblance to the rest of the family, no one ever questioned his parentage." Duilio leaned back against the beige sofa and crossed one ankle over the other. "His recent encounter with your sister made him . . ."

Her face lifted. "My sister?"

"Yes, apparently he'd seen her before, in his dreams. As long as ten years ago."

Oriana's brows drew together. "So he's a seer?"

"Exactly. Because it passes father to son, that indicates he wasn't fathered by Joaquim Tavares—the elder Joaquim, I mean—but by someone who's a seer."

"*Your* father," she finished. "Which would also explain the resemblance between you two. Is this a problem?"

"Not for me or my mother," Duilio told her. "I've always suspected, but thought I was wrong because he never showed signs of being a seer. Mother also guessed, but Father would never answer her questions about Joaquim's mother. And Rosa Tavares took the secret to her grave."

"Yet your mother took him in when his mother died," Oriana said. "Why?"

He laughed shortly. "Don't forget, my mother's a selkie. The harem shares a male and raises the children communally. Rosa Tavares was part of the extended family, therefore to Mother it would have been the only appropriate thing to do, no matter who fathered him."

"And how did that sit with your father?" Oriana asked.

That was a thornier issue. "Well, Father was never happy to see Joaquim and Cristiano when he arrived home. They were immediately shuttled off to *their* father's house—again, the elder Joaquim Tavares—as soon as the ships arrived. Joaquim says that Alessio used to harass him about being the bastard son, which was why the two of them didn't get along. Before Alessio went to Coimbra, he and Joaquim actually fought a couple of times. That taught Alessio to leave him alone. Joaquim never told me why they fought, though, because he didn't want to sow trouble between me and Alessio."

Oriana stepped away from the wall. "So Joaquim is your brother rather than your cousin. What does that change?"

"Nothing, actually," he admitted. "He was already my legal heir. I put that in my will as soon as I returned here last year. I knew he would take care of my mother, should anything happen to me. I've told him a dozen times that he's welcome to move back into this house, but he's balked. He doesn't want to mention this to his father, and Mother and I don't see any reason anything should change unless he wants it to. I suspect more than anything else, he just . . . wanted to have the truth off his chest."

"But if he's a seer, why doesn't he predict things like you and Pinheiro do?"

Duilio sighed. "I'm limited because I'm half selkie, but Joaquim is limited because he has the gift of finding. His seer's gift merely serves to reinforce his ability to find things. Or people—which is exactly what the police have had him doing for the last several years. He specializes in finding lost people. When other officers give up on cases, they turn them over to him."

Oriana shook her head. "But your father wasn't a finder."

"The gift of finding had to have come from his mother," he explained.

"Did he not know that? Did she never tell him?"

Duilio shrugged. "She was from Spain. The Church there makes witches disavow their powers, or they imprison them. Spanish witches ignore their gift, deny it, or leave the country."

"Should I pretend I don't know?"

"Joaquim knew I would tell you."

"Ah," she said. He opened his mouth to ask what had happened with her father, but she quickly turned the conversation back to him. "So when do you visit the infante again?" she asked with false brightness. "Are you going to be able to beat him?"

"Actually, there's something I need to discuss with you first," he told her. "I didn't want to bring it up in front of Joaquim, so I didn't mention it earlier, but he's asked me to serve him, after his brother passes, of course. I . . ."

"The infante?" She turned away toward the dark window again, laying one long hand on the sill. "Perhaps that's for the best."

What? Her resigned tone surprised him more than anything else. "Oriana, I didn't . . ."

She looked back over her shoulder. "I need to go back to the islands, and I don't know how long I'll be gone. Or if I'll be able to return."

Duilio stared at her, aghast. How could she think he was going to let her walk away again? She'd done so once and nearly died. "And you don't intend to take me with you?"

"Take you with me?" Her brows drew together. "If you're to serve your infante, you can't leave anyway, can you?"

Yes, there it was, the snap of anger in her voice. She was upset. Duilio grabbed her hand to draw her closer. She resisted for a moment, but then gave in, letting him fold one arm about her. She rested her cheek against his shoulder.

"I didn't promise him anything," he told her, stroking one hand over her tightly coiled hair. "I wouldn't take a step like that without discussing it with you first, and I never expected we would stay here forever. You've told me that's not what you want. I do listen, you know."

She pulled away, her hands clutching his lapels, which would give his valet fits if the man saw it. "It would be simpler to let me go my own way," she whispered, not meeting his eyes.

Yes, she's been working up to that all afternoon. She'd been stewing over whatever her father had said, and had come up with that solution, which wasn't going to work for *him* at all. "Are you going to tell me what your father told you?"

Her face lifted, her eyes meeting his. They glistened with unshed tears. She licked her lips and stepped back. She walked around the sofa to sit there, hands wrapped tightly together. And there was nothing he could do but follow.

Oriana tried to decide what to say. Duilio sat down on her left, close enough that she could feel the warmth of him. He'd refused to make plans without her, yet she'd convinced herself it would be best to go on without him. She'd displayed her lack of faith in him, and now she felt ill. And yet he waited, patient enough to give her the time to sort out her reaction.

Two months ago it wouldn't have occurred to her to want him to hold her. She hadn't known him then, and hadn't had anyone to rely on in so long that she'd forgotten what that was like. It was different now. She had the tantalizing prospect of having him near to support her, to care for her. She'd been certain last night that was what she wanted most, but then she'd learned one fact that had spun all of her newly formed plans out of control. She took a couple of breaths to calm herself, and said, "My father told me why he was exiled. It wasn't what I was told before."

Duilio regarded her with worried eyes. "You already knew you'd been lied to. Did this surprise you?"

She nodded. "Yes. I'd believed what I was told about him. I'd even visited with his mother and she didn't tell me the truth. They didn't want my life ruined the way his was, so they didn't tell me."

"Tell you what?" he prompted gently.

"That my mother was murdered. You see . . . if it all comes together the way I think it does, my mother was murdered because she knew something about a woman in the ministry. My father was exiled because he pressed for the ministry to investigate my mother's death. *That* was his crime."

Duilio licked his lips. "Secrets have a way of consuming lives. Does this have something to do with Maria Melo?"

He'd made that connection quickly. "When she came here to the house, she said my mother didn't know how to play the game."

"You think she killed your mother," he said, catching her implication.

"Yes, or it was done to protect her. It has to be her. There's something wrong with her, something my mother noticed."

It all came spilling out after that, everything her father had told her. He listened, his lips pressed together, until she reached the end of her words. Then he closed his eyes, brow furrowing. He was, she realized, trying to get his gift to tell him the answer. If he could only ask himself the proper question, surely he would *know*.

He opened his eyes and looked at her. "You're right. Eventually you will learn she was responsible."

At least I'm not crazy. "If she's planning to assassinate the prince, she's putting my people in danger. I don't know who's protecting her, who's giving her the authority to do these things, but they're acting against the interests of my people."

"That's why you need to return to the islands, isn't it?"

It was a relief that he understood. "Yes. She might be the one acting, but someone is sanctioning her acts. They gave permission to kill my mother, exile my father, and to execute me. Marina's legally dead, so she can't interfere there. I can't help but wonder if the farce surrounding her supposed death was done in part to assure that."

"Then again, *you've* been declared dead. You're not allowed to return. What can you do?"

"I don't know, but I'll think of something."

His hand settled atop hers. "We'll think of something."

We. He didn't even question involving himself in a matter that might cost him his life. "Duilio, you wouldn't like it there. Males don't have the same rights. It would be difficult for you. And if I'm expendable, you would be as well. I don't want you to get hurt in all this."

He shook his head. "That's not going to change my mind, Oriana. If you mean to tackle this hydra, then better you don't do it alone."

The Ministry of Intelligence was like a hydra, but there was one head of the beast who may still be in this city. "In the morning, I'm going to start looking for Maria Melo. Try to figure out who she is."

"I'll come with you," he said.

"No," she said firmly. "The people I need to speak with won't talk with you around, Duilio. I need to go alone."

He started to argue, but paused and asked, "Will you take the gun or . . . a knife? I'd worry less."

"I'll do that." She'd already decided the little revolver would fit into her handbag.

He took her hands in his own. "And you won't leave the city, not without me."

"I won't leave the city," she promised. "Not without you."

He smiled. "Good. This whole courtship process may not be settled, but you're not going to be rid of me easily."

Her heart swelled when he said that.

"How long, exactly," he went on, "does this courtship take?"

"Until both are sure that it's what they want." But he clearly had no doubts about taking her as his mate. He'd offered to make her his wife, even. She was the one dragging her feet. "It's only been two days, Duilio."

He lifted one of her hands to his lips, then turned it to press a kiss to her palm. "Yes, I'm impatient," he said, "but I will wait."

Oriana shivered. It still amazed her how he affected her. She raised her hand to his cheek and slid it around to draw him closer. His lips found hers and he surprised her by lifting her onto his lap, but that let her press closer. She felt the heat of his body against hers. She slid her hands inside his dinner jacket, running them down his sides.

She loved the way this felt, this warmth and closeness and that fevered need to press even closer. When she was touching him, all her worries slipped away. She believed this relationship would work and he wouldn't regret this in six months or two years or seven. It was as if the rest of the world and all its tangled webs of social expectations and politics no longer mattered. *Just the two of us.*

One of his hands lifted to her cheek again, then slid to touch her tightly braided hair. She could feel his fingers searching for her hairpins, and she laughed against his lips. "Let me do it."

She raised her arms to unpin her hair. His hands slid up her sides, sending a delicious shiver down her spine. Not content to wait for her to finish, he began kissing one side of her jaw, brushing close to her gill slits. She nearly dropped all the pins.

"Duilinho!" Felis' voice snapped from the doorway, startling both of them.

Duilio let Oriana go and she slid awkwardly from his lap back onto the sofa.

The elderly maid stormed across the room and cuffed Duilio's left ear hard enough that Oriana heard the pop.

"Behave yourself, boy!" She waggled one gnarled finger at him and grabbed Oriana's arm. Oriana rose, more out of surprise than anything else. "Come on, girl. You can't trust men to control themselves. They'll take advantage every time."

Oriana cast a helpless glance back at Duilio as the old woman dragged her away. He seemed torn between amusement and pain. By the time Felis had hauled her into the hallway, she heard him give in to laughter.

"Don't give a man anything until he's married you," Felis lectured as she pulled Oriana up the stairs. "That's all they're after, girl. Next thing you know he would have had your dress off. Yes, even Duilinho. I love the boy, but he's got the seal in him too. Not as bad as that Erdano, mind you. Still no excuse for putting his hands all over a trusting girl."

Trusting girl?

The tirade went on until Oriana was standing before her bedroom door. "Now lock it after you," Felis admonished, "or he'll try sneaking in here."

Oriana meekly went into her room and shut the door behind her, making a point of fetching the key and rattling it in the lock for Felis' sake. Then she leaned her back against the door and giggled. She should be grateful that Felis wanted to protect her honor. Having someone concerned for her was valuable.

But she'd been thoroughly enjoying herself. *What a shame.*

CHAPTER 25

Duilio and Joaquim stood in the hallway at the Royal Medical-Surgical School, waiting for the promised doctor to show up. Their inquiry here had taken far longer than they'd expected. Every doctor who might help them had to be fished out of a consultation, meeting, or class, and none so far had been able to help. They were waiting now on a Dr. Cruz, who'd attended the school in the same years as Dr. Teixeira, twenty years ago or more.

The officious clerk who'd been grudgingly helping them came striding back up the hallway toward them, a stern-looking older man in his wake. The gray-haired doctor looked down his narrow nose with a disdainful scowl. "Well, Officers, what do you need today?"

Joaquim patiently explained again that they were looking for information about a healer who'd visited the school years before to demonstrate his powers for the doctors. "Do you have any recollection of that?"

Dr. Cruz' jaw worked. "Yes, it was a farce—a waste of the students' valuable time. Why are you asking after ancient history?"

"We're following up on an earlier conversation with Dr.

Teixeira," Duilio inserted. "I believe he also witnessed that demonstration. Is there any record of the healer's visit?"

"I doubt it," the doctor said. "Professor Rocha—the one who arranged it—wasn't much of a record keeper. He was constantly losing papers and books."

"It would be very helpful," Joaquim tried, "if you could tell us anything about the healer who visited."

"I don't recall much, to be frank." The doctor crossed his arms over his chest. "He was a novice. I remember asking whether he was going to be a priest or a monk."

He? The doctor seemed sure about the healer's gender. Joaquim glanced over at Duilio as if seeking agreement, but they both knew what the next question should be. And they both knew the answer. Witches in the Church generally migrated to the same order.

"Do you recall what order?" Joaquim asked anyway.

"A Jesuit, of course," the doctor snapped. "Is that all, Officers?"

They'd come to the large house on Boavista Avenue that Anjos had rented for himself and the others of his team. The house sat across the wide avenue from the Dom Sebastião III Military Hospital. Built in a style favored in Spain, it had a small courtyard in the center, complete with a quince tree and a fountain on one wall. It had to have cost a small fortune, making Joaquim curious about the source of the funds. But it was spacious and served as both offices for their handpicked corps of two dozen or so Special Police officers as well as a dwelling for the four of them: Inspector Anjos, Inspector Gaspar, the Lady, and the frightening Miss Vladimirova. Perhaps it was just the Spanish blood in him, but Joaquim liked the house.

"There's no point in your approaching them," Anjos told them in a weary voice. He seemed to be having a difficult time catching his breath after climbing the stairs to join them. "They won't divulge anything about one of their number."

"I know a couple of the priests," Joaquim offered. "I might be able to approach them in an unofficial capacity."

Anjos looked doubtful. "I'll have the Lady make an official inquiry. She's been working with them for years. If they're going to give up anything, they'll give it to her."

The Lady's specialty was witchcraft, and she'd negotiated a tenuous truce between the Jesuits and the Freemasons. She had managed to keep the two groups working together in civility as they sought to unravel the web of spells left behind by Maraval's attempt to remake the world. If Anjos meant to use official channels, she would be the one to handle it. "Has Gaspar reported back in yet?"

Anjos took a deep breath, and then began coughing. He drew out a handkerchief and covered his mouth. Joaquim fought the urge to shrink back. Tuberculosis *was* contagious.

After a moment, Anjos had the coughing fit under control and tucked away his handkerchief. "Dr. Teixeira's secretary didn't report anything out of the ordinary in his schedule or his notes," he said as he lit a cigarette. "He did go out to lunch that day, meeting someone at a café on Santa Catarina Street. She didn't know who. Gaspar's gone to inspect the doctor's house."

Well, that didn't help. Joaquim took his leave of the ailing inspector, and he and Duilio made their way down the stairs to the ground floor. Joaquim stopped in the foyer, glancing up in time to see a black-draped figure watching them from a window across the courtyard. He shuddered and turned away, heading out into the street. It was overcast, but he felt better for being out of that woman's sight. "Did you see her?"

Duilio adjusted his frock coat, likely settling it over his holster again. "Yes. I felt that all over the back of my neck. I'd swear she was thinking about killing me."

Joaquim didn't argue. "She has barely enough power to stop him from dying, but when she kills something, she's stronger. That's probably why Gaspar decided she's not our killer. If she'd killed all these women, Anjos wouldn't look so bad."

Duilio shook his head. "The Lady told us she saved Anjos once before. He works with her, but does she strike you as caring about him? Or anyone?"

Miss Vladimirova's lack of emotion *was* eerie. Joaquim walked silently for a few steps, trying to decide whether he was slipping into gossip or merely discussing the case. But it was pertinent that Miss Vladimirova may have a motive to kill. "The rumor is that they are lovers—Anjos and Miss Vladimirova."

Duilio stopped and gaped at him. "No," he said in a flabber-gasted tone. "Truly?"

"It's true that the other officers *say* that," Joaquim allowed.

Duilio closed his eyes, concentrating. "Well, I'll be damned," he said a moment later.

"Duilio," Joaquim protested halfheartedly, "watch your tongue."

Nela ran a druggist shop on Bainharia Street, a narrow lane in the oldest part of the city. An exile rather than a spy, the old sereia woman had helped Oriana once before, despite the rules that forbade interaction between the two groups. Then again, Oriana wasn't a spy any longer. When she came inside, the old woman closed up her store, guaranteeing them privacy. "Now what brings you here this time, girl? The last time you were chasing a necroman-cer. I assume it was that Maraval?"

Oriana gave the woman a shortened version of what had hap-pened with Maraval's plan, and then told her about her near execu-tion. "So I'm hunting for this Mrs. Melo now," she finished. She described the woman to Nela, but Nela shook her head.

"I wish I could help you, girl," she said, "but I haven't heard of her. I can keep an eye out for her, if you think she's still a threat."

Oriana had spent much of the morning trying to track down other spies here in the Golden City. Most had refused to speak with her, but the two who had weren't any more helpful. They didn't know the name, nor had they recognized the woman's description. Oriana was beginning to think Maria Melo was a ghost.

"I do think she's a threat," Oriana told the old woman. "I think her secret mission is to assassinate the prince."

Nela brought over the pot of tea she'd had brewing, sat down at her table with its tea-stained cloth, and poured for both of them. She regarded Oriana over her cup of tea. "If so, that would be a catastrophe for our people. It doesn't make sense for the government to follow that path, so you're thinking that there's a faction within the ministry secretly supporting her."

Thank the gods that Nela had seen that possibility. It meant she wasn't unreasonable in her suspicions. "Exactly. But I still don't see the point."

Nela tapped one finger against her lips. "The question is who would profit. Who would most benefit by our going to war with Portugal?"

Oriana didn't have an answer.

Over dinner Duilio had divulged his and Joaquim's discoveries, along with a bit of gossip which, by comparison, made her day feel wasted. She'd gotten nowhere in her search for Maria Melo. Perhaps she was going about it all the wrong way, but she couldn't think of any other approach to finding the woman.

Fortunately she had one task tonight, and that was well within her abilities. She could surely locate Genoveva Carvalho and casually initiate a polite conversation. She armed herself for that by allowing Teresa to dress her hair and lay out her best gown.

The black dress was a fine one, certainly. The sleeves were puffed and the silk shantung had a luster that spoke of the high quality of the fabric. The silver satin cummerbund lent the outfit a dashing air that the high standing collar belied. It was well made, yet still suitable to a lady's companion. Oriana ran one of her hands down the front of the dress, admiring the sheen.

Teresa entered the room again, bearing a box in her hands, one too small to be another gown. "This got put in with Lady Ferreira's new dresses," she said. "It goes with yours."

Oriana crossed to the bed where Teresa laid the box and waited while the young woman opened it and spread the paper, revealing silver beading that sparkled in the dim light. "What is it?"

"A capelet," her maid said. "Felis says Lady Ferreira had this dress made to go with it."

Teresa lifted the item carefully out of the box.

It made sense of the choice of the silver cummerbund. The cape-let was meant to spread over the wearer's shoulders. Its beading simulated peacock plumes, only mostly in silver with the centers of the feathers rose and gold and burgundy. Teardrop pearls dangled from each multicolored plume, and Oriana saw the sparkle of gem-stones among the beads on the high collar. Surely those jewels were paste, not the real thing. Teresa unhooked the collar and held it out, waiting for Oriana to turn so she could set it in place.

She could argue that the capelet was too fine for her to wear. She *should*. It was too colorful, too eye-catching for a mere compan-ion. Oriana caught her lower lip between her teeth and turned about anyway.

Teresa set the overlay cautiously on her shoulders. It was surpris-ingly heavy, although with all that beading, she should have expected that. Teresa came around, closed the collar's hook, and grinned. "Felis says it's one of Lady Ferreira's older pieces, but the lady thought it would suit you. It does look good with your coloring, miss, and your hair."

Oriana licked her lips. This was Lady Ferreira's? She had trou-ble catching her breath for a moment. The chance that those spar-kling gemstones were paste had dropped dramatically.

Duilio fiddled with his silver cigarette case, wishing this whole night was over. He hadn't been out in society much in the last few weeks, partly because he wished to avoid Alessio's former lovers and partly because he hadn't had much enthusiasm for it. He'd been too worried about Oriana to spend his evenings listening to gossip and avoiding mothers desperate to find a wealthy husband for their daughter. But tonight he would have to wear his mantle of inane social hanger-on again, long enough for Oriana to catch Miss Carvalho and dissuade her from pursuing him.

Normally he didn't mind acting the fool for a night or two out of the week, passing among the aristocracy. Most thought him too stupid to pose any threat. They never gave him much notice as he stood on the edge of their world, talking as freely as they would in front of a potted orange tree. That had proven useful to the police. Even so, lately his enjoyment of these functions had dimmed.

But his mother was likely to cause a stir tonight, and the whispering behind fans might be fun to watch. She wore a new gown, a creation of silk in old gold with an overlay of cream-colored lace, the neckline framing her necklace of yellow diamonds. While many widows went draped in black for the remainder of their lives, when a woman decided to remarry, it was customary for her to leave mourning behind. His mother's choice of gold would be seen as a sign that she intended to find a new husband . . . or already had one in mind.

Duilio sighed and slid the cigarette case back into his jacket. Then he saw Oriana coming down the stairs, one of his mother's most prized possessions about her neck and shoulders. It had been a gift to her from his father on their tenth anniversary, and there was a small fortune in white diamonds studding the collar. "Mother, does she know where that came from?"

His mother's eyes flicked toward him. "I wanted her to have it. It suits her."

Yes, it certainly did. Not only did the beading on the capelet emphasize the burgundy tint in her hair, but he could only imagine how well all the silver beads matched the silvery scale pattern of her lower body. That thought brought forth a quick mental image of

Oriana wearing the capelet and nothing else, and Duilio had to remind himself that he was a gentleman and had promised he would wait. "Well, I can't argue that, Mother. It's as if it was made for her."

"It never suited my coloring so well."

True. His mother would have looked better in gold than silver, but his father hadn't been the most observant of men. Alexandre Ferreira had found the thing in Goa and purchased it to make up for one of his many infidelities. Oriana didn't need to know that part of its history.

Duilio went to the stairs to offer his arm. Oriana laid her hand on his sleeve, only the tips of her fingers visible beyond the edge of the silk mitts that hid her webbing. "You look lovely."

Oriana's eyes lowered. "If you picked any housemaid off the street, she would look lovely in this gown."

"Possibly," he said, "but I was speaking of you, not the gown."

She licked her lips nervously. "You look lovely, too."

Duilio smiled. "Thank you. I so rarely get told so."

She laughed, and then sobered. "I shouldn't be wearing this. It's too fine for a companion."

"Nonsense," his mother said from behind him. "I think it's perfect for you, and as you're *my* companion, it doesn't matter what anyone else thinks."

"Teresa told me this is yours, Lady," Oriana said.

His mother reached past him and straightened one of the beaded segments so that it lay smoothly along the black silk of Oriana's puffed sleeve, the pearls dangling down to her elbow. "I want you to have it, dear," his mother said. "Now, shall we go and get this performance over with?"

Oriana nodded jerkily, so Duilio laid one hand over hers and led her toward the door. The carriage already waited outside their gate, so they all made their way down to the street, and a couple of minutes later, they were on the way to the Simões house. Normally he would be mentally rehearsing his society chatter, trying to decide what to be when he arrived. But it didn't seem worth the effort at the moment. He spent the drive watching Oriana in the dim light of the carriage. He hoped she wasn't cursing him for getting her into this.

CHAPTER 26

Oriana sat in a chair next to Lady Ferreira, well aware of the speculative looks she was receiving from the matrons about them. It wasn't only that Lady Ferreira had appeared in public without her mourning garb. No, *she* was being watched because of her attire, too. Oriana raised her chin, determined not to flinch under their regard. She fixed her eyes on the center of the room, where a small group danced to the music of an eight-piece orchestra, Genoveva Carvalho among them.

Oriana watched the younger woman for a moment. Miss Carvalho was, without any question, a graceful dancer. It was a skill Oriana didn't have herself—her wide feet were made for swimming, not dancing. Lady Carvalho sat a few seats away and occasionally leaned close to speak to Lady Ferreira, so Oriana suspected she could snag the younger woman's arm when she came back to her mother's side after the set of dances.

Unfortunately, after that set ended, another gentleman arrived to sweep Miss Carvalho back onto the dance floor before Oriana had a chance to catch the younger woman's eye. She would have to bide her time. She glanced around the ballroom and saw Duilio near the far wall, chattering away at the corpulent Count of Viana, who wasn't making much effort to hide his boredom with his conversational companion. Duilio's hand—the one not holding a champagne glass—was waving in a slow circle as he talked, a sure sign that he was rambling on endlessly about nothing. It was a particular talent of his, one which served to convince many people that he had nothing other than feathers in his head. And how was he explaining the bruises on his cheekbone and jaw? She guessed the explanation involved walking into a wall. Or a tree—that would be more colorful.

For one second, Duilio's eyes met hers across the ballroom, and he winked. The count didn't seem to notice. Oriana hid a smile behind one hand.

The rustle of fabric warned her, and she glanced up to see the black-draped form of Lady Pereira de Santos approaching. The lady gestured to the empty chair next to Oriana. "May I sit down, Miss Paredes?"

There was no point in fighting this. "Of course, my lady."

The lady settled gracefully, half turning in the seat to face Oriana. Evidently they were going to have a conversation. "I'm grateful, Miss Paredes," the lady said softly. "I know you've no reason to like me, but I hope we can get along."

She hadn't expected the woman to say that. *Think it*, perhaps, but not say it. "I would like that, my lady, for my father's sake. And my sister's. She thinks very highly of you and your daughter."

The lady smiled. "Dear Marina. She does tend to pitch her entire heart into things, doesn't she?"

Oriana choked back the laugh that threatened to spill out. Clearly Lady Pereira de Santos knew Marina well. "I'm afraid so."

The lady shifted on the dainty chair and gazed out at the dance floor. Her tall daughter Ana stood to one side of a gaggle of girls, ignored as always. "Tell me, Miss Paredes. Should we be concerned about this young man Marina has decided to idolize?"

Oriana almost balked at the lady's interference. But if she was going back to the islands, who would watch over Marina but her father and this woman? She could tell the woman a great deal about Joaquim, but settled for saying, "He's a good man, my lady. There's no need to be concerned."

"Ah," the lady said. "He's asked to escort her to Mass on Sunday."

Oriana glanced over at Duilio, who was now boring another gentleman—Mr. Remigio. It would never have occurred to Duilio to escort her to Mass, which said a great deal about the difference between him and his cousin—no, his half brother. And about her as well, she supposed. "Marina will enjoy that."

"I believe so." The lady twitched one of the folds of her heavy black skirt. "You are looking particularly well tonight, Miss Paredes. Do you not dance?"

"I'm afraid not, my lady," she said. "In truth I've only come to speak to someone, and then we'll leave."

The lady surveyed the dance floor again. "To whom?"

"Miss Carvalho," Oriana admitted, gesturing toward the dance floor with her chin. "A personal matter."

"I see. After this dance, shall I fetch her for you?" The lady leaned closer. "Because otherwise I suspect she'll avoid you all night."

Oriana had to admit she was right. "That would be very helpful, my lady."

The lady touched Oriana's knee with gloved fingers. "I'll bring her back this way, and you can join us."

Oriana watched the lady rise and walk around the edge of the dance floor. *Everything* tonight would cause gossip. Now she'd been singled out by the daughter of a duke, and planned to converse with a young woman above her station. At least Lady Pereira de Santos would bring Miss Carvalho to her, which would make it seem less like she was hunting the other woman. Oriana folded her hands in her lap and tried very hard not to attract any more notice.

Lady Ferreira smiled, patted Oriana's knee, and softly said, "Everything will be fine."

Oriana nodded gratefully at her. Lady Ana had joined her mother and, when the dancing stopped, the duo somehow managed to be right next to Miss Carvalho and her young partner. Lady

Pereira de Santos engaged the young man in conversation, and a few seconds later he was leading Lady Ana—who stood half a hand taller than him—onto the dance floor. Lady Pereira de Santos chatted with Miss Carvalho as they headed back toward where Lady Carvalho sat. Oriana rose and began threading around the side of the dance floor toward them. She could tell the moment when, as the music began again, Genoveva Carvalho saw her coming. The girl flinched, but Lady Pereira de Santos kept her hand on the younger woman's arm.

"Miss Paredes," the lady said as Oriana neared. "You should take my place. I feel the need to sit down."

"Of course, my lady," Oriana said. She indicated to Miss Carvalho that they should walk on and, after a few steps, Lady Pereira de Santos wandered off to where the matrons were gathered. Oriana walked at Miss Carvalho's side in an uncomfortable silence. As she'd hoped, Miss Carvalho was too well bred to make any fuss in public, so they strolled around the end of the dance floor where Oriana spotted a pair of balconies, hidden behind heavy draperies. "Would you be willing to step out onto the balcony with me? Only for a moment."

"Certainly," Miss Carvalho said hesitantly.

Oriana drew aside the draperies, opened the glass door, and stepped out onto the balcony, the younger woman trailing her. These balconies faced out onto the Street of Flowers, and the smell of the damp cobbles filled Oriana's nose. It was chilly, but she didn't think they would be there long. When the draperies fell back, concealing them from the dancers, Oriana turned to her companion. "I need to speak with you about Mr. Ferreira."

Duilio watched Oriana walk along the edge of the ballroom with Miss Carvalho. He slipped farther back from the edge of the dance floor, hoping their conversation wouldn't cause too much of a stir. He'd spoken to a few gentlemen, boring them adequately to drive them away. Fortunately he was alone now. He took a sip of his wine, leaned back against the wall, and nearly leapt out of his skin when a voice spoke by his ear.

"I'm glad I caught you," the infante said in a low voice.

Duilio turned to face his previously unseen companion. The infante was dressed in clothes more suited to a casual dinner than this ball. "God above. What are you doing here, Raimundo?"

"Better keep your voice down," the infante said, smirking at his surprise. "People can't see us, but if we're overheard it would raise questions as to why the empty corner is talking."

Duilio shook his head in disgust. Yes, he'd been correct about the infante's talent. It was like the Lady's. Making certain to keep his voice quiet, he asked, "You're related to her, aren't you?"

The infante, his eyes on the few dancers in the center of the room, smiled. "You mean my aunt? Yes. I wondered how long it would take you."

That helped explain how the Lady and her associates had come to be serving the infante. "What are you doing here?" Duilio asked again.

"In truth, I wasn't planning on coming, but since I'd left the palace anyway, it seemed expedient."

The infante had a gift for talking yet leaving out anything meaningful. He would make an excellent politician. "Why leave the palace?"

The infante glanced at him. "My brother left. Middle of the afternoon on a Tuesday. He never leaves the palace, so I had to wonder why. But I lost his carriage and don't know where he went. Thought I would make the best of it and come to the ball."

He made it sound as if he did this weekly, randomly visiting balls and spying on the guests. *Perhaps he does.* "How did you know the Simões family was hosting a ball?"

"I read the newspapers," the infante said with a shrug. "Have you given any thought to my request?"

Duilio sighed softly, watching as Miss Carvalho accompanied Oriana out onto a curtained-off balcony. That would raise eyebrows, but it was all the privacy they would be able to manage here tonight. "I discussed it with Miss Paredes. She needs to return to her people's islands. I honestly don't know how long we'll need to remain there, so I cannot commit myself."

"Ah," the infante said. "My uncle told me to expect that response when he and I discussed your future."

Now I am being baited. "Your uncle?"

"Miguel Gaspar."

Duilio decided he wasn't going to parrot the man any longer. He'd already guessed that the infante and the Lady had to be related, given the similarity between their gifts. She must be the infante's aunt, and Inspector Gaspar his uncle by marriage. The infante *wanted* him to know that. "I see. I assume they, and Anjos as well, work directly for you."

"Yes, they do. I dined with Gaspar earlier, which is how I knew you were coming here. I assume your Miss Paredes has personal concerns to iron out, related to her exile? But my understanding is that exiles can't return there," the infante said. "They are, essentially, dead."

Ambassador Alvaro must have divulged that. "That seems to be the case."

"I might be able to help, then," the infante said. "But we can discuss that later."

How could the infante help Oriana? Duilio took another sip of champagne, wishing the man wouldn't talk rings around him. "So you have your answer," he said. "Is that all you came for?"

Genoveva Carvalho looked as if she knew what Oriana intended to say, her eyes downcast. "Miss Paredes, I'm not unaware that . . . that he prefers you to me. And I do understand how men are. I . . . I know that men will . . ." She gazed down at the darkened street below, where a puddle of light from the streetlamp made the wet cobbles glisten.

Oriana had seen this girl face down Paolo Silva, so she was surprised by Miss Carvalho's tentativeness. "Yes?"

Miss Carvalho took a deep breath. "I know men have . . . other women. If he were to marry me, I wouldn't interfere between you . . ."

A flush of anger heated Oriana's body. She forced her hands to stay on the railing. Her nails were too short now to do much damage anyway. "Do not say another word."

Miss Carvalho's head lifted, eyes wide. She'd clearly heard the threat in her voice.

"If this were my home," Oriana said tightly, "I would have the right to rip your eyes out for intimating you mean to steal my mate." That wasn't exactly true—he wasn't her mate yet—but Miss Carvalho couldn't know that.

"Mate?" Miss Carvalho repeated weakly.

"Yes, he belongs to me." Oriana blew out a slow breath, trying to calm herself. Although Miss Carvalho already knew Oriana was a sereia, the girl was obviously unaware of the offense her suggestion would have sparked within sereia culture. "Courtship runs differently among my people, but have no doubt that he is mine."

"You've married? I didn't . . . I didn't know. I . . ." Miss Carvalho's mouth fell open, as if she'd just realized what she'd implied.

Oriana swallowed her ire. Miss Carvalho's incorrect assumption wasn't entirely her fault. In human society, marriage was the observable sanction of a relationship. Without it, everyone would always assume Duilio kept her as his *mistress*. Oriana hadn't made her claim on Duilio clear in *human* terms. No, she hadn't made a claim on him at all, had she? She licked her lips.

She needed to resolve that. As soon as possible.

She gazed down at the younger woman, and said gently, "He has asked me to marry him, Miss Carvalho, and it will be done as soon as we can make the necessary arrangements."

"Oh," Miss Carvalho said softly. "I hadn't seen any announcement in the papers, so I assumed . . ."

She would have to take care of that as well. "We've been busy, Miss Carvalho."

Miss Carvalho turned her gaze back down to the wet street, where two people now stood in the streetlamp's glow. "You must despise me."

Oriana sighed. "No, Miss Carvalho. Social convention prevents him from being clear about his intentions toward me, making it easy for you to misunderstand. At least you had the sense to pursue him, when most women in society don't recognize his true quality."

"Too late, though." Miss Carvalho laughed bitterly. "I always see the truth too late."

Oriana felt a surge of compassion for the young woman. How many things had *she* not seen until it was far too late? The truth about her sister? About her father? Even Duilio. It had taken her time to trust him. She touched Miss Carvalho's gloved hand where it lay on the railing. "We all make that mistake. Wait for a man who holds you first in his heart, Miss Carvalho."

The younger woman sniffed. "I don't have that luxury," she said. "I need to marry before . . ." She pressed the back of her hand to her lips, holding in a sob.

Oriana felt her shoulders slump. Now she felt cruel. She'd made the younger woman cry. Then again, if Miss Carvalho had hoped to marry Duilio just to protect herself from scandal, she deserved no better. "Are you with child?" Oriana asked bluntly.

Miss Carvalho's face rose, her brows drawn together. "No! Why would you . . . ?"

"Because when a young woman rushes to find a husband," Oriana said patiently, "it's usually because she's with child."

Miss Carvalho let out a choked laugh. "That's what my mother did," she said. "I'm never going to make that mistake. But he says he'll expose me, and Father doesn't want the scandal. If I don't marry quickly, he's going to force me to enter a convent. He says it's for my own good, but I don't want that."

Wasn't that the usual punishment for a girl pregnant out of wedlock? Oriana found this conversation more confusing by the moment. "Who's going to expose you?"

"The man who . . . the man my mother . . ."

Oh, now I understand. Too scandalous for a girl of Miss Carvalho's good breeding to say aloud. "Your *true* father?"

Miss Carvalho nodded jerkily. "He's been following me about, watching me. He wants . . . he wants me to . . ."

Oriana's eyes slid past their hands to where the couple in the streetlamp's light argued. It wasn't two women, Oriana realized abruptly, but a woman and a priest, his wide-brimmed hat hiding his features. The woman walked a couple of steps past him and turned back, snapping off a few indistinct words with an angry shake of her finger.

Oriana instinctively grabbed Miss Carvalho's arm and hauled her back to the shadows of the small balcony. The younger woman gasped in fright, and hid her face with one hand.

"Quiet!" Oriana hissed. What was making her heart race? She squinted down at the couple, trying to place what had set off her wary reaction. The woman's clothing was dark and austere, her hat plain. She could be a widow or perhaps a lady's maid or . . .

The woman glanced up toward the window where they stood, revealing a handsome face with strong dark brows.

Oriana felt the urge to hurt someone swell back through her senses. She let go of Miss Carvalho, shoved the draperies out of her way and ran inside, cutting straight across the ballroom floor.

"No, I primarily came to apologize to you," the infante said. "I find that you're less useful to me in this particular guise."

Duilio chased that around in his head for a second. "Apologize for what, Your Highness?"

The infante chuckled. "I had Anjos . . ."

Cries of protest sounded from the dance floor. Duilio turned in time to see Oriana shoving her way through the dancers. She ran out of the ballroom and toward the stairwell.

Cursing, Duilio shoved his wineglass into the infante's hand and dashed after her around the edge of the dancing.

Oh, God! We are going to be in every newspaper in the city in the morning.

But it was too late to pretend insouciance, not when he was pushing through the crowd about the ballroom's door. Duilio reached the stairwell in time to see Oriana run across the marble floor of the foyer and shove on the front door. A footman jogged to intercept her. Duilio bolted down the stairs, shouting at the footman to stay back. He reached Oriana just as she managed to haul the heavy door open.

She barely even spared him a glance. Holding her skirts high with one hand, she ran down the steps and into the wet street toward a spot where a lamp spread its light in the darkness. She peered up the street and then down. "Damn! She was *here*, Duilio. She was right here."

He didn't need to ask. She had to mean Maria Melo. "Did she see you?"

Oriana looked at him for the first time. "Yes. I think so."

"She must have run, then." He surveyed the traffic. Pedestrians always moved along the Street of Flowers at night, but most preferred to wait for the tram, especially if the cobbles were wet and tricky. There were a handful of carriages coming and going, but nothing out of the ordinary. "No telling where she went. What was she doing out here this time of night?"

Oriana still held up the hem of her skirt. "She was talking to a man. A priest. He wore a cassock."

And the back of a cassock wouldn't tell them anything. Then again, what would a priest be doing out at this hour talking with Mrs. Melo? "A plain cassock? Black or brown?"

Oriana shook her head. "I wasn't looking at *him.*"

No, of course not. Duilio pursed his lips, and then scowled as the rain started up again—a quick, heavy downpour. He grabbed Oriana's arm and drew her toward the house.

"I can't go back in there," she protested. "They must all think I'm mad."

Since she'd been talking with Miss Carvalho, the gossips would surely think that young woman had said something to overset Oriana. His running after her would probably confirm that in their eyes. It would be the scandal of the month. Well, perhaps two weeks. "I'll send for the carriage. We can wait in the foyer."

He led her up the stairs and inside the house again. Her hair had partially come down in her flight from the ballroom, her braid loosened from its pins. The hem of her lovely gown was marred with grit from the street. And they were both of them rather wet now. Duilio beckoned over one of the footmen and asked him to summon their driver. As the footman left, Duilio saw his mother descending the stairs in a stately fashion on their host's arm, lending a belated touch of decorum to their sensational retreat from the Simões ball.

Duilio turned back to Oriana, who was trying to shake some of the grit off her hem. "You're sure it was her?"

Oriana's eyes lifted to meet his. "Absolutely."

CHAPTER 27

O riana strode up the walkway and into the warmth of the house. She felt worn and frustrated now. She'd managed to thoroughly upset Miss Carvalho, make a scandal of herself and Lady Ferreira by association, and alert Maria Melo to the fact that Oriana Paredes wasn't dead. All that and she'd gained *nothing* in return.

Fortunately, Lady Ferreira had taken her appalling conduct in stride. In the carriage on the way down the Street of Flowers, she'd laughed over the precipitous end to their evening and dismissed Oriana's attempted apologies. Duilio, sitting on the bench facing them, had worn a pensive look on his face but hadn't contradicted his mother's lack of concern.

As soon as she crossed the threshold, Lady Ferreira announced her intention to go on to bed. Oriana followed more slowly.

Duilio came abreast of her as she walked up the stairs. "Did you have success with Miss Carvalho?"

"Yes," she said, "although I walked into a different pit of eels."

His brows drew together as he stepped up onto the landing. "What?"

"Miss Carvalho is being blackmailed, I think, and she hoped that marriage might save her from either dishonor or the convent." She stopped outside her bedroom door. Lady Ferreira had already disappeared into her own room. "Pinheiro was right about her father pushing her to pursue you, so it wasn't necessarily about you."

He actually looked crestfallen. "I've been put in my place, haven't I?"

Oriana heard Cardenas locking the front door for the night. She opened her bedroom door, stepped inside, and grabbed Duilio's arm before he could get away. "Quickly," she said. "Before Cardenas comes up the stairs."

Duilio didn't fight her urging. He came in, shut the door behind him, and turned the gaslights near the door higher. "Felis is going to box my ears again if she finds out."

"Then don't tell her," Oriana told him.

He glanced toward her dark dressing room. "Where's Teresa?"

"I told her not to stay up. I'm capable of undressing myself, you know."

"I have no doubt of that," he said wisely.

Her heartbeat was throbbing in her ears now. She didn't know what she was doing. Well, she did know *what* she was doing, but she didn't have any experience at it. She began to pick apart her damp braid with trembling fingers. "I wanted to talk to you."

His lips twisted into a smug smile. "I would never have guessed."

She shoved her loose hair back over her shoulder. "About what Miss Carvalho said."

"Ah, yes, that I'm not even her second choice," he said. "I'm merely convenient."

"Don't pretend your feelings are hurt when all you wanted was to escape her."

"Just because I don't want her," he said, "doesn't mean I like hearing she doesn't want me."

Oriana gave him a flat look.

He heaved an offended sigh. "Very well, what is she being blackmailed over?"

"That's not important," she said. "I meant the part where she thinks I'm your mistress."

"Pulling me into your bedroom doesn't help dispel that notion, Oriana."

"On the contrary. I was being shortsighted, because our relationship will undoubtedly be interpreted that way by your peers."

"I'm not concerned about their interpretations," he said.

"I am." She tugged off her mitts and tossed them onto the low table set before the settee. "Since you don't have a wife, women like Miss Carvalho think they have license to pursue you. So I told her we intend to marry, and as soon as possible."

A smile curved his lips. He drew her closer, one hand under her elbow. "Did you actually mean that, or were you only saying so to put her off?"

Oriana took a deep breath. "I want to make my claim on you clear. Here in Portugal that means marriage."

"So you've decided you do want to claim me?" His fingers ran along her jaw and down across her gill slits.

Oriana shivered and her eyes drifted shut. Until Duilio, she'd had no idea what it was to want a man—not like this. It was as if he'd exposed an entirely different woman buried under the hard shell of isolation she'd always worn. She caught his musky scent under the smell of his shaving soap and wanted to lean closer to taste his skin. But she stepped back, took a careful breath, and said, "Yes. I am willing, if you want me."

When she opened her eyes, he was regarding her with his brows drawn together. "You said that before. Is that part of a ritual?"

"Yes," she whispered.

His expression didn't change. "And what does the man respond? What should I say?"

So much for the romance of the moment. "I do, perhaps?"

"Ah, that makes sense." His hands settled around hers, cupping her fingers. "Would you be willing to try one more time?"

Oriana kept her eyes on his hands. "I am willing, if you want me."

"I do," he said in return. And after a moment of silence, "What happens now?"

Oriana finally found the nerve to look him in the face. "What do you think happens?"

His eyes narrowed. "Is this where the elephants come in? Because there was something about elephants in that French book."

"Duilio," she began, exasperated.

"Did I mistranslate something?" He sounded perfectly serious, but the sly smile on his lips gave away his mirth. "I don't own any elephants, but I don't want that to cause problems."

"Where would my people get elephants?"

"Someone somewhere uses elephants," he said with his brow furrowing.

What? "Is 'elephant' some new slang men are using?"

"No, but it truly should be. I like it," he said musingly. "Perhaps I can start a fashion, although I'm not certain to what I should apply the euphemism."

Duilio chattered when he was trying to set someone at ease, so all this nonsense must be for her benefit. She pinched his palm. "Stop being silly."

His face went serious. "Should I go?"

He was offering her a chance to put him off. Oriana grabbed his hand and drew him closer instead. He came willingly enough and kissed her, his body pressing hers into the door as it had the day before in the library. After a second, though, he pulled away . . . only far enough that his fingers could reach the buttons of his coat.

She helped tug it off his shoulders, feeling breathless. "Do you realize I've never seen you unclothed?"

He glanced up, his eyes laughing. "You caught me with my shirt off once."

"You've seen me several times," she pointed out. "Completely unclothed. It's not fair."

"It doesn't count when you're in the water." He undid the cape-let's hook at her throat and carefully laid the beaded confection over the back of the leather chaise.

She sat to take off her slippers and stockings, and he settled next to her. When their shoes sat neatly aligned at the end of the chaise, he said, "Turn around and I'll undo your buttons."

She held her hair aside and his fingers nimbly opened the buttons down the back of her gown. His warm breath brushed her neck and his lips touched the few inches of skin he'd unveiled, which sent a shiver down her spine. His hand tightened on her waist. "You're not wearing a corset."

"I can't," she said, glancing at him over her shoulder. "My lungs are small, so I can't breathe if I do."

"Interesting," he said. "I should write that down."

"Later." She pulled away and stood to push the gown down over her hips. He stayed on the chaise, watching her, and she paused, feeling suddenly shy. Idiotic, since he *had* seen her nude before, several times. He'd held her naked in his arms. But he'd never watched her undress, and somehow that seemed far more intimate than the other. Or perhaps it was because she knew this would go further. Her mouth felt dry.

"Please," he said.

All her nervousness fled with that whispered request. If Duilio Ferreira was desperate enough to beg, she had nothing to fear.

Duilio swallowed. He'd promised her he would wait. He kept reminding himself of that. But if this was what she wanted, he wasn't going to quibble over whether this was appropriate behavior for a gentleman. He was *not* going to rush this either, no matter how much he wanted her.

Oriana let her fine new gown fall to the floor, stepped out of it, and picked it up to drape it over the armchair. She turned away from him, unbuttoning her corset cover. She slid that off her shoulders and tossed it over to the chair. Then she unbuttoned her underskirt and let it fall, leaving her in her camisole and drawers.

Duilio suddenly understood. She wasn't facing away from him out of shyness. She was permitting him to see her dorsal stripe, something she'd never intentionally done before. She'd always kept her bare back from view, hinting that there was a risqué aspect to a sereia's dorsal stripe. When she drew her camisole over her head, it bared the upper end of the stripe, a swath of black that came to a point between her shoulder blades. In the gaslight's flickering glow, Duilio could make out the rippled line of brilliant blue that separated the black of her stripe from the silver of her lower body. She untied the tapes of her drawers, pushed them down over her rounded hips, and let them fall.

That got him to his feet. The swath of glittering black rippled down her back, widest where it bisected each buttock, then tapering to a tip at each heel. He ran one hand along the blue edging and down to her waist. "Your stripe is beautiful," he whispered.

It was the right thing to say. She glanced over her shoulder at him, almost blushing. "Thank you. My best feature, I'm told."

He didn't want to think about how many men had previously told her so. He pulled her into his arms instead. "Are you sure of this?"

She gave him a knowing smile. "Please me."

His eyebrows lifted. *Yes, that's definitely an order.* "I'll do my very best."

CHAPTER 28

WEDNESDAY, 29 OCTOBER 1902

Dressed in one of her new ensembles—a rose-colored blouse and darker jacket over a full burgundy skirt—Oriana sat down on the edge of the bed. She touched Duilio's hair, but he barely moved in response. "Duilio, wake up."

That didn't rouse him either. He was evidently one of those people who didn't wake well. Admittedly, he hadn't gotten much sleep, for which she'd been partially responsible. She didn't feel particularly guilty about that. Oriana watched as he slept on, bemused by the fact that he was hers now. She wondered how long it would take her to become accustomed to the notion.

She had a lover. She had a *mate*. And a rather attractive one, too.

She levered herself down on the bed next to him to better see his face in the morning light. Even in his sleep, the corners of his mouth turned upward, as if his dreams were fine ones. His hair was too short to look overly disordered, but she was glad she'd had a chance to comb her own out before he saw it. His dark lashes lay against his skin. She wished she had such thick lashes. It must be a selkie trait. And his scent was more marked now, that warm smell of musk she found so intriguing. He would probably bathe immediately after rising and ruin it. There had been other women before her; she wondered if any had commented on it.

"You're rumpling your skirt," he mumbled.

Oriana shifted away to look at his face again, but he wrapped one arm about her waist and drew her closer to nuzzle her neck. "Duilio," she protested, "you'll have to get up sooner or later."

He pulled away again, his eyes dancing with laughter. His lips remained pressed closed though, as if he didn't dare let out whatever clever quip he had in his head.

She couldn't decide what he was holding in, and he didn't say.

Instead he reached across and ran a finger across her lower lip, and softly said, "Mine."

That assumption of ownership made her laugh. "It doesn't work that way. You belong to me now, not the other way around."

He rolled halfway atop her, pinning her by throwing one bare leg over her skirts. "Is that why you wanted to have it your way? So you would have the upper hand?"

From his tone he was joking, but she hadn't considered it in that light. "No, I honestly hadn't thought of that. But if I marry you, will I not have to promise to obey you?"

"If?" he asked. "There is no *if*, Oriana."

"When," she amended.

He touched her cheek. "You should know by now I would never try to hold you to that. I might . . . suggest, but no more."

"So if we ever get to the islands, you'll be a dutiful mate?"

"I'll do whatever you want," he promised rashly.

That was an enticing offer. "Will you grow your hair longer?" she asked. "Males don't wear their hair this short back there."

He returned to nuzzling her neck. "Hmmm. I could do that."

"You'd have to wear a pareu, of course." She'd told him about the traditional garb on the islands before, essentially no more than a length of fabric secured at the waist. He'd sounded intrigued, but then it had been a distant possibility. "And all the appropriate jewelry," she added, wondering how far she could get before he balked. "And you'll have to be tattooed as well. . . ."

That got his attention. "Tattooed?"

"A line tattoo," she explained, "so women will know which family you belong to."

He blinked down at her for a moment. "Where?"

She laid one hand over his heart. "Here."

For a moment, his eyes were serious. "I can do that."

She'd expected him to refuse. "We'll see."

He shifted his weight over to free one hand and ran a finger over her lips. "We could stay here today."

"You're wrinkling my skirt," she chided him.

"I want to see what your stripe looks like in the daylight." He leaned down to kiss her anyway. She laid her hands flat against his back, his bare skin warm under her fingers. For a time she let herself be lost in the joy of feeling his lips against her throat, what little of it was bared for his touch.

A strangled screech from the other side of the room—followed by the unmistakable sounds of china clattering on a tray and the door slamming shut—broke the warmth that enfolded them.

Duilio, still half atop her, wore a sheepish expression. "We didn't lock the door, did we?"

"No." She grimaced. "Teresa brings me coffee in the morning to help me wake up."

Duilio shifted onto his side again, his leg sliding off her. He rolled onto his back and ruefully said, "That is the first time I've shown my bare ass to any of the servants since I was about five years old."

Yes, that particular part of his anatomy would be the first thing Teresa saw. Oriana didn't know how she was going to face the maid after this. She scrambled off of the bed and gazed down at Duilio. He had one arm thrown over his face, hiding. "Well, now you have to get up."

He exhaled dramatically. "I suppose I'd better explain to Cardenas."

Even if Teresa said nothing, the staff would all figure it out eventually. How was he going to explain to them about spending the night in her room? This wasn't the same as when she'd been ill. They'd been willing to overlook his behavior then, but now? "I'll talk to Teresa," she offered.

"No, I'd better go straight to the top." Duilio rolled off the bed, got to his feet, and stood before her. "And now you can't say you've never seen me unclothed."

She smiled but didn't comment as he began to don his discarded garments from the night before. Everything that came to her mind to say would probably cause them to end up back in that bed . . . with neither of them eating breakfast. And she was quite hungry.

She eyed the coffee tray abandoned on the table next to the door. Miraculously, it looked as if nothing had broken. The bed was far more rumpled than she usually left it—there was no hiding that she hadn't been alone in it last night—and his bed would be untouched. She wasn't certain how he was going to explain it to Cardenas in a way that would appease the staff, but Duilio seemed confident he could smooth things over. She would have to trust him.

Although dressed, Duilio hadn't bothered with his shoes. He clutched them in one hand and beckoned her over to the door. "Will you look to see if the hallway is empty?"

She was impressed by his foresight. "Are you practiced at this?"

"No, I'm practical." He motioned toward the door with his head. Oriana went to look outside, but Duilio stopped her. He kissed her once more and let her go. "Couldn't help myself."

Oriana rolled her eyes and then peered out into the hallway. She didn't see anyone, so he slipped out her door and then out of her sight. Breakfast seemed a very long way away now.

Duilio felt starved. He was often hungry as it was, but he'd been awake half the night. Ignoring an affronted Marcellin, he bathed quickly and dressed in a casual tunic and trousers. Then he went to hunt down Cardenas before too much gossip spread below-stairs. He kept an eye out for Felis on his way, since she seemed to have a special sense that warned her whenever he did anything improper.

Cardenas harrumphed, but wasn't surprised by his misbehavior. The butler promised he would talk to Teresa, and Duilio hoped that would be an end to it, although he doubted he would be that lucky. When he got downstairs to the dining room, he found Oriana already there. She caught her lower lip between her teeth and tilted her head in his mother's direction as if to warn him. He nodded to the footman and took his usual seat.

His mother regarded him blandly. "Duilinho, honestly, a little discretion would have been preferable to cleaning up afterward."

So his mother *had* heard. That explained Oriana's cowed look. Household gossip certainly traveled quickly. Duilio shook his napkin out and laid it in his lap. "Has Oriana informed you that we've decided to marry?"

His mother's brows rose. "Yes. Don't change the topic, dear. My point is that I expect *not* to have a repeat of this morning's events until after the wedding."

Duilio stole a glance at Oriana, who gazed fixedly at her plate. She had one hand over her mouth, but her dark eyes danced. "Yes, Mother," he said. "I'll be discreet."

His mother picked up her newspaper in one hand and her coffee in the other. "That's all I wanted to hear."

The footman brought his regular breakfast and Duilio, after deciding he wasn't going to catch Oriana's eye, started in on his food. He had the feeling that if Oriana could blush, she would be doing so. His mother hadn't been forbidding him to share Oriana's bed. She just wanted him not to get *caught* again. "Have the two of you decided when the wedding will be?"

His mother put her paper aside. "If you're not averse, I thought it could be done next Saturday morning, the eighth. I believe Father

Januario would be amenable, human or not, and we're planning on having both families at the house that evening anyway."

Ah yes, the dinner party. Oriana didn't flinch at the hurried date, so Duilio guessed that she and his mother had been discussing this before his arrival. He picked up the newspaper that lay next to his plate and turned it to the social page. "I'm not averse, Mother. Whatever you and Oriana decide is fine."

"You'll need to send an announcement to the papers," his mother said. "*This* morning. And notify your man of business."

"Yes, Mother," he said absently, his eye captured by his own name printed on the page in front of him, among the columns of social gossip.

He'd fully expected to see his name in the paper this morning. He had. He'd expected to see a clever quip or two regarding Oriana and himself and Miss Carvalho.

What he hadn't expected was an entire column dedicated to a blatantly laudatory discussion of Duilio Ferreira and how he had spent the last six years working with police forces across Europe and here in the Golden City. It went on to talk about his involvement in the investigation of *The City Under the Sea*, even mentioning Oriana at one point. He stared at the page, aghast.

"Duilinho?" his mother said, sounding as if she'd repeated that a couple of times now. When he glanced up at her, she asked, "What's wrong?"

He handed the paper over to her. "I think the infante is responsible for this."

"For what?" Oriana asked as his mother surveyed the page.

"I've been exposed." He puffed out his cheeks, unsure whether he was upset about this or not. "I'm not going to be very popular in social circles for a while, I expect."

"Exposed?" Oriana repeated, eyes wide with worry.

"Sorry," he said quickly. She must think the article revealed his selkie blood. "Not in *that* way. Just that I work with the police."

"And look! You're called his *intrepid assistant*." His mother leaned across to show Oriana that line of the article. "See? Right there. That will undoubtedly cause people to rethink their interpretations of last night's abrupt departure from the ball."

"Oh, dear," Oriana said, taking the paper in her own hands. "You think the infante did this? Why would he?"

"He said something to me last night about my not being useful as I was. He had Anjos do . . . something. I've forgotten exactly how he worded it. But he apologized, so this must be his work."

His mother tapped her cheek. "The infante was at the ball last night? You neglected to mention that."

"Yes," he said, "although you shouldn't spread that about, Mother." They'd discussed Oriana's sighting of the Melo woman last night on the short drive back to the house, and after arriving home, he'd been distracted by Oriana herself. "He was more forthcoming than usual, and handed me some interesting information, although I don't know that it's pertinent."

Oriana was scanning the article again, as if she didn't quite believe the words printed on the page.

"Where was the infante?" his mother asked. "I didn't see him, although I'm not sure I would recognize him."

"Ah," Duilio said. "He shares the Lady's gift for disappearing. She's his aunt."

"The lady without a name?" His mother's lips pursed. "I barely remember the infante's mother, but I suppose there's some resemblance."

Oriana lifted her eyes from the paper. "Did you actually single-handedly find the murderer of this French duke?"

"Well, yes." Duilio shrugged. "The gendarmes had settled on his valet for the murder and threw him in prison without further investigation. My gift kept telling me he wasn't the killer, but since I hadn't told them I was a witch, I couldn't tell them that. I just kept looking until I found the actual culprit. Even proven innocent, Marcellin had no chance of employment after being accused of such a crime, so I took him on. I suppose those details about my time in France and Great Britain came from Alessio."

Oriana tossed the paper onto the table. "Well, they don't say how I came to be your assistant. What will we tell people about that?"

"That after my mother hired you to be her companion, you figured out that I worked with the police and offered your assistance?"

Cardenas came in, a salver in hand. "This was delivered for you, Mr. Duilio."

Duilio picked up the note, broke the seal, and read it. "Inspector Anjos is requesting our help today," he said. "I'm including *you* in that, Mother."

She grinned. "Do I get to be your assistant as well?"

I am never going to live this down. Never. "Apparently Anjos needs to discuss something delicate with Lady Carvalho, and thinks your presence might ease the way."

"With *Lady* Carvalho?" Oriana asked.

"That's what it says." Duilio wondered if there could be some link between the "delicate matter" to be discussed and the blackmail Oriana had mentioned last night. He could see Oriana was wondering the same. "I suppose we'll find out what this is about at eleven."

Lady Carvalho didn't refuse to see his mother, but sent down word she wasn't yet prepared to receive visitors, so the butler led them to the front sitting room to wait. Not only were the three of them waiting there, but Anjos and Gaspar had met them at the Carvalho house as well.

The front sitting room of the Carvalho house wasn't as garishly decorated as the library, but featured the same clashing colors, this time coral and pink floral upholstery that must surely be driving his tasteful mother to distraction. Then again, Lady Carvalho was her friend, and she was usually tolerant of the woman's foibles. Oriana and his mother sat on one of the loud couches, talking together, possibly plotting the details of the upcoming wedding, although from his mother's serious expression, Duilio doubted that. Perhaps they'd moved on to Miss Carvalho's blackmailer instead.

Gaspar came to stand near him, giving Duilio a chance to survey the Cabo Verdean inspector. The infante had told him that Gaspar was married to the Lady, but neither of them had ever mentioned that interesting fact. Duilio guessed they'd kept it secret because the inspector was *mestiço*—half African and half Portuguese. His marriage to a Portuguese lady, while it wouldn't be too sensational back in Cabo Verde or even down in Lisboa, would likely cause gossip in more conservative Northern Portugal. And while Duilio might be a half-breed himself, it wasn't the same. Selkie blood wasn't visible in the way that African blood was. He suspected Gaspar had to endure discrimination on occasion . . . or perhaps more than occasionally.

Gaspar returned his regard, one dark brow lifting speculatively. "So I see that you and Miss Paredes . . ."

His words trailed off, but Duilio had no doubt what the man was intimating. He felt a flush creep up his cheeks. While the infante seemed to enjoy confusing him, Gaspar preferred to shock. "Can you actually *see* that?"

Gaspar folded his arms over his chest and leaned one shoulder against the wall. "Yes. One of the more amusing aspects of my talent. There's a visual tie left behind that I perceive, although it's difficult to describe."

Now *that* would take some serious contemplation. There was a tie created when two people became lovers? "My brother must have been in the center of a web at all times."

"Some people are like that," Gaspar said. "I tend to keep my distance. They're often catastrophes waiting to happen."

What must it be like to know everything about every person he meets? Duilio guessed that was why he perceived Gaspar as old, even though the man was only five years his senior. He shook his head. "Did Anjos tell you the healer Dr. Teixeira saw all those years ago was a Jesuit?"

"Yes, although it's more pertinent that he's *male*," Gaspar said. "Male healers are fairly rare. I believe this solves a mystery I've been pondering since the first time I visited this house."

Duilio regarded him with a furrowed brow. He hadn't made the connection before, but he had an idea now why they were at the Carvalho house. Lady Carvalho's appearance at the doorway prevented him from asking Gaspar for clarification.

Lady Carvalho was the daughter of a noble family and near fifty like his own mother, but she hadn't aged as well. The yellow morning dress she wore made her seem washed out. Even so, she was a kind woman who'd always invited his mother to their family events despite the fact that his mother and father lacked noble pedigrees, and Duilio had always liked the woman better than her blustering husband. Lady Carvalho surveyed the inhabitants of her sitting room, wringing her hands together as if she were regarding her executioners. Then her quivering chin firmed. She entered the sitting room and ordered the butler to shut the door behind her.

His mother rose and crossed to Lady Carvalho's side. She took her friend's hand and drew her toward the sofa where she had been sitting with Oriana. "These gentlemen have come to talk to you, Luiza. It's a police inquiry, but I promise they'll be discreet."

Lady Carvalho sank down on the end of the sofa. "This is about Genoveva, I suppose."

Anjos came around the end of the sofa and sat in one of the chairs, several feet from the lady. "Indirectly, my lady," he said in a kind voice.

"I suppose he told you." Lady Carvalho's voice sounded dismayed. "He's been threatening to do so."

Yes, this was definitely about Genoveva Carvalho's blackmailer.

"He hasn't," Anjos said. "Inspector Gaspar has a special gift, one that allows him to see what gifts others possess. We've always known that Miss Genoveva is a healer, even though she seems unaware of it. As your husband isn't a healer, nor are you, that tells us your daughter is either adopted or had a different father."

Lady Carvalho pressed her hands together in her lap, knuckles white. "The second."

"Would he have been a Jesuit novice then?"

She shot a nervous glance at Duilio's mother.

She laid a hand over her friend's. "Luiza, I bore a child before I was married, so don't concern yourself about my opinion. No one needs to know about this."

"He's been threatening to reveal her if I don't send her to him to"—Lady Carvalho sniffed and tugged a handkerchief out of her sleeve—"to study his art. I don't want her around him, but he's going to ruin her reputation if we don't give in." She sniffed into her handkerchief. "On top of Constancia running away, it's too much. My husband is furious. He's threatening to send Genoveva to a convent instead."

"Oh, dear. Constancia has run away?" his mother asked gently.

Lady Carvalho took a deep breath. And then another. "Yes, she declared she was going to marry Tiago Coelho, and her father flew into a fury. So they ran to his family out in the country. They married last week."

Duilio couldn't help grinning when he imagined how much that would irritate belligerent Lord Carvalho. Tiago Coelho had been one of the family's footmen. A few weeks before, the young man had endured a severe beating trying to protect young Constancia. Despite his being a Freemason, whose prime tenets included Equality, Carvalho didn't epitomize that particular ideal. He'd probably been livid. No wonder Genoveva took his threat of the convent seriously.

His mother patted Lady Carvalho's hand. "I'm sure Mr. Coelho will do all he can to make Constancia happy."

Anjos waited until he had the lady's attention again. "Now, Lady Carvalho, we need to know everything you can tell us about this Jesuit. His name, what he looks like, where he's living. We need to find him."

Lady Carvalho sniffled again. "Why?"

"We need to speak with him regarding a death last week," Anjos said, choosing the least sensational route. "We believe he might have information."

"I don't know where to find him," she said. "I promise. He's come here three times, but I don't know where he's staying."

"Staying?" Anjos repeated. "He doesn't live here in the city?"

She shook her head. "I don't think so. He's only been coming around for a month. I don't know why he wouldn't have come before if he had been living here."

"And his name?"

"Pedro Salazar," the lady said softly. "I thought he was leaving the novitiate. He told me that, all those years ago. But then he left for Spain and didn't come back."

Well, they had a name now. Duilio still doubted the Jesuits would give them any information, much less help the police find the man. Lady Carvalho went on to describe a tall, lean man, just over fifty, with dark eyes and straight brown hair.

"He was brilliant, you know," she volunteered. "He believed that if healers and doctors worked together, anything could be accomplished. That illnesses could be defeated, injured parts could be replaced with new ones, and even the dead could be returned to life. That was why he went to Spain. There was a doctor there who wanted to work with him."

"Spain isn't very friendly toward witches," Duilio observed. "Why risk going there?"

"It was his *dream*," she said. "He was willing to sacrifice anything to chase it. His freedom, his life. Even me."

And a well-bred Portuguese girl who discovered she was with child would have to find a husband quickly—or enter a convent, as

Rafael Pinheiro's mother had done. Duilio doubted kindly Lady Carvalho had ever had much choice in her life after that.

"Does he still chase that dream?" Oriana asked.

"I don't know," Lady Carvalho whispered. "When he came here, I didn't let him stay long. He . . . his presence made my flesh crawl, as if there was something wrong about him—something evil. I can't imagine what, but I just wanted to run away."

Oriana leaned forward. "Miss Genoveva mentioned he'd been following her. Has he?"

"She told you?" Lady Carvalho asked, sounding amazed. "I don't allow her to go out alone now, because I fear he might steal her away."

Inspector Anjos nodded. "A wise decision, Lady Carvalho. I suggest you keep your daughter home until we have him in custody. We do suspect him of wrongdoing."

"What has he done?" she asked hesitantly.

Anjos seemed to consider for a moment. "Several young women have been murdered," he finally said. "We think he may be involved."

Lady Carvalho went whiter than before. She made the sign of the cross, covered her face with her hands, and sobbed. Lady Ferreira laid a consoling hand on her back. "You could not have known, Luiza, all those years ago."

"Wait a minute," Oriana said, looking over the back of the sofa at Duilio. "Miss Genoveva said he was following her. Last night when I saw Maria Melo, I pulled Miss Genoveva into the shadows. She seemed frightened, but at the time I assumed it was of *me*."

"The priest," Duilio inserted. "It was *him*." When Anjos gazed at him expectantly, Duilio clarified. "Pardon me. Last night from the balcony at the Simões house, Miss Paredes saw Mrs. Melo speaking to a priest. Miss Carvalho must have thought it was him."

Gaspar pushed away from the wall. "I think we need to ask Miss Genoveva, then."

Lady Carvalho rose, handkerchief clutched in her hands. "I'll go up for her."

With that, the lady left the room, while Anjos rubbed fingers against his temples as if his head ached. "So now we have two people we can't find," he said, "one of whom is tied to the deaths of the prostitutes, and one of whom is a spy who might or might not be an assassin. But apparently they're dealing together."

I'm missing something important, Duilio thought.

"Could Mrs. Melo be choosing victims for him?" Oriana asked. "After all, that was her function within the Open Hand."

"His victims are random," Anjos said softly. "Women one might find on the street alone late at night. They might believe a priest trustworthy and walk in his company, making it an excellent guise for a murderer."

"If he was on the street last night," Oriana said, "might he not have been looking for another victim?"

Yes, they would have to check the morgue later. Duilio hadn't talked to Joaquim so far this morning, so he hadn't heard anything. "And what does either of them have to do with the murdered nonhuman girls?" he asked.

"To our knowledge, nothing." Anjos rose when Lady Carvalho appeared on the threshold of the room, a red-eyed Miss Carvalho behind her. Oriana rose to let Genoveva have space on the couch, and Anjos stood until the women settled. He offered Oriana the chair in which he'd been sitting, but she shook her head and went to stand next to Duilio instead. "Now, Miss Carvalho," Anjos said as he sat again, "I believe your mother told you what we were discussing."

Genoveva lifted her chin. "Yes, Inspector. I was on the balcony at the Simões ball, and saw that man in the street below. He's been following me frequently for the last two weeks."

Anjos leaned closer. "We believe you're in danger from him, Miss Carvalho."

"How so?" she asked.

"When a healer goes bad," Anjos said, "they can kill with a touch. This man must not come anywhere near you or anyone in this household. Do you understand?"

Anjos might be using a gentle tone, but he'd delivered the truth in the bluntest terms. Miss Carvalho nodded jerkily, her shoulders rigid and her spine straight. "I understand."

Duilio was glad the girl seemed to grasp the seriousness of the threat.

"Now, I believe we've learned what we needed," Anjos said. "Is there anything you can think of that might tell us where to find this man?"

Miss Carvalho shook her head slowly. Anjos bid the two Carvalho women a good day and indicated that the group should vacate the family's home.

"What will happen if you capture him?" Miss Carvalho asked before they managed to get away. "Will . . . will I have to testify?"

Given the resolute look on her face, Duilio had no doubt she would. But she clearly didn't want to do so. Testifying would expose her even more publicly than the priest's earlier threats.

"We're going to kill him, Miss Carvalho," Gaspar said. "So it won't be necessary."

Anjos directed a narrow-eyed glare at Gaspar.

"Kill him?" Miss Carvalho cast a horrified glance toward her mother.

"I'm sorry, but that is likely," Anjos said more gently. "We cannot jail him. He would only kill the guards, so our choices are limited."

Duilio hadn't thought that through. He didn't like it. It offended his loyalty to the law, but pragmatism outweighed that. If the man could kill with a touch, there weren't many options. He definitely wished he'd brought his revolver along with him now.

They left the Carvalho house with an agreement to meet back that afternoon at the house Anjos and his team rented. Now armed with a name, Gaspar could take the Lady to meet with the brothers at the Jesuit house again and, given their suspicions, the brothers might help. None of them knew how the tie between Maria Melo and Pedro Salazar changed the case, but it was undeniable that it had.

"Where have you been?" Joaquim asked as they strode through the front door. He'd been pacing the front sitting room for half an hour, straining his mind to think of a place all three of them might go together.

Lady Ferreira embraced him and kissed his cheek. "We're pleased to see you too, Filho."

Joaquim felt himself flushing. "I'm always happy to see you."

She patted his shoulder and pointed toward the sitting room. "I'll go ask Mrs. Cardoza to put together a quick luncheon before Duilio gnaws off one of his flippers," she said. "Why don't the three of you talk? I know Duilinho has news for you."

Oriana went on into the sitting room, and Joaquim caught Duilio's arm. "News?"

"I can't imagine what . . ." Duilio's brows drew together. "Oh! Wedding next Saturday. The details elude me but I'll presumably need someone to stand up with me, and I would like it to be you."

"His mother's arranging everything," Miss Paredes said quickly.

"Congratulations," Joaquim managed, "to both of you, but . . ." He rubbed his hands together, gazing at the rug as if he might find the words there.

"Just say it," Duilio said.

Joaquim turned to Miss Paredes instead. "I don't know what provoked it, but someone I know from the Special Police sent word that they had orders from the prince himself. They're to pick up your father for violation of the ban."

Oriana sank down on the sofa, one hand pressed to her belly.

Duilio scowled. "Does Anjos not know?"

"My source said the order intentionally bypassed Anjos and his team. And Anjos can't refuse the order either, not once he hears it."

"Has anyone warned my father?" Oriana cut in abruptly. "Did you . . . ?"

"I went there first," Joaquim reassured her. "I gave him the keys to my flat. I don't think the Special Police know of any tie between him and me. My friend told me they're trying to drag this out as much as possible, Miss Paredes, due to your father's status in the business community."

Oriana turned to Duilio. "Can the infante not interfere?"

"Unless he can prove the prince is unfit to rule," Duilio said, "if he moves directly against the prince's orders, it would be treason."

"Everyone says the prince is insane," she protested.

Joaquim couldn't argue that. That was the reason the Special Police were willing to drag their feet at all. He understood her agitation, though.

"Knowing and proving are two different things," Duilio reminded her.

Oriana pressed her fingers against her temples. "This is my fault. Mrs. Melo saw me. That's why this is happening."

Joaquim shot a glance at Duilio, who explained quickly that they'd seen the elusive Mrs. Melo the night before outside the Simões ball, and that she'd seen Oriana. The woman had threatened Oriana's father before. Apparently she hadn't changed her tactics.

"Your father's too well connected for this to work," Joaquim told Oriana. "I'm sure Lady Pereira de Santos has lawyers competent enough to stall this in court indefinitely. Don't let this distract you. It tells me we're getting close enough to worry her."

She gazed at him, arrested by the import of that. After a moment of silence, she said, "Nela told me I needed to figure out who would profit the most from my people going to war with the two Portugals. That's what we need to know."

"And Melo's the key to that," Duilio said.

Oriana threw up her hands. "Short of my standing in the street and calling for her, I don't see how I can find her."

Duilio grimaced, his eyes sliding toward Joaquim. "I had an idea while we were in the carriage. There's one person Anjos probably hasn't questioned about her."

Immediately after the capture of Maraval, the hunt for his associates had included questioning all the servants who'd met with Mrs. Melo. None had any information on the woman beyond the false persona she'd created.

"Who?" Joaquim asked.

"Remember when Silva gave us information about the Open Hand? He got that information from Mrs. Melo. She came here afterward to ask Oriana whether he'd spilled everything she'd fed him. We couldn't tell Anjos that, though, without revealing that the woman was a sereia spy." Duilio took a deep breath and huffed it out. "I think we should go see my charming uncle, Silva . . . our charming uncle, I mean."

Joaquim groaned when he made the connection. "He's my uncle, too, isn't he?"

Duilio clapped him on the shoulder. "Lucky you."

Oriana strode back to the couch and picked up her handbag. "Let's go then."

Duilio's stomach rumbled. "Can we stop in the kitchen on the way out?"

CHAPTER 29

Oriana sat next to Duilio on the carriage's bench, trying to get her mind under control. She wanted to go look for her father. But he'd managed to evade trouble for ten years here. She had to have faith in him.

Duilio wrapped his hand around hers. "He'll be safe. I'm sure of that."

Ah, gods, I hope that's his gift speaking and not wishful thinking.

Joaquim sat across from them, watching the houses along the Street of Flowers as the carriage rattled along the cobbles. Over a quick lunch, Duilio had filled him in on the meeting at the Carvalho house. The fact that a priest might be involved with these murders seemed to disturb him. "If Pedro Salazar was interested in working with a doctor," Joaquim finally said, "I wonder if he's still doing so."

"How so?" Duilio asked.

"Well, the cuts on Felipa Reyna's throat were neat," Joaquim said. "We thought they could have been done by a doctor. That would give us another tie between the two cases."

"Why employ a healer to remove things? Dr. Castigliani didn't, did he?"

Joaquim shook his head. "To keep the victims alive longer? To study them longer? I don't know. We're still missing pieces."

Oriana glanced out the window, feeling cold again. They passed the Church of Santo Ildefonso with its whitewashed facade and obelisk and headed toward Bonfim Parish. The carriage bumped over the tram's tracks, and she grabbed a hand strap to stay upright. "Taking victims apart is the opposite of healing."

Duilio's brows drew together, his lips twisting into a scowl.

"What's wrong?" she asked him.

"I'm not sure. It's like the answer is just out of my reach," he said. "Or the question."

Oriana caught Joaquim's eye. He merely shrugged.

The carriage slowed, and Duilio peered out as they came to a slow stop. "Silva's probably going to be unpleasant."

Oriana wasn't certain whether he was talking to Joaquim or to her, but his bastard uncle liked to tear into others' fins just to see them react. She followed Duilio from the carriage and gazed up at a fine house on Pinto Bessa Street. Not as large as the houses on the Street of Flowers, it was still large by city standards. Three wrought-iron balconies crossed the granite facade. Masonry acanthus leaves decorated the eaves. Somehow she'd expected Silva's home would be less attractive. Then again, the man had always dressed well.

Asking the driver to stay close, Duilio walked up and rapped on the door. After only a moment, it swung open to reveal a very starchy butler who surveyed his three callers with a disdainful air. "We're here to see Silva," Duilio said shortly, handing over his card.

The butler looked at the card and back at Duilio. "You may come inside while you wait."

They followed the butler into a sitting room. The furnishings weren't new, but were in excellent condition, save for a discreet patch on of the upholstered chairs where a falling cigarette might have burned the brocade. It wasn't what she'd expected of the prince's former pet seer. "Will Silva actually help us?" she asked Duilio.

"Rafael will be annoyed if he doesn't," Duilio said. "So I expect he will."

"Ah." Whatever she thought of Silva, he did seem inclined to keep on good terms with his son. She didn't sit, hoping that would be a sign to the man that they didn't intend to stay. Joaquim picked up a book left on a side table to peer at the spine.

"I suppose you've come to gloat, pup?" Silva said from in the doorway, hands on his hips.

Duilio regarded him suspiciously. "I've come to ask a question. Why would I gloat?"

"How much did you pay the *Gazette* to publish that piece of drivel they ran this morning?" Without waiting for an answer, Silva turned and cast an appraising eye over her. Oriana did her best not to react to his rudeness. "And you've done well for yourself, fishling," he said. "More like a cat than a fish, always landing on your feet. Now you're his 'assistant,' I hear. I am impressed."

That didn't need an answer. Oriana folded her hands and waited.

Silva indicated Joaquim with a sweep of his hand. "And you've brought along the bastard, too."

Joaquim's cheeks reddened at that reference. Oriana guessed that Silva had long suspected Joaquim's parentage, especially since Joaquim and Duilio looked so much alike. It was an ironic topic with which to needle Joaquim, particularly since Silva was a bastard himself, and had fathered a bastard as well—Rafael Pinheiro.

"How charming you're all here," Silva said snidely. "Ask what you want and get out."

"We need to talk to you about Maria Melo," Oriana said. "Where can we find her?"

Silva spread his hands. "I don't know any Maria Melo."

Oriana wished they had Anjos with them. His Truthsaying abilities could sort the truth and fiction of Silva's words. "She's near my height, dark hair and eyes, older with heavy brows. She talked to you about the Open Hand. She told me she was your informant among them."

"I know about whom you're speaking, girl." Silva shook his head despairingly. "You don't even know her real name, do you?"

Duilio caught her eye. "What name do you know her by?"

"Iria Serpa," Silva said.

Well, they'd known "Maria Melo" was a false identity. "Can you tell us how to find her?" Oriana asked.

Silva sighed dramatically. "They live somewhere on Almada Street, although *he* generally remains up at the palace. He's been given rooms in the new building there, so he can be available for His Highness at all times."

"He?" Duilio asked cautiously.

"Her husband," Silva said, waving one hand dismissively, "although from what I've observed, there's not much love lost between the two."

"*Dr.* Serpa?" Duilio asked, eyes wide.

"Of course, him," Silva said.

The name meant nothing to Oriana, but she could see it did to Duilio. "Who is he?"

Duilio turned back to her, mouth pressed in a grim line. "Prince Fabricio's personal physician."

"Always whispering in his ear," Silva said contemptuously. "Serpa's a quack. He's only concerned with making a name for himself, but His Highness wouldn't listen to me when I said the man was trouble because Maraval vouched for him."

Oriana noted that Silva didn't seem concerned about his former employer's situation.

Duilio had closed his eyes, concentrating. *What is he asking himself?*

"It's already too late," Duilio said. "The prince has already made the wrong decision. He's going to die."

Silva's face hardened at Duilio's words. "I warned him. Well, I suppose I shall visit my tailor and order my black armbands."

Oriana swallowed. She should feel something, a hint of triumph perhaps. If the prince died, the infante would lift the ban on her people. Her father and her sister would be safe. Then again, if Maria

Melo—or Iria Serpa—succeeded, the sereia and the Portuguese might end up at war. She had to stop that. She didn't have time to mourn Silva's prince.

"Damnation!" Duilio pinched the bridge of his nose. "That's it! The chaplain at the palace. The infante said his name was Salazar."

Oriana blinked, trying to follow where his mind had gone. Wasn't Salazar also the name of Miss Carvalho's true father, the priest?

"Yes, the new one," Silva said, dismissing the man's importance with a sweep of his hand. "Maraval brought him in, which is a mark against him in my reckoning. He creeps about in the shadows. If I'm not mistaken, he knew Serpa back in Spain."

"Serpa came from Spain?" Joaquim asked.

Silva shook his head ruefully. "Aren't you supposed to be the detective, Inspector? Yes, Serpa might be Portuguese, but he lived in Spain long enough to pick up a lisp."

Oriana drew in a startled breath. *What if I've misunderstood all along. What if Maria Melo isn't a sereia at all?*

The afternoon sunlight as they stepped outside the doors of Silva's fine house seemed terribly out of place. Traffic moved along the street normally. No one knew that things had already gone terribly wrong. There was an assassin with access to the prince, a doctor who might have strange ideas, and a healer who was killing girls in the city.

Duilio shook his head, trying to parse out what had to be done first. They needed to get to Anjos and warn him of their new information; it tied together the two cases they'd been working on, *and* Oriana's assassin. It still didn't tell them what the trio was trying to do.

"Let's see if we can find Anjos," Duilio said as they climbed into the carriage again. He closed the carriage door and rapped on the wall to get the driver started.

The carriage began to roll, and Oriana sat back. "What kind of decision could the prince have made already? Something that will kill him?"

"I don't know the right question to ask," Duilio said. "We would have to think like the prince to understand what he's decided. I've only glimpsed him twice at the palace, but he doesn't look sane, so there's no telling."

"If we can't stop it," Joaquim asked, "what's the point?"

Duilio shook his head. "Rafael said we're needed to stop the . . . chaos that would follow, whatever that is."

"War between my people and yours?" Oriana suggested. "Could Spain benefit from that somehow?"

Duilio felt his brow furrow. "I suppose they could offer to defend your people's islands, but given their recent losses to the American navy, I doubt they could stretch themselves that far."

A few years before, an American ship had blown up in a Cuban harbor. There had been speculation that one of the Canaries serving with the Spanish navy had planted an "infernal device" on the American ship's hull, although that had never been substantiated. That incident, however, had provoked a backlash by the Americans that the Spanish hadn't expected, leading to the loss of some of their colonies and much of their navy as well. It had been a terrible blow to the country.

Oriana touched a finger to her temple, the sign that she needed a moment to think. Then she said, "But this plot is old, Duilio. At least fourteen years old—that's when my mother was murdered. Was Spain still formidable enough to be a threat fourteen years ago?"

"Yes," he guessed. "But what would Spain possibly gain from it? Your father told me they already trade with your people."

"I don't know," Oriana whispered.

Duilio closed his eyes, asking his gift whether this was all a plot of the Spanish throne, but it gave him no answer. *That must not be the right question.*

The carriage shuddered to a stop unexpectedly, and Duilio leaned forward to look outside. The traffic moved past them unusually quickly, but he couldn't make out why.

"What's going on?" Joaquim asked. "We can't be there yet."

"No idea." Duilio opened the carriage door and jumped down to talk to the driver. The horses stood unmoving, refusing to take a step farther. They shook in their traces, their heads tossing. The driver had no idea what was wrong either, but several other drivers seemed to share that problem. A mule-drawn wagon had stopped ahead of them. Duilio gazed down the street between the stalled carriages and carts, but couldn't see any reason for the disruption. When he turned back, Joaquim was helping Oriana down from the carriage.

"It's a sereia," Oriana said quietly. "In pain, or she wouldn't sound like that."

Duilio told the driver to turn the carriage around and go home. "Let's get out of the road." He guided Oriana to the edge of the cobbles. "You can hear her?"

"Yes," she said softly. "My ears are more attuned to it than yours."

"Could that be what's upsetting the horses?"

"They probably hear better than you."

Duilio was willing to accept that explanation. Their driver got the horses to back up and then began a wide turn in the middle of the street. Fortunately he managed to complete it before a tram approached.

"We'd better find out what that is," Joaquim said.

Oriana wrapped her arms about herself and nodded.

Duilio did a quick search of his pockets, but had nothing to stuff in his ears. "Will I be able to resist her?"

Oriana shook her head. "She's not *calling* you. She's. . . . screaming, for lack of a better term. She's inflicting her pain on everyone else. You'll have trouble getting close, rather than the opposite."

And it would probably be worse for Joaquim. He didn't possess a selkie's natural resistance to the *call*. "Well, we have to go anyway. Any advice?"

"Try not to listen?" she suggested.

Duilio puffed out his cheeks and started walking. As he neared, he could tell the disturbance was originating on the cross street—Almada Street.

"Isn't this the street that the doctor lives on?" Oriana asked, pointing at the street sign on one house's wall.

"Yes." This couldn't be good. He turned up Almada Street, a street narrow enough that two carriages couldn't pass easily. He hadn't gotten far when the edge of the sereia's sphere of influence became evident. A cluster of pedestrians, some with their hands over their ears, stood gathered in front of a pastry shop. An old woman broke away from the group and came toward them, waving the ends of her shawl to tell them to leave.

Joaquim intercepted her, saying that he was a police officer, but the woman didn't stop. She kept going down the street, hands waving in agitation.

Duilio made his way to where the gaggle of pedestrians stood in front of the shop. Surprisingly, he recognized one of them. Mr. Bastos, whom he'd met on his first visit to the palace, stood in the center of the small crowd. The elderly man's white hair was disordered and he seemed shaken, clutching at the arm of a young man wearing an apron. Duilio peered at him. "Mr. Bastos, do you remember me?"

"Mr. Ferreira. Please, I am not a madman. I have been to the police station already today, but they won't listen to me. I cannot go home." The old man reached up frail hands and tugged at his white hair. "The screaming is too terrible to bear."

Duilio patted his shoulder. "What has happened, sir?"

The old man gazed up at Duilio with watery eyes. "The flats above mine. I do not know the man who lives there or his wife. They do not talk to me. Last night I thought I heard crying coming from their flat. It crept into my dreams and woke me over and over, calling me to help. This morning it became screaming, pushing at me until I had to leave my own home. I covered my ears but it did no good."

No, Duilio didn't expect it would. "Which house is yours, sir?"

Bastos pointed down the street. "Number 339."

Some ways down, the pedestrians huddled past that house, clinging together on the far side of the street. Duilio wondered if they even realized they were doing it. There was an odd feel in the air, as if fear had taken a tangible form.

"You work for the police, don't you, Mr. Ferreira?" Bastos asked, glancing back and forth between him and Oriana. "Can *you* not find out what is wrong there?"

Evidently Mr. Bastos read the *Gazette*, too. Duilio cast an apologetic glance at Joaquim, who merely rolled his eyes in exasperation. "Yes, sir," Joaquim said. "We'll get to the bottom of this."

Duilio turned to the young man in the apron. "Do you have any cotton? Lint or bandages? I may need it to get closer."

The young man dashed into his shop and emerged a moment later with cotton bandages. Duilio thanked him and handed one roll to Joaquim before he pulled out some of the cotton and forced a small wad into each ear. He pocketed the remainder and tossed a couple of milreis to the young man, who tucked them into his apron. Duilio could still hear a bit, but it was as if his head were underwater.

With one last nod to Mr. Bastos, Duilio pointed toward the opposite sidewalk, and the three of them headed in that direction, Oriana in the lead. She wended her way between a pair of carriages slowed to a standstill. Duilio followed.

Several houses farther down, number 339 was a building of three stories, very similar to the others that lined the street, built onto each other in one long row, granite or color-washed plaster in white and cream and yellow with red-tiled roofs. Duilio approached the threshold of the building and stopped, almost paralyzed with apprehension.

He could hear it now, even through the cotton plugs—*the screaming.*

Oriana touched his face with her fingers, drawing his attention back. She gestured with her other hand, asking him to look at her. He kept his eyes on her face as she led him into that malaise of fear. Sweat trickled down his spine.

If his selkie blood lowered his susceptibility to a sereia's voice, then he could only imagine how difficult this must be for Joaquim, who didn't have that protection. Beads of sweat shone on Joaquim's forehead. Duilio gestured for him to stay outside the house.

He used Bastos' key to open the front door and it swung open, revealing a hallway with a narrow stairwell that led to the upper floors. On the other side of the hallway was a door to Bastos' ground-floor apartment. Oriana led Duilio up the stairs, forcing him to climb on while his skin continued to crawl. She paused at the second-floor door but signed for them to go up, so they moved on to the next floor. When they reached the top landing, she tried the door but couldn't get it to open.

Duilio gestured for her to move aside and kicked the door in. As the door crashed back, the fear intensified, hitting him like a wave. His stomach turned, and he leaned his head against the wall in the hallway, intent on keeping his latest meal inside, where it belonged. The worst of it passed after a moment. Oriana's hand touched his face again, her lips moving, and he realized she was singing to him, interference to that other voice. She took his hand and drew him into the apartment, throwing glances behind her every few steps.

Heavy draperies cut the light to a minimum, but there were no furnishings in the room. The smell reminded Duilio of the morgue, all antiseptics and stale blood and urine.

Oriana tugged his hand again, her eyes on his, and he forced his feet to follow. They passed through another empty room, and then into a wide room where the wood floors were lit by sunlight flooding down from a large hole cut in the ceiling . . . a makeshift skylight. A bed frame with no bedding or mattress stood on their left, and on the right another bed was set against the wall.

A girl lay in that bed, her eyes wide with terror.

Oriana dragged him the last distance to the bed, grabbed his hand and firmly set it over the girl's open mouth. Her breath almost steamed against his palm. The sound of her screaming continued, muffled, issuing from her vibrating gills. Duilio stared down into the girl's terrified face, the eyes red-stained but her face dry. Red inflamed lines crossed her skin, like fingers radiating up from her swollen throat.

Oriana sorted through the contents of a small cart at the foot of the bed. A moment later she returned to his side, a dark bottle in her hand. She picked up the sheet that covered the girl's body and poured some of the liquid onto the corner of it. Then she jerked his hand away and replaced it with her sheet-covered one.

And slowly the screaming eased . . . and then ceased altogether.

Duilio could feel it throughout his body. He hadn't realized how strong the reaction of fear had been until it was gone. He was chilled, his clothes drenched with sweat.

Oriana lifted her hand away from the girl's face, but the girl didn't move.

Duilio dared to pull the cotton from his ears. He could hear the distant sounds of the traffic moving again on the street below, but silence reigned in the barren room now. "What did you do?"

Oriana showed him the dark bottle. "Chloroform. I figured there must be something of the sort on that cart there."

His breathing was returning to normal. He smelled again the chemical scent of a hospital ward, with the smell of decay and urine mixed in. His eyes watered.

The young woman on the bed lay with a sheet covering her body, but she wore nothing more than that. Her dark hair had been cropped short. He could see more clearly now the red lines of infection that caressed her face, rising from a swollen seam that ran underneath her chin, down beneath her gills, and across above her collarbone. A blossom of bluish red under the skin showed on one shoulder. Duilio suspected that if they pulled the sheet back, they would find more of that. He could feel the fever rising from her. That was sepsis spreading throughout her body.

"Have you got it under control?" Joaquim called from the front room.

"Yes."

Joaquim came closer, peering at the girl's swollen neck with its inflamed gills. "I don't understand. I thought your father warned the exiles. . . ."

"She's human," Oriana inserted softly. "Look at her teeth."

Duilio leaned over and pulled back the girl's upper lip, feeling again the heat of her breath. The teeth revealed were blunt like his own. He stepped back and surveyed the inflamed rectangular seam in the girl's throat, his stomach turning. "That's not possible."

Oriana shook her head. Tears glistened in her eyes.

"Marta Duarte," Joaquim said abruptly, crossing himself. "Check her right arm. There should be a large birthmark just above her elbow. She disappeared from the same brothel as the otter girl, Erdeg."

Duilio tugged the sheet down a few inches to reveal a port-wine stain on the girl's arm, verifying her identity. He drew the sheet back up. "The gills were spliced in. Grafted in? Felipa Reyna's throat was removed and put in place of this girl's."

Joaquim turned pale. "Poor girl."

"We need to get her to a doctor," Oriana said.

"No, let's bring a doctor here," Duilio said. "Do you think Dr. Esteves would come?"

Joaquim nodded grimly.

"We'll stay here and keep her drugged," Duilio said.

Joaquim was out the door in an instant.

"What is the point of this?" Oriana asked.

"I don't know." Duilio looked about the room, spotlessly clean, barren save for the two beds and cart, then up at the hole cut in the roof. "This took planning," he said. "They did all this for some reason. It doesn't add up."

Oriana took a breath and then laid her free hand over her mouth. The smell was stifling. "What can we do for her?"

"Water?" Duilio went back through the flat and located the washroom. He had nothing to carry water in, though, so he returned to the back room and, after sorting through the bottles on the cart, located one that held gauze. He handed the contents to Oriana and went to fill the bottle. When he returned, Oriana was dampening a section of gauze with chloroform. The girl had started to move, coming back to consciousness. He dribbled some water into the girl's mouth, and she swallowed reflexively, her spliced-in gills flaring.

Then Oriana held the gauze over her mouth again. "I don't know how long chloroform lasts."

Unfortunately, he didn't either. He found some of the remaining gauze, folded it into a pad, and wet it. He laid that on the girl's burning forehead. Then he tidied the sheet, drawing it up about her arms. She'd soiled the bedding at some point, but surely she wasn't aware of it. He hoped not. He didn't think he could bring himself to do anything about it. He met Oriana's eyes. "I don't know what else to do."

"You're not a doctor," she said, still holding the bottle of chloroform in one webbed hand and the gauze in the other.

"I still feel like we should be doing *something* for her."

Oriana regarded him steadily, anger having replaced her earlier tears. "We're going to find them and avenge this horror."

CHAPTER 30

The girl continued to breathe fast and shallow, air rasping through her stolen throat. Duilio knew chloroform was dangerous, but neither he nor Oriana could recall exactly what danger it presented. It might be a mercy if it killed the girl.

Duilio paced, wearing a path between the door and Oriana's side. He itched to be in motion—his brain worked better that way. Oriana kept her eyes on the poor girl's face, watching for signs she was regaining consciousness. She'd removed everything from the top shelf of the cart and pushed the cart to the head of the bed. It looked uncomfortable, but she could sit on it and rest the bottle and gauze in her lap.

"Duilio?" Joaquim called. "I have the doctor with me." He appeared in the doorway, with Dr. Esteves and his receptionist behind him.

The older man pushed past Joaquim into the room. He came to the bedside, looked down at the drugged girl, and crossed himself. "My God."

The receptionist—Duilio couldn't recall her name—followed Esteves, her air of efficiency like a wall of iron about her. "Both of you gentlemen leave now," she said briskly. "The doctor doesn't need you hovering over him." She took the bottle from Oriana's webbed hands without sparing them a glance. "Now, miss, what have you given her, and how much?"

"I poured some on the gauze and held it to her mouth until she stilled," Oriana answered. "I don't know how much, exactly."

"And when was the last time you did so?"

"A few minutes ago, perhaps."

The woman harrumphed. "Well, not much you could do to hurt this child now. Go on, girl, let us see to her."

"Is there a washroom?" the doctor asked Duilio.

"I'll show you," Duilio said. Joaquim accompanied him and the doctor out of the room, pointed out the washroom, and then they made their way down the stairs to the building's front entry, where the clear afternoon air didn't hold the taint of decaying flesh.

"I'm going search the second-floor apartment," Joaquim said. "I've got legal grounds for going in there. You don't."

There were times that not actually being a police officer had its drawbacks. Joaquim had to do all the real work alone. Duilio watched Joaquim go up the stairs to the second floor and disappear inside. He closed his eyes and asked if Joaquim would be safe up there. His gift reassured him, despite the questionable circumstance of an unlocked door.

Oriana came down the stairwell. "I left them alone in there," she said, wrapping her arms about herself.

Duilio put his arms about her. "Don't worry."

The sun was lowering, sending golden color across the walls of the buildings, lending a false sense of peace to the street scene. The traffic had returned to normal, carriages now moving along the narrow street. People walked down each side of the street again, no few casting a shocked glance at the openly embracing couple. After a moment, Oriana pulled out of Duilio's arms. "So what do we do?"

"I was going to suggest checking the area behind the houses."

Most blocks of houses had a large open area in their centers, often overgrown with vegetation and filled with refuse and old stone. They descended the steps and walked around the buildings until they found a narrow gravel drive between two houses that allowed access to the center of the block. Behind number 339 they found a decrepit old stone outbuilding, empty at the moment, but ruts in the alleyway suggested a coach had been kept there. Recent manure told of horses. A large metal bin inside had been used to burn fabric. Sheets, Oriana declared, after finding an unburned piece of cotton no bigger than her finger. Duilio didn't know how much bedding and bandaging the doctor had bloodied in his surgeries, but he'd been thorough in disposing of it.

By the time they got back to the front of the house, Joaquim had come downstairs. "They intended for this all to be found. I'm assuming that applies to the girl in there as well—Marta Duarte. The doctor *wanted* people to know what he's done . . . and why. They left his notes, a journal, and several supposed letters from the Ministry of Intelligence of your people's islands."

Oriana shook her head. "I can't believe that."

It was too easy for Duilio's taste. Spies didn't leave out official letters to be discovered. That reinforced Oriana's suspicion that they were trying to start a war. "Let's go talk to Esteves."

They headed back inside and up the stairs. The door to the third-floor flat hung open, part of its frame torn away when Duilio kicked it in. "We're coming in," he called to warn the doctor.

"Come along," the doctor said. "I'll need you to look at this."

The room wasn't any brighter, but the doctor had replaced the contents of the cart, setting up a makeshift hospital. They had moved the bed away from the wall and closer to the light, and the receptionist sat near the girl's head, a watch in one hand and a dropper in the other. A cup of some sort had been affixed to the girl's forehead by a strap. They'd gotten organized quickly. Duilio's respect for Esteves rose.

"Well, now we know you were right about that book," the doctor said, his mouth turned down into a frown. "The doctor transplanted the Reyna girl's throat into this girl's body."

"Transplanted?" Duilio repeated.

Esteves cast regretful eyes over the young woman's unmoving form. "Doctors have long held that someday we will be able to re-place damaged organs. Some *have* experimented—with animals, mind you—and there's reportedly been some success with corneas, but something on this scale is the stuff of fiction, Mr. Ferreira."

"But they gave her a sereia's ability to *call*," Duilio told him. "We felt it."

"Temporarily," Esteves said firmly. "You didn't pull this sheet back, did you?"

Duilio glanced guiltily at Oriana. "No."

"This poor girl has been operated on *three* times," Esteves said. "Someone has tried to attach an otter's tail, and there's a square patch of selkie pelt grafted onto her abdomen."

"Is the patch about the size of a hand?" Duilio asked.

The doctor peered at him narrowly. "Yes."

"The selkie's missing pelt was eventually found," Duilio admit-ted, "and had a healthy patch that size. It was still alive, I suppose, because *that* part was."

"Well, that graft was done more than a week ago, judging by the growth of the fur and healing," Esteves said. "The tail was the first surgery, but the throat was in the last few days."

That matched up with their timeline. And surgery would have been done during the day, when that skylight would give them enough light to see what they were doing. Felipa had died early in the eve-ning, but the doctor might have used lamps to see his work that time.

Dr. Esteves again pointed to the girl's stolen throat. "None of these incisions allow for drainage. That assures death would be the end result."

Duilio stepped closer. "I don't understand."

"They hold any corruption inside," the doctor said, gesturing with his hands. "This doctor had to know she would die from sepsis eventually. He made the incisions *look* good, and I have to wonder if he involved a healer to aid in that."

"A healer only deals with superficial wounds," Duilio said. "They won't work on a puncture or anything deep."

"Yes, because their ability is limited. But a healer could have made the swelling around these . . . implanted parts go away *temporarily*. They could make it appear to be healing. I suspect that was what this was all about. This is for show. The tail isn't even attached to her spine in any way, only sewn on."

"She could *call*, though," Oriana protested. "She was *calling*, even if it was a warped version."

"Oh, yes," the doctor said to her. "*That* change was more than cosmetic. And it also suggests a healer. The healer could control the flow of blood while the doctor was replacing the voice box. That's the only way such a massive operation could be carried out without the patient dying from blood loss. Even so, I'm shocked this girl is still alive. The healer involved had to have been working herself to death to keep this girl breathing."

Oriana turned to Duilio. "Could that be why Salazar has been killing so often? Because he's using that strength to keep this girl alive?"

"Killing?" Esteves asked cautiously.

"We think he's been killing one or two women a night," Duilio told him. "Pedro Salazar is the healer Dr. Teixeira observed at the Medical-Surgical School years ago—a Jesuit priest. We believe Teixeira confronted the man, who later killed him to keep him from talking."

Esteves shook his head. "A healer who's a killer? And a priest?"

"I'm afraid so," Duilio said. "A cassock isn't a guarantee of goodness."

"Unfortunately true," Esteves said. "Neither is being a healer, I suppose, given how this girl has been tortured."

"Is there any chance Miss Duarte will live?" Joaquim asked.

"No," the doctor said. "The infection has spread to most parts of her body. I suspect she's been delirious for some time."

Joaquim's shoulders slumped when he heard that verdict. Duilio suspected he'd wanted to save at least one—but if the girl did survive, she would never be the same anyway. He set a hand on Joaquim's shoulder. Duilio turned back to Esteves. "Mr. Bastos claimed she was crying in the night, but screaming this morning."

"Apparently she was abandoned here. These sheets haven't been changed in more than a day." Esteves wiped his hands together. "I have been giving some consideration to your query about doctors who show an unhealthy interest in such things. There *is* one I recall from my school days. He talked about that book as if he'd seen it, read it. Eventually the doctors who ran the school sent him away."

"Dr. Serpa," Duilio said.

Esteves blinked at him, dumbfounded. "How did you know?"

Duilio set one fist against his mouth, trying to sort out what he knew about Dr. Serpa. He strode into the front room and paced its length a couple of times.

Oriana had followed him. "What is it?"

"I think I understand now what the prince decided." Duilio headed back to the room where the doctor waited. "Dr. Esteves, could she have looked normal *yesterday afternoon?*"

Esteves frowned. "A strong healer could have suppressed the visible symptoms of the sepsis. The girl would already have been dying inside, though."

"Prince Fabricio left the palace yesterday afternoon," Duilio said, trying to line events up in his mind. "I think he came here to see this girl, and only after that did they leave her to die."

The doctor looked as mystified as Oriana and Joaquim did.

"What are you talking about?" Joaquim asked.

"The prince left the palace yesterday afternoon," Duilio said. "The infante tried to follow him, but lost him."

"And what does that mean?" Oriana asked.

Duilio tried to work it out. "The prince wants to be like the sea god—the one on the palace archway—you've seen photographs of it, haven't you? I'll wager that between Serpa and Salazar, they convinced him he could be equal to a sereia, by taking a sereia's power."

"But his doctor has to know it would kill him," Joaquim said.

"That's the point," Oriana said before Duilio got it out of his mouth, understanding lightening her features. "The doctor is going to assassinate the prince, with his permission."

CHAPTER 31

The cab took them down to the Street of Flowers faster than Oriana could walk. When they reached the house, Duilio jogged up the front steps to bang on the door. Cardenas peered out a side window, and then hurried to let them in. Duilio pushed open the door and yelled past the butler down the main hallway. "Mother?"

"Lady Ferreira is in the sitting room," Cardenas said, "entertaining."

"I'll go talk to her." Joaquim said and headed that way.

Duilio set a hand on the butler's arm. "Have we heard anything from Monteiro this afternoon?"

"Not half an hour ago, Mr. Duilio," Cardenas said. "He's still at Mr. Joaquim's flat."

Duilio saw Oriana let out a tightly held breath. He'd felt sure that Monteiro was safe, but Serpa needed a throat to transplant into the prince's body, and Monteiro *would* be the first choice for someone as vindictive as Mrs. Melo. Even with Monteiro safe, they still had access to one male sereia: Ambassador Alvaro.

Duilio turned back to Cardenas. "Please have Marcellin bring up my revolvers and my oldest sporting jacket. And ask Mrs. Cardoza if there are any pastries we can carry off with us."

Cardenas repeated that to himself, lips moving, and went in search of the valet.

"How can you eat?" Oriana asked.

"In this line of work, we see a lot of unsettling things. Plus Joaquim threw up in the hallway back at that house, so he's got to be hungry. I know I am." She groaned, but walked with him toward the sitting room when he tugged on her arm. "Once we get . . ."

Duilio stopped on the threshold of the sitting room, startled. His mother did have a guest—none other than the infante himself, sitting on the couch like an old family friend. Which in a way, he was.

The infante rose politely when he saw Oriana standing at Duilio's side, but asked, "Where have you been, Duilio?"

Duilio stopped himself before he actually answered that question. He didn't want to blurt out the things they'd seen in front of his mother. "Miss Paredes, Inspector Tavares, and I have learned of a plot to assassinate the prince, Your Highness, and we were even now preparing to go to the palace to pursue those involved."

The infante's eyes narrowed. "Who are we looking for?"

"Dr. Serpa, Your Highness."

The infante's brows drew together. "Serpa? I don't like the man, but he's had plenty of opportunity to kill my brother before now."

Duilio thought he'd figured out the man's reasoning, as strange as it seemed. "Yes, but not in the sensational way they'd planned, Your Highness. He needed Father Salazar to do so."

"Please don't ask him to explain that," Joaquim said hurriedly.

The infante glanced at Joaquim, and said, "Perhaps we could discuss this elsewhere?"

"Yes, Your Highness. Why don't we retire to the library? Mother, if you can tell Cardenas we've gone there."

"I'd be happy to." She rose. "It's been so nice to chat with you, Your Highness."

The infante kissed her hand, and then followed Duilio and Joaquim from the room.

"The newspaper article wasn't amusing," Duilio whispered to the infante as they walked toward the library.

"Actually," the infante said, "I thought it was. And if you're to work for me, it will be better if the public doesn't believe you an imbecile."

Well, he couldn't argue with that logic, although he *hadn't* promised the infante that he would take a government position. Duilio shook his head regretfully, wishing necessity hadn't forced him to refuse. Once they'd settled in the library, the infante taking one of the chairs at the table, Duilio filled him in on their afternoon's discoveries.

When he'd finished, the infante pinched the bridge of his nose. "That's insane."

Duilio nodded. "The line between madness and genius is thin at times. The prince will die slowly and in great pain, and he will have consented to his own murder because he wanted more power than he was born with."

The infante laid his hands on the polished surface of the table. "Will die?"

"We're too late to stop it, Your Highness."

The infante sat back, presenting Duilio with his aquiline profile.

The library door opened, and Oriana stepped inside, now dressed in one of her old black skirts and a black shirtwaist. Over that she wore Duilio's brown sporting coat, a less-than-fashionable ensemble. She carried a low-brimmed hat under one arm, and her hair was tightly bound at the nape of her neck. She spotted the cherry box on the table and went to retrieve the small gun from within. She stuffed it into her leather cummerbund, picked out a handful of bullets, and slipped them into a coat pocket.

"I should be more upset by this," the infante said. "He's my brother, but . . ."

"He's had you under arrest for years," Duilio said. "And even though we're not supposed to say it, half the city thinks he's insane."

"And yet that doesn't make me feel better about it," the infante said. He rose when Joaquim stepped back into the library.

"The carriage is ready," Joaquim said. "Are we?"

Duilio looked around at the others. Stalling wouldn't make them any readier.

Anjos waited behind his desk at the house on Boavista Avenue, a grim expression on his face. Gaspar stood at one side of the room, the Lady seated near him, and in the far corner Miss Vladimirova sat, a black presence in her web of veils and stillness. Her hands were folded neatly in her lap, and Oriana didn't see the woman breathing. She shuddered, causing Duilio to touch his hand to her back.

"Raimundo," the Lady said, rising, "what are you doing here?"

"I got locked out of my room," the infante said ruefully when she embraced him. "I went out this morning, but when I came back there were guards on my door, ones I don't trust, so I left."

"Any idea why?" she asked suspiciously.

"No. I assumed I was in trouble with Fabricio again, although from what I've heard, something worse is afoot." He gestured toward Duilio, who proceeded to tell them about the information garnered from Silva and the horrible discovery on Almada Street.

The Lady had settled back in her chair. "Yes, Father Salazar was defrocked about five years ago. He'd been working with prisoners at the Unnaturals prison in Lleida, and it came to light that he and the doctor involved had been experimenting on them. 'Illicit medical studies of transplantation,' the Jesuit father called it. So we have the right man."

"Unnaturals prison?" Oriana asked. That didn't sound good.

The Lady turned her pale eyes on her. "In Spain they imprison nonhumans and witches who refuse to disavow their gifts. It was the perfect place for their experiments. They had a population of prisoners whom the Spanish government despised. It had been going on for years before the Jesuit order discovered their priest's involvement."

"And they defrocked him as a direct result," Joaquim said. "He should have lost the protection of the Church then, but it appears he managed to keep his expulsion secret."

Oriana frowned. She had missed something, some key that would unlock a door for her.

"I suspect it was in the interest of those running the prison to look the other way," the Lady told him. "Now that we've affirmed he's our murderer, I cannot stress enough how deadly he is. No one other than Miguel or Nadezhda should go near him."

That made sense, since Inspector Gaspar was immune to magic and Miss Vladimirova was, well, *already dead.*

"I have little to lose," Anjos added, grinding out his cigarette, "and little to attract him. I'll go with them to find Salazar."

For the first time, Miss Vladimirova inhaled. "I want you close, but do not approach him. You cannot run."

Anjos shook his head. "I can't help with the sereia woman, if she's there. That will have to come down to Ferreira and Miss Paredes." He turned to Joaquim. "You, Inspector Tavares, will stay with His Highness. You are to keep the infante safe until you can turn him over to the protection of his guards. Are you armed?"

"Yes, sir." Joaquim patted the coat pocket where he'd stashed one of Duilio's revolvers.

"Then we'll take a team through the front gates." Anjos turned to the Lady. "Once we get inside, I want you to find a quiet corner and stay out of trouble. Otherwise Miguel will fret."

Gaspar didn't argue with that assertion. The Lady merely inclined her head regally.

"So we'll all go together?" Duilio ask.

Anjos pulled out his cigarette case and scowled down at it. It was empty. He closed it and laid it aside. "While I would prefer to leave His Highness here, we need two entries into the palace to be sure someone gets in. The three of you will go with him the way he usually sneaks out—through the park."

The park around the palace was steep and heavily wooded.

There was no moon tonight, and in the darkness it must be easy to get lost. "How will we find our way?" Oriana asked.

"Trust me," the infante told her. "I do this regularly, Miss Paredes, and often at night."

Anjos rose, one hand on the desk for support. "Let's go before Serpa and Salazar get away."

Oriana realized what was missing from the discussion—Maria Melo. "Lady? Do they imprison sereia at that unnatural prison?"

Anjos looked to the Lady, as did the others. Her brows rose. "*Unnaturals* prison. Not exactly. My understanding is that there are sereia there, but they *run* the prison, since they can control others with their *call*."

"Canaries, you mean, then," Oriana corrected. "The sereia in Spain originally came from the Canary Islands. They're the ones who serve the Spanish navy. The sereia at that prison would be Canaries, not my people." Even if their service aboard Spanish naval vessels had been forced initially, over the centuries the Canaries had become the willing partners of their captors. Oriana could easily see how their talents could be used to control a prison. *This has to be part of the puzzle.*

The Lady inclined her head. "Yes. That must be the case. I doubt the Spanish would trust anyone from the Portuguese islands with such a responsibility."

If Mrs. Melo had been at that Unnaturals prison, she could have met Serpa and Salazar there. It explained the tie between them that hadn't made sense before. And Canary bloodlines bore visible differences, Oriana had heard—a small dorsal fin and ventral striping, either of which her mother might have accidentally seen. Or heard about.

Her people hadn't associated with the Canaries for centuries, distrusting both the Canaries' willing service to a human throne and their acceptance of the Christian religion. Canaries weren't allowed on the Ilhas das Sereias, so it was shocking that one could have infiltrated the Ministry of Intelligence. Oriana nodded slowly, thinking that she might have just found the key to her family's troubles.

"Maria Melo?" Duilio asked her, clearly tracking her thoughts.

"She's a Canary, a *Spanish* agent," Oriana whispered. "Hiding in my own people's Ministry of Intelligence."

That *would* be a secret big enough to destroy lives.

CHAPTER 32

Only the occasional streetlamp lit the rolling carriage now, creating brief flashes of illumination within. Oriana sat facing forward, her shoulder pressed against Duilio's. The infante and Joaquim shared the backward-facing bench, probably far more uncomfortable for Joaquim than his royal companion.

The infante turned out to be a handsome man with an expressive face that currently showed his inner turmoil. Oriana found him *likable*. He certainly lacked the distant superiority she'd endured from many of the social elite. In her time as Lady Isabel's companion, she had met far more of those self-important noblemen than men like him or Duilio. She'd clearly been traveling in the wrong circles.

She could make out Duilio's profile, but couldn't see his features to know what he was thinking. They were about to walk into the palace and try to arrest the insane doctor and his wife—who may very well be a Canary spy. Anjos wanted Serpa and his accomplices to stand trial for the murders of the four girls in addition to the prince's eventual death. Oriana doubted he'd get his wish. There was the issue of assassination . . . and treason. Against the enormity of those crimes, the citizens of the Golden City would care little about the deaths of four commoners, no matter how gruesome.

Sighing, she touched Duilio's hand where it lay on his leg. His head turned in her direction. She beckoned him closer and whispered into his ear what she hadn't managed to say to him before. She had practiced silently in the dressing room while Teresa braided up her hair, and yet it was still difficult. This time the words came out—no more than a whisper, but audible nonetheless. "I love you."

He set his forehead against hers. "That's the perfect gift."

She breathed in the smell of his skin and then sat back, not wanting to distract him—or herself—further. The carriage rattled along the cobbles, and all too soon it came to a stop. Duilio peered outside into the darkness, opened the door and stepped down. He folded out the steps and let the rest of them climb out.

The driver had stopped halfway between two streetlamps, which meant the darkness around them was thick. Oriana wasn't certain where they were, but clearly Duilio recognized the place. They appeared to be on a street near the back side of the palace, behind the man-made hill on which it rose. She lifted her eyes toward it, feeling a trickle of dread down her back.

On a moonless night, the palace was an intimidating shape in the darkness, its ornate merlons lit by myriad lanterns. She'd never been this close. Someone like her—a nonhuman and not welcome—would never voluntarily walk into that place.

"We'll go up through the park," the infante said. "It's steep, but there aren't many guards to hide you from."

Oriana gazed up at the hillside. She could walk forever, but climbing steep streets winded her. She touched Duilio's hand. "I may not be able to keep up."

"Don't go too fast," Duilio said to the infante. "We may have trouble with the slope."

"We can go ahead," Joaquim said. "Time's of the essence."

"We can't," the infante said. "We have to stay together for me to hide you from the guards."

"I'll do the best I can," Oriana promised.

"We won't leave you," the infante said firmly. "Let's get started."

The wall surrounding the palace had arches that gave visitors access to the gardens, allowing the citizens to use the lower parts as a public park. Oriana spotted one of those near the end of the street where they stood, across the wide avenue that separated the palace from the rest of the city. They walked back around to the alleyway to avoid the streetlamp, but then boldly crossed the road. A single carriage trundled along the cobbles, loud in the night air. A handful of pedestrians laughed as they walked along the roadside in the opposite direction. None seemed to notice the group slipping under one of the arches. They walked underneath it and onto an unlit pathway.

"Give me a moment," Oriana begged. They waited while she lifted her skirts and tucked them up into her tight cummerbund. Showing her stocking-covered legs might be shocking in Portuguese society, but necessity outweighed propriety. "That should help."

None of the men argued. They followed the infante through the dense foliage, keeping close together for fear of losing track of one another. After a climb that seemed to go on for half the distance up the hillside, Oriana felt worn out. But the infante's voice drifted back to her. "There's a rope here and a ramp to help us get the rest of the way up."

A second climb ensued, steeper this time. After a particularly precipitous patch, Oriana's lungs began to burn. Duilio slowed and drew her into his grasp, one arm wrapped about her waist and the other on the rope. He carried half her weight, so they managed to keep up, finally coming up into a clearing where a small domed building stood hidden among shadowy trees. A single pair of flickering gaslights on either side of an archway lit an inner door.

Oriana leaned against one of the pillars to catch her breath. "What is this place?"

"It used to be a studio, I believe," the infante said. "Forgotten now. The trees have grown so much that it can't be seen from the patios any longer."

In the faint illumination of the hissing gaslights, she spotted Joaquim gazing up at the remaining slope and turned to look at it herself. The last stretch to reach the palace walls seemed vertical. "How do we get up that?"

The infante reached into his waistcoat pocket and drew out a key. "There are stairs. Much easier, I promise."

For a moment she wanted to throw herself on his neck in gratitude. "Thank the gods."

He laughed softly and opened the door under the archway with his key. He handed the key to Duilio. "Lock it behind you."

A tight spiral staircase cut into the stone of the hillside led up from that spot. Lights hissed over their heads, casting wobbling shadows all about them, the gas pipes running exposed along the stone walls. The stairwell deposited them one story lower in a tunnel with a cobblestone surface. It had the same feeble lighting, but all of them could walk along it abreast. The tunnel sloped upward, then turned back on itself and ramped up another level. The air smelled musty.

"Is this the entryway tunnel?" Duilio asked softly.

The infante shook his head. "No, it mirrors the one on the opposite side of the palace."

"So we'll come out on the basement level?"

"Yes. We'll come out into the basement level of the old tower, below the entry level. We're actually under the new palace right now, but we can't get up there from here."

They continued walking along the dark tunnel until they reached another large wooden door. "This is where faith comes in," the infante said. "If the wrong guard is stationed there, we're going to have to incapacitate him."

On one side of the heavy wooden door, Joaquim drew his gun but flipped it about so that he held it butt out. Oriana pressed herself to one side of the tunnel wall, while Duilio did the same. The infante waited until they were all ready, and then knocked lightly on the heavy wooden door. When nothing happened, he rapped louder.

The rattling of the lock warned them before the door swung

inward. A big man stepped to the threshold, his old-fashioned blue uniform marking him as a palace guard. A wide smile crossed his face. "Your Highness, I had almost given up hope."

The infante relaxed visibly. "Bastião, what's happening in the palace?"

The big man surveyed them all quickly and said, "The prince and his doctor have been closeted since the noon hour in the new building. The guards have all been ordered to let them alone."

The guard caught sight of Oriana's tucked-up skirts and stocking-clad legs. He looked away, flushing. Oriana quickly tugged her skirts free.

The infante began to walk and the guard fell in next to him, with the three of them following. "Has anyone missed me?"

"I don't think so, Your Highness," Bastião said. "You're still supposed to be locked in your quarters. I have noticed that about half the guards seem to be missing, mostly yours."

Oriana walked faster to keep up with the men. *Yours* must mean guards who were sympathetic to the infante rather than the prince.

The infante scowled. "I was afraid of that. That means the remaining ones would stop us from entering the new building."

Duilio drew his revolver from his pocket. Oriana thought about her stubby gun, but decided to let Duilio do the shooting for now.

"Stay close," the infante said, "move slowly, and be quiet."

The big guard stepped around the infante so that he stood behind the man, and pointed to the ground next to him, apparently wanting Joaquim on that side. Oriana stayed behind them with Duilio, and the infante led the way, stepping into the tower room with a firm tread.

To one side of the huge basement room, another guard sat in a wooden chair, tied up and with a gag in his mouth. Oriana watched the man's eyes as they walked past him and toward the stairwell on the other side of the floor. The guard didn't spot them. The infante was, indeed, hiding them all from sight.

They crossed the wide floor, walked through another archway and into another spiral staircase. She was beginning to think the mazelike reputation of the palace was underrated. They wended their way up that staircase, and came out into a short hallway that actually led outside. The infante opened the door and strode down the steps to a wide patio. A guard patrolled the outer edge, pacing along its length, but he didn't notice their exit from the building, or even the door's movement. Oriana closed it as softly as she could, grateful their luck was holding.

The blue-tiled walls were ornate, but she didn't have a chance to look at them. They hurried past a pair of stone columns carved to look like giant ropes and up the stairs into a far more severe and plain part of the palace, a section that rose stories above the others—the new building, she guessed, where the guards had been told not to go. As soon as they walked through the arched doorway, she could tell something was wrong. A vibration prickled along her skin, so faint she might have thought she imagined it if she hadn't seen Duilio pause and shake his head.

The lighting in this section of the palace was brighter. A wide carpet runner muffled their steps but the stillness about them felt strange, as if that part of the palace was abandoned. Oriana didn't see any guards down the long white hallway before them. She leaned toward Duilio. "Are there usually guards here?"

"Yes," the infante remarked in a conversational tone. "I wonder where they've gone."

The vibration along Oriana's skin abruptly intensified until she could feel it in her bones, abruptly identifiable—the call of a *male* sereia, but uncontrolled and panicked.

It wasn't her uncle.

CHAPTER 33

A door slammed somewhere in the nearby halls and Duilio started. He felt more than heard that *call*. It rattled along his senses, making his teeth and his ears ache. It didn't pull him toward the source, but it was enough to make him jumpy.

The infante stood very still, one hand raised as a request they all stop. "What is that?" he whispered.

"Male sereia," Oriana answered. "Their timbre is too low to attract. They repulse, instead. That's why you never hear about them."

"Good God." The infante shook himself and walked on.

The sound of clipped footsteps ahead brought him to a stop. A woman dressed in a servant's austere black emerged from the main hallway about thirty feet away. She peered down the hallway in their direction.

Oriana instantly recognized her—Maria Melo, or whatever she called herself now.

"Be still," the infante whispered.

Mrs. Melo gazed past them, hands on hips, and called, "Heliodoro, I need you."

Oriana's hands balled into fists. Duilio grasped her arm to keep her from attacking.

The woman called for the unknown man again and walked swiftly back into the main hallway. Duilio let go a pent-up breath when she was out of sight.

"I suggest we follow," the infante said softly.

Oriana shook her head. "No, just Duilio and me."

Duilio turned to speak, but stopped. A heavyset man in a dark suit stood in the entry through which they'd just come, looking as startled to see them as they were him. The infante's ability to hide them must not extend in all directions, and the newcomer had come up behind them.

"Bastião, get him," the infante said softly.

Bastião didn't hesitate. Pistol in hand, the big guard pushed past Duilio and charged toward the man.

The man eyes went wide, and as he stumbled toward the outer door with Bastião in pursuit, he called out Iria's name in panic. The woman had to have heard his warning.

"We'd better move," Duilio said, searching for something in his pockets. "Our chance of surprise is gone. Raimundo, stay behind us."

The infante stepped aside, apparently well schooled in taking orders for his protection. Duilio and Joaquim jogged to the end of the hallway. Joaquim peered around the corner, gestured for them to come ahead, and proceeded down the main hallway. The odd vibration ceased abruptly, startling in its sudden absence. Then another sound replaced it.

Oriana heard the sereia's *call*—a female's voice this time. It had to be Maria Melo, reaching out to control them.

Mesmerized, the infante slowly turned and began walking that way. Joaquim had already disappeared around the corner. Duilio was the only one who hadn't gone. He held his hands over his ears, the right one clutching his revolver against his head.

The song flowed over and past Oriana, not pitched to entice her ears, but Duilio started walking after the other two men, slowly, as if fighting every step. With the other sereia this close, he didn't have much of a chance of defeating her *call*, even with his selkie blood and Oriana's claim on him. None of the males would be able to escape.

Oriana weighed the odds. If she stayed behind Duilio, Mrs. Melo might not notice her in his shadow, not if she was focused on the men. So she kept directly behind Duilio's slowly moving form, flicked open the cylinder of her gun, and dug a bullet out of her coat pocket. She hadn't fired a gun in years. She wouldn't do so unless she absolutely had to. The vibrations flared through her webbing and interfered with her senses. But she would do it if it meant bringing Maria Melo down.

Duilio walked on around the corner, his hands covering his ears, his footsteps slow and measured. Oriana shot a quick glance past him, but didn't see Joaquim or the infante anywhere. They must have followed the sereia through one of the doors that led off on either side.

Duilio started moving faster as they approached the *calling* woman, heading directly toward an open door on their left. Keeping as close as she could, Oriana tried to set a bullet into the cylinder, but her hands trembled and it fell to the runner. She hissed in frustration, located a second bullet, slid it into the chamber, and clicked the cylinder closed. She held the gun with both hands, praying it wouldn't have too much of a kick.

She pulled back the hammer as Duilio stepped over the threshold into a vast room. Maria Melo stood on the far side, a splash of darkness against a white wall, her head thrown back as she *called*. She'd pulled down the collar of her shirtwaist, and her gills vibrated visibly.

The infante stood before her, one hand reaching out to touch her face, trapped like a fly in amber by the strength of her *call*. Joaquim had almost reached her, but a man in a black coat stood next to him, grasping his arm. Oriana saw a knife in the man's hands, thrusting toward Joaquim's heart.

She stepped out from behind Duilio and fired. Vibrations from the recoil made the room spin about her, the reverberations in her webbing distorting her senses. Gasping, she dropped the gun, thrust her hands under her armpits, and fell to her knees.

Next to Joaquim, the man fell, too. He clutched his belly, his face wracked with pain. Oriana couldn't hear him over the *call* of the sereia, but she saw him roll onto his back and hold up hands covered with blood. The sereia continued to sing, Duilio still walking toward her.

Oriana clenched her teeth to fight the dizziness. She was *not* going to lose them.

Softly she began a song of her own, *calling* them to herself. Tearing males away from another sereia's grip was nigh impossible at this distance, but Joaquim stopped in his progress toward the woman. Duilio continued on toward her.

Why? Oriana gulped in another breath, mystified. She should have been able to reach Duilio more easily.

She changed her tone, hoping to reach him specifically, weaving his name into her wordless song, putting into it all her yearning for him. Joaquim turned away from her, but Duilio still ignored her summons. He walked on, by then only a foot or so away from Mrs. Melo.

The woman lowered her head to gaze disdainfully at him, the volume of her song decreasing with that motion. As if in a dream, Duilio lowered his left hand to hear her better, his right hand still clutching his revolver to his ear. The woman looked directly at Oriana and started sliding Duilio's gun from his hand.

Oriana put every bit of desire she had into her song, begging him to return to her. Where had her own revolver gone? She couldn't turn her head to look for it.

The gun slipped from Duilio's fingers.

The sereia woman turned his revolver in her hand, pulled back the hammer, and . . .

His right hand still firmly over that ear, Duilio punched her in the throat with his left.

A sharp squeal from Mrs. Melo's throat had them all clapping hands to their ears as she dropped the revolver to clutch at her neck with both hands. Her *call* was gone.

The infante shook himself and stepped back. Joaquim looked dazed, but quickly knelt down at the side of the man Oriana had shot.

Duilio reclaimed his revolver and turned back to Oriana. "Are you hurt?"

Oriana gaped at him. "Were you planning that all along?"

"More or less," he admitted. "I couldn't exactly tell you once she started up."

Duilio could always count on people underestimating him. As Oriana walked to where her revolver lay on the carpet several feet away, she surveyed their surroundings. It was a huge room, the walls draped with sheets, all reeking of carbolic. There were no beds in the room, no furnishings at all. It was as sterile as that flat, converted into a surgery. What looked to be a hundred lights glowed in the candelabra, adding to the stark whiteness of the room. The smell of stale blood hung in the air, and a bundle of dark-stained fabrics was collected near the door of the room.

Oriana swallowed, her throat aching. How much of that blood was her uncle's?

She pressed the back of one hand to her mouth, fighting tears. She'd known they would be too late to help him. She'd *known*. And she was horrifyingly grateful it wasn't her father's blood there.

For a moment it seemed everything was frozen in ice about her, the world gone still. Duilio shot a concerned look at her where she stood in the middle of the room, unmoving. He took a step toward her.

Then Joaquim rose from where he'd crouched next to the moaning doctor. "Gut shot. He's not going to make it."

The infante lunged forward and grabbed Mrs. Melo's arm, hauling her back to her feet. "Where is my brother?"

She hissed at him in response.

And the low vibration of a male sereia's *call* began again, this time from the doorway behind them. Oriana spun about. A man leaned against the doorframe, wearing a fine nightshirt marked with spatters of blood. His overlong hair looked wild, and his dark eyes were unnaturally wide. He opened his mouth, apparently to speak, but all that came forth was the soundless *call*, sending irritation throughout all their senses. Then he collapsed onto the hard floor.

"I'll kill him," Mrs. Melo gasped out.

Oriana jerked back around to see the woman holding a knife to the infante's side, the other hand twisted into the neck of his coat. The infante must have turned to look to the doorway like the rest of them, and she'd taken advantage of his distraction.

Joaquim moved toward her.

"I'll do it," she rasped. "Don't come any closer."

Oriana lifted her revolver again. "You're not going to hurt him. You have orders. What would your Spanish masters do to you if they found out you killed him?"

Mrs. Melo shoved the infante away and threw the knife at Oriana. Oriana deflected the flying blade with her arm, but her quarry ducked behind the draped sheets and disappeared. Hissing, Oriana pressed her hand over her arm. The knife had grazed her. She wasn't certain how badly. It stung like a salt-wrapped burn.

She ran over, grabbed the sheet draping the wall, and pulled hard, sending it cascading down about her feet. A narrow door was concealed behind the fabric, set into a wall where plaster leaves chased along delicate vines. Oriana jerked the door open and gave chase.

D uilio ran after her. He had no idea where he was going. Oriana was ahead of him, and there weren't any other doors leading off to either side. There was nowhere else for the Melo woman to have gone.

The hallway ended abruptly in another one of the damned spiral staircases. Oriana stood at the landing, leaning over the steps to look down into the center for her quarry. Duilio groaned. He'd hoped the new section of the palace would be free of this nonsensical architecture.

Up or down? Oriana gestured at him.

His lack of familiarity with this part of the palace meant he couldn't guess, but his hearing was better than Oriana's on land. Duilio listened, trying to determine which way she'd gone. He could hear a patter of feet above. Given how quickly Oriana tired while climbing, he figured Mrs. Melo's lead would quickly shorten. *Up*, he gestured.

The staircase continued upward through the floors, and Duilio stopped at each one to peer into identical narrow hallways. He didn't see her. At the highest point of the palace they came out of the stairwell into the fifth-floor hallway. Mrs. Melo was nowhere to be seen. He turned back to Oriana and spread his hands wide.

Breathing heavily, Oriana pointed to the door at the far end of the hallway. He guessed it would lead into a room that mirrored the one they'd left on the ground floor, but when he opened it, it only showed them four wooden walls, no larger than a closet, with a metal ladder leading upward. Duilio stepped inside and looked up . . . and saw stars in the night sky.

CHAPTER 34

Joaquim helped the infante maneuver the prince onto one of the torn-down sheets, preparing to carry the man somewhere safer. Across the room, Dr. Serpa had managed to prop himself against one of the sheet-covered walls, and held one hand pressed to his abdomen. His black suit hid the seep of blood, but his hands were red-stained, making Joaquim hope Serpa might simply bleed to death. Oriana *had* shot the man in his stomach. Almost no one survived that sort of injury. If the man didn't bleed to death, the infection would kill him slowly, which might be more just.

Serpa's eyes fixed on him. "I am going to be infamous," he said in an educated accent with a hint of a Castilian lisp. "Like Castigliani. Doctors will speak of my work for centuries."

"He's talking about the doctor in that book, isn't he?" the infante asked Joaquim, one hand pressed to his brother's forehead. The prince moaned, but his eyes remained closed.

Joaquim nodded. He wasn't going to satisfy Serpa by rising to his bait.

"There's a house on Almada Street," Serpa called toward them. He coughed and then said, "A girl is there. Tell the prince's guards they can find her in the back. Her body and my notes should be taken to the medical college."

Leaving the infante for a moment, Joaquim rose and went to

stare down at the doctor. "Her name was Marta Duarte. Did you even know her name?"

"They'll study her for years," Serpa went on as if he hadn't spoken. "The otter and the seal parts were only for show, so they shouldn't judge our work by that. The throat, though—that was pure genius. With a healer to control the infection, anything can be replaced. I've laid the foundation for transplantation of hearts and lungs, hands and feet and eyes. Doctors may never speak my name because they pretend they don't approve, but they'll copy my methods."

Joaquim felt his fists clenching. Surely the Medical-Surgical School wouldn't condone such experiments.

"Oh, they will," the doctor said, almost as if he'd spoken aloud. "Now they'll be able to give anyone gills," he rambled, the last few words beginning to slur. "I've made all the peoples equal."

Joaquim turned away, jaw set. This man would have ripped out the throat of Marina Arenias just to prove his claims and never once considered the vibrant life he was cutting short. No one had that right, no matter how groundbreaking the results.

Eager to get away, Joaquim went to the door. He peered out and, at the crossing of the hallways, spotted three guards approaching. He checked his gun, but when they got closer, he saw that Bastião led them. A moment later the large guard knelt before the prince's bloodied form.

"My God," the guard said, crossing himself. "Is *this* what they were planning?"

The infante lifted his hand from his brother's forehead. "Yes. A slow death, I'm afraid."

The guard visibly collected himself and faced the infante. "The other guards were locked in the gymnasium, Your Highness, along with a dozen or so of the servants. They claimed they were enticed there with magic."

"The sereia woman," Joaquim supplied. "She must have *called* them."

Bastião glanced up at him. "Yes. They're moving out to secure the palace now, but I've warned them not to fire on strangers because of the investigators from the Special Police."

"Good." The infante rose and pointed toward the doctor. "Rodrigo, keep an eye on Serpa. I don't care if he looks dead. I don't want to take any chances." One of the guards went to take a station by the doctor. "The rest of us can carry His Highness back to his rooms. We need to do it as gently as possible. Bastião, what did you do with the man you were chasing?"

Bastião rose. "I tied him up downstairs in the gymnasium, Your Highness. I left him in the chaplain's charge."

Mother of God! Drawing his gun, Joaquim ran for the stairwell.

Oriana climbed upward in Duilio's wake, the metal rungs cold under her hands. When she reached the top of the access shaft, she took a deep breath and pushed herself up onto the roof, trusting that Duilio would have their quarry covered. As she expected, he stood a few feet from the ladder, gun trained on the woman.

Maria Melo stood at the edge of the rooftop, peering over a low wall into the darkness at the wooded park below. Lights illuminated the white merlons that ringed this section of rooftop, each as tall as a man. Oriana yanked on her skirt to free it from the shaft and got to her feet on the flat graveled area, catching Duilio's eye.

Duilio settled his aim on the woman, and said, "Iria Serpa, you're under arrest."

That's not going to work. Oriana knew the lengths to which this woman would go. Iria Serpa—or Maria Melo—wasn't going to let herself be arrested. There was too great a chance she could be made to spill the truth eventually. No, the woman probably saw only two alternatives: escape or death. She'd retreated to the rooftop, though, which left her one option. Oriana tried to calm her breathing as she decided what to say.

Mrs. Melo glanced back over her shoulder. "It won't help anyone if you take me in."

"This is personal for you, isn't it?" Oriana asked. "A vendetta against the prince that required he die in the worst way. Make him a sereia, the very thing he fears most."

Mrs. Melo was intrigued. Oriana could see that in the smirk that lifted one corner of the woman's lips. She had little illusion that the woman would confess the truth to her, but her reactions alone might provide some answers.

"So you found yourself at that prison," Oriana said. "You met Serpa and his healer and insinuated yourself into their plans. You saw a way to get them to do your bidding. I'd bet they thought this was all about them and their dubious medical advancements. But you're smarter than they are. They must have been so busy dreaming of being immortalized that they never once questioned why you were helping them."

Mrs. Melo laughed. "Yes, his precious work. He wanted that girl preserved for posterity. I should have burned down the damned building."

"But now the police are there," Oriana told her, "collecting everything." Duilio took a step toward the woman, but Oriana put out one hand to stop him. How long could she keep the woman talking? "They have to have evidence to take you to trial."

"It would be a fair trial, of course," Duilio added.

Maria Melo laughed harshly, her lip curling. "A fair trial? Twenty years ago, your precious prince executed my parents just for living here. Are you old enough to remember that? They were charged as spies. Did your police even try to determine if they were before condemning them? No, your prince just had them hanged."

The acid in her tone made Oriana think she was hearing the truth. "And what did Felipa Reyna do to deserve your ire?" Oriana asked.

"The girl was in the wrong place at the wrong time, nothing personal." Mrs. Melo's head turned as she glanced over the low wall behind her. "In this business, people die. I would have preferred to kill that interfering father of yours for *his* throat, but the Special Police let me down again."

That *had* been the reason behind the arrest warrant then. The woman was still trying to eliminate the threat posed by Oriana's family. Duilio stayed still, gun trained on the woman, as Oriana stepped forward. Her head was swimming. What else could she learn before the woman acted?

"Tell me, did you kill my mother?" she asked, curious to see if Mrs. Melo would even answer. "Or did someone do it for you when she figured out that you're a Canary?"

Mrs. Melo laughed again. "You think you're a priest to hear my confession? You think I'll trade all my secrets to save my life? I'm not the fool you believe I am. I've always known the price. I know the rules of this game, far better than you do, girl." She hummed a few notes . . . just enough of a *call* woven into them to distract Duilio. His gun lowered only an inch.

"No!" Oriana shouted, jumping forward.

Duilio fired a split second too late, his bullet striking stone. Maria Melo tumbled off the roof. Oriana managed to get one hand on the woman's skirt, but the woman's weight began dragging her toward the gap between the two merlons.

"I can't hold her!"

Duilio dropped to his knees next to her, trying to get a better grip on the fabric or a limb, but Mrs. Melo hung limply, bent at the waist, both arms and feet dangling down. "Damn! She must have hit her head going over."

Oriana felt herself slipping closer to the edge. Her hand burned, the fabric twisting tighter around her fingers. Duilio reached over the edge of the precipice, trying to get a hand on the woman's jacket.

Cloth ripped with a hiss. Oriana let out a cry of frustration as the fabric in her hand suddenly came loose. Duilio tumbled forward in a desperate effort to grab Mrs. Melo, but Oriana grabbed at his legs to steady him.

He sat down hard against the side of the merlon, his breath coming short. "Thank you."

Oriana peered over the edge of the wall, Duilio's hand knotting into the back of her borrowed jacket to keep her from going over. He might not be able to see the ground, but sereia eyes were better in darkness.

On the rocks below, Maria Melo lay broken. She wasn't going to move anytime soon.

Oriana sat there, Duilio's arms about her as they both tried to catch their breath. She needed to remember every word the woman said. Maria Melo had given up a few pieces of the puzzle . . . and that was more than they'd had this morning, but she'd taken most of her secrets down with her.

Oriana grasped Duilio's arm, feeling dizzy now the confrontation was over. There was one thing she *could* prove. "We . . . we have to retrieve her body."

Duilio rose and hauled her back toward the doorway. "We'll get the guards to do that."

She pressed a hand against her aching arm, and then swayed. Duilio caught her before she could hit the gravel rooftop.

The stairs down to the basement level were dark, but Joaquim could see lights in the hallway below—the gymnasium where the infante kept beating Duilio. That thought made a brief smile cross his face. But it fled when he saw a black-garbed figure steal up the stairwell at the far end of the long hallway.

Anjos had ordered them not to pursue the healer, but he wasn't going to let this man get away. *I just won't get within arm's reach.*

As he passed the entry door to the gymnasium, he saw the stocky young man Bastião had left in the chaplain's care. Hands bound behind him, the man slumped on the floor, mouth agape and eyes staring. Joaquim leaned against the doorframe to peer at him. That left little doubt their chaplain was a killer . . . and was willing to kill again.

Determined not to lose his quarry, Joaquim made his way cautiously to the end of the hallway. He paused at the base of the stairwell, listening. Footsteps moved away on the floor above, so he started up. He came out on the ground floor, back pressed to the wall. His heart beat loud in his ears as he listened for movement.

Where was the man?

Then his eyes caught a movement, a black shape coming out of that center hallway as if he'd taken the wrong direction and had to double back. Joaquim chased the man down the hallway. Just before Salazar reached the outside doors, they swung open, and two uniformed officers of the Special Police stepped inside. Salazar retreated toward Joaquim.

"Don't try it," Joaquim warned, raising his gun.

Salazar spun around and ran toward the two newcomers instead, catching one with a hand wrapped around his throat. The officer gasped, his eyes wide and his weapon falling to the floor. The other raised his gun but didn't fire, saying, "Let him go."

Salazar began backing away, dragging his hapless hostage with him as a shield. He backed into a side hallway and into a brightly lit room, shutting the door behind him.

The outer doors opened again. Miss Vladimirova stepped inside, Anjos and Gaspar directly behind her, and Joaquim waved for the two inspectors to join him. "He went inside that room. He has an officer hostage."

"The officer's dead then." Miss Vladimirova's veiled head turned toward Anjos. "I will go."

She walked slowly toward Joaquim, setting his skin crawling as she neared. He glanced at Gaspar and Anjos. Neither argued with her. They merely checked their guns and headed for the door, Anjos grimacing as if in pain.

Joaquim turned the latch, pushed open the door, and Miss Vladimirova walked inside, the scent of river water drifting with her. The room appeared to be a sitting area with chairs and tables clustered in small groups, abandoned now. The police officer Salazar had taken hostage lay on the entry rug, eyes open. His throat looked scalded.

Joaquim crossed himself. "How many people can he kill?"

Miss Vladimirova's head swiveled toward him. "I do not know if there's a limit."

That didn't sound good. Salazar wasn't using his borrowed strength to heal now, so what could he do with that power?

"The energies will burn him if he doesn't use them," Miss Vladimirova volunteered. "So he will use them to strike."

No, that wasn't reassuring. *But we can't stop now.*

There were two doors on the far wall. Joaquim strode to the nearer, opened it carefully and peered out. It led onto a narrow dark hallway that must be a servants' passage, one that would take them right back into the main body of the old palace, judging by its placement. A hand settled on Joaquim's arm—Gaspar. He'd forgotten the man was behind him. "Find him," Gaspar said. "We'll follow."

Joaquim swallowed. He knew what the hard-eyed inspector wanted. Gaspar wanted him to prove he was a witch yet again, to use his long-buried abilities to bring down a man who'd done far worse with his witchery.

He didn't know *how* he was supposed to do that, but he had to try.

Joaquim clenched his jaw, closed his eyes, and forced himself to concentrate. This wasn't like finding Duilio whom he knew as well as himself. He didn't know Salazar at all. His name meant nothing, and all Joaquim could do was string together what few facts he had and his brief glimpses of the man. *Priest but defrocked, illicit. Torturer, despite being called to heal. A man with no respect for women.* That thought brought out a flash of fury and, for an instant, he could almost *see* Salazar as a faint light traveling away from him. He pointed in that direction before his sense of the man faded.

Gaspar nodded and pushed past, whispering, "Well done."

Joaquim followed, jaw set. This wasn't going to be pleasant. Gaspar meant to kill the man, but Salazar had killed two men in the last few minutes, which surely made him formidable enough even for Gaspar. Anjos and Miss Vladimirova followed more slowly.

When they reached the end of the hallway, Gaspar pulled the door open. They'd clearly ended up in the original palace, with a hallway heading both left and right, and to one side a spiral staircase led up to the next floor. Gaspar glanced back at Joaquim. "Well?"

Joaquim focused on Salazar again, gaining a sense of the man more easily this time. "Up."

"That's a strange choice," Gaspar whispered. Anjos hadn't quite reached them, so Gaspar made a gesture to tell him they were taking the stairwell. Gaspar started up, hugging the outer edge of the spiral. When they reached the top, they stepped out into the hallway and Gaspar gestured for Joaquim to be still.

"What are you doing here?" he asked the empty hallway.

Joaquim wondered if Gaspar had lost his mind.

The Lady abruptly appeared, her back pressed against the opposite wall several feet farther down the hall. She looked unusually pale and her eyes were wide and frightened. "He chased me up here," she whispered. "Thank God he couldn't find me."

Gaspar didn't spend time consoling her. "Where are the officers who were guarding you?"

She pointed toward a doorway. "Giving chase. They followed

him in there." She grabbed Gaspar's arm and gestured toward the wall a few feet away. "He touched that."

A handprint showed on the wall, where the plaster was scorched. Gaspar reached out and touched it. "Still warm. Stay with us," he told the Lady. "Tavares, guard her with your life."

Joaquim opened his mouth to argue, but didn't have any logical protest to make.

Gaspar opened the door and entered, stepping over the slumped body of a man in police uniform that lay next to the door. Joaquim followed, keeping the Lady behind him.

The room was some sort of waiting area with chairs lining two long walls. A red runner led up the center to a desk on a dais, and near that Salazar waited for them. A second police officer stood in his clutch, unresisting like a rag doll. It seemed to take no effort on Salazar's part to hold him up. Was that strength stolen from his victims?

"Come any closer and I will kill him," Salazar said, angry eyes on Gaspar.

Gaspar gestured and Joaquim obediently split away, crossing the aisle and pressing against the far wall. Then Gaspar raised his pistol and calmly took a shot at Salazar's head. The priest's head snapped back, a small hole appearing in his forehead. But before their eyes, he shook his head and the bullet hole disappeared. The police officer slumped to the floor instead.

What just happened? Joaquim gaped at the officer now lying on the red runner. A small hole showed on his forehead.

Gaspar tossed his gun to the floor and charged at the priest instead. Salazar held his arms wide, waiting for Gaspar to tackle him. Joaquim cast a quick glance at the Lady, then moved closer as Gaspar barreled into the priest, shoulder first. Salazar staggered back, but kept his feet. He slapped a hand against Gaspar's cheek.

And then he snatched it away as if *he'd* been burned.

Roaring in a guttural voice, he shoved at Gaspar instead, actually throwing the inspector back through the air. Gaspar slammed into the far wall with a loud grunt. He slid down and caught himself on a chair, surprise flickering across his features as he gripped his right side with his left hand. His jaw clenched in pain.

The Lady moved toward her husband, but Joaquim blocked her path. "Stay back. Please, Lady."

At the far end of the hall, Joaquim saw Inspector Anjos enter, the black-draped woman with him. Four palace guards in their old-fashioned uniforms followed them. One of them ran past Anjos, ignoring the inspector's order to stop. The guard tried to catch Salazar's arm, but the priest grabbed him instead, laying one bare hand to the man's throat. Joaquim smelled burning flesh.

Then Salazar saw Miss Vladimirova and his eyes went wide with terror. The man backed up against the wall, dragging the guard with him. Anjos stayed at her side, his gun ready. The other three guards spread out, cutting between Joaquim and the priest.

"This is simple," the woman said in her oddly flat voice. "You will come with us, or I will make you regret it."

Anjos dared a quick look down at the dead police officer just as the captive guard began to struggle in Salazar's grasp. The priest's eyes seemed fixed on the woman like the point of a compass, though. He didn't move either way. She raised one gloved hand. "Come now."

"I'd listen to her," Anjos said. "We have you surrounded."

Salazar's eyes snapped toward Anjos. "I can keep your prince alive. I can control the infection. So long as I'm with him, he won't die."

Was that his plan all along? To keep the prince tied to his questionable mercy?

"Yes, you can," Miss Vladimirova said. "Killing every day to keep him on his feet. But I could, too. We don't need *you* for that."

Salazar's eyes skimmed over the officers in the room, Anjos only a few feet away, Gaspar still hunched on the wooden chairs, Joaquim farther back. Then he shoved his current captive away and jumped toward Anjos, one hand snaking out to grasp the inspector's hand over the gun. Anjos didn't hesitate. He fired. The healer hissed in pain, but didn't release Anjos. "If you have any fondness for your protector, whore," he said to Miss Vladimirova, "you'll stay away. I'll kill him, inch by inch."

Anjos began breathing heavily, but didn't move. Blood dripped from his hand, as if all the vessels were rupturing. Anjos tried to raise his other hand to pull back the gun's hammer, but froze in place.

Joaquim watched Anjos struggle. If he shot Salazar, the priest could just transfer the injury to Anjos, couldn't he? That was why Gaspar had tried attacking him bodily. Joaquim stepped forward.

"Get back," Gaspar hissed at him, teeth clenched. "Don't interfere."

Joaquim cast him a horrified glance. Salazar was going to kill Anjos. Then he felt the Lady's hand on his arm. "Let *her* do this," the Lady whispered in his ear. "She's far more powerful than he is."

"He's killed four people now. How can she beat him?"

"He's got Anjos," she whispered, eyes fixed on the tableau ahead of them. "There's nothing in the world more important to her. Not even her own self-control. To save him, she might even come back to life."

He peered at the Lady's avid face, trying to grasp her meaning. She'd said she believed that Miss Vladimirova had stopped her own life, a matter of control. A healer had to have life to heal someone else, though, and Miss Vladimirova didn't. Had they put Anjos forward intentionally, to force the Russian woman's hand? Joaquim kept his gun trained on Salazar, just in case. Blood ran from Anjos' hand now, a steady stream.

"Let him go," Miss Vladimirova said to Salazar. "Your last warning."

The other guard jumped onto Salazar's back, breaking his grip on the inspector. The healer twisted in the guard's grip, wrapped a hand around the man's throat, and that guard went limp.

Released, Anjos fell to his knees, his right arm hanging at his side.

Joaquim stepped forward again. He could shoot, now that Salazar wasn't touching the inspector.

Miss Vladimirova held up one hand. "Don't waste him."

He spared a glance at her. *Waste him?*

Anjos now knelt in a pool of blood, his life bleeding away.

Miss Vladimirova stepped closer to Salazar. "You know what I am, don't you? You can feel it in yourself already. I am your death."

Salazar leaned toward Anjos, but before he could touch the inspector, Miss Vladimirova stretched her arms toward him.

A wind whipped through the room, and for a split second Joaquim's breath was stolen away. He felt strangled. Then the sensation released him, passing as quickly as it had come upon him. One of the two remaining palace guards ran from the room, bumping into Joaquim as he fled.

Miss Vladimirova stood with her arms outstretched. Salazar arched toward her as if a hook were buried in his stomach and she was reeling him in. Then he collapsed to the floor.

Joaquim felt cold all over. She'd taken Salazar's life without even touching him.

She gasped in a huge breath, sounding like she'd been underwater. Joaquim couldn't see her face, but she threw back her veil and ripped off her hat, revealing a golden braid fiercely pinned back in a bun. She continued to gasp for air, visible waves of heat coming off her body.

Then she spun toward Anjos. She cried out something in her own tongue, brokenly. She fell to her knees in his blood, grasped Anjos' wounded hand in hers, and ripped at his shirt with her free hand. She worked that hand inside his undershirt. Her eyes closed and she went still.

Joaquim had never watched a healer at work. *This seems . . . voyeuristic.*

He turned away. Behind him, the Lady knelt at Gaspar's side. The inspector perched halfway between sitting and standing, his right arm clutched close. Joaquim helped her get Gaspar situated on the chair, which earned a pained grimace from the inspector. Broken ribs, without a doubt.

Gaspar waved Joaquim away, so he went and checked on the downed men. The police officer Salazar had held hostage lay dead, a bullet wound to his forehead as if he'd somehow been given the injury in Salazar's place. One of the palace guards was stunned, but alive. His throat was red and burned, but he was breathing. The other hadn't fared so well, neck twisted at an awkward angle. The first police officer, abandoned by the entryway, was dead as well.

That left the healer. Joaquim didn't want to touch Salazar's body. He was putting it off. As if by agreement, he and the remaining guard settled for grabbing Salazar by his feet and dragging him away from Anjos and Miss Vladimirova. They left him near the door, and Joaquim asked the guard to keep an eye on the corpse, just in case.

"Take his head off," Gaspar hissed from his seat. "To be sure."

Joaquim cast him a horrified glance. *Is he serious?* The palace guard didn't hesitate, though. He drew his saber and swung it at the healer's throat.

"Little different than a vampire," Gaspar said. He pointed toward Miss Vladimirova with his chin. "That one's been walking around dead for decades."

Joaquim swallowed. He didn't have a good grasp of witchery, but it seemed a barbaric step. He was in above his head with these people. He looked back to where Miss Vladimirova still leaned over Anjos, speaking softly in a strange tongue. He could see heat rising from the woman's form, rippling the air about them, but it eased and then faded away. Joaquim eyed the pool of blood in which Anjos lay, wondering how much a man could lose and still survive.

The woman released Anjos' hand and fell to her hands and knees. Anjos began coughing. Surely that had to be a good sign.

"Help me turn him," she begged, one hand extended toward Joaquim. "Help me."

It was his first real look at her face. Her features startled him; Miss Vladimirova was only a girl, and a frightened one at that.

She tugged on Anjos' coat, trying to get him onto his left side. Joaquim leaned past her and dragged Anjos over. Anjos then began coughing in earnest. He didn't seem to be aware, though, and a second later Joaquim was grateful because the inspector started coughing up hideous phlegm, black and tarry. Joaquim knelt behind the man, supporting his back with his knee. "What is this?" he asked the girl. "Is this normal?"

"The consumption. It is coming out," she whispered. "Don't touch it."

Joaquim swallowed, eyeing the pile of sputum next to Anjos. *Oh, Lord, no, I am not going to touch that.* They'd better take up that whole section of the carpet and bury it at sea, or burn it, or whatever would keep that from passing to a new victim. "Will it hurt him?"

The young woman—no more than eighteen or nineteen, Joaquim guessed—sat back on her heels. Her forehead glistened with sweat. "No, he's cured now."

She'd cured him? Consumption was one of the illnesses he was sure healers couldn't handle. This was what she'd intended when she told Joaquim not to "waste" Salazar.

How many had the priest killed? His accomplice, the first police officer and a second, one of the palace guards, perhaps more. Joaquim shuddered. He'd lost count.

Miss Vladimirova lay down on her side, heedless of the blood.

One of her hands stretched out to catch the tips of Anjos' fingers. Then she seemed to slip into sleep.

She'd used the accumulated deaths to save Anjos' life, the thing she hadn't been able to do before . . . because she refused to kill. The Church wouldn't agree with her methods, but she'd worked a miracle.

CHAPTER 35

Oriana's coat sleeve had been hiding the worst of the bleeding. The cut on her arm was shallow and not terribly dangerous, though, so Duilio cleaned and bound the gash himself while she gazed at him sheepishly. He would drag her out to see Mrs. Rodriguez later and see if the old woman could help speed the healing along, but he suspected a few nights of unbroken sleep might be the best remedy. That was regrettable in its own way. He would far rather spend those nights with her.

Once he'd gotten her back down the ladder and the spiral staircase, a second contingent of guards showed up to help them sort things out. Apparently Maria Melo had seduced them all into the private gymnasium in the basement—and then locked them in. But Bastião had let them out, and they were now getting things under control. Joaquim had been sent with a contingent of guards to retrieve Dr. Esteves from the house on Almada Street, since the doctor was already familiar with what had happened to the prince.

It was a matter of time, though. That knowledge showed in the demeanor of the guards; they turned to the infante for orders. They knew their prince was as good as dead.

Since the ballroom was already ruined, the guards used it as their staging area, bringing all the bodies there for accounting. On one side of the room lay the sheet-covered bodies of Dr. Serpa, the driver Heliodoro, and the body of the healer, Salazar, which had been rather gruesomely beheaded. Apparently Gaspar had thought it the best way to be certain the man *stayed* dead. Duilio didn't want to think too hard about that logic. In addition there were three officers of the Special Police dead, as well as four guards, the prince's valet, and Ambassador Alvaro. They had found the ambassador's remains in the basement, waiting by the furnace. Like Felipa Reyna, his throat had been stolen.

Duilio accompanied Oriana when she went to cover her uncle's body. She seemed steady enough on her feet, but he didn't want her to be alone for this. The guards in charge of the bodies allowed her to touch his face one final time, and promised that his body would be returned to the sereia government with proper ceremony. Duilio then drew her back out of the guards' way.

"Poor Uncle Braz," she whispered as they moved back. "I was never close to him, but he was kind to me."

"Perhaps you should try to sleep now," Duilio suggested.

"Not until I see her," Oriana said firmly. "I need to see her."

He led her back into the area of the ballroom where the representatives of the Special Police had been sequestered, foreigners inside the walls of the palace. Anjos lay on one side, a sheet folded up for his pillow. Despite not responding to anything around him, he looked . . . *healthier* to Duilio's eyes. Laid out next to him was a young woman, not even twenty, he'd guess, a thick golden braid streaming over one shoulder. Blood stained one side of her face and her hair. She had troubled dreams, expressions of fear flitting across her pale features. If she hadn't been wearing the same heavy black dress he'd seen earlier, Duilio would never have believed that this girl was the terrifying Miss Vladimirova. The sense of dread he'd always felt when she neared was absent. And now he knew why she'd always gone veiled. No one would have been frightened if they'd seen her true face.

Gaspar sat stiffly in a nearby chair, a torn sheet wrapped tightly as a bandage around his chest. The Lady sat by his side, her worried eyes moving between him, Anjos, and the sleeping girl. She glanced up at Duilio and Oriana as they settled in their chairs.

"The ambassador?" Gaspar rasped, placing one hand on his ribs.

"Yes," Duilio told him.

"I'm sorry, Miss Paredes," Gaspar said with a pained grimace.

"I knew it would be him," she said softly.

They all looked up as Joaquim entered, Dr. Esteves with him. The pair crossed immediately to where the Special Police officers waited. The doctor's eyes were shadowed, as if the night's work had worn him down. Duilio was impressed by the man's dedication.

"The girl didn't make it more than a few hours," Esteves said when he reached them. He surveyed the various officers. "Who needs attention most?"

Gaspar pointed to the officer with the burned throat lying on the floor near Anjos, the one Salazar had left dazed. Esteves knelt at the man's side and opened out his bag.

Oriana rose again, and Duilio saw the guards were bringing in another body wrapped in bloodstained sheets. He followed her over to that side of the room. Once the guards laid the sheet on the damaged rug, they opened it at Oriana's insistence. Inside lay the broken body of Maria Melo.

Oriana gazed down at the body of her nemesis, fists clenched. Mrs. Melo had landed on her back, and the guards had lain her out as she'd fallen, so her body didn't seem overly broken. But the staining of the sheets showed that her back wasn't intact.

Anger warmed Oriana, despite her light-headedness. This woman had caused so much harm. Never with her own hands. Instead she'd stayed behind the scenes and manipulated and threatened others into doing evil for her. And she hadn't seemed to care who stood in her way.

"I need to see her thighs," Oriana told the two guards laying out the body.

They glanced at each other as if trying to decide whether or not to comply with such a shocking request, but one eventually knelt down and began to neatly fold back the woman's skirt and under-skirt, exposing bare skin above her stockings. *Striped* skin. Three blurred lines of black ran diagonally across each thigh, identifying the woman's bloodlines without doubt. "She's a Canary. I was right."

Duilio shook his head.

"A bird?" the guard asked.

"No, a sereia whose ancestors came from the Canary Islands. Her people serve the Spanish navy. She's an agent of Spain."

"You can tell that from those stripes?" the guard asked.

"Yes. The Canaries have markings like a skipjack tuna. I've never heard of anyone on our islands having those markings." Oriana knelt down by the body. "They also usually have a dorsal fin that starts between the shoulder blades. I would bet she had it cut away, though, like the webbing between her fingers."

The guard nodded and pulled the dead woman's skirts back down. "When we get a photographer in here," he said, "we'll make certain he catches those details, miss."

Oriana licked her lips. "I don't know exactly how the Spanish would benefit from a war between the islands and the Portuguese," she said, "but I have no doubt someone in Spain is trying to start one."

"I agree," the infante said from behind them, his face grim. "Miss Paredes, I'll do my best to make sure the information about this woman's origin is passed on to the Ministry of Foreign Affairs."

Oriana noted that he didn't promise. Either he was hedging his word . . . or he understood politics. "Thank you, sir."

He nodded. "I no more want war with your people than you do,

I suspect. I'd like to speak with you further on the matter in a couple of days, if you're willing."

With her? "I have no . . . sanction to speak for my people, sir. I am an exile now."

"Yes. I'd like to discuss that, too." The infante inclined his head to her, and Oriana felt the strangest impulse to curtsy to the man. With a nod to Duilio, he left them, gathering more of his guards as he went.

Duilio's lips pursed, his eyes caught by movement across the room. The palace guards were preparing to carry Anjos to a carriage drawn up onto the palace's patio. Apparently they were ready to usher the Special Police out of their territory.

Oriana took one last look down at the body of Maria Melo. "I wonder what they'll do with her."

"I suspect the Spanish ambassador might be brought in to take a look at her."

"He'll deny everything," she said.

"Of course he will," Duilio said. "Come on. Let's get out of here."

Oriana glanced at the place where her uncle's wrapped body lay and wished his spirit a speedy return home. Then she set her hand on Duilio's arm and let him lead her away.

Joaquim had carried out the sleeping Miss Vladimirova and set her in the carriage next to Anjos. He joined Duilio and Oriana as they stood waiting for the next carriage to take them down into the city. "I'm going to stop back by Almada Street," he said. "Dr. Serpa intended for a copy of his journals to be sent to the Medical-Surgical School, and the original book was back at his flat. Dr. Esteves and I discussed it during our journey up to the palace."

He was talking about *The Seat of Magic*, the book that had fueled the idea for all this death. "It's evidence now," Oriana said. "Isn't it?"

Joaquim's lips pressed in a tight line. "We'll see."

Duilio turned to her. "Given that you've lost some blood," he said, "you need to get some sleep."

"I'm fine," she protested.

"Humor me," he said. "I'll take you back to the house, then go back and join him. We have things to take care of."

CHAPTER 36

Oriana woke in her own bed with midmorning light slanting in from the skylight in the bathroom. Her arm ached and the bandage's constriction annoyed her, but she'd had worse. For a time she lay there, her mind rambling over the things that she'd seen. She wished the entire previous day and night could be dismissed as a bad dream, but she knew better. She sighed heavily.

"Are you going to get out of bed?" Duilio asked.

She lifted her head and spotted him sitting across the room on her leather chaise, a book in his hands. He was neatly dressed in a dark coat and trousers. "What time is it?"

"Almost ten." He rose and came to stand by her bed. "See, I've left the door open to keep the servants happy."

"To keep Felis happy," Oriana said. "You're afraid of her." She sat up in bed, trying to decide whether her appetite or any other urges were particularly pressing. She could wait. "What are you reading?"

"The French book," Duilio said. He held Monsieur Matelot's flawed volume on sereia culture. "Mother's right. There needs to be a more accurate book on your people's customs."

If they could return to her people's islands, he could easily write that book. But there was still someone within her people's government who'd been willing to sacrifice her, someone who'd funded Serpa's obscene plans and the murders of her uncle and Felipa Reyna. She didn't know if she would ever feel safe there, but she *needed* to find out who'd been involved. "Perhaps someday," she equivocated.

"We've heard from Lady Pereira de Santos, by the way," he said. "The warrant for your father's arrest has been canceled, so you can rest easy on his account."

She laid her hands over her face. "Thank the gods." Then she recalled their other unfinished business. "Have we heard from Dr. Esteves?"

Duilio came and sat down on the edge of the bed facing her. "Yes, he believes he found a copy of Serpa's journal at the medical school's offices. He should be over in a couple of hours. Will you want to join us in the library when he arrives?"

"Yes," she said. "And what until then?"

His smile grew. "Did you have anything particular in mind?"

Oriana cast a glance at the bathroom door where she could see sunshine streaming down through the skylight. "Do you still want to get a look at my dorsal stripe in the daylight?"

"Is that a possibility?"

"It is," she admitted. "Although I suggest locking the bedroom door first, in interest of being discreet."

Duilio didn't waste any time.

A worn-looking Dr. Esteves produced a pair of leather journals bound with black ribbons as soon as he entered the library. One was printed, the title on its spine in Spanish—*El sede de la magia*—verifying that the book *had* been translated into a human tongue. The second must be Dr. Serpa's notes, the handwritten pages filled with a tidy, flowing script.

"Do you think there were more copies?" Duilio asked, looking at the notes.

"No way to tell," Esteves said. "I read some of this. Serpa truly did believe he was creating something fantastic."

Standing against the bookshelves with her arms folded, Oriana stared at the books as if they were a nest of snakes.

Joaquim shook his head. "There's a limit to how far one should go."

"Which is why I'm here, son." The doctor nodded to the two books resting on the polished library table. "Are those the original?"

One was the copy his father had brought from the islands; the second one, Joaquim had found at the doctor's house. "Yes," Duilio admitted. "One of them has been sitting in this library most of my life, unread."

"Serpa left his copy on his desk," Joaquim added, "in plain sight. Waiting for someone to pick it up and admire his cleverness, no doubt."

"So what do you plan to do with these?" Esteves asked.

Joaquim shot a glance over at the library hearth, which one of the maids had lit that morning to battle the chill. The flames had died down to embers, but he picked up the doctor's journal, walked over to the hearth, and ripped out a few pages. Then he tossed them on the embers. The paper curled, the ink smoking. The edges caught fire. Esteves picked up one of the journals and went to join Joaquim at the hearth. Soon they were both feeding pages slowly into the flame, the smell of burning paper acrid about the room.

Duilio ran his hand over the last book, the volume his father had owned. "We're destroying knowledge. What if there's something important in here?"

Oriana set her hand over his. "My uncle died because of this. Those girls did, too. Nothing is worth that."

"Some things come at too high a price," Joaquim said.

"What they did wasn't a miracle, Mr. Ferreira," the doctor said, glancing over his shoulder at Duilio. "It wasn't even a success. It was butchery, and we know enough ways to butcher each other already."

Serpa had killed at least six people in his quest for infamy—although the sixth, Prince Fabricio, wasn't dead yet. There was no knowing how many Salazar had killed. And all they had created between them was death.

Duilio picked up the last volume and carried it over to the hearth. He didn't know if burning the book was the right decision, but it was what he was going to do.

Epilogue

Saturday, 1 November 1902

The afternoon air was crisp, probably one of the last fine days of autumn. From the patio overlooking the park behind the palace, Duilio could see the northern side of the city, the Street of Flowers stretching in one silver line down toward the river. Above them, the blue-and-white flag of Northern Portugal snapped in the breeze.

It was All Saints' Day, the day for honoring the dead. Not a day of mourning, but a day of processionals and celebration. They had even gone to Mass that morning and lit candles at the cemetery. But the infante had asked them back to the palace, a personal visit rather than a state one. The nobility were actively courting the infante's favors now that he would soon have power after all. Duilio was aware of the honor he'd bestowed on them, bringing a commoner, a former sereia spy, and a mere gentleman to the palace to take up his very valuable time.

"I would have preferred that the Special Police not expose that one of the conspirators was a sereia," the infante told them as he strolled along the patio with Joaquim on one side and Oriana and Duilio on the other, "but tomorrow the newspapers will carry the speculation about her being of Spanish origin instead, and remind readers that the Spanish navy has long used sereia from the Canary Islands to hide their ships on the ocean."

"Thank you, Your Highness," Oriana said. "That will help."

The infante wore mourning already, his blue-and-red sash the only indicator of his royalty. "And as for the disappearance of the girl's body," he said. "I am naturally appalled that evidence has been removed. But as there isn't going to be a trial for Serpa or Salazar, I suppose it doesn't make a material difference."

That had been their last job that night, to transport the mutilated body of Marta Duarte to the Brothers of Mercy. Serpa had believed the girl's body should be preserved so that the Medical-Surgical School could study her at length. Instead, the girl had been given a proper burial in a pauper's grave. Duilio had no regrets over that piece of lawbreaking, and neither did Joaquim. Unfortunately, the police were not as sanguine about it.

The infante caught Joaquim's eye. "There was a hearing scheduled for Monday about your possible involvement in that, Inspector Tavares, but after a discussion with Police Commissioner Ribandar, that hearing has been canceled. I do have some influence."

Joaquim shifted uncomfortably. "Thank you."

Duilio wasn't sure if Joaquim's discomfort stemmed from disregarding the proper channels of justice, or being overtly singled out by the infante. Probably both.

The infante acknowledged his thanks with a nod. "There's also the matter of the Special Police. Since the ban will be lifted, their previous directives are being . . . modernized. I have no use for a body meant to hunt nonhumans. I would be better served by a body helping manage discontent between the different races if we are all to be back in the same city. I think, Inspector, that you know all the right candidates to replace recalcitrant members of that force."

"I could make several suggestions," Joaquim said hesitantly.

The infante sighed heavily. "I meant that you should head up such a body, Inspector."

Joaquim shook his head. "No, sir. I'm not an administrator. Commissioner Burgos of the Special Police *is* the man for that position. He's inclined to support your mandate and is already familiar with those officers. But I would be pleased to work for him, should the opportunity arise."

"I understand." The infante stopped walking and turned to Duilio and Oriana. "I spoke frequently with your uncle, Miss Paredes. My understanding is that those who are exiled from your people's islands are no longer citizens. You are dead to them, and essentially have no home. Is that correct?"

"Yes, Your Highness."

"One of the things I intend to do is to offer citizenship to non-humans who've been living in the Golden City. They would become Portuguese citizens. I was hoping you would consider accepting, Miss Paredes." He held up one hand. "It would help to have someone come forward and accept citizenship visibly, to prove it's not a trap."

"I understand, Your Highness," Oriana said.

"In addition, Prince Dinis and I mean to jointly reestablish diplomatic ties with your people's islands. We will need to appoint an ambassador to take up residence there. We don't have anyone trained for that position, I must admit, but we intend to appoint someone for a temporary term, perhaps a year or two. I had hoped that *you* might be willing to accept that position."

"Me?" Oriana asked blankly.

"If you were willing to accept Portuguese citizenship, of course," the infante said. "I'm aware that your people are ruled by the women and would be more responsive to a female ambassador. And would you not be a better interpreter for us of the situation there? I, of course, expect Duilio to accompany you, as your legal advisor."

Duilio was taken aback by the offer. "Your Highness?"

"Alessio told me long ago that diplomacy might be your true calling," he said with a rueful smile. "Your relationship with Miss Paredes affords me a rare opportunity. You understand our laws and the political situations between the various countries of Europe. Miss Paredes understands the customs and beliefs of the sereia. And both of you know there's a threat looming over the relationship between our peoples. I cannot think of a better choice."

Duilio glanced over at Oriana, whose eyebrows rose expectantly, then turned back to the infante. "May we have time to consider, Your Highness?"

Bastião strode out of the door of the new part of the palace and crossed the patio to the infante's side. He leaned close and whispered into the infante's ear. The infante's lips pressed in a thin line and he nodded to the guard. Bastião walked on toward the clock tower.

The infante sighed and said, "Unfortunately, I have to leave you now. Please give your mother my apologies, Duilio. Bastião will be back in a moment to escort you to the gates."

His mother had invited the infante to the dinner party that would follow their wedding in a week. The infante had already sent a note excusing himself, but Duilio thought his mother would appreciate the personal apology.

After one more regal inclination of his head, the infante turned and walked back into the palace. The bell in the clock tower began to ring, a slow knell. Duilio drew out his watch to check the time. It wasn't the hour, or the half hour. Then another bell began to toll— the cathedral's. And soon the faint sounds of other church bells joined in. Prince Fabricio was dead.

From the palace's patios, Duilio gazed out over the city's red-tiled rooftops. Tomorrow the city's men would don black armbands as was proper, but this was still a day of celebration. "Long live Prince Raimundo," he said softly.

In the Golden City, everything was about to change.

ABOUT THE AUTHOR

J. Kathleen Cheney is a former mathematics teacher who has taught classes ranging from seventh grade to calculus, with a brief stint as a gifted and talented specialist. Her short fiction has been published in such venues as *Fantasy Magazine* and *Beneath Ceaseless Skies*, and her novella *Iron Shoes* was a Nebula Finalist in 2010.